CHAPTER 2

ROSE

I wouldn't care if people would watch, snicker, or whisper rude remarks. I feel free and happy and that's all that matters. My girls are dancing beside me while my brother is only a few feet away with his friends.

"Rose, I know you said you don't want to sleep with someone tonight, but please take him home," Darcy whispers, grabbing hold of my shoulders and knocking me out of my daze.

Confused and surprised, I look at her and a very enthusiastic Chloe next to her.

"Who the hell are you talking about?" I ask.

She rolls her eyes and leans in closer. "That guy staring at you and standing next to Daniel."

I look over at Daniel and that's when I spot Luca, staring at me with his beautiful eyes. His strong features and a devious smirk makes his gorgeous god-like face. Taking my eyes off of him quickly, I lean into both of my girls while making a circle.

"Not a chance in fucking hell! Are you both mad?!" I yell at them.

They look confused at my sudden reaction. He's my brother's friend for years, which is a no-no. Plus, how could somebody like him even want a broken mess like me?

"Why the fuck not? Let me judge you!" Chloe yells over and I'm slightly taken back.

She's not the kind of girl to just sleep around like Darcy and me. She doesn't really judge us, but she has had a few words with us when Darcy brings in two men to the flat. Neither me nor Chloe has gotten any sleep that night.

"Now I'm really confused. Since when have you been okay with one-night stands?" I question her whilst trying not to laugh. I can tell that Darcy's amused as I give Chloe a questioning look, waiting for her to answer.

"Since that beautiful boy first looked at you. Rose, he hasn't taken his eyes off of you."

My heart skips a beat. Could she be joking? Of course, she is. Like I said, why would he want a broken mess? I obviously hide it well.

"He's still looking!" I hear Darcy over the music.

Rolling my eyes, I try to ignore it. I know they're only being supportive. The last thing I need is someone like him in my life, but Theo broke my heart so bad I don't think I could ever fall in love again. Besides, I know that Luca is dangerous. If I take him home tonight, I wouldn't ever be able to forget Theo.

"Stop trying to make me feel better. He's way out of my league, plus he's cocky as hell!" I scoff to myself and thought I need a drink. Pushing my way through the crowds, I march over to the bar. Leaning against the cold, wet surface, I wait for my turn.

"Hello, sorry to bother you, but can I buy you a drink?" A confident and unfamiliar voice startles me slightly, but I'm impressed. I've never been approached so quickly at a bar with an offer.

"Of course, you can. I won't turn that down." I smile at him. *As long as I can see the drink being made and given straight to me.* I move to the right so he can slide in next to me and I could get a closer look at him. His facial structure is strong, but not too masculine. He has dark brown eyes and chocolate hair.

"What can I get you?" the bartender asks.

"Yeah, can I have a double vodka and coke and—"

He looks at me, and I realize I haven't given him my order.

"Oh, make that two," I answer quickly. I turn back around and watch the dance floor whilst he talks to the bartender. Everybody is sweating, including my girls at the centre.

"Who are you here with?" he asks me.

I wouldn't want to look like I'm ignoring him so I turn around to answer him.

"My girls, you?"

"My colleagues at work, they're a bit boring," he replies, laughing to himself.

I smile sweetly at him as he looks straight into my eyes. I watch the bartender make our drinks and gives them to us. The man pays as he has promised.

"Let's get some air," I whisper, holding his hand as I lead the way to the smoking area. I drag him to the farthest corner of the garden. Opening up my clutch bag, I take a cigarette out from my pocket. Lighting it, I look up at the stranger in front of me. His deep eyes are watching me as he inhales his already lit fag.

"So, what's your name, gorgeous?" he asks.

I realize how attractive he is.

"Well, aren't you confident? I'm Rose, and you are?" I ask with a light chuckle.

"Beautiful name. I'm Jacob," he answers with his eyes still on me.

I can tell he's nervous. Truth be told, so am I. I never know how to make a conversation, and I still don't know how I manage to bring guys home.

"Are you new to the clubbing scene?" he asks.

His question is catching me slightly off guard. "No? How old do you think I am?" I laugh.

His face falls slightly whilst I wait for him to answer. "I just haven't seen you out before. I would have recognised you anywhere. You're gorgeous," he compliments me again.

Trying not to roll my eyes, I lift my fag to my lips. "I've been out plenty of times. How old do you think I am, then?" I ask him again, raising my eyebrow, intrigued to hear what he is about to say.

"Twenty-five?" he replies hesitantly, obviously hoping it wasn't an insult.

It isn't. I've always been told I look older.

"Twenty-one. You're older than twenty-one, right?" I ask, hoping I'm correct that he's not younger than twenty-one. It's scary how many guys I have spoken to on a night out who use fake IDs to get in. I've nearly taken them home with me.

"I'm twenty-six." I nod as he answers with a heart-stopping smile.

We talk for a couple of minutes more, and I become more attracted to him as time goes on. I take his hand and drag him back inside to dance with me. All the alcohol I have consumed invades my bloodstream, and I just want to dance. It doesn't take me long to find everyone in the exact same place—Darcy's all over the long-haired guy from earlier, and surprisingly, Chloe is dancing against my brother.

"Come here." Jacob pulls me by the waist until I'm pressed up against his hard chest. I slowly grind up against him. The need is hitting me hard. I squeez my thighs together, trying to stop the ache from getting stronger. I know what I said earlier to the girls, but fuck it. Jacob is sweet and sexy, and I want to take him home with me.

I lean back and look up into his dark eyes, giving him a small smile. I grab the back of his head and pull him down until our lips collide. With the smell of cigarette and vodka, he deepens his kiss as our tongues match each other's movements: soft but needy. His hand slides down my back and cups my bum, my core painful for him.

I pull away from the kiss, standing on my tiptoes, and lean into his neck. "Let's get out of here," I whisper into his ear, and his eyes widen with lust before grabbing the back of my neck and kissing me again.

Letting a moan escape my lips, I pull away. "I need to tell the girls. One second." I breathe into him and he nods his head.

I look towards the girls, but my eyes instantly land on Luca. He's dancing with the same girl, but his eyes are still on me. I feel sorry for the girl. I look at Chloe still dancing with my brother whose eyes are shut. Grabbing the chance, I quickly walk over to her and slightly pull her away from him.

"I'm going home, don't let Daniel see us, please," I whisper.

She looks at me with a smile whilst giving me a wink, and I left her to dance with my brother again. Darcy's eyes are already eyeing Jacob and me with an amused and proud face.

"Rose!" I hear someone call my name.

I turn around to find Luca walking towards me with strong eyes and a clenched jaw. "Where are you going?" he asks, puzzling me.

"I'm going home," I say, turning myself away from him. I feel his hand wrap around my forearm, spinning me back towards him. His face is red, making me even more confused.

"Why are you going home with him?" His eyes move towards Jacob who looked jittery and still irritated.

If this carries on, he will not go home with me and probably thinking Luca is a jealous ex-boyfriend or something stupid.

"Because I want to. Because I can?" I growl at him. His protective questioning has me stunned and angry. Who does he think he is?

"Why pick him? He doesn't know how to fuck a girl like you."

His words surprise me. His face is still straight and now I'm flabbergasted. What does he mean? Does he want to come back with me? *No Rose, don't be so careless.*

"Oh, you can?" I ask, raising my eyebrow and kissing my teeth at him.

"You wouldn't know how to handle me if you ever got so lucky." His lips are leaning in closer.

I try to stop myself from shivering as his hot breath fans my neck. *Arrogant dickhead.*

"Lucky for me, I won't ever have to find out," I snap, pulling my arm out of his grip and walking away from him quickly. I grab Jacobs's hand, tugging him outside of the club before I change my mind and take Luca instead. *Yeah, right.*

"Everything okay?" Jacob questions me as we get inside of a taxi.

"Yeah, just my brother's friend being protective, that's all."

He nods at my response whilst I give the taxi driver my address. Why is he acting like he is jealous? Like he wants me to take him home? I don't even know him. Like that matters anyway. Daniel has always had a strict rule for his friends ever since school. "*Do not even think about trying it on with my baby* sister," he says, and nobody ever tries because they know he would kill them. Through the years and after everything that has happened, that threat has doubled, if only he knew what I got up to on the weekends. Like tonight.

Unlocking the front door, I walk in with Jacob gripping onto my waist and slowly kissing down my neck. I try to concentrate on slipping my heels off. I throw my clutch bag on the kitchen counter. "Did you want a drink?" I ask him in a dry voice and take a step away from him slightly. The more I look at him, the more attractive he becomes. He's at least six foot and lean. His brown eyes bore into mine as he shakes his head in response. Before I have the chance to blink, he's striding towards me and slamming me up against the kitchen wall. My breathing falters as his lips crash down onto mine. He cups my bum and lifts me up off the ground asI wrap my legs around his waist.

"Bedroom?" He pulls away from the kiss.

I point my fingers towards my bedroom door and he nods. His soft lips attack me again as he walks out of the kitchen and into the hallway. He finds my bedroom and within seconds, I'm being thrown onto my bed. I sit up quickly, pulling my dress up over my head and throwing it to the floor. His eyes widen with his hands gracing over my naked skin. Leaning his head down, he kisses me again with hunger and desire.

"You're so fucking sexy," he whispers against my lips as heat spreads between my legs.

I'm ready for him now. My fingers find the hem of his black T-shirt as I pull the material up over his head. He's fiddling with the button of his jeans. He finally gets them off his legs, before leaning down and kissing me hard. His arousal presses against my thigh, while my hands run over his prominent muscles. Hooking my fingers around his boxers, the pressure of his lips on mine harden as I tug the material down his legs.

Sliding off the bed, I walk a couple of feet away from him, unclasping my bra and using my forearm to cover my pebbled nipples, teasing him. His eyes enlarge. With my free hand, I pull down my black lace knickers and throw them at him, leaving me naked and ready for him.

He takes in a deep breath as I climb towards him, showing off my naked body. I kiss his lips quickly before falling to my side and lying down on my back. He impatiently climbs on top of me and begins to caress my bare chest. He lowers his head and wraps his lips around my firm nipple. I moan instantly at the contact.

"Condom," I whisper to him.

He sits up immediately, panic evident on his face. "I haven't got one. Please tell me you fucking do. Shit! I just never do this. I didn't think."

I giggle at his rush of worry as I lean to my bedside table. I pull out a condom and open the packet. His face instantly shows relief as I slowly slide the latex over his twitching cock.

I'm on the pill and I hate condoms, but I can't stand the thought of catching a disease because of my sleep-with-anyone-attractive-on-a-night out mindset. Once the condom is correctly on, he grabs my calves and forcefully pulls me to the edge of the bed. I squeal in surprise as he smiles at me in an almost arrogant way. *He is beautiful.*

"You ready?" His voice is soft but confident. His deep eyes watch me like I'm a piece of art whilst I am trying to calm my breathing. He stands up as he opens my legs wide and bends my knees towards my chest, leaving me in an awkward folded deck chair position. My heart is pounding. I'm nervous and excited to feel how powerful he can be. Let's see if Luca was right about him, as bad as that sounds in my head.

"Good baby." Holding his hard cock, he places his big tip at my sensitive entrance, soaking wet and ready. I can just about contain my excitement as my core aches for him inside me. With one thrust, his strong hips slam into me. I moan out in pure pleasure. I don't have a second to adjust before he slides out of me slowly and pounds into me again. He starts a hard rhythmic pattern, pleasuring me completely.

CHAPTER 4

ROSE

The week days go by so slowly. I'm adamant time is passing backwards. The clock ticks and ticks but I feel like I'm waiting forever. Just thirty seconds until I can leave the office for the weekend, and all I want to do is snuggle up in bed, drink wine, and smoke twenty cigarettes whilst watching "Romeo and Juliet" for the billionth time. Ever since I saw Theo and Lauren together on Sunday, I've been in hibernation. The news of them being together isn't fresh, but the news of their engagement hurts just as much as it did the day I caught them; maybe even worse.

I'm growing less in love with him every single day, and that's what kills me about loving Theo. I have been madly in love with him once. I know it never dies all in an instant, but all I can do is watch as it finally fades. I know I need it; I need to fall out of love with him completely.

Stepping outside into the fresh air, I take a deep breath and start walking. The best thing about working at Fallon Publishing House is that it's only a ten-minute walk from the apartment. I don't have to get on the tube or grab a taxi or drive in this hectic city. I'm ready to get out of my heels and slip on my fluffy socks.

"Hello Rose."

I jump out of my skin as Luca appears next to me with Ray-Ban sunglasses resting on his nose. He is wearing a plain black t-shirt and skinny black jeans with black combat boots. He looks flawless. His arms are bulging out of his t-shirt. His beautiful inked artwork is making him stand out like a sore thumb, but in the best way possible.

"Luca? What are you doing here?" I smile at him, trying to keep my calm.

He doesn't say a word but carries on walking next to me. I watch every woman who walks past us give him the eye or raise an eyebrow as he moves through the crowd. Starstruck by his beauty, his sex appeal is uncanny; he's every girl's fantasy but every parent's worst nightmare.

"I work just around the corner from here. You free this evening?" His face turns towards me.

I hesitate trying to think of an excuse but nothing comes out of my stupid mouth. What the hell is wrong with me? Why can't I speak to this boy? He's rude and arrogant, but holy hell, he does heart-pounding, addictive, hot sex.

"Great, let's go grab a drink." His lips curve into a smile that stops my heart in a second. His pearly white teeth show as he grabs hold of my hand and pulls me faster down the path.

Walking into a bar I've never seen before, we take a seat at a table as neon blue lights light up the modern and sleek room. People in suits sit around after a long hard day at work. I pick up the menu and decide on a glass of Pinot Grigio.

"What are you having?"

I point to the menu as I was unable to bloody speak. He nods and walks up to the bar. *God, his bum looks good. What is wrong with me?* He is only a boy. I've spoken too many of them before. I give myself a pep talk for a few more minutes before he's back at the table with our drinks.

"Thank you." I take my glass from his big tattooed hand, taking a sip to calm myself down. Oh, this is what I definitely needed after this week.

"What's the deal with you, Rose?"

My eyes shoot up in his direction. His eyes are curious and bright.

"What do you mean?" I ask, unable to understand what he's getting at.

"On Sunday, I watched you break down, acting vulnerable and weak to some posh twat and his girlfriend. What was that about?" His lips are smirking but his eyes are serious.

My throat is instantly dry that I pick up the glass, taking two big gulps before placing it back on the table. "I prefer the sensitive approach. Being called as weak and vulnerable isn't something I like being reminded off," I growl, giving him a stern face.

"Yeah, you're right I'm sorry. What happened to you? They really seemed to have a massive impact on you." His voice is gentle and welcoming.

I take a deep breath and play with my thumbs, refusing to look at his gorgeous face.

"We were engaged. I walked in on them having sex in my bed. I grew up with Lauren and she watched me fall in love with Theo." My voice is harsh and quiet. I pick up the glass, taking a few more gulps, holding in my tears as I wait. I wait for him to say something heartless or amusing to make me feel even worse.

"Look at me."

I slowly raise my head to look at Luca. His eyes are sad and his jaw is once again tense and bold.

"Don't you dare question your worth because of a cunt like him. I don't want you comparing your beauty. She hasn't got anything on you." He leans forward and holds his beer bottle tightly.

Is that a compliment? His eyes are boring into mine like he's trying to read my mind. He's right. I question myself every fucking day because of their betrayal.

"Thank you, Luca." I reach forward and squeeze his hand, only to pull away quickly and realize the awkward move I have just made as he sits back in his chair. Probably silently gagging at my touch.

"So, did you have fun with that Jason guy or whatever his name was?" he asks, lifting the bottle to his lips. Great, the arsehole is back.

"Well that's none of your concern, is it? Plus, it's not Jason, it's Jacob." I roll my eyes at his change of mood.

"Whatever. He seemed like a desperate nob head wanting anyone with a hole and tits," he speaks with venom and humour in his voice.

I can't understand if he was insinuating. I'm just a hole with tits, but I didn't like it nonetheless.

"He fucked good so why should I care?" Proud of my comeback, I cross my arms against my chest waiting for his answer. I watch him as he swallow hard and his eyes become serious.

"I fuck better." Leaning closer towards me over the table, his eyes are watching me with so much intensity.

I don't doubt that, Luca. But I can't tell him that.

"You're a bit sure of yourself, aren't you? You could be so wrong about that." I lean forward with our eyes still locked as my lips raise into a smirk.

"I know you'd love the chance. Keep dreaming, sunshine. You had the opportunity, but instead, you took Justin home." He laughs lightly, taking a swig of his beer.

He knows he's winding me up, trying to make me fall at his feet. Not happening.

"It's Jacob, you bellend. Stop trying to make yourself feel better because I turned you down!" I lean back against my seat further away from him.

He bites his bottom lip, which made me feel lost.

"I don't fucking care and you didn't turn me down. You just know you wouldn't be able to handle me," he snaps, picks up his bottle, and downs the rest of his beer with his eyes not leaving mine. His inked throat comes into view as well as all the details covering every bit of his skin.

I've never been a massive fan of too many tattoos, and Luca is covered head to toe from what I can see but holy shit, it's perfect to look at. He puts the empty bottle back onto the table with his eyes watching my every shift and pant.

"Stop looking at me like that," I snap at him. His stare is making me blush and somewhat uncomfortable.

"I enjoy looking at you. It's funny seeing what I do to you." He begins to laugh again.

I roll my eyes, trying to think of something smart to say but nothing comes to mind. I look down at my phone as the screen lights up.

Text Message [From: Jacob] Hi Rose I hope you're well? I was wondering if you wanted to have dinner tonight? Jacob X

"Speak of the devil and he shall appear," I say proudly looking up at Luca whose jaw is tensing.

He knows Jacobs has texted me.

"What does he want?" Rolling his eyes, her tries to act unaffected but something tells me it's bullshit.

"He wants to take me out for dinner tonight," I answer, not sure whether or not I should even consider it. He is lovely and a really good shag, but I'm not ready for any type of commitment.

"You're with me though!" he growls, crossing his arms. He doesn't look happy about it, but the thought of trying to wind him up gets the better of me.

"I still have time to get ready and have dinner though, don't I?" I raise my eyebrow making a point.

He closes his eyes whilst his nose is flaring. His breathing is deep. "You won't have sex again, will you?"

His question confuses me. Why is he always so on edge?

"Why do you care if I do?" I look at him waiting for an answer.

He stiffens as our eyes lock the entire time. "I just think you're wasting your time with someone like him."

I can't seem to read what he's really thinking. What does he want from me? He's impolite, brash, and a massive flirt.

"And I'm not wasting my time with you?" I ask, knowing what I've said may come across as rude, but I'm hoping he's honest with his answer. I just want to know why he's taken me to a bar. I want to understand what his problem is.

"No, but apparently I'm wasting mine." He stands up quickly from his chair, squeezes his knuckles tight that cause them to go white.

"What's your problem? Why do you have a problem with Jacob?" I ask, shocked with his reaction when Jacob hasn't done anything wrong. I haven't done anything wrong. Since I left the club with him, Luca's been on my case about the poor boy.

"Because I saw you first and you still picked him. Have fun tonight, Rose." Slamming his chair behind the table, he storms out of the neon-lit room and leaves me struck by his words.

What the fuck does he mean by that?!

Applying my red lipstick, I look at my reflection. My hair pin is straight for once, my silver silk cami and my black skinny jeans look casual but classy. Pulling on my leather jacket and my knee-high boots, I wait for the doorbell.

"Anyone home?" Chloe's voice echoes through the flat.

I open my bedroom door and step out into the hallway. Leaning against the front door, she peels her heels off her feet, in obvious pain. She looks ready for her nightly routine of a bubble bath and Netflix. Her bright blue eyes look at me up and down.

"Where are you off to looking like that?" she asks, winking at me.

She's well aware I'm meeting a guy; probably thinks I'm going out to get pissed and have sex. I might have to, if the night is awful.

"I'm meeting Jacob for dinner," I answer.

She stops mid walk and turns back to look at me. "I thought you didn't want to do the whole dating scene?" Her hands are now on her hips, waiting for an answer.

To be honest, I have no fucking idea why I said yes to him.

"I don't, but I just thought, *why not?* He was really nice. Oh, Luca took me out for a drink after work. He kicked off that I was meeting Jacob and stormed off. Weird, right?" I tell her, trying to fix my zip on the side of my boot.

"No not really, Rose. It's obvious he has a crush on you." She approaches me, shaking my shoulders like she's trying to make me see sense.

"Chloe, we are not twelve years old anymore for fuck sake. He probably just wants to fuck and chuck," I answer. All he talks to me about is not being able to handle him or whatever.

"Why haven't you fucked him then? Since when have you been against that?" she snaps, laughing slightly.

She knows exactly what Daniel would do to me and him if he finds out.

"No, I won't bow down to him and his gorgeous good looks." I'm not sure if I even believe what comes out my mouth but god, I hope I don't falter.

"We'll just have to wait until Darcy does then," Chloe says whilst I roll my eyes.

She isn't wrong. As much as she loves us, I know she can judge us sometimes; even when she doesn't admit it. I used to be like Chloe before my heart got broken by Theo. Wayne had technically taken my virginity and that was it, but Theo helped me and made it better on our first sex. Lauren is a lot like Darcy. We have swapped roles, I guess.

The doorbell rings and pulls me out of my thoughts. I walk over and look through the peephole, slightly gutted that Luca is not on the other side. Why would I even want him to be here? I hesitate before opening the door. Jacob, with a wide smile and as handsome as ever, stands in the doorway. He's wearing a smart navy-blue button up shirt with black skinny jeans and smart black shiny shoes.

"You ready gorgeous?" His voice is soft but I can hear it slightly shaking.

I smile up at him, feeling a slight warmth. "Yeah, see you later Chloe."

We both wave at her as she leans up against the sofa and watches us walk out. His fingers intertwine with mine, and I instantly want to pull them out of his tight grasp, but I hold my breath. *Be nice.* Leaving the apartment building, we walk across the carpark towards a black Audi Q2.

CHAPTER 5

LUCA

Opening a bottle of Budweiser, I let my body fall into the leather sofa. I need a distraction instantly. Grabbing the remote, I turn the TV on, hoping to find something interesting. *Nothing.* Resting my elbows on my knees, my mind wanders to the drink I just had with Rose. That Jacob lad and that fucking women are driving me mad; I don't even know why. I've only met her a couple of times and she will not leave my brain. Running my hands over my face, I try to ignore the headache starting to form.

"Hey, you alright man?" Daniel walks into the living room, still in his work uniform. Sitting down in the armchair across from me, I give him a slight nod before taking a swig of the cold beer.

"Work stressful or something?" he asks again, and I try not to roll my eyes. I need to figure out what to say. He shouldn't know how much I'm thinking about his sister. I cannot even explain it myself. She's annoying, attention seeking, and rude, but I can understand why. She's broken, hurt, and cheated just like me. Maybe we're more alike than I thought.

"Yeah it's been a long day. I bumped into Rose after work." I admit to him. He looks at me immediately with wide eyes.

"Did you speak to her?" he asks wearily. *Why is he acting so damn weird?*

"Yeah we had a quick drink. She's going out with that Jacob," I answer. His face relaxes at the mention of Jacob.

"That's good. She needs to get out of her low, and meet someone who will treat her properly." He turns to face the TV again.

"Her ex damaged her that bad, huh?" I ask, wanting to know more. Rachel has broken my heart when I find her having an affair. I have loved her so much but she has shredded me completely. Maybe I can help Rose? *No don't be stupid.* We both screw around to try and forget, that much is obvious.

"He's not the only problem. I just want her to be happy." He doesn't take his eyes away from the TV. I don't want to pry and be nosy, but what more could've happened in her life to make her so low? Dragging my fingers through my hair, I am frustrated that I'm even thinking about her this much. She's just a girl I've met a handful of times; a girl who actually doesn't want me. Ever since Rachel, I've found a buzz from women. I've never been turned down, until Rose.

"You think he will treat her properly?" I question. I'm getting more pissed off with myself by the second. *Just shut your mouth, Luca.* I can find plenty of women who are willing to do it without the challenge. She's not even my type. I don't go for the natural blondes with a curvy figure with no tattoos. I like a girl with ink and she doesn't have one, but she's still breath-taking.

"I hope so. She's been through a lot with our dad and Theo. She's had it rough." His face is full of concern. I don't want to dig too much into her past, and I know their dad died about five years ago in a car accident. I don't know why that would be tougher on Rose than Daniel? Wouldn't it be a mutual amount of pain for both of them? I nod in response, trying not to bring back any bad memories for Dan.

"Can I make something clear, Luca?" Daniel leans forward with a straight face. Lee bursts through the door with a wide grin and a plastic bag from the Chinese takeaway down the road.

"What's up motherfuckers? I got dinner!" He slams his butt next to me, trying not to laugh at this dude who is impossible sometimes. He's a funny fucker.

"Have I interrupted something here?" Lee looks at both of us wearily. Daniel takes his eyes away from me and smiling back at his friend.

"No man, I was just about to explain my rule to Luca." Daniel's voice is calm, removing his eyes from Lee and back on me.

"Oh shit, you haven't told him yet?" Lee snaps and I turn to look at him with musement on his stubble-covered jaw. Raising an eyebrow, I look at them. *What fucking rule?*

"There's a rule I don't know about?" I ask confused and laugh awkwardly. I've known these boys for a few months now and there's a *"rule"* I don't know about? What is going on?

"I'm kind of always been protective of Rose, and I have a strict rule that no friends of mine are allowed to have any kind of relationship with her apart from friendship. Like Lee, for example, he wouldn't dare do anything." I almost spit the beer out of my mouth. *What the fuck! Really?*

"Isn't that kind of old school?" I question him and he laughs lightly. He knows it is so why does he do it? Did something happen between a friend of his and Rose that ended badly?

"I just know what my mates can be like. I can't stand the thought of one of you man whores sleeping with her or anything." His body is tensing up at the word *"sleeping"*. I mean, I guess I get it. If one of my dickhead mates had sex with my little sister, I would kill them. We all know how we can get and have drunken conversations about a girl we had the night before. It's pretty gross and distasteful.

"Not saying you're a sleaze ball, but you like the ladies," he confirms and he's right. It would be disrespectful if I made a move on her. To be honest, from what I can tell, she wouldn't touch me if her life depends on it.

"You have nothing to worry about man, she's just a friend." He fists bump me and I down the rest of my beer. I've only sorted my life out after Rachel makes it a living hell. I've made two new great mates and get lucky when they ttell me about a spare room. I can't jeopardize that over the idea of fucking Rose. No matter how much my body reacts whenever she's around. *I can't do it, even though I want to.* I can't even work it out in my own head. It's the excitement I get when I tease her because I know I make her hot. Some innocent flirting can't be that bad, can it?

"Let's go out tonight, Lust had me buzzing last weekend." Lee pipes up, swallowing a mouth full of chicken fried rice. I wait for Dan to speak. I'm down for a night out, dancing girls, alcohol, fuck yeah I'm in.

"Sounds good," Dan answers, sipping on his beer.

"I'm down," I finally agree. Maybe I can get my mind off things.

"Nice one. Get ready and we can start drinking. We have a load of beer." Lee walks over to the dishwasher and places his plate inside. A few minutes later, Daniel and I do the same before disappearing off into our separate rooms to get ready.

Looking at my reflection in the mirror, I ruffle my wavy hair with some gel. My grey t-shirt is tight against my broad upper body with black ripped jeans and my favourite combat boots. Slipping on my leather jacket, I leave my bedroom and towards the kitchen for a drink.

The music is attacking my eardrums as we make our way through the club. This place is even busier than last weekend. Leaning up against the bar, I order three bottles of Corona for us before leaving the swamped dance floor towards the chilled outdoors. Finding a free table, we quickly sit down with my eyes scanning the smoking area as I light a cigarette.

There are a lot of girls here tonight, and I'm not trying to be too picky. I know what I really like and a few girls sitting out here have already caught. My eyes find somebody with a pair of knee-high boots. Her slender legs, wide hips, and round bum shaped by a pair of tight black jeans. I can see the shape of her tiny waist underneath her thin silk top. Her long blonde hair is as straight as a pin, and she's curvier than what I would go for. God her ass is incredible!

"Isn't that Rose?" Lee's voice interrupts my thoughts. I take my eyes off the blonde girl to look at the boys. *Rose is here?* I follow Lee's stare, and of course they're staring at the blonde. *Are you fucking kidding me?*

"Rose?!" Daniel calls from across the smoking area. I watch wide eyed as she turns around and my heart stops. Her intense blue eyes are brighter than I've ever seen them. Her eye makeup is dark and sexy and her plump lips is Rosie red and vibrant. How the hell can she look so sexy? I thought she was beautiful, but now I also think she is sexy, too sexy. She needs to wear jeans more often. What a sight to see.

Her smile is bright as she walks over to our table. I clock Jacob walking behind her with a light grip on her hand. *Are you fucking kidding me?* I watch Jacob as Rose hugs her brother. They really look good together. He's clean cut and dresses well. Unlike me with a body head to toe in tattoos. *Fake smile, be nice, don't try to knock the fucker's teeth out for no reason.*

"Hi guys." Rose approaches Lee and me whilst Jacob shakes Daniel's hand. Taking my eyes away from them, I look back at Rose. Her skin is glowing in the light and her blue eyes sparkle slightly. I take it all back. She's not my type, but Jesus Christ, I think she could be now. I give her a quick smile whilst Lee wraps his arms around her waist. *He's such a flirt.* Jealousy is hitting me slightly.

"Nice seeing you all again," Jacob speaks up with a genuine smile on his stupid face. I give him a nod and go back to smoking my fag in peace. As the rest convulse in conversation, I check my phone. Its only eleven thirty, and I already want to get out of here now knowing she's here with him. The smell of her sweet perfume invades my nose, and I close my eyes as she takes a seat next to me.

"I'm sorry about earlier Luca." My head snaps up to my left and see her sitting close to me. Beautiful and vibrant, her skin looks radiant under the heater.

"Sorry for what?" I ask in confusion.

"For wasting your time earlier." She looks down to study her perfectly manicured fingers as her cheeks turn into a pink blush. She really is stunning.

I nod, remembering our bicker at the bar earlier this evening. She shifts her eyes back to my face as my heart rate starting to increase. Her blue orbs are taking me in, but I have to look away. I can't disrespect Daniel. He has made a strict rule about his beautiful sister, and I can understand why. She's a goddess that every guy out here would practically want her to bed. I can't deny my attraction towards her, she's exquisite. I won't go back on my word though. *I will not.*

"Don't worry about it." Giving her a genuine smile, trying so hard not to act like my cocky self. I can't flirt and confuse her into wanting me like I do with all the girls. I can't fuck her like I'd like to. I want to worship her gorgeous body. I won't be that guy to her. I'll treat her like a friend and not like a challenge because I know I will lose and ruin my friend's trust.

My body warm as alcohol runs through my bloodstream. The music is pounding throughout the large dancefloor. Everyone's dancing and swaying their hips whilst the fluorescent flashing lights are making my eyes blur. Lee and Daniel are dancing next to me. I'm trying not to laugh at their ridiculous dance moves; they keep pulling out of the bag.

Scanning the room, my eyes land on Rose, who is only a few feet away grinding her luscious hips against Jacob. Her golden skin shimmering in the light as he holds her tight, moving his hands all over her body, he's taking in every detail of her and loving it. *Bastard.*

"Hello sexy." I turn my head slightly to see a petite girl standing only inches from me. Her lips are close to my ear as she stands on her tiptoes. She had long wavy auburn hair hair and her dark brown eyes covered in black eye makeup. Septum piercing and multiple tattoos are scattered across her slender arms. She steps back, knowing she has my full attention. Her tiny black dress is hugging her slim frame and surprisingly, her large breasts are taking in the shape I can tell they're fake, but still so sexy. This girl is definitely my type. Smiling down at her, I lean in close to her ear.

"Hey gorgeous," I whisper. Her body shivers in response as my finger glides over her waist. I look into her mysterious eyes as she smiles at me and grabs her hand.

"Want a drink?" I ask her.

"Please," she replies. Her voice is deep and seductive. I pull her with me to the dance floor and see the lads watching me with this sexy woman. I clock Rose standing next to Daniel without Jacob. Her eyes look curious yet sharp. I can't tell what emotion they hold but I don't care right now. *Let's have some fun tonight.*

Finding an alleyway around the corner from the club, I scan the area before pulling my zip down my jeans and grabs the foil packet I keep in my wallet at all times. I slide the latex over my throbbing arousal. Her lips presses hard against mine as my fingers holds her naked thighs.

"Quickly," Emily moans against my lips. I lift her up as she wraps her slim legs around my waist. Pulling her tiny thongs to the side, I quickly slide myself deep inside of her. Kissing her hard to stop her loud cries from getting us caught, pounding into her petite body feels so good. I haven't had sex in nearly two weeks and that's a record for me. Holding onto her knees, I lift her legs over my shoulders and bury myself deeper inside her pussy as her back presses up against the brick wall.

I'm trying to focus on my movements as I slam myself inside her over and over again. Her sobs are becoming louder with each thrust. Sinking deeper and hitting her sweet spot every time. I turn my head to make sure nobody is around, and my eyes land on Rose, standing at the end of the alleyway obviously frozen in place.

I grind my hips harder into Emily as I keep my eyes on Rose, her eyes are wide with embarrassment. I want to show her exactly how I fuck. I want her to see how much fun she could have with me even if it's so wrong.

CHAPTER 6

ROSE

His bright blue eyes watch me the whole time as his strong tattooed arms hold the girl up against the wall with her legs over his shoulders. His strong, powerful thrusts and control, and hearing her moans of pleasure are burning into my brain. Getting the images out of my head is nearly impossible; they're getting worse the harder I try to block them out. It's becoming more intense and detailed, and I'm imagining myself instead of the random girl he's slamming his lower body into.

Why wouldn't he stop? I watch him become more dominant with every thrust whilst his eyes are boring into mine the whole time as she screamed out. My body freezes in its place when I enter the alleyway looking for Jacob, but catches Luca instead, showing no mercy towards the tiny girl. What must have felt like minutes is only seconds before I ran off, humiliated beyond belief. I don't even know why I'm the one embarrassed catching him having sex.

"You alright girl? You're up early today," Chloe asks, walking away from the counter with two mugs of coffee in her hands. I haven't even noticed her in the kitchen with me. *How out of it am I?* Sitting down next to me, she slides the mug in front of me. I smile at her, lifting the drink to my lips and taking a small sip. I don't even know what to say to her. How can I explain about last night?

"Sorry. Last night was just weird. Jacob disappeared half way through the night," I tell her, trying to figure it out myself.

"He disappeared?" Her perfectly shaped eyebrow is raising slightly.

"We had dinner and decided to go back to Lust. We danced for a while and then he went to the bar but never came back to me. Dan, Lee, and Luca were out though." I close my eyes thinking about him again and the way he grinds his hips has my core instantly aching.

"What happened with Luca? Don't say nothing. I can see your brain ticking away." She grabs my arm with excitement in her voice. Sighing to myself, I try not to laugh.

"I caught him having sex in an alleyway." I cover my mouth with my hand as the embarrassment still overwhelming. She instantly bursts out laughing.

"What the fuck, that's actually hilarious." Her body is shaking with amusement. I bite my bottom lip and try to stop the image from reoccurring, but it won't go away.

"Who fucks in an alleyway next to a club?" I ask her as she calms downs.

"I do." Darcy walks in with her head held high. Her makeup is flawless and her hair is sleek. We both roll our eyes, she's probably had sex in that alleyway already. My phone begins to ring on the counter in front of me. Snapping out of their conversation, I see Daniel's name appearing on the screen. Picking my phone up, I accept his call.

"Hello," I answer, slightly confused that he's calling me so early in the morning. He's normally asleep until at least two on a Saturday.

"Hey smelly, you free today?" he asks. His voice is surprisingly chirpy. Maybe he's still drunk.

"I can be, why? What's up?" I'm hesitant. Even more concerned why my twenty-four-year-old brother wants to hang out with me again when he has seen me so often recently.

"Us three are going to the beach, you girls want to join?" he asks as excitement takes over me.

"I'm game, let me just ask." Taking the phone away from my ear, I look at both of my girls who are watching me already.

"Beach today? The lads are going." I smile a wide smile and look at them.

"Fuck yes!" Darcy squeals, running off down the hallway.

"Yes! I need to shave my legs though!" Chloe's voice is full of panic as she jumps up off the stool. Darcy walks back in and grabs a water bottle from the fridge.

"Sounds good, who's driving?" I ask him.

"I am and one of you girls can?" I look straight at Darcy. I still have a little alcohol in my system, and I know it's at least a two-hour drive to the beach.

"Darcy will drive," I tell him, giving her a cheeky wink. She rolls her eyes, but nods in agreement before rushing off back down the hallway.

"Okay we will be outside in thirty minutes!" he says.

"See you soon." I hang up the phone and find both girls have already disappeared to their rooms.

"We have thirty minutes!" I call out. Forgetting my coffee, I walk down the hallway towards my bedroom. Rummaging through my drawers, I can't decide what bikini to wear. I didn't even know I owned this many.

"I'm sorry but if Luca's coming, you need to look sexy. Wear your yellow bikini!" Darcy barges into my room and attacks my drawer until she pulls the tiny thing out. Is she kidding me? My brother will be there. I shake my head in protest. I didn't even know I still owned that thing.

"I cannot wear that, it's so revealing." I pick it up, studying the material. It's like a luminous yellow eye patch and the pants are just as small.

"That's exactly why you need to wear it." Darcy snatches it from my grasp. I notice Chloe leaning up against my door frame watching us with obvious amusement, already dressed and ready to go.

"Fine, but if I get a nip slip, you tell me!" I yell, pointing my finger at them both. I pull my shorts off with my baggy t-shirt over my head revealing my naked body. Quickly slipping the tiny bottoms on and even smaller bikini top, I look at myself in the mirror.

"I would, so fuck you." Darcy's inappropriate words make my eyes roll as comes behind me in the mirror, checking me out. I shove her away as I walk towards my wardrobe and grab my red maxi dress.

"I agree. If you won't fuck, Luca then you can at least tease him," Chloe says with a smile. She knows why I won't even consider having sex with him, but I can secretly dream, *right?*

"He's going to die, you have the most insane body." Darcy's now checking herself out in the mirror, her tiny figure is hidden under an oversized tie-dye t-shirt and shorts.

"You two are the worst influences ever." I snap, pulling the dress over my head. I pack a towel, a random book off my shelf, and my purse. My phone vibrates in my hand and see a text message.

Text Message [From: Daniel] Outside, let's get going x

"Let's go girls! They're here." I walk out of my bedroom.

Chloe locks the front door behind us. My body instantly becomes hot as we make our way outside the building. The sun is beaming down on us as we walk to Darcy's red Citroen. Daniel has parked up next to her car, and I catch his eyes watching Chloe with lust. Her tight little shorts are showing off her bum as she climbs into the car. I try so hard not to look for Luca whilst remembering last night's events. Staying strong, I get into the passenger side.

"Follow me Darcy. If you lose me, I'll get Luca to send Rose directions. I've given him your number just in case Rose!" Dan yells out of the window before driving off. Why give Luca my number for fuck sake?

After more than two hours of driving, Darcy has almost killed us twice whilst Chloe is singing to James Arthur at the top of her lungs we finally arrive. My nerves are getting the better of me as I get out of the car. I catch Luca stepping out of Daniel's car, wearing a white t-shirt and washed out denim shorts. Shit! He looks good in white.

Making small talk with my brother seems easy as we make our way over the hill and onto the sandy beach where families and friends scatter all over. We spot an empty patch and put our stuff down. Laying my towel on the sand, I sit down and place my bag next to me.

"Shit. Has anyone got sun cream?" I ask in panic and look around the group as they get settled.

"Yes." Luca's deep voice makes my skin tingle. I watch him open a carrier bag next to Daniel. Passing me the bottle, I smile as our eyes meet. For the first time since last night, we look at each other. His eyes are almost silver in the sunlight.

"Thank you," I say before looking away. Opening the lid, I pour the white liquid into my hand and start to rub it onto my arms.

"Need any help?" Lee asks, wiggling his eyebrows, and I smack his arm. The sun cream splatters across his t-shirt. Everyone laughs except Luca. I can feel his eyes taking me in as I rub the cream into my skin.

"I'll do it." Chloe stands up. Her slender figure is already on show in a black bikini. I turn my attention back to the boys, watching her with pure desire especially Daniel. I join her standing up and passing her the bottle as she leans in to my ear.

"Take that dress off and show him what he wants, tease the fucker." She's confident and adamant it will work. Holding my breath, I grip the dress and pull it over my head. The warm air is hitting my skin as I expose myself. I throw my dress to the floor and wait for Chloe to pour the cream into her hands. I don't know what's gotten into her. She's never been so supportive about this sort of thing. *Ever.* Her parents are so strict and overwhelming growing up; she has never experienced anything until she started University. She is free but she's still strict on herself.

I start to rub it onto my stomach and chest, making circular movements. Chloe's hands are massaging the cream into my back and shoulders. Bending down, I pour the cream into my hands and running it over my legs. Unable to stop myself, I look towards Luca. His face is full of amusement. I smile at him and he returns it with a raised eyebrow. He really is something else.

"You girls sure know how to put on a show." Lee stands up next to me, wrapping his arm around my shoulder.

"Tell me about it." Darcy stands up, fanning herself with a big grin. She knows well what we are up too. I can feel his eyes still lingering on my body, and I've never wanted to break Dan's rules so bad. He may be an arrogant arsehole but what I saw last night has me aching for him, but I don't want to ruin his friendship with Dan. I need to cool off so I leave the group and walk towards the calm water. I need to clear my head as nobody has made me feel so hot and overwhelmed before. Not even Theo has that effect on me.

Lifting the cigarette to my lips, I look out towards the beautiful water. The sun is shining so bright I can feel my skin tingling.

"That was impressive." His husky voice appears beside me. I turn and look at him, holding my breath. His chest, stomach, back, and arms are completely covered in tattoos, and I've never been more blown away. Not one bare bit of skin is on show. It's beautifully intricate and detailed, plus, his body is gorgeous.

"Like what you see?" He nudges my shoulder gently. I roll my eyes and look back out towards the water.

"You wish." I scoff, trying not to make it obvious that I actually want to pounce on his muscular body and hump him forever.

"I like what I see that's for sure." My head snaps back to him, giving me a toothy grin as I slap his arm. I can feel this overwhelming sensation in the pit of my stomach. Whatever he's doing to me is dangerous. I think he's probably the most gorgeous human I have ever seen, and it scares me that I can't have him. I know it's only one sided.

"You wish." I repeat myself. He cannot know what he's doing to me. He'll find it hilarious and tease me about it forever and all he's doing is standing next to me. *Shirtless and gorgeous.*

"I really fucking do." His words are baffling me. A slight smile is tugging on his lips.

"You're such a weirdo," I answer him, nudging into his shoulder. He leans in closer with his lips only centimetres from my ear.

"A weirdo you want to fuck?" My whole-body shivers and the mental image of him pounding that girl last night has my legs weak. Squeezing my eyes shut, I try to ignore it and shake myself out of my daydream. I put on a front once again.

"You're such a cocky fucker, aren't you?" I snap at him. Acting unaffected is what I have to do, he can't know how badly I wish that was me last night and that he has no idea.

"Who gets what he wants that's for sure." His minty breath is fanning my face as he steps closer to me once again. I can feel my heart slamming into my breast bone and my stomach flipping.

"Keep dreaming." I look into his topaz eyes. They look back at me and he's pushing me. I know it. He knows what he does to me. He has known it since the night I met him.

"I don't have to dream, you'll come running." Holding every bit of strength I have, I lean closer.

"Doubt it hunny," I whisper, biting his bottom lip as his eyes widen. He knows I won't go down without a fight. I will not bow down to his sexiness. Secretly, I want to jump on him and kiss him.

"We'll see, darling." His soft lips linger close to mine as our eyes get connected. If my brother isn't in sight, I'd probably let this fucker win, and I would give in to him eventually.

"Let's get in the water, I'm fucking melting!" Darcy screams running towards the water with Lee, I step back from Luca just in time for Lee to wrap his arm around my waist and knock me into the cold water with him. I yelp as laughter fills me. Lee is holding onto me and begins to swing me around and soaks me in the water completely. I look up at Luca standing at the edge of the water. His eyes are sparkling in the sunlight with a powerful glare as he looks at Lee thrashing me around playfully. Chloe appears out of nowhere throwing herself on Lee's back.

Finally getting out of his tight grip, I swim further out before dunking my head under the water, away from Luca's watchful eyes. I know he'll still be there when I come back up so I ready myself. I'm sure his stare alone may stop my heart so I need to stop his.

CHAPTER 7

LUCA

The cool water is running over my feet as I watch Chloe and Darcy jumping around on Lee, but Rose is under the water. What is she thinking? Could it be the same thing as I am? How hard it is not to kiss her, not to have my way with her. I could tell she is struggling to compose herself too. After last night, I have wished it was her I had against that wall. Seeing her today in that incredible bikini, I want her even more. Keeping my eyes trained on the spot of water, she disappeared from where I am.

She appears out from the water slowly with only a feet away from me. She whips her hair back and pushing it away from her face. She's soaking wet, and I don't think I have ever seen something more beautiful. Fucking hell this is cruel. She's so cruel for wearing something so tiny. Her toned stomach is flexing and glistening with water droplets. I can't help but look at her small bikini top; it's tempting and tormenting me I just want to rip it off her. She's doing this on purpose, I know it.

I've never been with someone with a body like hers before, I always go for tiny petite girls but Rose is a curvy goddess. She's womanly and sexy, her marble blue eyes open catching me instantly. And then she smiles. She fucking smiles and I feel myself harden, are you fucking kidding me?

"You alright mate?" Daniel appears by my side. Covering my junk in a casual way, I turn myself towards him quickly before he catches me having a mini heart attack over his sister's incredible body.

"Yeah, this is a nice beach," I lie. Like I care what the fucking beach looks like. There are probably hundreds of girls across the beach with their bodies out, and all I want to do is look at Rose. I turn my head slightly to take her in. She's now on Lee's back and all three of them are climbing on him trying to dunk him under the water playfully. Her round arse is in full view and my cock twitches at the sight. Sucking in a deep breath through my teeth, I turn on my feet and walk back towards our bags.

Minutes later, everyone comes back to their bag. I watch Rose as her bouncing tits come into my view. Her stunning face is glistening in the sun. I look away quickly before someone notices my excitement. I wrap my towel around my centre, trying to hide it. *This is not okay.*

"How did your date go last night?" Daniel asks. Rose wraps the towel around her body to dry herself. She's hesitant and when her eyes roll, my interest heightens further.

"It was okay. He disappeared hallway through the night. I tried calling and texting, but nothing." She shrugs her shoulders like she's uninterested. So that's why she found me last night; she was looking for Jacob. *What a cock*!

"So, he ditched you?" I spit out before I can stop myself. Rose looks at me with a smile. How could someone ever ditch a girl like Rose? I don't think I could after having her in bed. I think I would keep her naked forever.

"Exactly, he ditched me." Her watchful eyes study me, and my heart starts to pound in my chest. What the hell is Rose doing to me? Daniel has banned me from trying anything. She's forbidden, but I have no self-control and she really is reeling me in.

"Where the hell did you wander off too last night, Luca? Did you get lucky?" Lee nudges my shoulder, wiggling his eyebrows at me. All of the girls burst out into fits of laughter. *Great. So she told them.*

"Maybe I did." I wiggle my eyebrows back.

"Yeah in the alley." Rose scoffs. My eyes shoot to her and everyone starts to laugh but I don't care. I know Rose has enjoyed watching me. Her eyes are lingering onto mine. I've only met her a couple of times and she's the hardest person I've ever had to resist.

Finishing a quick phone call with my boss, I head back over to the group. Lee and Darcy are nowhere to be seen. Daniel is texting whilst Chloe is applying more sun cream. I take my eyes away from her and land on Rose, lying on her back. The sun is beaming down on her curvaceous body and teasing me further.

"Hey man, we are just going for a walk," Daniel speaks to me as I sit down. He stands up leaving his phone on the towel where I am seated. I give him a nod as Chloe joins him. Watching them walk away and towards the water, I spot Darcy and Lee splashing around like children.

I look down at Rose again. Her eyes are closed wearing headphones in both ears. Her soft, flawless skin is darkening by the second. Taking her all in, I try so fucking hard not to touch her. I turn away to light a cigarette to distract myself.

It doesn't work. I just can't take my eyes off of her. My eyes follow down her body until I notice something on her outer thigh, a scar. At least seven inches long. It doesn't look new but it's obvious and dark.

"Can you stop staring at me?" Her voice startles me, making me look at her face. I can see playfulness in her curling lips.

"I'm sorry but if you could see what I'm seeing, you'd be staring too," I tell her, scanning her body again. *Wow.*

"Yeah right, get your head out of the gutter for five minutes." She rests her body onto her elbows and looks up at me again.

"You love it," I reply, unable to keep my eyes away from her plump chest and soft stomach. My eyes travel down to her tiny bikini bottoms and my cock starts twitching. I bet her skin tastes delicious. *Jesus, I sound like a creep.*

"If my brother ever heard the things you say to me, you'd be dead meat." She scoffs. I turn back to face her slightly. She is right, I can't deny it. I know I should stop, and I do know I can't.

"Well, what he doesn't know won't hurt him," I tell her, feeling bad for saying those words because his brother is a friend. He's helped me so much, but god, his sister is so fucking hot. It's unfair that he has a rule when she looks this good.

"Don't you respect him?" she asks. Taken back by her words, I think about it. I see how she watches me and how she struggles to control her breath whenever I'm around.

"Don't you respect your brother?" I ask her. She raises an eyebrow and her face twists in confusion.

"What's that supposed to mean? Of course, I fucking do." She snaps at me. I let out a loud singular laugh.

"I see how you look at me. Don't try to deny it, you want to fuck me." I look at her, raising my lips to form a cocky smirk. I want to get on her nerves and hit the jackpot when she opens her mouth in shock, rolling her eyes again.

"You're a pig." She scowls whilst lying back down and shoving her headphones back in to block me out, which is what I expected. I am pushing the boundaries which I can't seem to stop. I normally get what I want and this girl and her brother are making this hard for me. Rachel is the only girl who has ever held me down. I have been an arrogant arsehole before meeting her, and I'm an even bigger one now.

I shut my eyes lying down and trying so hard not to climb on top of her gorgeous body and giving us what we both want. A phone pings next to my head and pulls me out of my dirty mind. I look at Daniel's phone screen and that's when my heart sinks.

Rachel Silva's name appears on his screen—my ex-girlfriend—the girl I unexpectedly have fallen in love with—the girl who cheated on me and broke my heart.

Text Message [From: Rachel] I can't wait to see you tomorrow baby. Don't feel guilty about Luca! He will understand one day. I love you xxxxx

Confusion and anger are hitting me hard at the same time. Daniel and Rachel are a thing? Is he the guy she has been sleeping with and has carried it on even after meeting and befriending me? He knows it the whole time? I'm going to cause this boy some fucking damage.

By the time we arrive back at the girl's apartment building, I'm beyond livid and tired, but apparently the boys want to go up and drink for the night. Being around Rose is having an effect on me. She's driving me fucking mad. I've never been banned from fucking anyone before, and knowing I can't have her is making this more of a challenge. She's difficult but I'm going to win her one way or another, or I'll just go insane.

Once we are upstairs, the boys take a seat in the living room. Dan has already got the TV on, texting his precious Rachel. I want to launch myself at him and beat the crap out of him, but that's not what I'm going to do. The girls disappear into their bedrooms to shower or whatever whilst I'm trying so bloody hard not to imagine Rose soaking wet again.

I want to find her and fuck her brains ou btut I need to stay in control, for now. Walking to the kitchen, I grab a beer from the fridge. Staying away from her is proving difficult. I don't want Daniel to find out that I know, for now. He will find out, and hitting him will not come close to what I have in store for him.

"Am I allowed one?" Rose's soft angelic voice appears to the left of me. *Angelic?* She's walking over to the counter where I have the crate of beer. Her wet blonde hair is flowing down her shoulders and her sunkissed face is free of any makeup. She's wearing black runner shorts with an off the shoulder crop white sweater. *Those shorts are so small, Jesus Christ!*

"Sure." I pass her a Budweiser and watch her open it effortlessly. I can see her tight stomach as she climbs onto the counter next to where I'm standing. She gives me a big grin as I watch her every movement. I move away from her slowly so I can stand opposite her with my body resting against the island in the centre of the kitchen.

"I'm sorry about earlier. I'm trying to respect your brother." I say, trying to sound genuine. Oh, Daniel you're in for it.

"Do you always get what you want?" Her beautifully-shaped eyebrow raises and she bites her plump pink lips.

"Almost always." I rest my elbows against the counter looking at her and imagine sucking on her bottom lip.

"Even if the rule wasn't in place, what makes you think I'd give into you?" She takes a sip of her beer and looks at me, and I'm hesitant for a second. I look around the room to make sure nobody is around and step towards her.

"Because I saw how you looked at me last night, pounding into that girl so hard." I lean into her ear. Her delicious smell of grapefruit fills my nose, and I try so fucking hard not to fuck her on the counter. I rest my hand on top of her warm tanned thigh I could feel her body tensing against my touch.

I begin to stroke her soft skin gently, making small circular movements. Her breathing is increasing by the second. I rest my face into the crook of her neck, gently kissing the silky skin above her collar bone, then step back.

Her face is flushed and heated as her eyes widen. Her teeth is biting hard into her juicy bottom lip. "But we can't," she whispers. I shrug my shoulders trying to act chill.

"Like I care if we are not allowed," I reply calmly taking a swig of beer. She's jumping off the counter, budging past me and almost knocking me off my feet.

I follow her into the living room where everyone is sitting. The girls look clean and fresh. My eyes wander over to Darcy and Chloe. Darcy's eyes linger on me, and I smirk to myself. I've heard she's easy and fun to be with. She is more of my type than Rose because she's petite and tattooed with a crazy *"I don't give a fuck"* attitude. Chloe, on the other hand, is very pretty. Her eyes are insane but she's natural and too innocent.

My whole opinion on Daniel has changed now. I am so sure he was crazy in love with Chloe. Secretly anyway, we could all see it. He had us fooled, he has Chloe fooled. I know I'm an arsehole too, but he acts like a saint. I'll show him what his careless actions can do.

We spent the rest of the night drinking, ordering four pizzas from Dominos, smoking, and talking. I tried to stay away from Daniel and Rose. By the time it hits two in the morning, Lee is beyond smashed so we decide to crash on the sofas for the night. It hasn't seem like the worst idea until all I could think about is going into Rose's bedroom. My thoughts are starting to creep me out now.

I lay on my back listening to both Lee and Daniel snore like pigs. I am really trying not to smother Daniel's head with a pillow for going behind my back and being a snake of a best mate for not even telling me the truth. Banning Rose from my reach is totally unfair; I guess two can play that game.

My brain won't shut off. Daniel's betrayal sucks, and all I can think about is hurting him. *Bastard.* My body jolts up when an earth-shattering and excruciating scream coming from the hallway pulls me out from my dark thoughts. I look around the room in serious confusion. Daniel and Lee jolt up and run towards Rose's bedroom. *What the fuck is going on?*

CHAPTER 8

ROSE

Resting my head against the passenger window, I look up into the sky and see the stars shine furiously as the night drops like a heavy curtain; it's beautiful. The absence of light makes the shadows impossible to survive.

"You okay babe?" The sound of my dad's soft voice turns my attention towards him. He looks at me and then back at the winding road in front of us. His hands are gripping tighter against the leather steering wheel and his knuckles are white from the pressure.

"Yeah, just tired." Giving him a reassuring smile. Silence is falling upon us again. The truth is, I'm tired—so tired, tired of my life.

"What's going on in that brain of yours?" He questions me again with a big grin on his kind face. I've always felt close enough to tell my dad about everything, and he accepts my plans and wants me to chase my dreams.

"I'm just so tired of mum treating me like a child. I know it's a while off, but I keep telling her I want to leave and study in London. She thinks I should stay with her and work at the office." His grip tightens and his face falls.

"I know she only wants you around because Daniel's gone, but she needs to accept you want a life and you have a career goal; a dream and you should pursue it." His voice is strong and full of pride. I shake my head at him, looking down at my fingers and rubbing my thumbs together.

"Well, don't worry for now. We have two years to figure something out." Dad knows how badly I want to work for a book publisher. I have tried

to talk to her about it, but for some reason she can't let me go. She struggles with Daniel, but she hates the thought of me going.

"I am so proud you are going after what you love. I just want you to have the best life." His face is full of sadness as his grip tightens up against the black leather again. Holding back my tears, I give him another nod.

"Maybe you need to mention it to her again. Have you spoken to Wayne about it? Could he help?" I shudder thinking about him. My disgusting step dad could rot in hell, but I can't tell him that so I just shake my head to avoid an unwanted conversation.

"I think you have so much potential Rose. *You just need to believe in yourself." His big hand reaches out and ruffles the back of my head. He always knows what to say. He makes me feel like I can do anything if I keep at it; anything in this whole world.*

Silence floods the car again. Looking out towards the empty road, I spot a bright light in the distance that seem to hide in the fog. As it gets closer, it starts to form into two headlights. The speed of the vehicle is going too fast in the country lane that there is no space for both cars to pass through in time. My dad's voice is full of fear as he yells my name. Instantly, everything goes black, but the ringing of my dad's scream lingers longer.

The strong smell of a burning chemical hits my nose, and my vision blurs as I open my eyes slowly. I slowly manage to move my head to the right. My dad's sat still in his seat facing me. His warm brown eyes is full of fear and pain covered in blood and not a single breath leaves his partially open lips.

"Daddy?" I whisper, but no movement is coming from him. I feel bile rising in my throat and my heart beginning to speed up in terror. Trying to keep myself calm, I reach out and touch his face. His body is still unresponsice whilst his kind eyes are watching me.

A burning sensation is ripping through my throat as I scream out in pain. I move closer to him, trying not to hurt him. Touching his face and arms do nothing; I need to get a response. Anything. He needs to wake up; he has to wake up. Trying to move even closer to him is now impossible as an excruciating pain is hitting my left thigh, and the pain is making me gag instantly.

The more I try and control my breathing and shuffle closer to my dad, the worse my body hurts. Everything begins to hurt more and more by the second. It's unbearable and the pain is blinding me as it shoots through my whole body.

I cannot contain myself from screaming at the realization of what has happened. The sound of distant blurred voices and sirens become more visible. My door is suddenly pulled open and a fireman is cutting through my seatbelt. My vision is blurring as I feel myself getting weaker and weaker.

I close my eyes and feel my body being lifted out of the car and onto a stretcher. Trying to stay awake, I watch the fireman check my dad's body as I'm being pulled further away from him. I'm trying to fight away from the people who are taking me but I'm strapped to the gurney as I scream out for him. I have the worst feeling that I will never see him again, and I was right.

I jolt up from my bed with tears falling effortlessly down my cheeks. Within seconds, Daniel, Lee, Chloe, and Darcy are running through my bedroom towards me. Daniel reaches me first and grabs hold of me and pulls me to his chest. I couldn't stop the tears from falling as I cry into my brother's top.

"Is it dad?" he whispers, and I cry even louder as I remember everything.

"I miss him so much." Every now and then, I would wake up screaming and crying for my dad; the nightmares are life shattering. It's not just a nightmare but a memory I will never forget. As the years pass, they became less frequent, but it still hurts the same.

"I know, I do too, I'm so sorry." His body is shaking as I squeeze his top for a better grip. My bedroom is silent for a few minutes as I try to control myself. I look up to both of my best friends. Their faces are sad for me. They understand, they all understand. I've never been the same since that night, and Theo knows that too. The night that took the best man in the entire world will haunt me forever. He died beside me, and I wish I died instead.

"I have a glass of water if this helps?" Luca's voice is soft and full of concern as he walks over to me and Daniel. He bends down and passes me the cold glass. His eyes are bloodshot as I sip the water carefully. The cold liquid feels amazing as I gulp down the entirety of glass.

"Thank you." I place the glass back into his hand. His smile is gentle and his eyes are studying me that seems to wonder what has happened to me?

"Any time." He places his large hand on mine before standing up and walking out of my room.

"Want me to stay with you?" Chloe sits down on the bed. I shake my head and move my body away from Daniel.

"I'll be okay, I'm sorry for waking you up." I apologise as Daniel kisses my forehead before standing up.

"Don't ever be sorry for that." I slam my body back into my cushions and close my eyes, hoping it won't keep me awake.

I refuse to get out of bed, as the nightmare I haven't experienced in months has taken over my sanity. The memories from that night have left me unnerved and ruined; my dad is my best friend. The night he died has my life turned upside down. I was left with two broken ribs and a large cut on my thigh. My father has lost his life instantly, and every day I wish it was me who was taken instead of him.

Wayne is my grotesque step-father who my mother finally decides to divorce shortly after my father's death. I tell Daniel and mum what he is doing. He is sent to prison with only a five-year sentence, and he'll be out soon.

Everyone couldn't believe he has only gotten five-years for rape and sexual assault of a minor. I haven't thought about him in a while, and I have never told anyone what he has done to me—how he touched me, made me vulnerable and weak, until I lost my father. Theo doesn't even know even when we first started dating. I have lost my father and myself. I don't care how people look at me; I need to let it out.

Maybe that's why Theo have cheated on me. I'm sure he can't be that cruel because he has defended me in court against

Wayne and has supported me through my father's death. He has supported me through fucking everything.

CHAPTER 9

ROSE

Spinning around my work chair, I am trying to block the visions of my nightmare—my past. Everyone has heard and saw me have a breakdown,and it's nothing new to them except Luca. I stay in my bed the entire sunday, sulking and hiding from embarrassment. Daniel comes in and speaks to me for a while. I don't know what he have told anyone but he knows how badly I suffered; how I couldn't sleep for months and months. Looking down at my phone as it vibrates on my desk, an unknown number has messaged me.

Text Message [From: Unknown] what are you doing after work?

I'm hesitant, unsure who it could be.

Text Message [To: Unknown] Who is this?

Only seconds pass when my phone vibrates in my hand again.

Text Message [From: Unknown] It's Luca. You want to go get food?x

I stop typing before I hit send. Is this a bad idea? I can't deny we have some weird chemistry going on. We probably just find each other attractive, but we don't act on it. Surely that's not a bad thing like Lee and me? Maybe he just wants to be my friend? Or he wants to know about Saturday night?

Text Message [To: Unknown] Yeah, I'm game. Where and what time?x

I bite on my acrylic nail, waiting for him to text back. I know the sexual chemistry we have is stronger than some innocent flirting like Lee and me. I know my brother will not be pleased but I'm also my own person, and I don't shy away from meeting men.

Text Message [From: Luca] I'll pick you up from work, five-thirty okay?x

This is a bad idea.

Text Message [To: Unknown] Perfect x

At five twenty-nine, I make my way over to the toilet. I need to check myself over before I meet him. My tight dress is squeezing everything in I can hardly breathe. My black heels is killing my feet but I'm used to facing pain with a straight face. I run my fingers through my wavy blonde hair as I take one last look at myself. I don't look too bad for a full day's work.

Stepping out into the warm evening air, I come to a complete stop. I watch him from a few feet away, leaning up against a black 4x4 Mercedes. He's wearing a black bomber jacket, skinny jeans, and light brown Chelsea boots. This is so not fair; he's fucking beautiful and I can't even have him. Faking the biggest smile possible, I stride towards him, trying to ignore the possible blister on my left heel.

"Well don't you look lovely." He smiles at me with his face beaming. He wraps his arms around my waist for a hug, lets me go and opens the passenger door for me. I somehow manage to climb into the car without ripping my dress. The scent of cigarettes and cologne fill the air as he climbs in and shuts the door beside me and turns to face me.

My heart is pounding and my core is throbbing as his minty breath fans my face. *Hold yourself together Rose, you can do this. He's a god but you can do this.* "What do you like to eat?" he asks. I divert my eyes from his stunning blue orbs to look out of the window.

"I'm not fussy," I reply quickly. I feel awkward and shy being around him in such a small space,and I just want to pounce on him but I can't.

"Italian, good?" I can feel his eyes watch me as I lift my head up to look at him.

"I love Italian," I answer him happily. The thought of creamy pasta makes my mouth water.

"Sorted, I know a great place," he replies, giving me a smile worth a million pounds. He turns his engine on and begins to drive through the busy London whilst the journey is silent. My heart is pounding aggressively in my chest, and I'm not sure how to act. I don't know what to think.

We enter a dimly lit restaurant that smells divine, and my stomach rumbles as the smells invade my nose. As the waitress guides us over to a table, I look at the details of the restaurant with cute fairy lights scattered across the walls. For a friend, this place is pretty romantic. *Why am I here?*

I order a Pepsi max for our drinks whilst he orders a jug of water. I stare at the menu quietly hoping this doesn't go bad. "Can I ask you something?" He breaks our silence. I keep my eye on the menu, waiting for my answer. I'm scared to say "yes," what does he want to know?

"Yes." My heart speeds up at the anticipation; I take my eyes away from the menu to meet his blue ones.

"Why is Daniel so protective of you?" he asks. I'm slightly surprised by his question. I take a couple of seconds to think of every reason why he should be protective.

"At school, all the boys were gross and inappropriate. His friends used to be a bit too forward so he made the no dating rule. It's a little bit silly but it worked," I answer. He nods his head and looks down at the table. The waitress brings over our drinks and gets her note pad out to write down our orders.

After giving her our orders, he stops smiling at the waitress and pulls his full attention back to me, back to the serious questions.

"What about Theo? Why didn't he hate Theo?" he asks. I think back to the day I introduced Theo to him and mum. It has been a shock to them as I was only fifteen when we got together and Dan was eighteen.

"Well, Theo was polite and genuine, nothing like a typical sex hungry lad and he was the perfect boyfriend." I roll my eyes at the thought of my stupid fucking ex, Luca becomes quiet again. What is he thinking?

"What about your dad?" My throat instantly becomes dry. My heart beat is going wild in my chest at the word "*dad*." I grab my glass taking two massive gulps, trying to keep my breathing steady as I look at him. He's watching me looking intrigued, concerned, and guilty?

"What about my dad?" The lump in my throat worsening by the second.

"Was he protective?" he asks, crossing his arms and leaning back against his chair.

"A little, but when he died, Daniel's protective instinct heightened," I answer, remembering how worried he is in the hospital, he has never left my side.

"Why?" He carries on with the questions. Maybe he doesn't know I am involved in the accident?

"I guess after the accident he felt like he needed to keep an extra eye on me, amongst other things." I take my eyes away from him for only a second, thinking about Wayne.

"Sorry, I don't mean to be nosy; I just want to understand why I can't have you." He's confident with his words and my mouth instantly becomes dry again. Why does he want me? He only means sex, but I honestly believe I wouldn't stop him if he tried.

"He doesn't mind if they're not a friend of his and they're respectable, something to do with knowing what his mates get up to with other girls." I shrug my shoulders taking a sip of my drink, I get it. Boys will be boys, us girls can be just as bad.

"Makes sense, what do you think of it?" My eyes go back to Luca, who is leaning in closed. I'm not giving him what he's trying to get out of me; I won't do this to myself as much as I want to.

"What? The rule? I'm used to it, I've never had a problem with it," I answer whilst keeping a straight face. My eyes are still on him. Holding myself together is hard with the sight of him and the way his lips move or the shape of his jaw.

"And now?" he asks. His eyes are watching my every breath, and I don't take my eyes away from his too.

"Still no problem." I just want to laugh and give him the ego boost he deserves, but I won't let him know he's that gorgeous.

"You don't have to lie to me." I scoff at his arrogance. Even though I am lying, he's still a cocky bastard for assuming that.

"I'm not." I roll my eyes, looking anywhere but at him. If he looks at me long enough, he'll be able to see right through me.

As soon as our food arrives, we hardly say a word. I can't stop our recent conversation running through my brain, scanning every question, and remembering each reaction. I want to know what he wants from me, what reason would he have for taking me out for dinner? Questioning my brother's rules? It doesn't make sense.

"What are you thinking about?" I chew my garlic bread before looking up at him.

"Why did you ask me to dinner? And be honest because I am slightly confused," I say before putting my fork down to look up at his calm face and twitching lips.

"I want to know what happened on Saturday night. I've seen you break down twice since I met you. I just want to understand you that's all; you're hard to read." He rubs the back of his neck, looking a little bit uncomfortable.

"Wow Luca. You have feelings?" I joke. He slaps my hand placed on the table. Laughing with him, I find him cute when he is embarrassed. *No Rose, be serious.* Taking a deep breath, I decide to give him the answer, he might understand me more.

"My dad died in the driver's seat, I was in the car. I came out with two broken ribs and a deep cut on my thigh, he died instantly. I had a nightmare, that's all it was." I look down at my thumbs as I rub them together.

"I'm so sorry, I get why Daniel worries so much now." He places his strong hand over min. I look up into his sparkling eyes and smile at him.

"There's a lot of shit I've had to deal with, I'm a strong girl I guess," I say.

"I think we need to be friends, nothing more." He removes his hand from mine, placing it around his glass and taking a sip of water. I'm shocked, where is the arrogant flirt? Why do I feel slightly pissed off? I know what I've just told him has heightened his respect for my brother.

"That would be great." I give him a warm smile as I continue to eat my dinner, feeling slightly awkward with how tonight's events have turned out.

"So where do you work?" I ask him, trying to get my mind off everything. I also don't know anything about him or what he does for work. He finishes chewing his food before replying.

"I'm an events manager for Carter Corp. It's giving me good pay so I don't mind." He makes eye contact with me whilst he explains his job description. I am impressed that he's doing so well for himself at the age of twenty-four. Trying to listen to him is hard when all I can think about are his godly features, but we agreed that we can only be friends.

After arguing for at least ten minutes over who will pay for the bill, Luca wins whilst I leave a nice sized tip for the waitress. I feel bloated and disgusting, I just want a warm shower and to wrap up in my fluffy pyjamas. I somehow manage to climb into his car again, fearing that I will in fact tear my dress.

"Thank you for coming out with me tonight," he says whilst I look over at him. He moves his eyes from the road to me quickly with a slight smile on his gorgeous lips. I look back out of the passenger window, feeling off. I'm not sure how I should feel at all.

"Thank you for the invite," I finally answer him. The gentle tapping of his thumb against the steering wheel as the radio plays with music with a low volume. I close my eyes as I rest my head against the glass. Shortly after we are pulling into the car park and finding a space, he turns the car in and shuts the engine off. I sit up straight and feel his eyes on me, but I don't want to look.

"We can't tell Daniel about this can we?" he asks. I shake my head; I know Daniel will kick off if he finds out I'm been hanging out with Luca.

"Thank you again Luca." I give him another smile before opening the car door and sliding out. I shut the door behind me and begin to walk through the car park.

"Rose!" I hear my name being called from behind me. I stop in my tracks and take a deep breath. *Stay calm, everything is fine.* I turn around watching Luca stride towards me with his hands in his jean pockets.

"When can I see you again?" he asks, stopping a couple of inches from my face. I hold my breath, trying to think of anything to say. *I thought he only wanted to be my friend?*

"What about my brother?" Is all I can manage to say. My anxiety is rising with every passing second. This boy is seriously confusing me. *Can he just kiss me already?*

"I didn't say as anything more than friends, did I?" His lips form a cheeky smirk. My heart sinks slightly. I swear this boy can't make up his mind, or he's having way too much fun trying to confuse me.

"Rose?" I turn around and notice a dark figure walking towards me from the flat, and Jacob's face come into view. What the hell is he doing here?

"Have you been waiting for me?" I ask him as he stops in front of me.

"Yes, I need to talk to you," he answers with his eyes holding so much emotion.

"You have got to be kidding me." Luca scowls. I roll my eyes trying to ignore him.

"What are you doing here Jacob?" I walk towards him, trying to get further away from Luca.

"I wanted to apologise for Friday night. I kind of bumped into someone I haven't seen in a while and well, I saw my ex in the club." His apology is pathetic, no excuse whatsoever.

"Well that's what a phone is for a genius—to let your date know you've gone home to fuck your ex-girlfriend. I suggest you do that next time." I snap back. I feel Luca walk up behind me with his hand on my back. Why is he touching me?

"I know, I'm sorry." He steps closer.

"Okay but I'm not interested, it was fun but I'm not interested anymore." I say, feeling slightly bad but I don't want to lead this guy on.

"But—" He begins to speak but Luca cuts him off.

"Just fuck off, she's not interested." Luca growls through gritted teeth. I turn and look up at him. My anger is boiling. Who does he think he is to be involved like that? Why hasn't he left me yet?

"Okay man. Jesus Christ, I'm sorry Rose, take care." He smiles at me sweetly and turns on his heel. I watch him pace towards his car and speeds out. I step away from Luca.

"What was that about?" I hiss at him, looking at me with wide eyes.

"Doesn't he understand a hint, you don't want him?" He raises his voice. His jaw is clenched as I glare at him.

"How do you know what I want, Luca?" I put my hands on my hips, looking up at him angry and tired.

"Because I see how you look at me." I'm once again being backed up into his stupid games.

"Don't start please." I close my eyes, begging for him to stop. He's so right but I can't let him know that. I'm scared of any type of commitment, but just being friends with Luca will be a challenge. Especially if he acts like this.

"I can't be friends with you," he blurts out. I open my eyes quickly and scan his beautiful face, feeling a slight pain in my chest.

"Well that's your problem." I push past him; I need to get far away and this night has been a weird and confusing mess. His bullshit is tiring.

"I either want nothing to do with you, or I want more. I know I can't have that." His comment has my blood boiling. I spin around on my heel marching back towards him. Looking up into his blue eyes, my neck is aching slightly. God he's so tall.

"Have what? Have sex with me?!" I press my body up against his, hoping I can get a reaction out of him.

"Yes, did you really think you could have more? How stupid of you." He smiles at me, not even realising how disrespectful he is. I clench my fists, holding myself back from smashing his face against the concrete wall.

"You're a fucking Pig. Is that why you took me out? To try and get me weak at the knees just so you can bone me and disappear like every other fucking immature boy." I push against his chest to hopefully wake him up from his arrogance.

"Maybe, like I really care about your feelings." He turns and walks away from me. I stand in the empty car park as he reaches his car. Slamming the car door behind him, he revives his engine; I flip him my middle finger and stomp through the car park. Hearing his car speed off out of the car park and down the road, I try to calm myself knowing he is gone.

CHAPTER 10

ROSE

The weekend doesn't seem to come around quicker. I need to get out, get pissed, and maybe have a mind-blowing sex. Chloe is busy with work so I go straight to Darcy, who of course wouldn't even hesitate on suggesting to come out. As soon as I get home, I take the shower to make some shaving and moisturising just in case I get lucky.

"Let me do your makeup." Darcy waltzes into my bedroom on her running shorts and a thin crop top.

"You're seriously not wearing that, are you?" I am stunned looking at her and praying she's not thought it honestly doesn't surprise me.

"Obviously not. I don't want to get makeup on my outfit, so is that a yes then?" She sits down in front of me before hearing my answer and begin her work. Thirty-five minutes later, she begins to scrape my hair back into a tight bun.

"Okay, have you decided what to wear?" I open my wardrobe and pick my mid-thigh long-sleeve bodycon dress—elegant, but sexy with a neckline to show off my assets.

"You look gorgeous! You need to wear big earrings with your hair up. Let me go see what I have." Darcy hurriedly goes out of my bedroom. I slip the dress on and check myself at the mirror. I usually don't wear dark make-up, but I approve of it anyway.

"Wear these," Darcy says, wearing a tiny white dress showing off her petite frame. She's holding a pair of sparkly silver hoop earrings. I'm surprised with how pretty they are, and I put them in quickly.

"You look sexy as fuck! Right, let's have some shots. I'm desperate tonight after last week." Darcy drags me to the kitchen and makes a couple of drinks. We smoke a couple of fags in the balcony whilst listening to music through the speakers.

We decide on going to Lust. I order two Jaeger bombs and we knock them back quickly. The music is pumping through my body as we make our way to the dance floor with sweaty people everywhere.

We sway our hips and grind to the music allowing the alcohol to flow through our blood, ignoring the stares of a few creeps as the club pounds tune after tune.

"You okay girl?" Darcy leans in and I nod my head in response. I move my body to the beat of the music as a new song starts to play.

"You look insane tonight." Luca suddenly shows up with his hands and touches my waist. He holds me close against his front with my bum against his groin as I grind against him. I'm startled and confused like always.

"What are you doing here? I thought you hated me?" I ask him, ignoring the fact that his touch is making me feel weak and vulnerable.

"I came out with some work friends. I saw you and wanted to come over and apologise," he says with his lips touching my ear. I pull myself away from him and head towards the smoking area. I see Darcy with a new lad so I walk away without telling her where I'm going.

"Look, I'm sorry I'm such a cock all the time," he says with his voice irritating me. He wraps his hand around my upper arm and turns me towards him. He looks straight into my eyes like he's trying to tell me something.

"You really look beautiful." His words surprise me, but I roll my eyes trying not to believe all the shit that comes out of his mouth.

"Oh, you really want to act like this? Real mature." He steps closer to me. I take a step backwards and try to keep a safe distance from this dangerous guy until I hit the brick wall,

"What do you want from me?" I ask.

"I want you to do what you really want. Tell me, what is it?" he says, making me startle. His face approaches mine with his icy blue eyes and it seems like I have forgetten all about everyone, the cluttered smoking area, and the people who may be watching us.

"I tell you, I don't want romance or love shit, I just want to fuck you so bad," he says with lustful eyes. I shall be disgusted and disrespected, but I want all of that too. That's all I've been doing for six months, and he has been doing it too after breaking up with Rachel. He's a broken mess just like me.

"Luca, I can't go behind Daniel's back," I stammer.

"Fuck what Daniel thinks." I push him against his shoulders as I storm past him.

"Where are you going?" He steps in front of me. Aware that people are watching us, I try not to cower and hide from this dickhead.

"Away from you. You are not God's gift so get your big head out of your arse hole, and go fuck yourself! Your pathetic mind games are tiring, and frankly, I don't give a shit to actually care!" I yell at him, slightly surprised that I have said it out loud.

"You wish you were that special sweetheart but trust me, you are not." He leans in, smirking with arrogance. God! Just punch that cunt in the face, Rose. People surround us as they watch with enjoyment, flipping him and everyone as I try to get out from the club.

"Can I just get some fresh air for a few minutes?" I ask the security team at the entrance of the club. They give me a nod before I step outside and lean up against the wall. Contemplating on going home, Darcy disappears with some bloke, and I feel like shit about Luca. The smoking area is too crowded, and I'm trying to hide away for a bit.

"Can you stop being a fucking princess, Rose?" Luca appears next to me. His jaw is tensing.

"You are such a bellend, you know that, right?" I push myself off the wall towards him. His lips are curling, making my blood boil even more.

"Of course I do, sweetheart." He laughs, and it makes me want to kick him in the nuts.

"Don't call me that!" I walk past him, but he grabs my shoulder to make me stop and turn to him.

"You really are a hard work, you know," he says with his face a few inches away from mine.

"Why bother? I don't see what your game is and what you're trying to achieve."

What does he want from me? He flirts to the ends of the earth, but talks to me like I'm a piece of meat he wants to devour and then throw me in the bin after he's had a taste.

"You really want to know?" He raises his eyebrow and stares at me. Don't cower, Rose. Show him he is not in control of whatever this is.

"Yes." I shrug out of his grip but he steps in front of me, making me unable to escape as my breath intensifies. Why do I constantly feel like this around him? Is it because he's gorgeous? I could even take him to bed whenever I want to.

"I can't stop myself, Rose," he whispers in my ear. Why can't he just be honest? He pursues any girl he wants in that club, but he keeps on coming back to me.

"Stop it, Luca!" I snap in his face and meet his eyes. His body slams against mine and gives me a consuming kiss. His heavenly scent is taking me over as our lips work in unison, then I open my mouth inviting his tongue. He pushes me against the wall and holds me in place as his kiss becomes stonger and dominant.

This isn't right. I'll ruin his friendship with my brother if I let this carry on. I can't even utter a single word when our lips are together, and I'm afraid I won't be able to stop. His hands travel down to my lower back, and I suddenly realize what's happening. I use all of my strength and push him off me. His face falls in shock as he staggers back. I look at him trying not to freak out. That was insane!

"You are Daniel's friend, I can't." I look at the concrete floor to avoid his eyes.

"What is so wrong about kissing you?" He steps closer. I step back, and I'm against the cold wall once again, looking at my feet and finding the words to say.

"You're his friend. He will kill you," I said calmly.

"I honestly don't care, Rose. You have this magnetic pull that I can't tell you what I want from you, but I know I will find out," he says softly. His hand caresses my cheek. I take a sharp breath and look at him. His god-like face is making me flutter.

"I don't want anything serious, Luca. I'm sorry, but I'm not ready for any commitment. Ever again." I won't allow myself to fall in love again no matter how gorgeous he is. Fuck heartbreak!

"I didn't say I want that either. I don't," he says. I don't know what I want from him. As gross as it sounds, I just feel anxious and horny whenever he is around.

"What do we do then?" I ask him.

"We can fuck." He smiles confidently, throwing me completely off focus as I remember how cocky he is.

"Don't ruin the moment by being a fucking dick." I punch his arm and giggle, hoping he's not angry for calling him a dick. To my surprise, he laughs with all his might. I would rather see him laughing than in a rage or being arrogant.

"I'd say let's go back but your brother lives there." He chuckles at his own words whilst I smile at him.

"He normally works on Fridays." I shrug and wait for his response. I know he will be shocked.

"And if he's not at work?" His eyes grow wide in surprise that I'm considering it. I can't imagine him being home on a Friday night.

"The bar gets pretty busy on Friday nights, live a little." I grab his hand to walk with me towards the chain of taxis waiting.

"If I die, you are coming straight to hell with me." His words excite me as we climb into the taxi and give the driver his address. I know this might be a big mistake, but I'm done fighting my urges. Bring it on.

CHAPTER 11

ROSE

Not a single light is on as we step inside the flat. There is no sign of Lee or my brother as we sneak out through the hallway into his bedroom. “Nice,” I whisper as I walk around. The white-colored walls are filled with pieces of artwork. His bed is covered with grey and black beddings. A bookcase filled with classic books impresses me even more, he must be a bookworm.

He rolls his eyes at my comment and marches towards me. His hands grip onto my waist and pulls me into his muscular body as our mouths collide.

I let him push me onto the bed whilst struggling not to moan as I lay down. Sliding his jacket off and pulling his T-shirt over his head, my eyes widen at the sight of his toned chest and arms covered with ink.

Keeping his jeans on, he crawls on top of me. He breathes heavily with his eyes still on me. Leaning down, he hungrily kisses me that I couldn’t stop myself from kissing back. His irresistible touch consumes my every thought and whole being as he clutches my waist. I wrap my legs around him before he pulls my body up into a sitting position.

He takes my hair tie out and makes my dark blonde hair flow messily down my shoulders as his fingers caress my cheek.

"I've wanted this since the night I met you," he whispers and continues to kiss me passionately. I look back at him without feeling awkward.

I tangle my nails into his hair and start to grind against him. Sharing the same sensation, he breathes into my mouth. His hands grab my calves, opens my legs, and throwing me on the bed.

"Take that dress off," he demands as he takes his jeans off, and I obey him quickly. I am happy for choosing a tiny black G-string and a lace bra.

"Fuck, Rose." He moan as I stretch my body on the bed showing off my stomach. Twitching with arousal, his tight black boxers are ready to burst.

"Seriously? Luca, how the hell are you so goddamn perfect?" I raise my eyebrow, unable to believe seeing his huge bulge.

"I can't help it." He winks at me before crawling over. My legs instantly open as I push my hips up and put pressure on his extremely hard cock that makes him moan with pleasure. Teasing him, I reach down and grasps his cloth-covered member as he hums in response.

His lips dive into mine and I'm taken back by his hungry kiss once again. He grabs my chest and squeezes my right breast whilst I try to keep up with his movement. I feel his hand wandering between my legs and my heartbeat pounds faster as he pushes my underwear aside and teases my wet opening before easing two fingers between my folds. I gasp in pleasure and arch my back as his fingers pump in and out slowly with his lips caressing my neck.

"Luca? You in mate?" The familiar sound of my brother's voice echoes at the door after knocking twice. Luca instantly jumps off me whilst I rush to grab my dress and slip it on.

"Shit, shit, shit," I whisper to myself and run around his room like a mad woman to look for a place to hide. I find a spot under the bed and roll underneath it.

"You alright? Thought you were at work?" Luca says. My heart is racing at the sudden realization of what I am fucking doing.

"Yeah just finished. Just wondering if you were still out," my brother answers.

"Nope I just got back," Luca answers confidently and pretends to be calm.

"Whose shoes are those?" my brother asks and my eyes widen at my idiocy. I left my fucking heels in the middle of the room! I'm dead. Luca's dead. I haven't heard Luca reply, and all I can imagine is that cocky smirk plastered on his gorgeous face. He's not helping the situation at all. He's going to get us caught, and I'm going to break his nose.

"Oh, shit. Sorry, I'll leave you to it, I'm going out." His words have made me feel relieved and realized I should leave immediately.

"Who are you meeting?" Luca asks abruptly.

"A girl from work," my brother replies. I cringe at the thought and have been slightly pissed off, thinking he has a thing going on with Chloe? *Dickhead.*

"Have fun," Luca's blunt reply makes me confused. I have been thinking that boys cheer and rev each other on to get lucky with any girl, but he doesn't sound pleased at all.

"You too, mate," my brother says before the bedroom door shuts. I get out from under the bed as soon as everything sounds clear and walk straight to grab my heels. I slide them on without looking at Luca, but I know he's watching.

"You going?" he asks.

"Look, I know we have this weird connection but you are Daniel's mate. This was a mistake and it wouldn't be fair on him, would it?" I pick up my clutch bag whilst he's standing in his boxers with his arms crossed and leaning against the door frame.

"I didn't ask for your opinion, did I? I couldn't care less," he mutters back, and my heart sinks a little at his choice of words.

"I'm sorry if I've pissed you off somehow. We can still be friends like, right?" I say as I walk over to him. I don't want to leave on bad terms. That always happens and I'm bored of it. His bright eyes have no emotion as they look at me, I almost want to slap some reaction onto his gorgeous face.

"We were never friends, but whatever, you know where the door is," he says as if he doesn't care and his eyes glare at me. *He really doesn't care at all, does he?*

"I'd tell you how I really feel, but I wasn't born with enough middle fingers to express myself in this case, so fuck yourself, cunt." I push my way past him making sure to unbalance him. He falls against the wall as I stalk out, slamming his bedroom door shut, and storming out of the flat.

After thirty minutes, I get a ride through Uber and contemplate on finding Darcy but end up texting her that I'm home. I open the front door, surprised to see Chloe still awake watching a film. She turns her head, confused that I am alone. I haven't said a word as I sulk over to the empty space next to her and slump myself down.

"Rough night?" She passes me a can of Strongbow cider. I smile at her, taking it and opening it quickly. I slide my stupid heels off my feet and run my fingers through my matted hair.

"Very," I reply after gulping down half of the can. I feel her bright eyes watching me with concern, but I can't decide if I should tell her or not. *Fuck it.*

"I nearly had sex with Luca." I decide to come straight out with it, and her eyes widen as she quckly jumps up on her knees.

"Wait, what? How?" She leans into me; I can't tell if she's shocked or annoyed.

"We saw each other feeling with lust, and I went back to the flat," I tell her, regretting every second of it.

"Daniel's flat? Did you want to get caught?" She laughs in utter disbelief.

"Well, we nearly did. Daniel knocked on the door whilst Luca had his hands in my pants." I chuckle to myself.

"Does he want a death wish?" Chloe, still in shock, asked in a louder voice.

"Fucking hell, I did bring it on myself." I realize it to be amusing, and Chloe and I are unable to stop laughing at my stupidity.

"So, why was it bad?" She calms down and looks at me. I winch and remember at the thought of what Luca has done.

"I told him it was a mistake because of Daniel, and he told me he doesn't care and that I know where the door is. So I told him to go fuck himself and do something smart before slamming the door." I chuckle to myself, but I can't deny feeling hurt remembering how cruel his words are.

"What a c*ck! But go, girlfriend." Chloe leans back into the sofa, smiling to herself. I rest my head on her shoulder, watching the film she's binging on with my mind wandering. It is indeed stupid, and I don't want anything but I can't deny the fact that I want more than just a one night of stupid wild sex from Luca. The thought alone scares me to fucking death.

CHAPTER 12

ROSE

It's been seven days since the incident with Luca, and I haven't heard from him or even Daniel for that matter, but I don't care—I couldn't care. What's the point in caring? He's an arrogant arsehole with a fucked-up mind set on love, just like me. How the hell could it possibly ever work? Fucking him is in fact a terrible mistake, and I would have had so much guilt for Daniel.

"Hi! Rose, isn't it?" A girl I've only seen a couple times around the office walks over to my desk. I snap out of my thoughts and realize the time. I look up at the petite girl with auburn hair and an almost perfect smile as she waits for me to answer.

"Yeah, Emily, right?" I answer quickly, turning my computer off. I slip my jacket on and pick up my handbag.

"Yes, I was wondering if you wanted to grab a drink? You probably have plans but you've only been here a few months, and we've never spoken. I don't want you to think that you have to but—" Her face reddens as she plays with the hem of her tiny skirt.

"Sure, but the first round is on you," I answer quickly with a wink and give her a genuine smile. Her full lips smile brightly as she swings her bag over her shoulder. Strutting round my desk I walk next to her as we make our way through the office, only a couple of people are still sitting and working and will be 'til the late hours off night.

"How do I not recognise you?" Emily asks whilst taking a sip of her wine; I shrug. Our University is huge, but you always see the same faces after a routine kicks in for most people. Emily seems familiar. In fact, I think I've seen her recently but not at work.

"Surely, we might have some common friends, huh?" she says. I try to think of anyone I know who could possibly know Emily, and apparently she is a year before me, so it could be possible.

"Lauren Mettam?" I ask, intrigued to find out if she remembers my old best friend, who used to sleep with older students and got a name for herself. Everyone knows her and at that time I didn't mind it, but I guess I've followed her footsteps.

"Yes! She had a threesome with the guys named Harry Bell and Donnie Richards. Oh, isn't she engaged to Theo Saxby now? Lucky girl, he is so hot." Her words instantly shake me that I stopped breathing, but she doesn't notice. Everyone knows Theo. He is popular in secondary school and even at the University. He has this compelling and charming personality.

"He's not so special," I mutter; her face falters in confusion.

"Oh god, did I say something wrong?" she asks anxiously. My heart is racing thinking of Theo and Lauren.

"Well, he's my ex-fiancé. He was cheating on me with my best friend, Lauren." I manage to say, looking down at my thumbs. God, I need to book an appointment to get infills.

"Oh shit, I'm so sorry." I hear her gasp before she leans over and grabs my hands, squeezing them tight.

"Don't worry, I'm recovering." I chuckle, trying to sound sure of my words when I know it's a bunch of bullshit. I know I'm a mess—an unstable mess.

"If a girl like you can't keep a man, then the rest of us are screwed." She giggles. I take a moment to look at her. Her bright hair is straight as a pin and her dark eyes somehow look bright and full of life. Her lips are full, which obviously look articifial; but still,

I'm jealous of them. I can't help but wonder if septum piercing hurts.

"Don't be stupid. You must've gotten attention with your tiny frame; you're making me jealous." I look down at my massive chest and thick thighs.

"Yes I do. I met the sexiest guy the other week in that new club, lust. I'll be going to him after this." She closes her eyes in a lustful way. God, he must be something.

"I go to Lust often. I'm surprised I haven't seen you," I reply, not really wanting all the details.

"We can go out sometime." She smiles at me.

"Yes definitely." I smile back at my new friend. She seems sweet. My eyes scan her tattooed arm of floral artwork and detailed to perfection.

As I wash my hair and letting the warm water run all over my body, I keep thinking about Luca—how his lips and fingers feel with mine even just for a few seconds. I know it's not right, but god, I miss his face. I could sit and just look at him and never get bored.

Stepping out of the shower, I wrap a towel around my body and take a long hard look in the mirror. My hair is soaking wet as I comb it away from my face and letting it run down my back. My skin is still glowing from the sun, making my complexion look flawless. I hear my phone *ping* as I walk into my bedroom.

Walking towards my bedside table, I pick up my phone. My body stiffens as Luca's name appears on my screen. *Why the fuck has he texted me? I thought he doesn't care?*

Text Message [From: Luca] I'm sorry about last week, friends? x

I take a couple of seconds to think about it. Do I want to be friends with a jumped-up prick like Luca? I don't know if I can trust myself around him, especially now, more than ever.

Text Message [To: Luca] Now you want to be friends? Make up your goddamn mind.

I stare impatiently at my phone for his reply.

Text Message [From: Luca] I know, I'm sorry. I had shit going on in my head when Daniel interrupted us. What are you doing? x

Maybe he feels guilty as well and takes it out on me? Fuck, I didn't even think about that.

Text Message [To: Luca] If you say so, I just got out of the shower, you? x

For some reason, I can imagine Luca's eyes widening at the thought of me soaking wet. I chuckle to myself and wait for a reply.

Text Message [From: Luca] Sexy, I'm bored. Can I come over? x

My heart rate goes wild with excitement but my brain is telling me *no*. Fuck off, brain.

Text Message [To: Luca] Friends, Luca. If you want to. x

I throw my phone onto the bed, rolling my eyes. I'm such an idiot. Why couldn't I just say "no"? Maybe we can talk about what happened and just be friends like we should be. Yes, that's it. Believe it, Rose. Just friends.

Text Message [From: Luca] See you soon ;) x

I rush around my room, thinking what to wear. How should I do my hair? I'm rummaging through my draws and picking out my black satin pyjama shorts, and the matching strap to. No bra and tiny knickers, just in case. I know I'm being a massive hypocrite, and I'm bringing this on myself but I can't stop it.

I let my hair dry naturally with a wavy mess, and I apply the smallest amount of mascara and lip balm. Within thirty minutes of me texting him, the doorbell rings. I open my bedroom door watching him walk into the flat, talking to Chloe and Darcy who look surprised to see him.

"She didn't tell us you were coming." Chloe looks confused, but Darcy just keeps staring at him, mesmerised.

"Yeah, I only text her about coming over a few minutes ago," he answers without being fazed by Darcy's constant staring.

"Right, okay," Chloe says with a hint of uncertainty in her voice as she turns my way whilst I give her a confused look. I make my way over to them as his eyes take in my full appearance. I watch as his Adams apple bobbles in his throat and his eyes linger on my figure.

"Rose," he whispers. Chloe and Darcy chuckle, and Luca's reaction is exactly what I wanted.

"You want a drink?" I walk past him and into the kitchen. He follows me like a lost puppy as I open the fridge pulling out two Coronas.

"You want to stay in here? Or, we can go into my room," I suggest. His topaz eyes are lustfully lingering all over my body. Shaking his head slightly, he looks at my face.

"Yeah, the room sounds good," he replies as I lead the way back into my bedroom. He shuts the door behind him as I climb onto my bed and him following me. Soon, we are both sitting awkwardly on my bed whilst I nervously sip my beer, anxious to even look at him.

"I'm sorry, Rose," he whispers as our eyes meet.

"I'm sorry too. I didn't mean it. It was a mistake," I reply. His eyes sparkle like the brightness of the bedroom light as he swallows and stares at me.

"It was a mistake Rose, but I don't regret it." I laugh at his words.

"I don't either, but as Daniel's friend, I feel like you should be loyal and concerned on how he would feel about us," I answer, unsure of what his reaction might be. His body is tensing slightly before taking a swig of his beer.

"You're right. I should be loyal to him." His face is emotionless but his eyes can't fool me. I see a glimpse of something in them, and I'm not sure if I would like it.

"Friends?" I say.

"Friends sounds good." He smiles at me and leans back onto my bed.

For the next hour, all we have done is talk. He tells me about his job and how he moved from a little seaside village in Kent. He has a younger sister and his mum and dad are still happily married. He draws his tattoos himself which surprised the hell out of me. All of the artwork in his bedroom are his. I tell him as much as I could about me: my role at Fallon Publishing House and my relationship with my mother. Of course, I leave out my old step dad Wayne and we don't touch the subject of my father's death. It is nice to see Luca let loose and be a normal person, instead of the cocky persona he likes to put on.

"Maybe I could take you to Hythe sometime?" he asks me with a genuine smile.

"I would love that," I reply. His hometown sounds cute with a pebbled beach and a canal running through the village.

"How about tomorrow? If you're free." He bites his bottom lip and my stomach flips.

"I'm free." I smile, instantly calming his nerves.

"Great. I should head off but I can pick you up around nine." He stands up off my bed. I follow him out of my bedroom and down the hallway. Chloe and Darcy are under one throw on the sofa watching Scream on Netflix.

"See you tomorrow." He opens the front door. I stand watching him leave when his big hand grips my waist, pulling me in for a hug. Standing on my tiptoes, I wrap my arms around his neck. His breathing is fast, and I can hear his heart pounding erratically, or it could be mine. Letting go, he smiles before I shut the door, and face my best friends.

"Explain please." Chloe has her hands on her hips, looking slightly unimpressed. Darcy, on the other hand, has a proud grin and is slightly nodding her head.

"We just talked, as friends," I say, budging past them and walking swiftly back into my bedroom.

"Friends who fuck." Darcy chuckles to herself whilst I and Chloe send daggers her way. She raises her arms in surrender before walking back into the dim living room.

"Are you okay with just being friends?" She leans against the door frame as I pick up my hair brush and run it through my wavy hair.

"Yeah, we get on surprisingly, and I'm seeing him tomorrow," I say.

"Where you going?" she asks.

"Hythe," I answer as she shakes her head.

"The fuck is Hythe?" she asks, confused.

"His home town. It sounds cute." I shrug. I know she doesn't agree with all of this especially that Luca and I are getting closer. At first she thought it was fun but since my last encounter with him, she believes he's bad news. She has always cared about me and Daniel.

"I just don't want this to end badly and you end up broken again with an enraged brother." She unfolds her arms with a sympathetic face.

"We are just friends." I come out of the bathroom two seconds later with a toothbrush in my mouth.

"If you say so." She smiles at me before slowly shutting my bedroom door. leaving me with my own thoughts. *We are just friends, right?*

CHAPTER 13

LUCA

Her body feels fucking insane as a low groan escapes her throat whilst I kiss her as hard as I can. Shredding her tiny dress off her petite frame, I exhale at the sight of her. Her skin is smooth and pale and her tits are perfectly plump and perky. What would you expect from plastic? *Still perfect.*

Holding my hard cock, I plunge myself deep inside her, stretching her without wasting time satisfying both of our needs. I begin to thrust against her tiny body, making her moan and scream louder and louder.

"Yes!" She yells as I grab her breast with one hand, pulling her even closer into my body. I watch her eyes roll as I carry on pounding her aggressively. I hold her waist, picking her up and flipping us over placing her on top of me. She slids her warm and wet pussy along my shaft. I moan as she slides my cock deep inside her whilst I kiss her juicy lips. She whimpers as I raise my hips hitting her deep inside. She then moves up and down slowly, teasing me, and driving me wild.

"You like this?" she asks, whispering into my ear.

"Fuck, Emily," I wail as she begins to grind her body, holding onto her hips. I lift my waist up pounding into her again, hearing her cries of pleasure almost defining.

"Fuck! Fuck! Yes, oh my god!" She screams as I hold her, taking full control as she stiffens in gratification. I stop moving, putting all of her body weight back onto my cock. Her senses overload as her eyes roll back moaning with intense desire. She begins to rub her clit whilst slowly grinding on me, whimpering, and moaning my name.

Unable to take much more of her teasing, I flip her off me and have her on her hands and knees, making her completely surprised. A surge of electric sentation ignites through my body as I slam my cock back inside her, her back arched with her head in the pillow, and her arse moves high up in the air. Pulling her hair, I pound into her. Knowing I'm going to cum very soon, I see her rubbing her clit again as I carry on.

"Cum for me, baby." I moan to her.

"YES!!" She screams out as her pussy tightens around my cock. I groan as I slam myself into her one last time, spilling out into the condom. I crane my neck taking a moment to calm down before pulling out of her.

"Wow," she whispers in shock as she collapses on her back with her body glistening in sweat. I lay down next to her, sliding the condom off, and wrapping a tissue round it before aiming for the bin.

"Better than the alleyway." She chuckles like she's out of breath.

I suddenly think about Rose—how we haven't spoken in seven days—how much that frustrates me. Sitting up, I lean over to my bedside table and pick up my phone. Though hesitant, I scan through my contacts for Rose's number.

Text Message [To: Rose] I'm sorry about last week, friends?x

Impatient for her reply, she probably thinks I'm even more of a dick than before. I wouldn't blame her if she does, I can't let anything get in the way of what I want to do though.

Text Message [From: Rose] Now you want to be friends? Make up your goddamn mind.

She seems pissed and I've ruined my chances. Couldn't I be nice? I type out a text hoping she gets the hint that I want to come over; to make her see me as a good guy after all.

Text Message [To: Rose] I know I'm sorry, I had shit going on in my head when Daniel interrupted us. What are you doing?x

It has only been seconds when my phone pings.

Text Message [From: Rose] If you say so, I just got out of the shower, you?x

I hold in the thoughts of her body dripping wet, and I close my eyes trying to ignore the images. She really is a goddess, and I haven't seen her naked but I can imagine how perfect she looks.

Text Message [To: Rose] Sexy, I'm bored. Can I come over?x

Please, please, please.

Text Message [From: Rose] Friends Luca. If you want too x

Fucking score!

Text Message [To: Rose] See you soon ;) x

I send a reply before Emily walks out of the Bathroom still naked, with her dark eyes seducing me. "I'm going out," I say casually. I can see the change in her eyes; she could be hurt or pissed off. I jump off my bed and walk over to my clothes lying on the carpet. Two minutes later, I walk out of the flat with a sulking Emily behind me.

Daniel has proved who he really is. I have been planning to knock him down and there may be a few injuries along the way. I'm toxica and he has just met his match. If he can't be loyal, then neither will I.

CHAPTER 14

ROSE

Waking up early, I jump out of bed rushing around my room trying to figure out what I'm going to wear. Luca will be here in an hour and a half, and I still need to shave everything. If it's hot enough, I plan on taking a bikini.

After taking a shower, I slip on a black bikini, and pack a spare pair of knickers. I decide on a high waist denim shorts and a black crop top. I look at my phone to see Luca's text message.

Text Message [From: Luca] Be there in five minutes xx

My stomach flips, and I can't understand why when it isn't a date but just a day at the seaside with a friend. After brushing my teeth, I make sure I've packed my purse and towel before leaving the room. Darcy and Chloe could possibly be sleeping when I enter the kitchenI grab a water bottle and an apple, heading out of the flat and down the lift.

Two minutes have passed, Luca's gorgeous Mercedes pull into the car park. Butterflies start to fill my stomach as my anxiety goes through the roof. *Just chill out, Rose. He's a friend. A very, fucking sexy friend.*

The shiny black car halts to a stop next to me. Luca surprises me when he jumps out of the car and comes over to where I'm standing. My knees weaken at the sight of him in a knee-length denim shorts and a black vest top, with a Ray Ban giving him the bad boy attitude that fits him perfectly. *Lord give me strength.*

"Hello, beautiful!" He beams, giving me a genuine smile before wrapping his arms around my waist and hugging me quickly before stepping away.

"Morning," I finally say back after catching my breath.

"Shall we?" He gestures his right arm to his car. We have the day for ourselves, and I'm honestly so excited. I smile at him as he opens the passenger door and watches me hop inside.

"Nice bum." He chuckles, flipping him the finger I watch him from inside the car, he's grinning to himself as he makes his way to the driver's side.

"So how long does the drive take?" I ask him, intrigued.

"About two hours depending on traffic, it's not too far from that beach we went to," he replies, suddenly remembering signs to Hythe or maybe even driving through the town as kids.

As Luca begins to drive, we sit in silence, not sure if I could call it an awkward silence, or maybe it's my stupid nerves kicking in and making it difficult to talk. As the radio plays at a low volume, I lean forward and turn it up a little, and realised that the song playing is my favourite. I close my eyes and smile to myself as I listen.

"Of course, you'd like this song." I hear Luca scoff to himself. I open my eyes, giving him a stern look.

"I don't "like" this song, I "love" this song and it's surprising what a song can do to help you figure yourself out." I scoff back at him. Everything I've ever been through traumatised me for fucking my life, but listening to this beautiful song keeps me calm. *"Just stop your crying, it'll be alright."*

"No, you just like Harry Styles," he says, and I couldn't stop laughing.

"Hell, yeah I do, he's fucking sexy," I answer, rolling my eyes at his disgusted face.

"You like a guy with tattoos, huh?" His question surprises me; I thought it would be another dig about Harry.

"With the right guy? Yes," I answer, and he smiles to himself whilst watching the road.

"Am I that right kind of guy?" he asks. God, he's arrogant.

"Don't push your luck, you're lucky we're friends." I playfully smile at him whilst he opens his mouth in shock but chuckles instead.

"You're feisty, I like it," he says as our blue eyes meet.

"Friends." I snap back at him. Even though I hate it, I have to do it.

"God, you don't need to beat me down so harshly." He laughs. I watch his shoulders move up and down as he giggles. He has got to be one of my favourite things to look at, ever. He's naturally flawless.

Random conversations about work, favourite books, favourite types of food, favourite colour and anything we could think of throw into the mix. We finally arrive in Hythe, watching out of the window as we pass through the cozy village filled with houses of different styles and roads full of people under the sun.

"You did bring a swimming costume or something, right?" He gives me a worried look.

"Of course, I did. I'm making the most of this weather," I reply.

"If it's anything like the one you wore last time, we might have a problem with our new-found friendship and the boundaries that come with it." I scowl at him whilst he seems amused.

"Don't be such a dick." I gently slap his arm, giggling to myself. Wishing to have worn an even sexier bikini because this might let him down.

"I'm joking, kind of." I roll my eyes at his comment. Looking back out of the window, he parks right opposite the beach.

"Are you not parking at your parents' house?" I ask confused that he'd rather spend money on a parking ticket.

"I'd rather not see them today," he answers. I get it, and without pushing any more questions that he obviously doesn't want me to know the answers, I step out of his car.

We walk in silence looking at the beach, families, and couples scattered across the pebbled floor as the sun shimmers against the calm water. Whilst walking down the wooden steps to find a perfect spot, the sun is beaming and making me want to dip in the water

"Here, is it good?" Luca looks at me. I sit onto the towel he's already laid out for me on the spacious ground. I watch him throw his towel down next to mine, pulling his t-shirt over his head revealing his gorgeous tattooed body.

"Stop staring at me. Friends, remember?" His voice pulls me out of my imagination. I stand up to hide my face from embarrassment, and pull my top over my head before taking my shorts off. I look down at him and see his eyes gawking at me. I chuckle.

"Stop staring at me, friends," I say. He slightly laughs before pulling down his denim shorts. Standing in his trunks, I take him in again. Jesus, I can't believe he designed his own ink.

"Smart ass." He laughs. I know he doesn't care about being caught, and he's never embarrassed or bothered about anything. I start to walk towards the water slowly, taking in the view of the bright ocean and feeling the summer breeze. My eyes are fixed on the water when suddenly, I feel something wrap around my waist and lift me up.

"Let me go!" I scream. Luca's laughter fills my ear with so much happiness, and I can't help but reciprocate. He looses his balance and falls down, taking us both under the waters. I come out from underneath and jump at him. I instinctively wrap my legs around his waist as he falls back into the splashing water.

"You do realize there are jellyfish in here." He laughs harder and I know he's kidding me.

"Bullshit." I raise my eyebrow. I feel like he's being serious but I don't want to freak out. His warm body presses against mine as my fingers lock around his neck.

"I wouldn't dare lie to you," he whispers.

"I reckon you would lie to me Luca," I whisper back with our faces getting closer together, smelling his minty warm breath.

"Don't stop yourself, Rose." His fingers are stroking my left cheek as he moves closer whilst his eyes linger on my lips. My mind is going wild, and all I could think about is kissing him. Looking at his beautiful eyes, he softly smiles at me before locking our lips together and perfectly in sync.

My arms tighten around his neck as his hands grip my thighs. He brings me closer to his body, letting out a soft moan as I let his lips take over. My stomach is flipping as my breathing intensifies. His fingers are gripping harder into my flesh, leaving possible bruises but I don't care.

"Jellyfish! Save yourselves!" A group of kids suddenly scream in fear, pointing into the calm waves. I pull away in shock and realised he wasn't lying about the jellyfish.

"Are you okay?" he asks with my legs still around him.

"Are you okay?" I ask with a raised eyebrow. I can't believe how natural he is with me. No arrogance are displayed or signs of being inappropriate. He's so gentle and it scares me. Why isn't he pushing me away?

"I'm just trying to catch my breath," he answers calmly. I can feel his heart pounding against my chest. Have I really made him feel like this?

"Me too." I rest my forehead against his with our eyes still locked together. I couldn't ignore the feeling that something is happening between us. Even though we're "just friends" and without commitment, I know something's going on.

"You know, Rose, I can't get you out of my head." I pull away from him unsure of what to say, but I know what he means and this weird chemistry between us.

"Same here, Luca." I smile at him as he looks back at me.

"Jellyfish!" The kids scream again. I pull my eyes away from Luca and realise the jellyfish are only inches away from us. I spring my body out of Luca's hold and scramble out of the water. He laughs noisily, casually walking out behind me.

"You are such a poser, you know that?" I smirk at him as he lays down on our spot. He leans on to his right side propping his elbow up with a pouting facial expression.

"How come?" he asks.

"You try to act like a hard nut but you're not fooling me," I say whilst laying down next to him.

"Ssh, don't tell anyone I'm scared of jellyfish." I can't help but giggle like a stupid little school girl. Reaching out, he grabs my arm and tugs me closer, wrapping his arm over my shoulder. I rest my head against his chest. *God, this feels so good.*

"Rose, what are we doing?" I think for a second but can't put my finger on it.

"I don't know, but I like it." His chest is vibrating as a sound escapes his throat.

"Are you laughing at me?" I lean up on my elbows, looking at his topaz eyes watching me with amusement.

"You are just adorable." He chuckles.

"Adorable? Are you kidding?" I slap his chest and roll my eyes before laying flat and ignoring him.

"You are sexy too. So fucking sexy, Rose," he whispers with his lips lightly brushing against my neck and slowly sliding up to my jawline. Biting my bottom lip, his hands graze up my waist to my neck, holding me tight before his lips smash against mine again. Growling and gripping my waist tighter, I let myself claim his dominance. Unable to breath, I push him away leaving him breathing heavily. He sighs before dropping his head.

"I'm sorry, Rose," he whispers.

"Don't be sorry, I'm just so confused," I reply. I don't want to like him; I really don't want to, but I can feel it happening, and it's happening so fast.

"Your brother is going to kill me," he says anxiously and runs his fingers through his hair.

"He won't ever find out, Luca," I assure him.

"What if he does? What's my excuse?" His jaw tenses as he closes his eyes.

"Why do you need an excuse for this?" I ask, confused.

"Why else would I be kissing his baby sister? Because you're perfect and I can't stop myself." He reaches into his bag and pulls out a cigarette before lighting it quickly.

"Don't get yourself all worked up, Luca. He won't find out." I place my hand on his shoulder squeezing it. He turns his head to me with troubled eyes and displeasure. Did I make him angry?

"Maybe he should find out," he mutters before placing the fag to his lips again. I watch as the grey smoke dances in the air.

"If you have a death wish, then go for it," I answer, lighting a cigarette. The tension between us is odd and uncomfortable. I do not understand why my brother should find out? What's that going to do? A fucking fight that I don't want to see?

"You know, I didn't bring you in this date for you to ignore me," Luca says.

"I'm not ignoring you, it's not a date." I snap back, rolling my eyes.

"Wow, that hurts." He looks at me, disappointed. I push him away and stand up.

"W-where are you going?" he asks.

"Just stretching," I answer, standing up to stretch my body. I feel the soft touch of his fingers making circles on my mid-thigh. I look down at him as he stares at the scar on my leg.

"You okay?" I question him, trying not to burst into laughter.

"Yeah, sorry." He pulls his hand away.

"Do you want to go home?" He stands up next to me, towering over my short frame and answer him with a nod.

At the car park, I look out of the window and see Chloe and Darcy's cars. Luca turns the engine off as silence takes over.

"Thank you for today," I say, awkwardly.

"Pleasure," he replies. I unbuckle myself and unlock the front door, when his arm holds me down.

"What are you doing?" His strong blue eyes stare at me with so much intensity. Without a clue, I jump out of my seat and straddle his lap as our lips smash together. His fingers grip my waist as my crop top scrunches up to my chest.

"Rose, we need to stop, or I won't," he whispers as I grind my body against his already rock-hard cock. My eyes bolt open at the size of his mandhood, making me moan louder. *Shit, he's huge*! I have no intention to stop. I would do anything right now to feel him deep inside me. My whole being aches for his body.

"Rose, please." He groans as he reaches my bum and palming both cheeks.

"Fuck." He breathes raising his hips when suddenly his phone rings, instantly stopping him. He pulls his phone out of his pocket.

Incoming Call: Emily

Who the fuck is Emily? I give him a confused look as he hesitates before ignoring the call. I climb off his lap, picking up my bag and swing the front door open.

"Rose, wait!" I hear him yell as I march through the car park.

"Why are you acting like a psychopath?" His hand grips my arm, whipping me round to face him.

"Don't fucking call me a psychopath! If you already have a girlfriend then tell me now!" I push him in his chest, making his grip on my arm loose.

"She's my manager at work. I'm probably needed in, and I should call her back," he answers me. I manage to calm down, realising how crazy I must have looked.

"Fuck, I'm sorry. Shit." I look down to the ground, watching his feet shift from one to the other. I turn and run from him and out of sight. Why do I react like this when I don't have feelings for him? If I do, I need to be careful.

CHAPTER 15

ROSE

Spinning around my work chair to pass my time is the only thing I could think of. I still couldn't understand why I acted the way I did on Saturday with Luca. If we are becoming friends, then I'm definitely putting myself in the shitter because there is no way he would want to be around a psychopath like me.

I groan as I cover my face with my hands and slump over my desk, just waiting for this awful Monday to be over so I can go home and groan some more.

"Hey Rose, how was your weekend?" Emily's sweet voice pulls me out of my mood. I sit up and look at her, smiling at me.

"I can't complain, how was yours?" I dodge talking about me and my stupid problems. A massive grin appears on her face. Do I really want to know?

"I saw him again on Friday night, Saturday night, and we hung out all day yesterday." Her voice is smooth and her eyes are vibrant with happiness.

"Well I'm jealous, are you serious or?" I question her and sit up straighter.

"Not yet, but I think he likes me." She scrunches her face up with the biggest smile I'd probably ever seen.

"Do you like him?" I ask, feeling more and more nauseous by the second.

"So much Rose, the sex is insane!" She rambles. I shut my ears to avoid too much information. I've only hung out with this girl once, and 'I don't want to hear about her sex life.

"Well that's good, Hun. I better get back to work. See you later." I wave her off as she struts her body through the office and make a few heads turn from the men. I roll my eyes and thump my head back down onto my desk. I can't tell why I feel so shit and why I can't stop thinking about Luca. I need a fix.

Text Message [To: Jacob] Hi Jacob, I know this is random but are you free this evening?x

I rush to the kitchen to make a coffee with my phone in hand as I wait patiently for the lady in front to finish with the machine before I make mine. Checking my phone, I tap my heel on the floor. My patience wearing thin.

Text Message [From: Jacob] Hey you, I'm free tonight, what are you thinking?x

I relax slightly as my thoughts wander since our last encounter. I really like Jacob. He is so sweet even if he fucks up a little bit. I'm not in it for the long haul but he's sweet enough to hang out with.

Text Message [To: Jacob] Come round mine? Get takeaway or something?x

Once Carol or whatever her name is moves out of the way, I make my coffee quickly. My phone suddenly vibrates on the counter as I finish stirring my steaming drink.

Text Message [From: Jacob] How does seven sound?x

I don't even wait a couple of minutes to reply.

Text Message [To: Jacob] Perfect, I'll see you then x

I walk back to my desk and sit back down and then place the mug on my desk. I feel relieved that I have plans after work. I hate not having anything to do in the evenings. I need to get my mind off Luca too. I really don't like that I'm thinking about him so much.

I don't know how the girls will feel about this, but Chloe definitely seems to like the idea of Jacob more than the thought of me getting it on with Luca. I'm not sure if that's for Daniel's sake or if she still gets a bad vibe of Luca even though I told them we get on—kind of.

Wrapping the towel around my body, I walk into the kitchen to grab a glass of water whilst Darcy and Chloe are sitting on the stools in a deep conversation. "Hey, I didn't know you were home?" Darcy looks up at me whilst holding a bowl of pasta. The smell of cheese and garlic is hitting my nose.

"Yeah about twenty minutes ago," I reply, opening the glass cupboard. I walk over to the sink and turn the tap on and fill my glass.

"Any plans tonight?" Chloe asks me, walking towards the dishwasher. I move out of her way as she places her plate inside.

"Yeah Jacob's coming over for a takeaway," I mutter, waiting for their reaction. Chloe's eyebrows raise in shock.

"Oh, I thought it ended badly between you both?" She folds her arms and leans against the counter. I take a sip of from the glass and feel the refreshing liquid slip down my throat.

"Yeah well, I guess we can sort that out, right? I mean we are friends," I answer, stepping away from the sink.

"Maybe but I thought you had a thing going on with Luca," she says, walking back over to the stool and sitting back down next to Darcy.

"No, we're just friends. I'm not even sure if we are friends. Anyways Jacobs nice, but why can't I hang out with him?" I say, looking at both of my friends. Chloe's face is blank, but I can tell her head is ticking with many questions or major judgement.

"I like Jacob, he's pretty hot," Darcy speaks up with food in her mouth.

"Darcy, you think everyone's hot." Chloe rolls her eyes making me chuckle.

"I'm not picky, sorry about that," Darcy replies, making me laugh more. I finished my food and place the glass in the dishwasher. "He'll be here in ten minutes, I better get changed." I smile at the girls before walking out of the kitchen.

"What's the point? You'll be naked again soon!" Chloe yells from the kitchen and hear her scoff before shutting my bedroom door. She may be right, but I honestly don't care at this given time.

I brush my straight hair taking in my reflection. I decide on a pair of black leggings, a casual plain black t-shirt, fluffy pink socks, and a long grey cardigan. It may be summer, but the flat is always freezing, which I love.

"Rose!" I hear Darcy yell from the hallway. I think of how attractive Jacob looks in his black tracksuit bottoms and a plain white t-shirt. I walk towards him with a beaming smile on my face.

"I swung by the Indian place just around the corner. I hope you like Korma?" He lifts the white plastic bag up, and I can't help myself from weakening at his thoughtfulness.

"I love Korma," I answer. He places the bag on the counter and steps towards me. He then wraps his arms around my waist. I squeeze him tight and feel his heart pounding against his chest.

"It's so good to see you Rose," he whispers.

"I'm sorry about everything," I whisper back. I know my friends are watching and it's awkward as hell. I step back from him and towards the kitchen cupboards to grab two plates, two knives, and forks, and a couple of spoons.

"Want a drink?" I ask him as he stands in the hallway watching me awkwardly.

"Sure, I'll have what you're having," he answers. I walk over to the fridge grabbing two cans of Pepsi max and passing them to him.

"Let's eat in my room." I pick up the cutlery as he picks up the bag and follows me down the hallway.

"Have fun!" Darcy calls out from the living room.

"Be safe!" Chloe follows shortly after her. I roll my eyes shutting the door behind me. I place everything on the bed before sitting down.

"Sorry about them. They're so weird." I chuckle to myself as I watch him sit next to me.

"Don't even apologise. My mates are exactly the same," he answers, ripping open the bag of food he begins to pick out a few containers of food. My mouth waters at the sight in front of me: Korma, Tikka Masala, Bombay potatoes with spinach, rice, Keema naan bread, Peshawari naan, two poppadom's ,and a bag of chips.

"Okay Jacob you've truly outdone yourself. I'm now a very happy girl." I don't even care how that comes across as I start to pile the food onto my plate.

"I'm glad," he answers. He picks up a spoon and fills his plate. I turn the TV on and watch his face light up as F.R.I.E.N.D.S. comes onto the screen.

"Oh, I love F.R.I.E.N.D.S.! Who's your favourite character?" He asks with his face beaming before shoving a spoonful of rice into his mouth.

"Chandler all the way!" I answer proudly, taking a bite out of the keema naan. My eyes rolling in pleasure. *Damn this food is good.*

"Same! Why is everyone so obsessed with Phoebe? She annoys the hell out of me!" he yells with excitement.

"I cannot stand her. I like you even more now." I smile at him before taking another bite into my food. We sit in silence whilst watching the show. I feel his eyes linger on me a couple of times which makes me stiffen.

"Thank you so much for getting that. Let me give you some money please?" I put the plate on the floor before taking my purse out from my handbag.

"Don't you dare." He stands up and marches towards me. I freeze and drops my purse on to the floor.

"I just feel bad. This wouldn't have been cheap." I pick up my purse and place it back into my handbag.

"It was my idea to surprise you with the food," he answers.

"I guess so, but I really don't mind," I say.

"No Rose," he says and steps closer towards me. I can't help but look at his plump lips. I know it's not right, and I only invited him for food and company but I also want more. Being touched and kissed by Luca has made me a crazy, sexually frustrated animal. I need Jacob to calm me down.

Without a second thought, I launch myself at him and he instantly catches me. He smashes his lips against mine, but all I can think about is how Luca has worked me up.

CHAPTER 16

ROSE

Typing on a keyboard is irritating me, the sound of my acrylic nails making too much noise is making me feel tense, wanting to rip them off. Squeezing my eyes tight I take a deep breath before opening my eyes again. I'm so unsure what to make of last night, I had sex with Jacob and it was good. Really good. I still don't understand why I can't seem to get Luca out of my bloody mind though.

Jacob is engaging and funny but after last night, I know it wouldn't ever be more than sex, maybe just friends. I don't know how he feels and that worries me because I don't want to lead him on, I'm just confused. The sound of my phone ringing pulls me out of my thoughts.

Incoming calling: Mum

I hesitate for a moment before accepting the call. "Hello sweetie I hope you're not too busy." Her voice sweet, I smile to myself. I haven't spoken to her in a while.

"Hi Mumma, no it's fine. Are you ok?" I question her, slightly concerned that she's calling me randomly, she never really calls.

"Are you free this evening, I'm going to Daniel's for dinner, I would love it if you joined." Her voice tense but still loving. I can imagine her bright blonde hair curled to perfection and her smile as bright as ever.

"I am free, I'll come straight from work." I reply.

"Good baby, I'll see you in a couple of hours then, love you." Her voice cheery making me smile.

"Love you Mumma." I hang up the call, confused. Why is she coming to London? She hasn't seen us in ages. Why was she inviting me? Daniel's the golden child, I'm the child who witnessed her father die and caused a divorce between mum and Wayne.

I watch the clocks in anticipation, the longer I watch, the slower time is taking until five thirty. I need to get out of here and find out why my mum is really here? Or am I just overthinking everything? Probably.

Knocking on the apartment door I wait nervously, I tuck my strands of hair behind my ear and push the remainder behind my shoulders. Watching the wooden door open, my heart stops. How could I possibly fucking forget?

"Hey Rose, you stalking me?" Luca leans up against the door frame with a smug look that I just want to punch.

"You wish." I push past him knocking him back as I stomp through the living room.

"Leave her alone mate." Daniel scoffs at Luca in a joking way. God if only he knew.

"Where's mum?" I ask Daniel as I give him a quick hug.

"Your mums coming?" Lee waltzes into the living room, I give him a quick nod knowing exactly what he's going to say next. What he has been saying for at least thirteen years.

"Your mum is so fucking hot." He sits back into the armchair wiggling his eyebrows at Daniel.

"Don't start, not my sister, especially not my mum." He scowls at both Lee and Luca. I watch Luca raise his hands in defence.

"Wasn't me." Luca laughs awkwardly. Daniel rolls his eyes and marches towards the front door at the sound of a knock.

Luca's eyes catch mine as I watch him, his blue orbs have me mesmerised as he keeps them attached to me. Stop it Rose. He thinks you're psycho.

"Hello sweetie." I turn my head, my gorgeous mum strides through the bright room in a pair of black skinny jeans, Chelsea boots and a tight black t-shirt, a leather jack covering her curves, the same curves that I have.

"Hey Mumma." I instantly smile running over to her, she wraps her arms around my waist.

"You look so slim!" She pulls away from me holding my shoulders, open mouthed looking at me in shock.

"I haven't done much." I answer casually.

"Starving yourself has done something." Daniel scoffs before putting me in a headlock, I fight away from my brother flattening my hair back into place.

"Hello boys, Lee so good to see you again." I watch as my mum gives Lee a quick squeeze before she walks over to Luca, who is watching her with bright eyes.

"Nice to meet you, I'm Ms Wilkinson but you can just call me Sonia." She gives him a quick hug.

"Luca." He replies sweetly. My mum studies him for a few more seconds, fixed on his beauty I can imagine. I don't blame her.

"So, did you guys want to order some food?" She looks directly at me.

"I could eat." I answer her, I shrug my long coat off and walk into the hallway to hang it on the coat rail. I look at myself in the floor length mirror. I'm wearing a mid-thigh black dress with cropped arms. I do look slim, my stomach flat but my boobs prominent.

"We are ordering Indian, is that okay?" Daniel asks me as I walk back into the living room.

"I had Indian last night but I'm happy to eat it again." I answer him, sitting down on one of the sofas.

"Oh yeah Chloe said you had Jacob round again, he seems like a nice lad." Daniel blurts out, my eyes shut in annoyance, my mums going to start asking twenty questions and I don't even want to know what Luca's thinking. Why would Luca care anyway? *He doesn't care.*

"Who is Jacob?" My mum asks with a smirk on her face.

"He's just a friend." I answer rolling my eyes. Please drop it.

"Yeah a friend you have sex-"Lee begins to speak.

"Finish that sentence and I will end you." I jump off the sofa and pounce on him sitting on the armchair. He begins to laugh as I fail to shut him up.

"Well I'm happy you have found someone, Theo was a wanker." My mum scoffs whilst reading through the takeaway menu. Luca laughs instantly at my mums' words, almost impressed and surprised. She looks like she has manners and she does, but she also has a potty mouth.

After ordering our food we all take a seat in the living room and wait, I know it's bad but I could eat Indian every single day for the rest of my life. So, knowing I have it again has my mouth watering, or its Luca sitting across from me that has me all hot and bothered.

"So, what brought you to London?" Daniel casually asks my mum.

"Well I haven't seen you both in a couple of months and I have something I need to talk to you both about later." I watch her face sadden and I instantly worry.

"Don't worry." She looks at me instantly, her face full off bother and now I can't help the pounding in my chest. I try to think of everything and anything it could be. Daniel's phone begins to ring, as he looks down at the screen, he instantly panics but calms quickly before answering and walking out of the living room.

I stand up and casually walking to the toilet to calm myself down, shutting the door behind me I take a few deep breaths trying to let all my worries clear. I open the bathroom door and standing in front of me is Luca, towering over me with eyes showing lust and anger.

"Can I help?" I question him with a raised eyebrow. He doesn't even answer me; his eyes just bore into mine. I take a step back as he takes two forward.

"Luca, Daniel's just in the other room." I whisper, leaning against the sink. I'm stuck as he takes another two steps towards me. His chest pressing up against mine, I'm trapped and vulnerable to him.

"I don't fucking care." He whispers back harshly, as I'm about to speak his hands grab hold off my face, leaning down his lips find mine in seconds. I just about hold back a whimper as his tongue dances with mine passionately, his hands move to my waist squeezing me tight and pulling me closer into him.

"Fuck Rose." He moans into my mouth as I lower my hand to his crotch, I know it's a stupid idea to touch him but I can't fucking stop myself. Putting more pressure onto his growing length, his kiss becoming wild as I feel my panties soaking between my thighs.

"We need to stop." I whimper into his mouth but I carry on kissing his soft lips.

"Rose I can't, I need you." I moan as his lips find my neck, my knees weaken as he plants hungry kisses all over my neck and jaw.

"Come over tonight." I whisper into his ear, he pushes himself off me. His eyes wide, probably matching mine.

"Tonight." He leans down and kissing me hard, before storming out of the bathroom. I take a couple more seconds to calm down, to sort my reflection out. My lips swollen and my cheeks a shade of red. Taking a few more deep breaths I walk out of the bathroom, back into the living room where everyone is talking. Daniel gives me a questioning look, I shrug it off and place myself next to mum.

Zoning out of the conversation as I eat my food, my mind even more frazzled and confused then it was before. Trying to enjoy my curry is easy, but knowing Luca is only a couple of feet away from me is far too overwhelming.

"So, what did you want to talk about mum?" Daniel asks, I look up from my food. Her eyes on me, she looks unsure and hesitant.

"I'd rather tell you both in private." She answers slowly.

"That's no problem Sonia." Lee stands up quickly picking his plate up, Luca joining seconds later. His topaz eyes watching me, he's unsure? Maybe even worried?

"We'll eat in the kitchen." Lee gives her a warm smile before walking out, followed by a confused Luca. I look back towards Daniel and my mum.

"What is it?" He asks concerned as her eyes brim with tears, oh shit what's fucking happened? I drop my fork and reach out to squeeze her hand.

"Don't worry about me darling, I came to tell you something, I don't want you to start freaking out but-" She begins to speak; I feel bile rising in my throat at the sudden realization of what she's telling me.

"No, no, no please don't say it." I begin to cry frantically.

"What's going on?!" Daniel runs over to me and squeezes me tight, my whole body beginning to shake in fear.

"It's Wayne, he was released today." My mum whispers, but we both hear clear enough. My brother's arms tense as his eyes begin to water.

"Fuck, I didn't realize it was this soon." He slams his fist on the table making mum and I jump.

"I'm sorry baby, but he doesn't know where you are and I'm hundred percent sure he won't even do anything, please don't worry!" She's next to me, holding me close as I cry.

"Daniel please don't let him find me." I beg, squeezing onto my brothers' arms, knowing well enough he will protect me from anyone.

"Always." He embraces me, I feel exhausted, petrified and nauseous all at the same time. After a few minutes of silence, I pick up my plate and walk into the kitchen to tidy up.

"Hey no you don't." My brother grabs the plate from me, Luca and Lee watch us muddled and concerned. Possibly by the amount of mascara smeared across my face.

"I'm okay to clean up." I snap at him taking the plate out of his grip.

"I don't want you too." He takes the plate out of my hand again and marches towards the sink. I collapse onto the kitchen stool next to Lee, I lay my head on the cool counter and watch mum, Daniel, Luca and Lee from a side view.

"I should head off, it's a long drive. Thank you for letting me have dinner." My mum tries to sound cheery, but I know she's far from it. Her husband played her like a guitar, cheated, assaulted her daughter and now he's out of prison. Hopefully he leaves her the fuck alone.

I stand up wrapping my arms around her waist, unable to control myself. I sob into her chest; the familiar smell of my mums Michael Kors perfume fills my nose and I feel at home. I don't want her to leave suddenly, I want her to move out of the house she lived in with Wayne and come stay in London.

"Please stay safe sweetie, call me if you need me please." She whispers into my hair as she squeezes me tight.

"I love you Mumma." I pull away from her as she kisses my cheek.

"I love you too darling." I smile at her warmly as she gives Daniel a massive cuddle.

"Look after my little girl." I hear her whisper into his ear, from the corner off my eye I see Luca stiffen. I turn my head to face him, his eyes on me with concern and I know he wants to come over and ask why I'm a blubbering mess.

Once my mum has left the flat, I walk towards my bag and coat ready to leave.

"Rose did you want me to come with you?" Daniel is standing in the hallway, his face full of worry, both Luca and Lee are lingering around the apartment unsure what is happening.

"No Daniel its okay, I'm sure he's not here." I answer honestly. I can't imagine Wayne is waiting for me at the bottom of the lift ready to snatch me.

"Who?" Lee abruptly asks. Daniel gives him a serious look.

"Don't start." He snaps at Lee.

"Woah Daniel its okay, he knows about it anyways." I give his hand a tight squeeze and a reassuring smile.

"I'll tell you later mate, it's about Wayne." He looks at Lee; I hold my breath, hoping he doesn't freak out. That won't help me right now.

"Shit ok." Lee's eyes wide with panic, I see his head ticking away before his eyes find mine instantly.

"Can one off us drive you home?" Lee asks, he understands. He's worked out the situation.

"No, I'm happy to get the tube." I pick up my handbag and walk towards the front door. Luca steps forward picking up his car keys and slipping his shoes on.

"I'm dropping you home, I'm meeting someone soon so I might as well." I look at his face trying to work out what he's up too.

"Thanks mate." Daniel smiles at Luca, I decide not to fight back so I give both Dan and Lee a wave, before stepping out into the hallway and towards the lift. Once we are inside its awkward and silent, it's killing me, but I don't know what to say to him.

"Are you ok?" His voice deep but soft as his eyes look down at me, I give him a slight nod.

"Who are you meeting?" I ask, more concerned about that. Trying to stay away from the sensitive subject. He said he would be coming over mine but is he really meeting someone else now?

"Nobody, I'm taking you home." He answers, he turns his body to face me. His fingers rest underneath my chin forcing me to look into his gorgeous face.

"Okay, thank you." I lean back against the wall as he towers over me. Silence fills the lift, I bite down on my bottom lip. The door opens and we walk in silence towards his 4x4. I watch as his light grey tracksuit bottoms hang loosely around his waist, his bum still juicy. He is a god even from behind.

Opening the passenger side door, he helps me into his car holding onto my waist, my breathing speeds up as he lets go. I sit still, waiting for him to join me. Seconds later he's slamming the driver's side and starts the engine, the smell of musky cologne hits my nostrils and I sigh in pleasure. God, he smells good.

"Ready?" He looks towards me with a straight face.

"Yep." I answer short, giving him a warm smile. I look out of the window as he drives out of the car park and into busy London traffic.

Throughout the journey home, all I can really think about is the sexy male sitting next to me, driving me home and possibly coming upstairs with me? It's not like I need a distraction from the whole Wayne shit that was thrown at me this evening. I guess I could talk to him about it? Maybe? I don't know, but I want him to stay with me for just a while longer.

CHAPTER 17

ROSE

He turns the car engine off whilst I reach for my handbag. Trying not to make any eye contact with Luca, I don't know if I should invite him up? Does he even want to come with me? I have no idea.

"Can I go with you?" he whispers. Well, that cleared that up for me.

"Sure," I answer. His face is tensing and his eyes are glassy.

We walk silently heading for the lift. Once the doors are closed, he slams me into the wall, leans down, and kisses me. I grip hold of his hair and pull him closer.

With his hands squeezing my waist, I moan in pleasure as my heart pounds in my chest at a faster speed. I want him. I need him, but I know I shouldn't be doing this.

"I want you," I whisper into his mouth as he squeezes my bum and lifts me off the ground. I wrap my legs around his waist whilst his cock rocks hard against my thighs. I could feel the cold air hitting my skin as my dress begins to ride up.

"Fuck Rose." He moans. I lean my head back as he kisses my throat. The lift comes to a stop and so does our kiss. He drops me gently, and I can't help but smile up at him. His face is red and flushed and his lips are swollen. I pull my dress down to its normal length and strut out of the lift.

I fish for my keys out of my hand bag whilst he grips both sides off my waist. His lips are lightly touching the side of my temple. I lean back against his body unable to control my smile until I finally I unlock the front door.

The flat is dark and quiet. I'm surprised that the girls aren't here, but I shrug it off and step inside. "Want a drink or anything?" I ask him and place my keys on the kitchen counter.

"No, I'm ok thanks," he replies.

I walk over to the fridge and grab a bottle of water. I twist the lid off taking a couple of sips whilst Luca's eyes watch me intensely.

"Shall we?" I ask him as I walk towards my bedroom. My nerves are kicking in as we enter my room with the lights still off. He grips my waist and pull me towards him with my back pressed against his front.

"Are you ok with this?" he whispers. Without answering, I face him and reach for the switch behind him to turn the lights on. Unable to control myself, I pull him towards me and kiss him.

He growls in response as he strides and pushes me on the bed with him, and fall on the soft mattress with him on top of me. I feel his cock throbbing against his tracksuit bottoms, and I try not to moan as he presses himself against my thighs but his lips make their way quickly down to my legs.

"You look gorgeous in this tight dress. I can't imagine how gorgeous you look naked," he whispers. I hold my dress and pull it over my head aggressively. His kisses are overwhelming as he makes his way up my body.

"Please," I beg. He kisses my stomach and stops at the band off my thongs.

"Patience baby," he says, looking at me. I just want to grab his head and push him in between my thighs, but I can't act too eager just yet. My breathing is loud as his fingers wrap around my thong and slowly pulls the material down. I raise my legs and watch as it slides down my calves and over my ankles.

"So beautiful," he whispers.

I want to speak and tell him to stop teasing me. I can't speak and I can't breathe. My hands grip a cushion behind my head as he raises my thighs and bends them against my chest. He then spreads them apart, showing my vulnerability. My core clenches in every second that passes.

My back arches and a loud moan escapes my mouth as he presses his lips against my clit. His circling tongue on my spot causes me to shudder in insane pleasure. His hand goes up my inner thighs before pressing two fingers against my entrance and make me moan ecstatically. My fingers grip his hair forcing him closer to me whilst he sucks my clit as his fingers curl and thrust inside me.

His tongue runs along my wet slit as he teases me. I know I can't take much more off this before I cum. I try to calm myself, but his tongue and fingers working together make it impossible. It's pure bliss.

"Luca!" I moan as his tongue flicks my sensitive bud. I have never felt such intense pleasure than this before. My body is overtaken by insane sensation. Luca looks incredible between my legs. His muscles are prominent as he pumps his fingers inside me.

"You are so fucking delicious, Rose," he whispers, taking his mouth away from me. He can see me struggling, and I just want my release. Smirking up at me he touches me with his tongue again.

"Fuck, Luca!" I breathe as he groans. Heat surges throughout my body as my legs begin to stiffen. He holds my legs in a bent position and flicks his tongue fast, trying not to scream with this unexplainable experience.

"Are you fucking kidding me?" I chuckle to myself as I sit up on my elbows looking at him. He crawls with a proud look on his face.

"You enjoyed that, didn't you?" He leans down to kiss me gently.

"There has to be something you can't do." I smile with a raised eyebrow still in shock with what he can do with his tongue.

"I'll show you what I can do." He kisses me once again and grinds his hard cock against my wet core.

Knock! Knock! Knock!

"Rose are you in?" Chloe's voice echoes from the other side of the door.

"Are you fucking kidding me?" Luca moans in annoyance as the door opens with Chloe and Darcy in shock.

"Girls, look away for fuck sake!" I yell, throwing a cushion at them. I jump up and slip my thongs back on. Both are still unable to take their eyes off the scene in front of them. Darcy nods her head in approval and gives me a cheeky wink which has me amused.

"So, we spoke to Daniel and he asked us to come check on you, but you seem happy," Chloe mutters. I open my drawer and grab an oversized t-shirt. Luca is lying casually on my bed looking at both girls with a pissed off expression.

"Well, thank you but I'm fine." I snap back at her. I know this isn't going to go down well. She has no brain filter when it comes to being honest sometimes.

"You know shagging Daniel's best mate isn't going to help." She growls. Why is she so fucking angry?

"I'm not shagging him!" I hiss back at her whislt standing up and cross my arms.

"Well, we would if you didn't open the door," Luca says. I roll my eyes but I agree with him.

"I can't keep up with you, Rose. Last night was Jacob. Now it's Luca? Don't say you didn't fuck him because I heard you." She raises her eyebrows, and I want to launch myself at her stupid face. Maybe I would have lied about Jacob, but god, what if Luca didn't know about Jacob? She wanted to drop me in the shitter, but lucky he doesn't care.

"Just get your nosy arse out of it. For once, just stop being such a prude." I take a couple of steps back and sit on the edge off my bed. She screws her face in anger whilst Darcy from behind is trying not to laugh at the situation.

"Fine. I'll be in my room when you're ready to grow up and stop being such a slag." She scowls at me. I am so ready to ring her neck in, but she decides to speak again before I can think of a comeback.

"Daniel is worried sick about the fact Wayne is out of prison. Your safety comes first. God, you'd think you would be terrified of sex, but no. You like to fuck any guy that gives you attention. He really was a confidence booster, wasn't he?" She slams my bedroom door, and I can't help my mouth from opening in shock. My eyes brim with tears as I collapse in a heap on the floor and begin to sob uncontrollably.

"Rose, what the fuck?!" Luca jumps to my side in a second, holding me against his chest. He strokes my hair as I feel his fingers shaking with anger.

"Chloe, you went way too far! How could you be so insensitive? Completely fucking cruel, you need to apologise to her right now!!" I hear Darcy screaming at Chloe from the other side of my door.

"No, she deserves to know what everyone thinks of her!" Chloe yells back. Is that what everyone thinks about me? I'm an easy slut because of my fucked-up past. I know I can sleep around but for my best friend to judge me, maybe I really have fucked up.

"Well if you don't speak to her, then I don't want to be near you. You are one evil bitch!" Darcy wails before opening my bedroom door. I look up and see Chloe for a second as she looks in. Her face is full of regret but I don't care. She can fuck off right now.

"What is going on?" Luca asks Darcy as she sits down next to us both. I squeeze onto his arm as I don't want him to know just yet. He might go away from me, and I don't want him to leave me.

"It's a long story. She'll tell you when she's ready." Darcy rests her hand on my shoulder.

"Rose I want to stay with you tonight, please?" he asks. I nod in response and feel his arms wrap around me. My brain is overwhelmed with everything that has happened today. Finding out that Wayne is out scares me to death, but for some reason, my feelings for Luca scare me even more.

CHAPTER 18

ROSE

Rolling over I reach for my phone, I press the home button as the screen lights up, three in the morning. I sigh to myself rolling on my back, my hair still damp from my shower. I still can't get over what happened a few hours ago, I'm not sure if I can ever forgive Chloe. She knew everything that happened with Wayne, she met the fucking guy. Wiping my face as a couple of tears fall from my eyes, trying so hard not to break down again.

"You alright?" Luca's husky voice startles me, I slowly turn around to face him. His eyes sparkle in the dim light off my bedroom.

"Yeah, sorry if I woke you." I whisper back at him.

"Come here." He reaches out, grabbing my waist and the back of my thighs, pulling me effortlessly to his body. I rest my head on his chest, his arm wrapped around my shoulder. The pad of his thumb stroking my cheek gently.

"You know what's crazy." He speaks gently.

"Hmm what?" I answer, raising my head slightly to look up at him.

"I like you." He tells me. His words have my heart racing, he likes me? Luca likes me? He's joking.

"Don't joke about something like that." I slap his chest lightly in a comical way. He holds my wrist looking down at me with a straight face, no sign of amusement evident.

"Why would I joke about that? I like you a lot Rose." His face serious and beautiful. Oh, my fucking god.

"Do you like me?" He asks, I'm silent for a second. All my thoughts and feelings are jumbled; can I bring myself to like someone again? What if I fall in love with him? I can't do that to myself.

"I do like you." I answer honestly. I've only known him for about five weeks, but I have spent so much time with him. I can't deny the feelings there.

"I knew it." He squeezes me tightly.

"Don't kill the moment, dickhead." I slap his chest again as he chuckles underneath me. We lay in perfect silence for a couple of seconds, I'm not tired anymore. My mind wandering, trying to figure shit out, what's going to happen now?

"Rose can I ask you something?" I raise my head to look at him, concern scattered across his face. I sit up and wait for him to go on. He wiggles himself into a sitting position next to me.

"Who's Wayne?" He asks, I turn on my bedside lamp to sit up straighter. Do I tell him? I guess after everything he heard earlier, I have to tell him. Either way he might find out. Taking a deep breath.

"My mum's ex-husband, he's been in prison for five years." I answer truthfully, waiting for all the questions to come.

"So why is everyone so worried about you?" His face full of confusion.

"He went to prison because he-" My voice shaking, the lump in my throat making it harder to speak.

"Hey, its ok you can trust me baby." He leans across pecking my lips softly. I take in a deep breath, calming myself after his affectionate action.

"He was arrested for rape and sexual assault." I almost whisper, tears prickle my eyes and fall down my cheeks instantly. Luca grabs my waist picking me up and wrapping my legs around his waist.

"Calm down, I'm here." I wrap my arms around his neck crying into the crook of his shoulder. He grips me harder pulling me closer, I can feel his heart pounding against his chest.

"He fucked my life up for so long Luca and now he's out." I cry, trying so hard not to be too loud. He hushes me gently stroking my hair.

"I won't let him anywhere near you, I promise you Rose." He murmurs into my ear before kissing it gently. His words calm me down as I feel my heart flutter, he's promising to protect me and I cry out again as he holds me tight.

"Rose?!" My door bursts open and both Chloe and Darcy come running in, they both stop mid run.

"Are you ok?" Darcy strides over to me whilst Chloe stands still. Jesus, I need to buy a lock for this door at this rate, I can't seem to get any privacy with this boy.

"Yeah I'm ok." I smile up at her, wiping my soaking face.

"What are you still doing here Luca?" Chloe asks from the other side of my room.

"I'm here for Rose, I also thought you would be too." He snaps back at her, I don't even want to stop him.

"Excuse me? You have no idea what I have been through helping her!" Chloe marches over to us full on raging.

"After everything she has been through, I would never expect a friend to speak to her the way you did earlier!" I sit up, climbing off him as he yells back at Chloe. *Touché Luca.*

"Look I'm sorry about that but it makes me so angry how she-" She begins to scream back at him, right now I've had enough.

"Don't fucking start acting like a victim Chloe, Luca is here because he cares about me. What you said earlier has me questioning your loyalty towards me, I would never say something so revolting to you!" I stand up walking towards her, tears falling from my eyes, hands shaking as I stand inches from her.

"I'm sorry Rose I just don't trust him." She looks towards Luca, his eyes piercing and angry as he looks at Chloe.

"Well I do, so deal with it" I glare at her, she needs to know when her opinion doesn't count, right now I couldn't care what she thinks about me or Luca.

"I'm sorry, night guys." She slumps out of my room and out of sight.

"You ok? Seriously?" Darcy holds onto my shoulder and looks at me full of concern.

"Yeah, I needed to tell him." I give her a quick hug.

"Good, I like him." She smiles at me warmly; I crawl back onto my bed and into the open arms of my favourite tattooed boy.

"Night guys" Darcy shuts the door behind her.

"You are one feisty girl, I like it." He whispers into my cheek before kissing it hard, I squirm as he begins to tickle my waist. Trying to forget about the argument as I relax in his company.

"Luca stop!" I laugh into his chest as he carries on, trying to get out of his grip. I throw myself on the other side of the bed getting away from him.

"No chance." He jumps onto my back pinning me down. His chest hard against my back, his breath in my ear, I instantly feel hot. Feeling himself harden against my bare thigh has me wanting him. So badly.

"What are you doing to me Rose?" He whispers into my ear; my senses kick in as a shiver runs down my body.

"I don't know." I answer shortly, trying to control my urge to jump on him. His body doesn't move from mine, I arch my back pushing my bum against his rock-hard cock.

"Fuck Rose, don't do that baby." His moans make me push harder until he's kneeling and I'm flat on my face, with my bum high in the air. I know my arse is on full show in my thongs, my baggy t-shirt ruffled showing off my bare back.

"Do you honestly realize how beautiful you are?" His hands graze over my bum cheeks, stroking down my back and reaching my t-shirt.

"No." I answer honestly, my thongs soaking at his touch. His hands slide back up to my bum.

"Can I show you baby?" He asks, I flinch at the sudden contact off his lips kissing my left bum cheek.

"Please." I whimper, his fingers hook round my lace, pulling my thong down my thighs, I lift my knees off the bed as he glides the material down. His hands grip both thighs spreading them apart, I push my face harder against the mattress as he begins to stroke my bum cheeks slowly.

"You're soaking for me?" He asks, his fingers gently touch my slit making me moan with the contact.

"Yes!" I cry out in pleasure as his lips start to kiss my cheeks, teasing me until they reach my soaking core. I flinch as his tongue circles my clit, pushing myself deeper into the mattress. His hands hold my thighs open as he begins to pleasure me like I've never felt before.

"Delicious." He whispers into my soaking slit making me shiver as my clit vibrates with his words.

"Jesus Luca." I moan into the bed, he carries on with his work as I wail and whimper, trying to keep my body up.

"I want to see your face when you cum." He stops the contact, making me want to scream. He takes hold of my calves and flipping me on to my back.

"Woah" I start to laugh in shock, his smile bright as his lips glisten from the dim night lighting. Without warning he tugs on my thighs raising them above my head, sinking his face in between my legs again.

"Fuck, yes." I sob as his mouth working wonders; I feel the pressure of two fingers enter me. Trying so hard not to cry in desire he starts to pumps his big fingers. Don't wake up the girl's you idiot. I cover my mouth with my hands as he flicks his tongue and pounds me with his fingers until I come undone.

"Beautiful." He expresses wiping his mouth with the back off his hand, trying to control my breathing and dizziness, I sit up and climb on top of him.

"We're not done." I say, his eyes wide with shock as I force him to lay down on his back. Feeling brave I pull my t-shirt over my head and undo my bra revealing my breasts, straddling his thighs I look down at him with my bare skin only inches from his face.

"Holy shit Rose." He reaches out, caressing and squeezing gently. He sits up taking my hard nipple in his mouth, sucking and flicking his tongue. I bend my neck back in pleasure as he stops, moving on to my other breast and continuing the same action.

"Delicious Rose." He groans with a very happy smile on his face, I raise my eyebrow at him.

"Why do you keep saying that?" I lean forward, my face centimetres from his.

"You're delicious in every way possible." His eyes bore into mine as I feel my heart flutter, the way his eyes look into mine, making my pulse rate quicken. I really fucking like him. I want to show him without telling him.

I slowly begin to kiss down his toned chest; his body twitching as my lips gently graze his warm inked skin. Reaching the edge of his black boxers, his throbbing member bursting to come out. I gaze up at him, trying to calm myself and show him what I'm made of.

"Don't look at me like that or I'll cum in my boxers." He groans, impatient and turned on. I smile to myself as I tug the boxers down, trying not to gasp at the size of his hard penis as it slaps against his abs. Pulling the material down his toned legs and throwing them across the room, running my fingers up his legs he growls.

Leaning down I kiss just above his tattooed belly button, teasing him as he twitches under my kiss. My fingers still running up and down his soft skin, making sure I use just the right amount of acrylic nail to tickle him slightly. Taking a hold of his penis I slowly start pumping my hand around his hard skin.

"Yes, baby just like that." He moans at my touch as I move my hand up and down, catching him off guard I lean my face down. I close my eyes, feeling a moment of panic that I don't want to disappoint him. Pushing that thought aside, I take a deep breath and relax as I slide his very swollen dick in my mouth. Hitting the back of my throat before slowly raising my head and bringing it back, flicking my tongue and suckling my lips on the head of his cock. He starts to thrust his hips in pleasure.

Taking a deep breath when I pull away and relaxing when his cock presses against the back of my throat, then taking another breath again when I pull back. All traces of doubt gone as I watch him roll his eyes to the back of his head. His hand gripping into my hair keeping a hold of me as I move my head up and down.

Swirling my tongue on the end of his cock tasting his salty pre-cum, his breathing changes as his thrusts against my throat fasten. His dick hitting the back of my gorge, feeling it grow even harder that I almost struggle to keep taking him in my mouth. I carry on using my tongue to lick around his shaft as he thrusts deeper and deeper, his body tensing as I cup his balls gently squeezing them.

"Fuck baby I'm going to cum!" He screws his face up in ecstasy as beads of sweat appear on his forehead. I remove my mouth from his cock, using my mouth I take both balls and begin to suck whilst pumping his wet cock with my hand. I make a noise in my throat as I continue to massage his balls with my mouth and tongue.

"Oh, fuck yes!" His breathing changes again as his shaft grows even harder in my hand, his body shudders, his legs shaking with one final pump cum shoots out of the slit as I aim towards my chest. His body twitching with pleasure as his liquid covers my breasts. Looking at him with my eyes half-closed, my brain still unable to focus for several seconds. His eyes wide and his body stiff, he looks at me in pure shock.

"Where have you been all my life? That was insane." Topaz eyes shining, I shrug my shoulders climbing off the bed.

"Where are you going?" He sits up on his elbows. His body glistening with sweat, his tattoos more beautiful than ever.

"I'm going to shower, I won't be long." I reply giving him one last look over.

"Can I join?" He wiggles his eyebrows.

"No!" I answer shortly before shutting my bedroom door behind me. I'm in heaven, I'm falling fast.

CHAPTER 19

ROSE

I somehow make it to work on time. Luca left around six this morning to go home and get ready. I put more makeup than usual to cover my puffy swollen eyes, tied my hair up in a messy bun, and choose to wear a navy blue bodycon dress and black heels.

"Happy hump day." Emily bounces over to my desk, wearing the cutest baby pink dress. Her bright ginger hair is curled perfectly,

"Morning, you ok?" I sit myself down smiling up at her. She rests her elbows against my desk looking at me.

"Yes, you seem cheery this morning." She raises her perfectly shaped eyebrow, pouting her plump lips.

"Yeah I guess I am," I answer, though hesitant and slightly confused.

"You had sex last night, didn't you?" She slaps my hand and opens her mouth in approval.

"No! No, I didn't, I did have company though," I answer. Why am I telling her this? I'm not that close with her, am I? I question myself confused.

"Yes girl, get over that stupid ex!" she preaches. I chuckle as she stands up straight and rolls her shoulders.

"So, what's happening with you and that guy?" I ask, intrigued. Her face falls slightly and she swallows hard. Uh-oh, sensitive subject. Shit.

"I haven't heard from him since Sunday. I like him a lot. I might try and meet him tonight."

"Well if he's being like that, then maybe good riddance." I try to cheer her up and give her my biggest fake smile.

"His best mates are super-hot so I might just shag him." I burst out laughing. God, she sounds like Darcy.

"Maybe you should," I joke before she waves at me and walks to her desk. I can't help but think about Luca. What has just happened last night? What does this mean now?

Trying to keep myself occupied, I block out any thoughts of Luca and the incident with Chloe. I'm still in shock, and I don't know how we can resolve it. I think of speaking to her tonight, but I'm just taken back.

Text Message[From: Luca] You free after work?x

My stomach flips with happiness as I look down at my screen, but I'm not sure how to answer him.

Text Message [To: Luca] Might have to get back to you on that one, need to fix my friendship x

I bite the tip of my pen, waiting for his reply. Since when did I get like this over a boy? After Theo, I would never text a guy after a one-night stand, apart from Jacob, but that's just because he's such a genuine guy.

Text Message [From: Luca] Ok let me know and I'll come round tonight? x

I smile to myself, and the thought of seeing him again really has me feeling giddy. I know I like him in some way and it's only been a few weeks, but he just has something pulling me in.

Text Message[To: Luca] See you tonight x

I get back to work with no distractions and do all the work assigned to me for the day before it hits five-thirty. I stand up, pulling my dress down to the appropriate length as I watch as Emily makes her way over to me with a massive smile on my face.

"I'm seeing him. He's coming over mine for dinner." Seeing her look this happy makes me warm.

"Good, let me know how it goes!" She grins at me before walking out of the offce with a bounce in her step. Leaving my office, I decide to quickly pop into Tesco express to buy a packet of cigarettes. Standing in the queue waiting to be served, I notice Lauren standing outside, I roll my eyes stepping towards the counter asking for my usual Pall Mall double capsule.

Taking a deep breath, I step outside walking past the bitch, hoping she doesn't see me. "Rose!" I hear her yell. *Great.* I come to a halt and turn around. She's almost jogging towards me. Her brown hair wavy and low her jeans are showing off her incredibly toned stomach.

"What do you want, Lauren?" I scowl at her, lighting my fag. She looks hesitant and weary.

"I really just wanted to say sorry." I roll my eyes turn to walk away from her.

"Sorry doesn't cut it, Lauren, and you know it!" I yell back at her.

"I didn't mean for it to happen. You must understand what it's like to want someone you can't have." I stop to face her.

"Yes I do get it, but it's how you betrayed me. That's what hurts." I feel my eyes tear up but I refuse to let a single tear fall.

"I know and I'm so sorry," she begs. I ignore her and continue to walk until I find myself at my front door.

The sound of the TV on makes my heart pound, hoping to see Chloe as I walk into the living room. Darcy is cuddled up in her blanket watching "Pride and Prejudice," as I slip my heels off and slump down next to her.

"Hey girl." She smiles at me. I smile back and snuggle myself under her oversized blanket.

"Shit, this is soft." I moan as the fluffy material soothes my skin.

"Rose can we talk?" Chloe's voice appears. I look up and see her standing uncomfortably in her work uniform.

"Sure," I answer, not making any effort to move from my now comfortable spot.

"Okay. I just want to say that I shouldn't have said what I said about Wayne. I just don't trust Luca at all." She speaks too fast, but she has me raging that's she's mentioned Luca for some reason.

"Why don't you trust him?" I shift in my spot, agitated.

"He's treating you like a challenge it's obvious." I lean my head back to close my eyes. My nostrils flare as I try to calm myself down.

"How do you know?" Darcy asks.

"He just seems too keen." She shrugs. *Is that all she can say? Wow.*

"So, it didn't occur to you that he might just like me?" I snap.

"I guess, I don't know. Look I'm sorry I'll just have to accept this, but I don't like it. He's Daniel's mate." She looks at me in the eyes, but I roll mine and cross my arms.

"He doesn't have to know right now. Either way, my brother cannot control who likes me and who I want to be with," I answer.

"Fine, fine, but I'm sorry I shouldn't have said it." She raises her hands in defence.

"Its fine," I reply. I don't feel like I can forgive her completely, but I guess it's better than last night. She sits down next to me in silence as we watch Keira Knightley on TV.

"This has to be my all-time favourite film," Darcy breaks the ice.

"I thought it was Dirty Dancing?" I look at her. There is no way "Pride and Prejudice" is her favourite.

"No, that's mine." Chloe says. I look at her and smile softly. Feeling my phone vibrate on my lap, I look at it as Luca's name appears on the screen.

Text Message [From: Luca] I can't make this evening I've been held up, tomorrow ok? x

Sighing to myself, I type out a quick reply before hitting send. I don't know what's gotten into me, but feeling this cheery and fluttery over a boy doesn't happen, ever. "I'm going to see if Daniel's free," I say, standing up. I walk into the kitchen calling his phone. After a couple of rings, he answers.

"Hey Rose, you ok?" His voice is comforting yet concerned. I knew he would be like this. I really appreciate having a big brother like him.

"Yeah, I was just wondering if you were free?" I answer, praying he is. The girls are awkward to be with around, and I feel like I really need to talk to him about Wayne.

"Yeah, I am. I was going to head out shopping if you wanted to join?" he asks.

"Where are you thinking?" I ask.

"Oxford Street. I need some new clothes, and I work this weekend so this is my only chance," he answers. I'm sold straight away and rush to my bedroom to change.

"Ok. I can meet you outside River Island in like forty minutes?" I suggest.

"Yeah sure, see you soon," he says.

I slipping into my high waisted denim jeans and my crop grey sweatshirt. Deciding on my white converse, I take one last look in the mirror before leaving the flat.

After getting the tube to Oxford Circus station, I stand outside River Island with a fag in my hand. The air is still warm as I look through the crowds.

"Hey you." His voice appears behind me. I turn around giving him a quick cuddle. His light brown hair in need of a haircut as he pushes it away from his forehead.

"Right so what do you need?" I ask and take in a deep drag of my fag before passing him the rest to smoke.

"I need some new jeans and a few t-shirts, I'm running low," he replies. I wait a few minutes before he's finished before walking inside the huge shop.

"You know, I saw Lauren earlier. She really doesn't know when to stop." I roll my eyes as I walk past a silk dress, feeling the material against my fingertips.

"Just ignore her. They're both a waste of space." He chuckles. I follow as we walk through to the men's section and begin our search.

Two hours later and with many shops down, we are finally finished with handfulls of bags. I bought a couple of cute tops and some new knickers as we walk through the crowded city. "Hey Luca!" My brother randomly yells and cause a few heads to turn. I see him in his camo bomber jacket, skinny black jeans, and a plain black t-shirt. *He is fire.*

"Alright, mate?" Luca walks over to him with a smile on his face and fist bumping each other. Luca is followed by a slim tall guy. His pale skin is covered in tattoos, including a tiny cross on his right cheek bone. His face instantly scares me not because he isn't ugly, but because he is far from it and has this evil look. I'm trying not to stare at him but his grey eyes makes me freeze.

"Hey Rose, you doing ok?" Luca asks. I look away from the creepy dude to look at Luca. My heart rate quickens as I see more than just a friendly look in his eyes; an emotion nobody else will catch.

"Yeah I'm better, thank you." I smile at him, trying so hard not to give anything away.

"I'm Daniel, and this is my sister, Rose." Daniel shakes the tall guy's hand, and he returns the gesture.

"Nick, your Luca's flat mate, right? I've heard a lot about you both," he answers my brother, and I look back at Luca. His piercing eyes are making my legs feel like jelly.

"Us?" My brother questions Nick, gesturing his hand between us both, and looks at Luca in confusion.

"Yeah, you've all been hanging out together right?" he asks, feeling slightly intimidated by Daniel.

"Yeah I guess so," Daniel speaks up whilst Nick looks at me.

"You are much more beautiful then I imagined." He reaches out for a handshake.

"Thanks, I guess?" I say. Luca's face clenches as he watches Nick's hand still holding mine.

"Right. We best be off. Rose. I'm starving." I nod at my brother, then we wave goodbye to the boys.

"See you soon," Nick whispers as I walk past him. His eyes are hinting something odd, but I shudder to myself as I follow Daniel. I turn one last time to see Luca and Nick still standing and talking amongst themselves. Luca turns to look at me with a small smile appearing on his gorgeous face.

"He was fucking weird." Daniel leans in and whispers to me before opening the door at McDonald's.

"I know, right. Super freaky," I reply. I try to ignore the look he gave me as my mind flashes bright red with warning signs.

CHAPTER 20

ROSE

"You know last night, he tried to end things with me," Emily blurts out.

I almost choke on my coffee as I lean up against the kitchen counter. She plays with her fingers and her face is full of emotion. I wait for the perfect moment to answer whilst I wait for Claire to finish making coffee. Once she leaves, I walk over to the round table and sit opposite her.

"So, you didn't break up?" I ask her.

"No, the power of seduction keeps a man coming back." She wiggles her eyebrows.

I'm taken aback. That doesn't work but I can't tell her that. "So, you are still together?" I ask.

"We aren't together but it's getting close, I think," she answers. So they and hang out and have sex, but are not exclusive? It almost sounds familiar without the sex part, yet.

"Has he said that he likes you?" I ask.

"Yes, but that was like two weeks ago now. He will be mine."

I try not to laugh at her confidence. I don't understand this girl. I like her, but sometimes I just want her to shut up. Just because she can seduce the bloke does not mean he will stay around, unfortunately.

Turning off my computer, I slide my heels back on and pick up my handbag ready to just get home.

"Night girl." Emily waves at me as she crosses the office.

I wave back and stay behind for a few more minutes, hoping to dodge her.

Ping

Text Message [From: Luca] I'm outside x

I smile to myself as I walk out of the lift. I can see Luca through the glass windows as I pass the reception area. He lights a cigarette in his mout with a proud smile plastered on his face. I take a few deep breaths and step out into the cool air, but the smell of smoke and aftershave hit my nostrils as I approach him.

"Hello beautiful." He smiles.

I wrap my arms around his neck as he pulls me in by the waist and holds me tight.

"Well, this is a surprise. I have to say," I as he keeps his hold on my waist before letting go. I watch him smoke the cigarette before he puts it out.

"Your place or mine?" he asks with a wink, and I slap his chest.

He bursts out laughing before cupping my face.

"Is that all I am to you?" I joke.

He looks at me whilst his thumb lightly strokes my cheek. "No, not at all." He gives me a warm smile.

Do I believe him? Should I believe him? "Good," I say with a smile. Walking towards his parked car, I can't help the butterflies in my stomach.

"Can I take you out for dinner, Rose?" He stops by the passenger side door, looking at me with his topaz eyes that seemed to shine in the sunlight. How could I ever say no to him? That thought alone scares the crap out of me.

"Why not?" I answer, trying to keep it casual, and not act like I'm jumping up and down inside like a little girl.

I watch out of the window as we drive farther from the city. The city lights disappear as we arrive in a town I've only heard about—Sevenoaks.

"This looks cute," I say.

He turns the radio off and nods in response before parking his car outside a gorgeous restaurant with fairy lights twinkling outside. The weather is still warm as the sunset beautifully lights up the sky with bright colours of purple and pink. As we step inside the cosy little cottage, Luca asks if we can sit out in the back garden. The hostess agrees and leads us through the restaurant. A tree in the centre of the garden sparkles as fairy lights wrap around its trunk.

"This place is beautiful." I lean across the table. This is the first time I've seen Luca so radiant and happy. His hair is slicked back perfectly. He is wearing a navy blue short sleeved button up shirt, and black skinny jeans.

"Wait until you try the food. I recommend the Josper chicken." He looks at the menu and then back up at me with a genuine smile.

"Hello. My names is Amy, and I'll be your waitress this evening. Can I give you some drinks?" The bubbly blonde girl says as she stands next to our table. She has a cute bob haircut and wears natural makeup and looks probably sixteen years old. I look back down at the menu, looking for the drink section.

"Yes, can I get a Pepsi max please. Rose?"

I look up from my menu. "Sorry, can I have a porn star martini please?"

Looking at the sweet girl writing on her notepad, I watch her eyes light up when she looks back over at Luca. I don't blame her, he is pure heaven.

" I think we're ready," I say.

She looks at me smiling, but I can see the envy in her brown eyes. "Yeah sure." She gets her pencil ready to write down our order.

"I'll have the Josper chicken with the lemon and Thyme sauce." I hand her the menu after she writes my order.

"Make that two," Luca orders, before handing her the other menu.

I can't help but admire the cottage. You don't see a lot of these in London. Amy brings us our drinks. I almost moan after taking a sip of my drink. Jesus this is good.

"You have fun last night?" Luca asks me, taking a sip of his Pepsi max.

I hesitate to answer, trying to understand what he means. Clocking on to his question, I remember he saw me last night with Daniel.

"Yes, it was nice. So, who was Nick?" I ask. Nick gives me the shivers; he is creepy and someone I don't think I could ever trust. I'm not being judgemental because of his tattoos because Luca has them too. He just had this look in his eyes that really didn't sit well with me.

"Nick is my best mate from school. He recently moved to London." His face is emotionless. He looks like he doesn't care, but I can see he's uncomfortable with the conversation.

"Don't take this the wrong way, but he seemed a bit . . ." I scrunch my face up, trying to figure out how to continue this without insulting Luca.

"Creepy?" Luca asks chuckling.

I take a long sip of my cocktail before looking back at him. "Kind of," I answer.

"I get it. People get that vibe with him. He is odd but he's had my back many, many times." He plays with his glass, reminiscing his old days possibly? We both go silent for a moment with his eyes still watching the liquid in his glass. I don't even know where to go from here as he is in deep thought.

"How was work today?" he asks. His eyes linger on me as I try to think what to say and play with my nails.

"I can't complain. I love it. One of my colleagues keeps giving me the low down on this guy she's been sleeping with." I roll my eyes.

He smiles at me obviously amused. "Go on," he says.

I watch as his plump lips touch the glass and takes a sip of his drink. The way his Adam's apple bobs up and down with every swallow is intoxicating.

"Well, to me it sounds like he's not interested in anything but sex whilst she wants more," I explain, trying not to think too much about it.

"Is that wrong?" he asks.

Is he trying to get on my nerves? Is he telling me that we are nothing but some weird fling?

"Not at all. He just needs to tell her the truth before it blows up in his face. She's a feisty girl," I answer, crossing my arms and leaning back in my chair.

"Dare I ask, but what do you want from me, Rose?"

His words have my heart racing and my mind blowing up with different thoughts. I don't want to fall in love and have a relationship, but can I control it?

"I know I want something good," I whisper, trying to ignore his watchful eyes. I'm not even sure what my own answer means. What is "good?" What does that even mean?

"We have two Josper chickens." Amy's voice interrupts our awkward silence.

"Thank you so much." I smile at her, still trying to dodge any eye contact with him. I feel stupid for answering that question.

"Is there anything else you guys need?" She looks at Luca, whose lips form into a smirk. Trying not to scoff, I take a big gulp of my cocktail.

"No, everything's perfect. Thank you, Amy," he replies, giving her his pearly white smile.

I watch her walk off with her blushing cheeks, and I know exactly how she feels.

"She is definitely going to be telling her friends about you later." I laugh, trying to slice through the silence. I cut though the creamy chicken.

"You reckon?" He chuckles to himself before shoving a potato in his mouth.

"If I served you at sixteen, I would be telling my girls." I carry on laughing as I chew my food. Damn, this is good.

"Not now then?" he questions me, raising an eyebrow.

"No not now," I lie. *Badly.*

"Why not?" He opens his mouth in shock and touches his chest in a playful manner, acting like I've hurt his feelings; he knows damn well how attractive he is.

"You're not my type." I roll my eyes, and he lets out a real laugh. I can't help but smile at him. I'm beginning to worry how this boy has got me so good. It's like he's breaking down my walls even when I tried so hard not to let it happen. I can see it happening, one brick at a time.

We sit in silence, and I'm enjoying my food way too much to even bother talking. I watch him every now and then, shovelling down food. That alone stops me from making any type of conversation.

"You can just take a picture if you want?" He raises his eyes onto me but I hesitate.

My cheeks are heating up whilst I hold back a response. I watch as he reaches out for my hand with his right one and places it on top of mine. My body is frozen against his touch, and his hand looks so big against mine. I raise my eyes to look at him.

His thumb is running small circles across the top of my hand as I try to eat my food with just one fork. I can see he's struggling, but I don't want him to remove his fingers from my skin. Unable to carry on eating, I finally place my fork back on the plate. I take a glance at the glistening tree.

"Does my touch make you uncomfortable, Rose?"

I snap my head back at him. He has also finished his meal.

"No, why would it?" I ask.

"I can tell you're scared of commitment; so am I. But I don't want this to just be a fling. I don't do that," he says, and my legs start to shake under the table.

"What about the girl in the alley?" I smirk at him with a raised eyebrow, trying to catch him out.

His eyebrows quickly rise in surprise but he relaxes seconds later. "I'm not saying I haven't had one-night stands. I don't take girls out for dinner just for the hell of it, Rose." His eyes are full of emotion—emotions that I can't read.

"I don't want this night to end," I whisper and see his eyes widen. My feelings for him are growing with each day that passes, and I really do not know if I'm ready for it. I don't want to fall for him, but I can't stop myself. What is it about him?

"Are we done here? Anything else you need? I can get the dessert menu." Amy appears out of nowhere with her overly excited smile and watchful eyes.

Way to kill the moment.

"Just the bill, please?" Luca sharply replies before giving her a warm smile.

She nods her head and about thirty seconds later, she's back with the card machine.

"Let me pay, Luca." I grab my purse, but he gives me a look that could kill so I back out before even trying. Standing up, I pull my pencil skirt down and fixing any creases on my white blouse. I feel his eyes on me as we walk out of the garden and towards his car.

"You know wearing an outfit like that tonight is a dangerous game," he whispers into my ear as I'm pushed against the side of his car. His body is pressing against my back, and his warm breath is fanning the side of my face and neck. The feeling of his lips gently kissing my neck is causing my legs to shake.

"Please, Luca." I moan against his touch as his hands wander from my waist to my bum, lightly squeezing both cheeks.

He steps back, leaving me cold and lost. “Rose, I don’t know how much longer I can go,” he whispers.

I turn to face him and see him biting down on his bottom lip as his fists clench together.

“Take me home please.” I smile, hoping he gets my hint. Opening the car door, I help myself inside. He climbs inside and sits next to me, only seconds later. His body tenses as he turns on the engine and begins to drive back to the bustling streets ofLondon.

CHAPTER 21

ROSE

"Are you coming in?" I look over at him; his hands are tightly squeezing the steering wheel. I watch his sharp jaw tense before he looks over at me.

"Ok," he answers. Why does he seem so eager? Unlocking my seat belt, I open the car door and slide out. Our fingers are touching as we walk through the empty car park.

The way up to my floor is filled with awkward silence. As we reach the front door. I can sense something is wrong with him.

"Rose, I'm sorry but I can't do this." His voice breaks, making me take a deep breath.

Trying not to take it personally, I turn to face him. "Why? What's wrong?" I ask him, letting every doubt fill my head.

"It's not you. I need to sort some things out. I haven't been completely honest with—" His phone rings, and

I roll my eyes trying so hard not to let any anger boil over. I watch him as he pulls his phone out of his jean pocket.

Incoming call: Emily

"Do you need to go back towork?" I ask, getting the hint that something really isn't right.

"Emily is not my boss." He ignores the phone call and looks at me.

Why didn't I question it when we went to the beach? Why would somebody call him so late on a Saturday evening?

"I can explain, Rose." His hand reaches for my face, but I smack it away. I let every ounce of anger spill over.

"Who is she then?" I growl, taking a deep breath to calm myself.

"Can we go inside? And I can explain everything," he asks.

"Only if you tell me everything." I roll my eyes as I unlock the front door. Darcy is wrapped up on the sofa watching some horror film whilst Chloe is on the armchair with her headphones, reading a book. They both wave at us, and I give them a weak smile before going to my bedroom.

I sit down on my bed and watch him as he slowly closes the door behind him.

He walks over to my bed and sit on the edge. "Emily isn't my boss. I'm sorry I lied about that." He looks at me and my stomach flips.

"Why does she keep calling you?" I find myself asking, which I soon regret. Do I really want to know? Do I really care that much? Of course I care.

"I've been sleeping with her for a couple of weeks," he whispers.

I watch as he runs his fingers through his hair and my heart starts racing. Has he been playing me this whole time? Why has he been on my case, but shagging some girl at the same time.

"So, you've been trying to get into my knickers this whole time whilst sleeping with some poor girl?" I ask.

He nods his head without looking at me. "At first, yes. I will be honest and admit that, but it's different now. It's not just about having sex with you; I like you, a fucking lot!" He tugs at his hair.

I keep my eyes glued on to him. How can I believe a word that he says? He's probably told her the exact same thing about me.

"Who is Emily?" I ask.

"The girl from the alley."

I lean back a little bit. He told me just over an hour ago that he doesn't have flings—that he doesn't do this kind of thing, but he has been doing it for weeks.

"You liar, you're such a liar. How many times has it been?" I ask, feeling sick.

"Only a few times. Last night was our most recent time. I promise you, Rose. I really want it to stop." His eyes are full of sadness. My stomach drops after hearing what he just said. After spending the night with me, after comforting me, after doing stuff to each other, he runs back to her—after I poured my heart out to him about Wayne.

"Last night?" I ask. You have to be fucking kidding me! How is this possible? "This is seriously fucked up. You've been sleeping with Emily Cooper, haven't you?" Just my luck. I'm hurt, but I don't want him to see it. "How do you know her?"

His eyes widen, watching me as I try to control my emotions.

How can he have no idea where she works when has been fucking her for weeks? "I work with her. She's been talking about you nonstop, and you're her favourite topic of discussion at lunch," I say.

Humiliated is an understatement. He doesn't say anything; he just watches me. I lean my head against the headboard, trying to understand everything.

"I'm sorry, Rose," he whispers as I close my eyes.

I'm not really sure how to take it in. Do I let it get to me? Or do I just let it go? It's not like we are dating really; we haven't spoken about it. Do I have a right to get so pissed off? I know I feel hurt and betrayed.

"It's just typical. You're the first guy I have let in since Theo," I say, trying to avoid his eyes. Can I trust him?

"I like you, Rose. I promise you," he says, reaching over and placing his tattooed hand over mine.

"How can I believe yo when you say shit like that to other girls?" I ask, losing all hope I had for him and hating myself for thinking it was a good idea to open up.

"I know I've messed up, but she's not you, Rose," he whispers.

I look into his eyes, trying to hate the sparkle that they hold. "Obviously not. She can't see how big of a tool you are," I growl at him.

"Rose, I'm sorry. I didn't want this."

I stand up. I need him out of my bedroom. I'm done with the conversation, and I'm done with him. He can have Emily. "Can you leave?" I snap. I just want to go to sleep and dread tomorrow.

"Ok, I'm sorry. Please just believe me when I say that." He stands up.

Refusing to look him, I swing the door open and gesture for him to leave.

"I'll see you around Luca," I whisper. I look up at his tall frame.

He is hesitant but nods his head. He steps closer, and I hold my breath as he leans down. "Please believe me, I'll sort this. I want you, I'll prove it," he whispers against my ear, gently kissing my cheek and leaving my room.

***

The office is too bright. I could hardly sleep last night. My mind is trying to work out what I should do; I feel tense and unsure. The thought of seeing Emily makes me feel nauseous, and I refuse to tell the girls. Chloe would laugh in my face and make me feel like shit about it. I couldn't work out in my head if I acted like a jealous, crazy "girlfriend" or if I was way too calm about everything. I know in some way I have no right to be angry. I've have been having sex with Jacob when Jacob and I first met.. We haven't labelled ourselves as anything, but now I've probably scared him off.

"Rose, can we talk?" Emily's voice knocks me from my Luca-centered thoughts. Her mascara is smudged as she walks towards me.

"Yeah, sure," I answer casually, giving her a warm smile. I stand from my desk and follow her into the bathroom.

She lets out a loud sob before wrapping her arms around my shoulders.

"Hey, what's going on?" I ask, trying not to feel guilty. Of course, I know it has something to do with Luca. It always does.

"He dumped me, Rose." She cries into my shoulder.

I hope she's not staining my red blouse.

"What happened?" I ask intrigued. I know it's not good of me, but I want to know what he said for my bruised ego's sake.

"He said he can't see me anymore. Apparently there's someone else." She shakes with each tear that falls.

If I never met Luca, I would think he's a total cock. I do know him but as much as I hate to admit it, I still like him. I know it's wrong.

"I'm sorry Emily." I squeeze her one last time before I step back with guilt rising in me by the second.

"It's ok. I know I'll get over it. I knew it was just sex. I guess I just wanted more." She wipes the tears away, giving me a small smile.

I feel awful; I really do.

For the rest of the day, I couldn't stop my mind from wandering off to everything that's been happening, Luca has been sleeping with Emily this whole time. The hours I have spent with him have been for nothing. Does he regret it? Does he like me? Or was that a lie as well? I knew we were getting closer, but do I really care enough to stop seeing him? We've both messed around with other people since meeting; maybe speaking to him is the best option.

Text Message [To: Luca] Please come over tonight? x

I bite down on my bottom lip nervously. I hope I haven't blown it. We've both been messing with each other; we need to talk everything out. I know I like him. I cannot deny that.

Text Message [From: Luca] I can pick you up after work, I've just left x

I smile, trying not to get too excited. I will not let him know. He needs to explain himself; we both need to decide what we are going to do. I finish in fifteen minutes and I have no idea what I look like, it's been a long day.

Text Message [To: Luca] Ok, see you soon x

I hit send and watch as the minutes go by. I check my appearance a couple of times, hoping I look decent. I don't know why I feel like this. Even after finding the truth I'm still running towards him, and I hate it. I told myself I wouldn't let this happen.

As soon as the clock hits five-thirty, I'm springing from my seat and out of the office in a heartbeat. I look like an idiot, eager to get outside so I can see him. Why do I want to see him? I step outside into the cool air, and that's when I see him. Leaning up against his black Mercedes, he looks beautiful as ever with his hair slick back, black t-shirt, and blue denim skinny jeans or [illegible] takes a few steps towards the building and meets me halfway.

"Hello," I speak, walking up to him slowly. My heart feels like it's going to burst as his eyes watch me.

"Come here," he whispers as he pulls me to his chest.

I wrap my arms around his neck as he holds me tight. The smell of cigarettes and aftershave fills my nose, and I instantly feel calm.

"Can we please talk?" I ask, taking in his scent.

"Please, I will be honest." He pulls away from me with his hands on either side of my face.

Our eyes are locked and the emotion is evident in his stare. He leans down and kisses me hard. My legs tremble as I invite his tongue into my mouth. It was passionate and raw as he holds my face. Trying to hold back a moan, I pull away from his lips. Remembering, that we need to talk before I let this really happen.

“Sorry,” he whispers, resting his forehead against mine.

I wrap my fingers around him giving them a tight squeeze as we walk back towards his car.

“Where do you want go?” he asks me as I climb into the passenger side.

I wait for him to walk around and get in on his side before answering. “Mine,” I tell him, as he buckles himself in.

Smiling at me and turning his engine on, he pulls out of the car park. The drive isn’t too long even with the typical London traffic, and before I realize, he’s parking outside of the flat.

“Ready?” he asks.

Taking my seat belt off I climb out of the car and we walk silently through the building towards my room. I wait for him to speak first.

“I really want to say sorry, Rose,” he says whilst playing with his fingers. His voice is quiet and shy which strikes me as odd. Luca Haynes is never shy or quiet.

“[illegible] get it Luca. We aren’t together. I don’t know what we ar[illegible] it’s ok to sleep with other people.” I decide to tell him as I walk over to the bed and sit down next to him, hoping my trousers don’t tear at the crotch.

“I don’t want that Rose. We said we didn’t want commitment at first, but I-I want it to change.” He looks at me and his sharp features send my heart fluttering and core aching. Is he serious?

“What do you mean?” I ask. My voice is shaking as I try to come to terms with everything. Do I want commitment? Do I want it with Luca? More than anything.

“I know I messed up, but I like you so much Rose and to be honest, that scares me.”

“Why did you dump Emily? She’s pretty upset,” I ask him, though I’m so happy he did.

"I didn't dump her because we weren't a thing and she knew it," he snaps, obviously not happy with my question.

I just want to believe him.

"You still led her on Luca, she wanted more from you," I retort as he needs to know that what he did to her is not okay.

"You slept with Jacob. I slept with Emily. It's done." He sits up straight.

I can see the veins in his neck bulging. "I didn't lead him on the way you led her on, Luca. You've been having sex with her for weeks. Yes, I had sex with Jacob and I will admit I'm wrong, but I haven't done it since telling you everything!" I climb off the bed, leaving a couple of feet between us. I don't know what I'm capable off with my emotions all haywire.

"She knew what she was doing. She's been fucking Nick for about a week!" he yells at me.

I stop myself from getting angry at the mention of Nick. "Nick? How does she know him?" I ask. She told me his best mate was hot, and that was Nick—Luca's best friend, Nick.

"She isn't the Goody Two-shoes she acts like, Rose. I think she even tried it on with Lee and Dan a couple of times." He chuckles, trying to make light of the situation as I smile at him.

Now it makes sense really. She's loud and flirtatious, walking around the office in the most revealing outfits.

"Honestly, Rose, I know this started off wrong but can you just tell me how you feel about me. I'm sitting here waiting, and I don't want to waste my time." His voice is strong and his eyes are piercing into mine. His words knock the wind out of me. He doesn't want me to waste his time?

"You've wasted mine as well. I'm just scared because I don't want to get hurt again," I whisper.

"I want you, trust me please." He stands up off the bed and walks towards me with his broad body towering over mine. For the first time, I feel nervous and scared because I really want him so I just let myself go.

CHAPTER 22

ROSE

I can't seem to put my thoughts into words. I need to show him. The desire in his ocean blue eyes show me what he wants and what we both want. I pull him down until our lips crash together. I feel a fire ignite within me that I have never felt before. I'm pushed onto my bed and watch with hooded eyes as he takes his clothes off quickly, revealing his ink-covered skin.

"Don't look at me like that, Rose. You take my breath away," he whispers before climbing on top of me and kissing me hard.

Moaning against his lips, I try to take my clothes off. He unbuttons my blouse quickly, revealing my white lace bra. I slip my trousers down my thighs and he tugs on the bottom pulling them down my calves and over my ankles.

Moving towards my neck, his lips leaves warm kisses making me hot and bothered with each touch. His fingers unclasp my bra. I slip it off, revealing my naked chest.

"You are so goddamn beautiful," he whispers before placing his hot lips over mine. His hand is tugging my thong off, leaving me naked and ready for him.

"How wet are you for me, Rose?"

I'm unable to answer, as my core ached uncontrollably. His fingers touch my wet folds and cause my back to arch with pleasure. His mouth finds my pebbled nipple and begins to kiss and suck them gently. I squeeze my eyes shut and let him take full control of my body as he moves down further, kissing, and licking my skin until he reaches my naked pussy. Slowly parting my thighs, his eyes linger on my pink slit. He leans down and gently pecks the skin just above my bud before slowly moving his lips to meet my core.

"Delicious," he whispers against folds as a thousand sensations overtake my body as he latches himself onto my clit.

"Luca!" I cry out unable to take the pleasure, hearing my own wetness as he sucks on my pussy turning me on even more. This boy is driving me wild. I sit up quickly as he looks up at me with a proud smirk on his face. The pressure of his tongue has my legs trembling. Inserting two fingers into my pussy, I arch my back and spread my legs wider for him. He begins to pound them inside me whilst working with his tongue and lips against my clit.

"I'm so close, don't stop!" I beg him whilst he flicks his tongue against my bud. My fingers clutch onto his hair as my climax builds higher and higher until it reaches its peak. My orgasm rocks through my body as I cry out in ecstasy. My legs are twitching with insane pleasure as I squeeze my eyes shut. My heart is pounding as I soften into the bed.

When I open my eyes, he's hovering above me with a small smile on his lips. He leans down and kisses me hard and deeply. I can taste myself on him and I don't care. The way Luca makes me feel is indescribable. Watching him get up, he pulls his black boxers off. I hold my breath looking at his tattoos detailed against his tanned skin. His muscles are defined and gorgeous. I could never get use to this; he's perfect. His arousals thick and hard, ready for me. I can't help but gulp at the sheer size of him.

"Holy shit," I whimper, my eyes tracing over every inch of his cock. Remembering how hard it had felt in my mouth.

"I know right," he whispers moving towards me again. His lips form into a proud smile. I can't seem to take off every popping vein and the pre-cum seeping from the head. He is large, very large, and I know I'm in big trouble. He puts every person I have been with to fucking shame, and I don't know how I'm going to handle this.

Leaning down, he kisses me again. My heart is slamming against my chest as his cock touches the inside of my thigh. "Are you sure you're okay with this?" he whispers, hooking his fingers under my chin.

"Yes," I instantly reply, not even thinking about it because I didn't need to. I need him so much.

"Do you have any condoms?" he asks.

I nod my head. Sitting up, I open my bedside table and grab a foil packet for him. I watch him as he slides the condom on and I lie on my back as he kneels between my parted thighs. Holding my breath in anticipation, I watch as he holds onto the back of my thighs pushing my knees against my chest and slowly sliding himself inside me. Squeezing my eyes shut, he stretches me fully asI try to get over the pressure inside me.

"Rose?" he whispers.

I catch him watching me carefully; I could not decipher the emotion in his eyes, but I could feel a wave of something.

"Don't stop," I beg as his thumb is circling my cheek and smiles.

The head of his cock teases my pussy, dipping in and out slowly. I can't help but moan in frustration and sheer pleasure it brings me. He grips hold of the back of my knees and thrusts his entire length inside me, and I gasp. Lifting my hips higher off the bed until my bottom half is being held up in his arms, the sounds of pleasure coming from his mouth is endless as he pulls out slowly. Slamming himself inside me, I grip onto my thighs to keep them still as he deepens with each thrust.

"Fuck!" I scream, unable to control the incredible sensation.

I look down at his throbbing cock, my toes curling tight as he begins to pound into me at a speed I've never experienced. I scream louder than I have ever screamed before, as his skin slaps against mine. My sensitive muscles are twitching as his controlled thrusts become wild. The way his hips move with each pound is fascinating yet incredibly sexy—he really knows how to please.

"Fuck, Rose. You feel so good." He moans as his eyes rake over my boobs as they move with each thrust. Letting go of my thighs, he grabs hold of my breasts and use them for support as he slams into me.

Wrapping my forearms under my knees, I keep my thighs high and wide for him. "I can't—Fuck, Luca!" I cry at the intense pleasure his cock is giving me whilst hitting my sweet spot over and over. The intense pressure in my stomach is blinding as I clench my toes. My eyes roll as his stamina continues to surprise me.

He lifts my legs towards the ceiling and spreads them as wide as they can go. I fist my hair, trying to control my moaning as he shows me no mercy. His toned body is shimmering with sweat as he grinds his body against mine. Feeling slightly light-headed, I tense my body trying to hold in every scream possible as I don't want the neighbours hearing this.

"Fuck, Rose." He groans leaning forward and smashing his lips against mine.

I drop my legs, wrapping them round his waist as he slowly thrusts and kisses me with passion. I continue to moan into his mouth as he slams his cock against my wall.

"You ready?" he asks, pulling out of my kiss and sliding himself out of my drenched pussy.

I look at him with a confused face before squealing in shock as he flips me over onto my hands and knees. I arch my back, resting my face against the mattress. Luca kisses slowly down my spine causing me to shiver. Slowly, his lips move down my spine until he reaches my bum cheek, making his way further down until his tongue flicks against my exposed core.

My whole body is shivering and pulsating with pleasure with every touch. Panting hard, I curl my toes at the blinding pressure of Luca slowly as he enters me again. I could feel every inch inside me as I moan.Holding both hips, he begins to grinds into me. My body is tingling and my stomach is aching as he continues to fuck me effortlessly. I reach down between my legs and rub my clit as I feel a build-up deep inside me—one I've never felt before.

"Harder, Luca!" I sob into the mattress as I feel the pressure in my stomach. I spread my legs wider for him as he places himself even closer against my body.

"Are you sure baby?"

I feel his hand reach out and grip into my hair.

"Yes!" I answer.

The anticipation is killing me. I cry out, raising my hips into his rock-hard cock as he rams into me. I rub my clit aggressively as he beats against my arse. My toes are curling tightly and my neck arches as he pulls my hair. I scream his name whilst he continues to rock my body hard against his. His balls are slapping against my hand as I rub my clit.

"I'm going to cum!" I scream into the bed as my walls clench tight around his shaft. My nerve endings have my knees wobbling as my body comes undone.

Luca continues to slam himself inside me before moaning my name and collapses on top of me. His cock jerks inside me as he cums into the condom.

I've never been fucked the way Luca fucked me—raw and passionate. Jesus. He's so fucking gorgeous.

"Fucking hell, Rose," he whines, shocked and out of breath as he crawls on top of me.

I roll onto my back and look at him. He falls down next to me and rests his head against the headboard. I can't help but smile and my heart is going crazy in my chest as I come down from my climax.

"Why are you so fucking beautiful?" he asks, gently stroking my cheek with his thumb.

I shrug my shoulders, not sure how to answer him. "Worth the wait?" I ask, almost embarrassed as I try to hide my face in the cushions.

He grips my chin, pulling me to face him again. His eyes are shining with something I haven't seen before. "Honestly?" he asks.

My eyes widen and my heart rate doubles. His face is strong but full of happiness, and I nod my head, scared to hear what he's really thinking.

"It was insane. You are incredible." He smiles.

I cover my face, trying to hide my smile. He pulls me over to him with my body resting against his. My fingertips are gracing over his inked patterns against his chest. Looking up into his topaz eyes, I can't help but lose myself in them whilst a soft smile is playing on his lips.

"Rose, you really are something special."

I sit up quickly, straddling his waist and kissing him hard. His fingers are scrunching the back of my hair and keeping my head in place as our tongues dance together. Pulling away from the kiss, I take in his world-stopper smile.

"Already eager for another go?" Luca laughs at me.

He loves how much he affects me. I sit up straight with my hands holding onto his shoulders. I listen out for voices, and I could hear my brother's voice travelling through the flat. I quickly jump off Luca's body and quietly walk towards my bedroom door.

"Who's that?" Luca shifts on the bed, tugging the duvet cover over his naked body. His eyes are wide trying to listen.

Pressing my head against the door, I look away from him but I can still feel the hole burning in the back of my head as he looks over my naked body. I roll my eyes as I try to concentrate.

"Is Rose home?" Daniel asks.

My hands begin to shake with fear as I look over to Luca.

"I don't think so. She's been in and out of here a lot lately," Chloe answers.

I scoff at her comment and walk back over to my bed. I catch Luca's watchful eyes, taking in every step as I approach him looking as gorgeous as ever.

"Get your head out of the gutter. We have a problem. My brother's here and he's asking if I'm home." I sit down next to him.

He jumps up frantically, nearly knocking me off the bed.

"Calm down." I laugh.

He's running around like crazy, slipping his boxers and jeans on in under ten seconds. I watch in fascination at how quickly he moves. He then scans my room for anything that may have fallen out of his pockets.

I walk over to my drawers and pull out my oversized navy Tommy Hilfiger t-shirt and a pair of runner shorts. He looks up at me still worried more than I am at this moment.

"I'll sort this. You can't leave my room without being caught, so just chill." I walk over to him and kiss him softly. Cupping his face, I press my lips against his one more time before turning and walking to the door.

"Hey, where have you been?" Daniel leans up against the kitchen counter with a raised eyebrow. Nick and Lee are standing on the other side of the counter whilst Chloe and Darcy are looking at me with a concerned look on their faces.

I gaze back at Nick. Why the hell is he in my kitchen? Unless he's now bum buddies with both Daniel and Lee too? I thought he gave Daniel a weird vibe?

"In my bedroom?" I answer, slightly worried he already knows.

"I've been calling you for like an hour," he answers.

I take in a deep breath, trying to think of something to say. "I've been sleeping," I reply, trying to come up with something believable.

Lee bursts out laughing, and everyone's eyes turn to him.

"Bullshit, Rose! That's sex hair!" He walks over to me and grabs my oily ruffled hair.

I push Lee off me whilst taking a couple of steps back. The girls look at me with wide eyes. I watch as Darcy mouths something to me. I squint my eyes and just about make sense of it. *"Luca?"* She nods her head discretely towards my bedroom. I nod slightly, just enough that only she can see.

"Right, let's leave this girl back to her sex antics, McDonalds, anyone?" Darcy chirps up, everyone straightens but Daniel and Nick keep their eyes on me.

"Who is it?" Dan asks with a smirk.

Why does he care? I'm pretty sure he doesn't want to know the answer to that. If only you knew.

"Jacob!!" Chloe burst out, surprising me.

We all look towards her, and I give her a look of appreciation. She smiles back at me probably understanding the situation.

"Oh-uh. He's nice, I like him." Daniel nods his head before walking towards the front door.

Everyone waves goodbye, but Nick stops me from shutting the front door as I hear the muffled voices of everyone leaving down the hallway of the building.

"Luca is one lucky boy," he whispers into my ear. His hand grips hold of my waist tugging me towards his chest.

I push him off me and step back.

"Excuse me?" I ask quietly. I try not to make a scene, though my blood is boiling as I tighten my fists into a ball.

"I know he's hiding in your bedroom. I'm not stupid like everyone else, love." He takes another step towards me, and I scowl at him.

"You have no Idea what you're on about," I growl.

His creepy face lights up in a smile causing me to shiver. "Oh, but I do, princess. Would be a shame if your brother did too." He smirks.

I push him against his chest until he stumbles out of the front door. Flipping him the middle finger, I give him a sarcastic smile before slamming the door in his face.

Things dawn on me as I slump back to my bedroom. I just had incredible sex with my brother's mate. Luca is meant to be off limits, the same way I am to him. We just had fucking sex. If Daniel ever finds out, we are both a toast. Have I tremendously fucked up and ruined everything? I honestly can't stop my feelings anymore.

CHAPTER 23

ROSE

Walking back into my bedroom, I feel tense and unsure.

Luca's eyes are on me as I walk back over to the bed. "Everything ok?" he asks, moving a strand of hair behind my ear as I kneel down beside him.

"They've left to get McDonald's, it's best if you go." I look up, his eyes shining down at me.

"Why do I need to leave then? Who was it?" he asks.

"Dan, Lee, and your friend, Nick." I scoff, still confused that my brother is hanging out with him.

"What did he say to you, Rose?" Luca's eyes widen in panic.

Why does it matter what he said to me? What could've worked Luca up so quickly? Maybe Nick isn't as loyal as Luca thinks.

"He knew you were in my bedroom and that we had sex." I raise my eyebrow at him.

His face is blank and I see his Adam's apple move as he swallows hard.

"How did he know it was you?" I ask him, trying to figure it out myself. I cross my arms, feeling uneasy with everything.

"I may have told him I like you, but it's nothing to worry about," he answers.

I won't think too much about it so I crawl away from him and off the bed, heading towards my bathroom.

"Want to join?" I ask him.

He smiles and quickly pulls his clothes off. Walking towards me, I pull my T-shirt over my head just as he reaches for my shorts and tugs them off quickly. I pressed my body against him, tracing his lips over my jawline.

"Don't tempt me, Rose." He breathes into my ear.

I can feel his cock hardening against my waist as he pushes himself further against me.

"Don't work yourself up too much, we have all night for that." I wink at him before pushing him out of my way into the bathroom.

Stepping into the shower, I turn the power on, waiting for the water to warm up. His body trembles as he takes in my naked body, water soaking every inch of me. He steps in and takes hold of my waist, pinning me against the tiled wall.

"What are you thinking?" He presses his chest against mine. I lean up, my lips demanding against his. The water pounds down on both of us as we kiss passionately. I want him all over again, I couldn't ever get bored of this.

"Should I feel bad about my feelings for you?" I look up into his glistening eyes with water trickling down his sharp face.

Stroking my cheek gently, he shakes his head smiling at me. "No baby. I don't feel bad so neither should you."

He presses his lips against my forehead as I wrap my arms around his waist, hugging him tight. Maybe I shouldn't. He might assume that we are serious about each other. Is Luca serious about me? Am I ready to be serious with anyone again? *Probably not.* But I want him so much.

***

Luca leaves and I grab my fluffy throw from my bed. I slip on my favourite hoodie and walk into the living room, ready for a night of Netflix. I place a can of Pringles on my lap whilst watching my favourite horror film. Of course, that is just wishful thinking. Within twenty minutes of watching the film, Chloe and Darcy enter the living room.

"Are you going to tell us what happened earlier?" Chloe steps in front of the TV and crosses her arms. She's obviously not impressed with me.

"What do you mean?" I pause the film to look at her, trying to keep a straight face. What is her problem? I just don't get it. She's never acted like this way around me before.

"You totally had sex with Luca!" Darcy jumps next to me on the sofa reaching for my pringles.

I roll my eyes, trying to ignore her wiggling eyebrows.

"Rose!" Chloe raises her voice again, taking a deep breath I look back at this evil friend of mine.

"Yes! Okay, I had sex with him! Why is that such a fucking problem?!"

I push thethrow pillow off me as I walk away.

"Because you know it's wrong! He's Dan's friend!" They both follow me as I march into the kitchen.

I need a fucking drink if this is what I have to deal with.

"You've probably fucked my brother!" I snap back at Chloe as I open the can of cider. I would never judge or be angry about that. If you like someone, you like someone. End of conversation.

"I haven't. I don't jump at the opportunity as easily as some." She leans up against the counter with her arms crossed and an intimidating look on her face.

Bitch. "Why is it so hard for you to be happy for me? I really like him." I keep my eyes on her, hoping to see a battle within herself. Nothing seems to change.

She scoffs as she rolls her eyes and walks out of the kitchen.

"You need to tell Daniel before somebody else does." I hear her mutter under her breath.

"God why is she such a fucking cow?" I rest my head against the fridge door.

Darcy raises her shoulders in defeat. "She's jealous because Daniel hasn't made a move," Darcy answers.

Thinking about it, Chloe's wanted my brother for years, and nothing has happened that I know of. I leave the kitchen and sit back into the warm sofa as I rewrap myself in the throw. Pressing the play button, I let Darcy sit next to me whilst sticking her hand into my Pringles.

***

My fluffy sliders tickle my toes as I lean over the balcony, watching the beautiful city lights. Putting my cigarette to my lips, I think about Luca's lips, when I inhale and I exhale the smoke. He has invaded every single thought I could possibly think off. Looking down at my phone as it vibrates, I can't stop the smile on my lips.

Text Message [From: Luca] Hey baby, I can't stop thinking about last night x

I think about every intense second of it and the way my body lights up when he touches me.

Text Message [To: Luca] Hey you, you've been quiet today, me either it was incredible xx

Bringing the fag to my lips again, I wait for him to text back. The night is calm and mild as I try to avoid any possible contact from Chloe. We haven't spoken since last night, and I'm trying to dodge her at all costs. I really can't understand it. Darcy and I can be a lot more precarious than her, but she's never had a problem. I know it's because she cares about Dan too much.

Text Message [From: Luca] Yeah, sorry I've been busy today! I hope you've had a nice day? I miss you, how soppy am I? xx

I feel my whole body twitch with excitement and butterflies hit my stomach. I can't stop the joy ripping through me. The undeniable feelings that I'm starting to feel for him scare me, but I also feel so optimistic. My phone begins to vibrate in my hand again and pulls me out of my thoughts as I look down expecting a text.

Incoming call: Luca

"Hello?" I answer. My heart is pumping as I wait to hear his husky voice on the other end.

"Hey baby, I hate texting. What are you doing?"

Oh lord, give me strength. Luca Haynes is calling me "baby." Trying to control my breathing suddenly seems impossible.

"I'm out on the balcony, why?" I ask.

"Daniel's not home. Lee and I are going to order some food in. Please join. I can see you without looking suspicious," he says.

I smile into the phone, but I realize he can't actually see my reaction.

"Yeah sounds like fun, I'll leave now," I answer him, stubbing my fag into the ashtray and opening the sliding doors. I jump in fright at the dark silhouette standing by the front door.

"Hey baby." Luca steps out into the dim light. I end the call without even taking my eyes away from him.

"How did you get in?" I ask, taking small steps towards the gorgeous man.

"Chloe let me in. She seems pissed." He chuckles, reaching out and grabbing my waist.

"Yeah, don't start with her." I roll my eyes at the thought of my best friend.

His eyes glisten as he looks at me. "You are breathtaking."

His warm breath fans my face and the smell of mint invades my nose. My legs wobble as he gently places his lips against mine, pulling me even closer to his body.

"Hmm," I hum as he steps away from the kiss

"Let's go then, shall we?" he asks, intertwining his fingers with mine.

I walk over to my oversized bomber jacket hanging up in the hallway and sliding it on quickly.

"Yes, let's go." I smile up at him as I open the front door and we walk out with our fingers interlace.

CHAPTER 24

ROSE

"Don't eat any of my chicken balls, Rose!" Lee jumps at me from across the sofa.

Whilst I shove the last chicken ball fully into my mouth. Trying so hard not to choke as I burst out laughing. His face is full of disgust as I chew it slowly.

"Damn." Luca laughs next to me. His hand is secretly on the small of my back as Lee sits next to him with a sad face.

"You're such a bitch. If you weren't Dan's sister, I would beat your ass," Lee growls.

I finish swallowing the greasy food and reach over to slap him across the arm.

"That's fucking bullshit, mate." Luca chuckles shaking his head in amusement.

"Fucking hell." He holds his arm in pain whilst Luca and I laugh even more. His hand is squeezing onto my waist.

"Where is my brother?" I ask both of them, trying to distract myself from my sexual thoughts.

"I think he's at work. I'm not sure actually," Lee answers, finally over with his drama queen state.

I don't think he starts work for at least another two hours.

Lee's phone begins to ring. I watch as he picks it up with a smile on his face.

"Speaking of the devil." Lee shows Dan's name flashing on his screen. He stands up answering and walking out of the living room.

"You have no Idea how badly I want you in my bedroom." Luca leans in with his soft lips skimming my ear.

I let out a low breath as I watch his eyes linger on mine. "Don't tempt me, Luca," I whisper back. I can feel the pool of desire, and I know I will not be able to hold out for much longer. I lean back as Lee walks into the living room, hanging up the phone.

"Did you guys want to go grab a drink? Dan's out with some work friends." He looks at Luca desperately.

I hope he says "no," please say "no."

"No man, I'm pretty tired but you can head off." Luca smiles with a glimmer in his eyes as they quickly glance my way.

My lips tug into a sly smirk as Lee pulls his jacket tighter round him.

"You okay getting home, Rose?" Lee looks at me with concern.

I nod my head smiling up at the sweet boy.

"I'm sure Luca will drop me home?" I look over at him, trying to act as casual as possible.

"Yeah no problem," Luca answers and shrugs.

"Make sure you do, man." Lee scowls at Luca, trying to act like the protective big brother for me.

We wave him goodbye as he walks through the flat and out the front door.

"So," I whisper, trying to break the silence that surrounds us.

Minutes have passed since Lee has left, and all I can hear is the sound of my heart pounding in my chest. His face turns to look at me. His eyes are piercing into mine, causing my stomach to flip flop.

"What are you looking at?" I frown as his eyes linger on my face. I stand up quickly and walk to the mirror hanging in the hallway, panicking that I have sweet and sour sauce on my face.

"Rose." He appears behind me.

I turn to face him once I'm sure I have nothing on my face. My heart begins racing as his topaz eyes starts to linger on my chest before scanning over my body. His eyes catch mine again as a sexy grin appears on his face before pushing me backwards and pinning me against the wall.

My breathing erratic, my body begins to burn and crave his touch. He presses his body against mine before kissing me passionately.

He leans away from me and takes my hand. I slam the door as his lips crash down onto mine again whilst he's pinning me against the wall. His hands hold onto the hem of my top before pulling it up and off over my head. He unfastens my bra, letting my breasts fall quickly. Tugging my leggings and thongs off my legs, he strips himself bare in front of me.

Holding my arms over my head as I try to reach for his throbbing cock, his eyes look at me filled with hunger and makes my body come alive for him. He removed one of his hands and pinned both of my wrists with one single hand, keeping my body held against the cold wall. His other hand glides down my stomach and over my throbbing core. His fingers rub against my sensitive clit as he leans down, kissing me hard.

"Ah!" I moan out as he puts pressure onto my aching bud.

My legs begin to shake as he trails my neck with kisses and sucks it gently. I grind my hips, trying to build up the sensation as he moves his hand away and releases my wrists from the wall.

"You are so beautiful baby." He strokes my cheek gently as I close my eyes at his soft touch.

"Wait a second," he whispers.

I open my eyes and watch him walk over to his bedside and picking out a condom packet. He strides back over to me whilst removing the condom from the foil. He rolls the condom onto his length and stands in front of me again.

"Have you ever been fucked up against a wall, Rose?" His fingertips trace over my thighs as I feel them tremble again.

"No," I whisper, anxious of what's about to happen next.

He doesn't even answer. He lifts both of my thighs up, and I naturally wrap them around his waist. He slowly pushes inside me, and I whimper as he stretches me perfectly. With both hands gripping my arse, he begins to thrust up into me with my back hitting the wall as his hard body slaps against my vibrating skin.

My fingers dig into his shoulders as he pounds into me deeply whilst my body is shaking with indescribable pleasure. He repeats his movements faster. Unable to keep my eyes open, I don't notice him moving across the room until I land safely on the bed.

Spreading my legs as wide as possible he places himself in between me, slams into me over and over again.

"Luca!" I scream out as his large member hits my g-spot like never before. He holds onto my calves spreading them even wider as he pounds into my tiny frame.

"Fuck yes, Rose!" He moans, sitting up straighter and grinding into my body.

I try to fight the tears away at the newfound pleasure building up inside me.

My legs tremble as he continues to hit my spot. He leans down, grabbing hold of the back of my neck firmly and pulling me up towards him. I lean on my elbows with my legs wide for him as he kisses me hard, whimpering into his mouth as his solid cock presses against my wall. His hips move in perfect rhythm as he slams inside me whilst I trace my fingers over the soft tattooed skin underneath his belly button.

"Yes baby, that feels so good," he whines into my mouth as I touch his skin.

Clinging to his hips, I pull him closer towards me as his cock hitting my wall. His stamina continues as he pounds deep, and all I can do is scream his name and grip onto his arms. His dominance is making me tense as he rams into my body.

He stares down at me as he thrusts perfectly. Clenching around him, I take a moment to acknowledge how beautiful he is. He tosses his head back and moans in ecstasy whilst I reach down rubbing myself aggressively. Raising my hips, my body is mixing with satisfaction as he glides his body against mine.

"Luca! I'm going to cum!" I scream.

"Cum for me, beautiful," he whispers.

His breathing becomes unsteady and hot against my neck. My body is tensing underneath his glistening skin. His dick hits my spot even harder as I go over the edge and curl my toes. I could hear them crack as I cum hard, clenching him tightly. He pulls out and quickly slips the condom off. I watch him in a dazed state as he rubs himself, biting his bottom lip as he shoots his seed onto my stomach and breasts.

His face twists in pleasure as he drops his hips slowly, collapsing next to my sweaty and cum-covered body. He reaches out and wraps his strong arms around my waist and tugs me closer to him. I tilt my head up, looking into his topaz eyes. I can see hundreds of emotions flooding through them.

"Rose, don't freak out but I think I'm fall—" he whispers.

Just then a pounding sound at his bedroom door pulls us out of our state. I naturally pull the covers over my body as his door swings open.

"What the fuck is going on here?!" Nick leans up against Luca's bedroom door with a devilish smirk on his face.

"What are you doing here, Nick?! I told you not to come over tonight man," Luca spits at him, quickly standing up and pulling his boxers on.

Nick's eyes linger on me longer than I am comfortable with. I pull the duvet up higher staring him down. "I wanted to see the show, but I guess we are too late."

His voice is deep, dark, and creepy. My pulse is racing whilst his dirty eyes rake over my duvet-covered body. Who does he mean by *"we?"* I feel my blood boiling as he continues to watch me, but I turn to see Luca's face full of panic.

"Well what do we have here?" A voice I recognise far too well comes from behind Nick's tall frame, and my heart beats erratically as Emily steps out from behind him.

"Hello, you sneaky little bitch." She leans up against Luca's bedroom wall with arms crossed, glaring down at me in hatred. *Fuck.*

CHAPTER 25

ROSE

"Emily? What are you doing here?" I ask. She rolls her eyes and steps into the bedroom with her dark eyes lingering on Luca's chest.

"I have known about you two for a few weeks now, and I knew you watched Luca fuck me in the alley." She sits down on the edge of the bed, glaring at me like she wants to rip my head off. So this whole time she's been playing me for a fool?

"H-how?" I stutter, totally confused.

"I have eyes, you idiot. I saw you two snogging outside of work. Plus, it was fun acting like a clueless victim. You really are a terrible friend if this is what you do behind their backs." She scoffs. Her nostrils are flaring with anger taking in my post-sex appearance.

"You don't know what you're talking about, Emily." Luca steps closer to me with his fists clenching against his side.

"I knew you were playing me, Luca. I thought I could be the girl to change you, make you fall in love, and all that bullshit. You picked the pathetic girl with a fucked up past instead." Standing up, she walks over to Nick's side as his arm wraps around her waist.

"Don't you dare act like you know anything about me!" I snap. She laughs—a real humorous laugh. *God! If only I am not naked.*

"Does poor Daniel know about this?" She looks back at Luca, ignoring me completely.

"Don't even think about it." Luca seethes.

"I think he has the right to know his mate has been fucking his silly little sister behind his back." Nick chuckles next to Emily.

"Fuck you!" I hiss at the creepy boy in the doorway.

"One day, baby." Nick winks at me. I growl at him, contemplating on attacking him butt naked.

"Back off, mate." Luca takes a few steps towards his so-called best mate. Nick squares up to Luca, trying to imitate Luca's stand but fails miserably.

"Don't think this thing is going to last much longer. You know far too well what will happen when everyone finds out the truth," Nick speaks loudly. *The truth*?

"I said, back off Nick." Luca steps closer and glares at Nick. I fear a fight would rise between these two.

"I'm just warning you, mate. This is getting a bit out of hand now. Surely you agree?" he says. Luca anxiously turns towards me.

"You need to go home, Rose. This was a bad idea," he whispers. I close my eyes, trying to calm myself down before I blow up.

"Everyone get out then so I can find my clothes!" I yell. They close the door behind them whilst Emily's chuckles can be heard from the other side of the door as I quickly change.

Swinging the bedroom door open, I come to face to face her. Her smile is bright and fake that I want to claw her dull eyes out.

"Should've thought about everything before you did something as stupid as falling in love with this boy. He will drop you like the piece of shit that you already are." She points towards Luca who is whispering in Nick's ear a few feet away.

I take a step closer until her breath is fanning my face as I dare her to say another bad word. "I'm not in love, Hun. If I'm correct, he's already dropped you so that makes you the piece of shit here." I scoff before nudging past her and slamming my shoulder into her side as I walk towards the boys.

"I'm out!" I call, sliding my shoes on.

"Let me drive you." Luca rushes over to me, leaving Nick and Emily watching. My body is shaking with rage, and my mind is multiplying with different thoughts and feelings that I didn't know I could ever have.

"No, I'll get the tube," I retort, not in the mood to be anywhere near this boy or anyone for that matter.

"Please, Rose, I can explain," he begs. His eyes are full of panic as I shake my head, taking hold of the door handle.

"This was a huge mistake. They are right." My face softens as he flinches with my response. His face falls to the floor as I open the front door. I look at Nick and Emily with amusement on their faces.

"Night, fuckers." I wave before slamming the door behind me and rushing down the hallway towards the lift quickly.

* * *

The warm water powerfully covers my body as I sit on the shower floor, cuddling my knees. I can't help but feel a little broken. By the time I had made it home, the girls were asleep, and all I wanted to do was break down and cry but I won't let myself do that. I will not cry over a boy or anything to do with a boy ever again. Surely, those three are just playing a sick little game with me. Nick knew I was in there with Luca. Why would he bring Emily into this? I'm so done with messy relationships or whatever this is.

Wrapping a towel round my body, I sulk back into my bedroom and watch my feet sink into my fluffy carpet. "Baby, I'm so sorry." Luca's voice makes me jump. My towel unravels and falls to the floor. I pick it up quickly covering myself, embarrassed and surprised as hell.

"What the fuck are you doing here?" I stride towards him sitting on the edge of my bed.

"The front door was unlocked. I came to explain myself properly and to apologise to the ends of the earth." He reaches out for my hand and I oblige, letting him pull me closer to his body. I step in between his thighs as he looks up at me.

"What happened really fucking sucked, Luca," I whisper, looking at his thumb as it traces circles along my wrist.

"I know, baby. I am so bloody sorry and you didn't deserve it."

I may have been a bit of a backstabber to Emily, but I didn't mean for any of this to happen.

"Do you think we are stupid for doing this? For liking each other?" I ask. My voice is quivering, hoping to God he says "no."

"I think we are mad, but fuck what anyone says or thinks. I adore you and I worship you Rose." He reaches his hand up and cups my cheek as I lean into his touch. Stepping closer, I rest my knees on either side of the bed, straddling his body. His breath is deep and hot as I lean my body against him, taking my full weight as he holds me against him.

"This is a risky move, Rose," he whispers. I smile into the crook of his neck as I wrap my arms tighter around his shoulders, feeling contented and happy.

"I obviously like taking risks, Luca." I kiss the soft skin of his collarbone with his body trembling underneath mine. His hands are stroking up and down my back with my towel as the only thing keeping me from being completely naked.

"Be mine, Rose?" I lean back and look into his eyes, searching mine for something—for my answer—for anything that will give him some hope. Biting my tongue to calm my excitement, I close my eyes to take a deep breath.

"Only if you'll be mine?" I pull myself closer to his body and kisses me—this is his answer. Our lips move in sync as we kiss harder than we've ever kissed before. Real emotions flood my eyes as I feel a tear trickle down my cheek. Trying not to ruin the moment, I pull him closer to me. I'm finally ready to let myself fall again and be happy even if it's against my brothers wishes. I want *Luca Haynes.*

My towel lay in a pile on my floor along with Luca's clothes. His body grinds into mine slowly as my legs wrap around his body. He buries himself deep inside me I can barely breathe as he worships my body.

"You are something special, Rose." He moans into my mouth as he picks up his pace. I moan in response as he hits my G-spot perfectly with every thrust. I sit myself up and he allows me to do so. I push against his chest as he lays down on his back. His topaz eyes are watching me with anticipation as I straddle his bare thighs and sink onto his hard cock.

"Oh f-fuck, baby." Luca groans, squeezing my eyes shut at the pleasure building inside me as I grind my hips against him and his large cock stretches me fully.

"Baby, I'm going to cum." He moans into my neck as I carry on moving until he reaches his climax. My walls are clenching around him as orgasm hits me. Rolling my eyes in pleasure, I slump against his wet skin.

"Fuck, baby, tense again." He groans into my ear. I repeat the same action and slowly grind my hips. Unable to take any more of the pleasure, he shoots a load into the condom before collapsing backwards into the pillows.

* * *

Sunday evening plays out better than I thought it would. Luca turns up to the flat with a rose and a bag of crisps and sweets. I lay across him with my legs outstretched. My head rests against his chest whilst watching the film playing out in front of us. I watch his hand as he begins to trace circles along my wrist.

"Well, I think you're cute." Darcy brings her attention back to me as I'm cuddled up against Luca's warm body.

"At least someone thinks so." I scoff as she gives me a genuine smile before facing back towards the film.

"I guess I'm going to have to get used to being cute then?" Luca looks down at me with his killer smile and a raised eyebrow whilst I laugh at him before nodding.

"God, fine. But only for you," he whispers into my ear, kissing my temple gently. Though his heartbeat is calm and his breathing is strong and collected, I can still feel my heart erratically punching against my chest. I'm sitting on the sofa, cuddling with my brothers' friend and falling helplessly more into his trap. I just hope and pray that this isn't a sick joke.

CHAPTER 26

ROSE

Emily has made the entire week her personal mission to piss me off. I do not trust her intentions. As happy as she may be now, she's apparently dating Nick. I believe she has some unfinished business to handle—me.

Luca and I have never gotten on so well. He's been round mine almost every night. Has Chloe started to warm up to the idea that Luca and I are dating? In a relationship? I haven't got a clue. All I know is that we are exclusive, which scares the crap out of me. I never thought I would feel like this ever again. The feeling of fancying the hell out of someone, or maybe even more. I'm not so sure yet on how I feel. I just know that I don't want this to end. I feel finally happy.

"Slut." Emily's voice appears behind me as I slam into the wall. I turn to face her, but she's already strutting down the corridor towards the lifts. I roll my right shoulder, trying to ignore the shooting pain. *Fucking bitch.*

Five-thirty hits the clock, and I'm finally ready to leave this bloody office for today. The weekend has come around so fast, and I need a break from Emily's knocking about. Trying to keep my calm and not rip her head off is killing me, but I cannot jeopardise losing my job over her pathetic games.

"Hello, gorgeous." I look up from my desk to see Luca leaning down, his white T-shirt hugging him tight, black skinny jeans, and his hair flopping over his eyes slightly. I stand up, pulling his T-shirt towards me as he takes hold of my waist and presses his lips against mine.

"You're both disgusting." Her bloody voice rips through my happiness. I pull away from Luca to glare at the evil bitch leaning on my desk with her face full of amusement.

"Shove it, Emily," Luca growls at her, and I roll my eyes whilst picking up my handbag. Luca's hand held out for me to take his fingers as he pulls me out of the office and into the lift.

"How many times has she shoved into you today then?" He raises his eyebrows as I slap his arm before giggling myself.

"Fuck off. It's not funny and I'm starting to bruise." I rub my sore arm, making him laugh even more.

"A new record. Yesterday, was four." He laughs with a genuine laugh whilst I stand on my tiptoes, glaring into his beautiful blue eyes. He pinches my chin with his fingers, holding my face in place.

"You are so gorgeous."

"I guess you're not so bad either." I wink at him as the lift door opens, and I walk out first, leaving him openmouthed.

"Baby, I know you don't think that." He catches and holds me with a big smile on his face.

"Of course, I do." I smirk. God I don't think that at all. He is honestly the most beautiful person I have ever seen, and I believe he knows it too.

Driving our way home, I can't help but think about Emily. As much as I want to kill her, I can see why she hates me, and I pity her. She's just being childish like she wants me to retaliate and lose my job. It wouldn't surprise me.

"Can we pop into Tesco please? I need some fags." Luca parks his car in the flat car park, and I jump out with him. Reaching over and wrapping his arm around waist, we walk towards Tesco express.

"I'll be outside." I stop in front of the shop, lifting my fag packet and hinting that I'm going to have a smoke. He kisses my forehead before stepping into the busy shop.

Lighting it, I inhale the strong chemicals and blow the grey smoke into the air. Taking a deep breath, I feel better instantly. Today with Emily has just been a nightmare. I study the shop through the glass doors. I can't see Luca, and he's probably in the sweet section or grabbing some beers for tonight.

"Hello, gorgeous. Could I pinch a cig?" I turn around and face a man in his late forties with curly brown hair, reminding me of Wayne.

"Um, y-yeah sure," I stutter as I pick out a fag from my packet and pass it to him. I lend him my lighter and watch as he lights the end. Smoke is blocking his face from my view as he passes my lighter back to me.

"Why is a pretty thing like you out here alone?" He keeps his eyes on me, trying my hardest not to shiver as he traces my body with his disgusting eyes.

"I'm not alone. My boyfriend's inside." I point towards Tesco, hoping he will leave at the word "boyfriend."

"He is one lucky fucker." He whistles to himself before inhaling more smoke from his cigarette.

"Thanks?" I give him a questioning look, feeling more uncomfortable by the second whilst his eyes are still watching me with so much intensity. I take a few steps backwards, wondering what he was talking about.

Bringing my fag to my lips, I face away from him and hope he gets the hint and jogs on. *Hurry up, Luca.* "Where is this boyfriend of yours then, baby girl?" I jump out of my skin as I feel the man's breath on my neck. I turn around, ready to dropkick him in the balls.

"Get the fuck away from me." I scowl in disgust. He chuckles at me, taking a step closer. I look around at the people passing by, but no one is taking any notice of the creepy man cornering a young girl.

"How have I never seen such a beautiful girl like you around here before?" He takes another step closer to me, my fist balling by my side and ready to swing into his twitching jaw.

"You really need to get away from me" I growl as he corners me against the wall. Luca needs to step out of the shop right now.

"I can't do that now, princess. I'm trapped in your spell." He smirks at me. His voice is coated in lust and amusement.

"Please," I whimper, trying to calm my racing heart as his breath fans my face, stinking of smoke and whisky. Of course he's a drunk. I turn my face to the left and see Luca walking out of Tesco with his eyes full of rage. Running over and grabbing the man by the throat, he slams him against the wall next to me.

"Get your slimy body away from my girl!" Luca holds the man's T-shirt. His eyes are bloodshot and his jaw is clenched.

"I'm guessing you're the boyfriend?" The man laughs at Luca's face. *Uh-oh.*

"Goddamn right. I fucking am! What the fuck were you doing?!" Luca's putting more of his body weight against the man. People walking by begin to stop and watch out of curiosity or for their vulgar entertainment.

"You are one lucky son of a bitch." The man slurs. I wince at his words and get scared as Luca's face turns red. If the man doesn't shut up, I'm worried Luca may kill him.

"Get the fuck out of here before I break your jaw." Luca spits at him before slamming him against the wall one more time. Luca walks over to me, taking my hand and pulling me far away from the drunk man.

Once we arrive back at his car, I'm gently pushed against the door with his soft hands cupping my face gently. "Are you okay, baby?" His face is flooded with concern. I nod my head standing on my tiptoes. He rests his forehead against mine as I close my eyes trying to calm down my rapid heartbeat. Everything about that incident was too familiar. I haven't felt like that in years, and I believe Luca knows that too.

"When I saw him pressing up against you, I wanted to snap his neck remembering what you've been through. I'm so sorry," he says. I look up into his eyes, trying not to let any tears fall.

"Thank you," I say, trying not to think about it. My hands are shaking as I remember how Wayne once had his body against mine many times before.

"Everything's okay now. I'm here." He kisses my temple before opening the car and grabbing his bag ready to spend the night.

* * *

"Hey, girl. You okay? You seem shaken." Darcy jumps up onto the kitchen stool opposite me and Luca and places our food in front of us.

"Yeah, just some creep trying it on with me earlier." I fake a laugh, wanting to lighten the situation.

"Ew, gross." She pulls a face before relaxing and placing her hand on top of mine as her lips form into a soft smile but her eyes tell me more.

"I could've killed him." Luca spits. I chuckle before looking up at him. He smiles gently and my stomach flips at the sight of him looking at me.

"I don't doubt that for a second." Darcy laughs, picking up her pizza slice.

"Where's Chloe?" I ask, trying to change the topic. Watching her bite into her pizza, I hold back a laugh as tomato sauce drops onto her white top. She grabs a napkin, trying to wipe it off but makes it worse instead.

"Why am I so fucking messy? I think she's with Daniel." I nod slightly. This is what I think is unfair—she can do whatever she pleases with my brother, but I can't be near Luca without her calling me a slut. *Hypocrite.*

"Does she really like him then?" Luca asks Darcy. I watch him in awe as he pops a chip into his mouth.

"She's been in love with the boy for like ten years. I hope to God he likes her as well," Darcy answers. I feel sad for Chloe. I don't know if he does but one time whilst hiding under Luca's bed, I heard he was meeting a girl. Luca's eyes meet mine, and I can tell he knows stuff that Chloe wouldn't like to know.

CHAPTER 27

ROSE

"I love you too, bye." I hang up the phone after talking to Theo. I flop my back against my cushions with happiness. I could hear my mum's faint voice while talking downstairs before she leaves for work.

"Rose, I'm off!" I hear her call out my name. I jump off my bed quickly, running out into the hallway and down the steep stairs.

My mum is standing by the front door looking as gorgeous as ever in a blazer and pencil skirt. I give her a tight squeeze, not wanting to let her go. Daniel is in his girlfriend's house whilst Wayne is standing in the doorway watching mum. I hate the summer holidays because Wayne works from home, and Daniel is never around. I meet up with the girls as often as I can but not today.

"I'll see you tonight, baby. Love you both." She lets go of me and opens the front door.

"Bye, darling." Wayne leans down kissing her quickly before she waves and shuts the door behind her. I look at him before rushing down the hallway and back up the stairs again. I look out from my window as her car pulls out of the driveway and down the road. I know he's watching from downstairs, waiting a few minutes before he comes upstairs.

Hearing the light tap of his fingers against my bedroom door, my body begins to shake with fear as he swings the door open, standing tall and pleased. I cover myself with my duvet, trying to hide from him. "Don't be like this, princess." He walks into my bedroom, slamming my door shut behind him and sitting down on the edge of the bed.

"Please, can you leave me alone?" I whimper. His fingers stroke up and down my bare arm.

"Tsk! Tsk! Tsk! You know I can't leave you alone," he whispers, leaning close to my face. I tug on the duvet but his strong hold pulls it down, uncovering me completely. My pyjamas are hiding my body, thankfully.

"Why? Are you not ready for me yet, baby?" He raises his eyebrow in disappointment. I cross my arms over my chest, hoping he just gets bored. My heartbeat is pounding faster by the second as his fingers touch the hem of my T-shirt, pulling it up slowly to show off my stomach.

"Leave me alone, Wayne!" I yell at him as he caresses my skin. I try to pull my top back down but it does nothing.

"Stop fighting this, Rose. You know you'll get it. You bloody love it." He leans close to my face, attacking my lips with his. I scream against him whilst his hands grip my waist, forcing me against the bed. Hot tears fall down my face as he starts to pull off my T-shirt, breaking our kiss.

"Stop! Please stop!" I cry out as my bare chest comes into view. His dirty eyes are taking in every inch of my chest whilst he smiles at me. I try to sit up and grab my T-shirt, but he throws it to the floor, slamming me back against the bed.

"Stop fighting me, princess! You won't win!" he yells in my face. His fingers are pulling my pyjama bottoms and knickers. I bawl into my pillow as I lay naked and vulnerable as his rough fingers trace my body.

"You get me so hard every time, princess." I look up at him in horror as I hear his jeans fall to the floor. Wrapping himself with a condom, my head pounds as he climbs on top of me whilst holding my arms above my head. I fidget underneath his strong body, trying to get out of his touch.

"Stay still. It will hurt more if you do this," he whispers against my neck, and I'm unable to control my breathing as he positions himself.

"NO! PLEASE!" I cry out as he enters me. I could hear his groans mixed with my cries as he takes complete control of my body. With every thrust, I scream out and beg for anybody to come save me—neighbours, anyone walking past the house, or anybody.

"Stop your fucking crying!" His hand wraps around my neck. My throat closes up as he begins to move faster. I can't breathe, and I feel light-headed and ready to just fade into darkness. His hand lets go as I become limp under him. I feel weak and unable to fight anymore.

"Please stop," I beg one more time. His breathing is heavy as he attacks my delicate body even more. My eyes widen in fear as he leans down, biting my chest and leaving a dark purple "love"' bite.

"I hope Theo doesn't see this." He growls whilst I cry out. Theo's going to think I'm cheating on him. Oh my fucking god.

"PLEASE STOP!" I scream out again. I need to get away from him. I can't live like this anymore. I need someone to save me.

"Stop being such a brat!" Wayne leans up, swinging his hand down and slapping me across the face. My throat burns as I cry in pain.

"Rose?! Rose! Wake up, baby!"

"Nobody can save you, princess." Wayne crashes his lips onto mine again. I fight to get him off me.

"ROSE!"

I jolt up in bed with Luca sitting next to me. His eyes are frantic with worry. I jump up and wrap my arms around his neck. I let myself cry onto his shoulder as I shiver with fear. He strokes my hair as he kisses my temple. "I'm here, baby. I've got you . . . always," he whispers as I begin to relax under his touch.

"Always." He breathes into my ear as I feel myself fall into a deep peaceful sleep.

CHAPTER 28

LUCA

I can't get her screams out of my head. She looks so peaceful curled up next to me, and I haven't been able to fall back to sleep since her nightmare a few hours ago. Hearing her crying and screaming wakes me up, and knowing she's been in pain all these years breaks my heart. If I could get my hands on Wayne, I would cause him so much agony just like Rose has had to carry around with her for years.

I reach out, stroking her naked back as she sleeps—soft and perfect. I know being with her as much as I am is wrong and being Daniel's sister has made this so wrong. I promised myself I wouldn't let this happen when I met her but goddamn. She dazzled me from the first moment, but she took my breath away the moment we kissed. I just hope this lasts. Of course, it won't. She'll find out eventually. She'll find out I'm not what she deserves. *I'll ruin her.*

"You okay? Why are you awake? It's five o'clock." Her angelic voice cuts through my thoughts as I look into her marble eyes. My breath is suddenly knocked out of my body as I take her in.

"You are so beautiful." I stroke her cheek and feel her soft lips smile at me.

"Did you want to talk about your nightmare?" I ask her, hoping she doesn't get upset again. Her face falls for a split second before she nods her head.

"Yeah, I'm sorry I woke you up." She gives me a sad smile. I lean over to cup her face with both hands.

"Don't say sorry. I was so worried about you. I couldn't wake you up for like two minutes," I say, remembering her thrashing around screaming the words "no" and "please stop."

"It was Wayne. It was just a memory," she answers as I look deep into her eyes. My heart is sinking for her. I can't even begin to imagine what she went through because of him.

"H-he used to make the most out of my mum's absence, and Daniel being God knows where, summer holidays were the worst. He worked from home so I couldn't escape him." She looks down, her voice shaky and nervous.

"You don't need to tell me if you can't, baby," I say softly, not wanting to force her into anything she's not comfortable with.

"No, it's okay. I was eleven when he first touched me. He was amazing when he married my mum, and I was nine when he moved in with us until I started to wear bras. It's like he changed into a hungry animal every time he looked at me. On my eleventh birthday, he snuck into my bedroom and everything fell apart from there." A sob breaks through her voice, and I pull her into my chest as she softly cries against me.

"He will never hurt you again. I'm so sorry." I stroke her silk hair with my eyes stinging. Her pain is ruining me. I never cry, but right now, I'm trying so hard not to break down for her.

"I know. Well, I hope not." She pulls away from me, and I look down at her.

"You want to know something?" she asks with a wide smile appearing across her luscious lips. I can't help but smile back at her as she beams at me. Using my thumb, I wipe away the warm tears still rolling down her flawless face.

"Go on then." I roll my eyes with amusement. She slaps my arm before snuggling in closer.

"I reckon everything will work out between us. Whatever this is, it will." She's almost hesitant. I look down at her fingers as they trace my tattooed chest. *God, baby, I hope so. I need you.*

"Same," I answer, trying not to think too much about it all. When everything spills, when Daniel finds out, and when Rose finds out the truth. *I've seriously messed up and it's killing me.*

"Kiss me," she whispers, pulling me out of my painful thoughts. I look into her eyes as my emotions skyrocket. I plunge my head down, finding her lips. My fingers grip into her hair, and her body responds against my touch. She climbs on top of me, kissing me harder with my cock twitching against her warm thigh. She moans into my mouth, and my body shivers. How can this girl be so perfect? I can't handle her like this. I need to take her now.

I sit up pulling her with me, flipping us around and making me on top. She chuckles into my mouth as I run my hand down her gorgeous breasts slowly. Her erratic breathing is matching mine, then I move my fingertips down to her soaking slit.

"You seem happy this morning." I pull away from the kiss, giving her my smirk. I know she can't seem to resist.

"Can you blame me? I have you naked on top of me." She raises her eyebrow.

"Touché." I laugh before kissing her again, her skin smooth as I slowly rub circles over her clit. Her back immediately arches for me as I move my lips from her mouth down to her neck. Her moans in my ear have me going wild. I use my other hand to cup her left breast as I gently kiss and suck her pebbled nipple, moving my face to her other breast and repeating myself.

"I'm so lucky." I glide my lips back up to her mouth, kissing her again. She kisses me back with so much passion. Sitting myself between her thighs, I reach for a condom in her bedside drawer, using my knees to push them wide open for me. I move my fingers to open the foil packet, and slide the latex over my hard cock. I begin to tease her soaking pussy. Her pink lips are glistening and ready for me.

"Please, Luca." She looks at me, her voice desperate and weak. I smile down at her as I thrust my hips, slamming into her. My eyes roll back as her tight walls clench around me. I move out slowly before slamming myself back inside her.

"Fuck!" She moans in pleasure as I continue this movement a few more times. Grabbing a hold of the back of her knees, I raise her legs high so I can fit my whole length deep inside of her. I look down at her perfect body as I grind my hips, picking up a rhythmic pattern and watch her big boobs copy my movements.

"Fucking hell, Rose. Your tits are so gorgeous." I groan as I carry on, her eyes half open but her moans loud. Stunned by her luscious body, I can't help but wonder how I ever became so lucky to get a chance like this—to fuck a girl so exquisite—to feel like my heart is going to explode whenever she looks at me.

"I can't handle this, Luca!" She screams as I raise her legs higher and over both my shoulders as I pick up my pace. My heart slams into my chest as the pleasure is almost unbearable. I don't know how much longer I'm going to last. Her pussy is clenching around me, and her stunning and curvaceous body is underneath me.

I slowly remove her legs from my shoulders, then she wraps them around my waist as I lean down, kissing the skin between her breasts whilst making the most of her beautiful body. My stamina surprises me as I continue to grind without faulting a single movement. *I want to spoil her and show her how much I care. She needs to see how much I care. God, I care so fucking much.*

"I'm going to cum, Luca!" she whimpers into my ear as I kiss up her neck and back onto her lips as her warm tongue invites me into kiss her harder.

"Cum for me, baby." I moan into her mouth as I feel her walls clench around my sensitive cock.

"Ah! Fuck!" she screams. Her moans shock me to the core as I shoot out into the condom. My groans mix with hers as I collapse next to her. She looks at me with a smile so bright my stomach flips, and I reach out kissing her with everything I have.

"Wow," she whispers out of breath. Her chest is rising and falling at a fast pace.

"Tell me about it. That was insane!" I answer her. My voice is dusty as I control my breath. Resting my head on my hand, I turn to face and watch her as her breathing slows down completely. Her eyes begin to flutter and she looks so happy and content.

I stroke her flawless face studying her. Her long dark lashes move with each breath I take as well as the beauty mark positioned above the left side of her lip. I run my thumb over it. She's so delicate; she's an angel. My heart drops as I look at the beautiful girl who has let her guard down and trusts me after everything she's been through. This can't end. How could I have ever been so heartless and stupid?

CHAPTER 29

ROSE

Daniel has called me late last night, asking if I wanted to go spend the day with him and mum, but I was hesitant. Especially after the nightmare I had Friday night. After a lot of persuasion on Dan's part, I decided I might as well see mum. I'm getting picked up in exactly one hour, but I'm still wrapped up in Luca's warm body with our legs intertwined as I lay on his chest.

"I really need to get going. If Dan sees me here, he will freak out." Luca sits up on his elbows. His hair is falling over his eyes as he looks at the time on his phone.

"I don't want to go." I sigh, rolling onto my back. Leaning down, he kisses me quickly before standing up. I watch his toned naked body walk over to his bag on the floor.

"What are you doing today?" I ask, climbing out of bed myself and rushing over to my underwear drawer.

"I'm seeing Nick. I need to have some words with him about everything." He appears behind me as I slip into my pink knickers whilst his hands wrap around my waist, tugging me close to him.

"Good luck with that. For a best mate, he's a snake,I say. His body vibrates from behind me.

"That is exactly why I'm seeing him." He laughs from behind me. I get out of his strong grip, ready to dress myself for the day. I'm wearing my black skinny jeans, a mustard yellow top, and black vans. I decide on straightening my hair and applying my usual amount of makeup as Luca sits on the bed behind me. His eyes linger on his phone before switching to me, so on.

"I need to get going, baby." I turn to face him. His bag on his shoulder as he stands by my bedroom door. I walk over to him and kiss him hard, secretly not wanting to let him go.

"Let me know when you're home, beautiful," he says after pecking me one last time and before opening my bedroom door and walking out.

I go back to my bedroom mirror after hearing the front door close behind him. My skin is looking brighter than usual, and my cheeks are aching with the constant smile I feel on my face. I'm happy—surprisingly happy.

*　　*　　*

"Why do you look so cheerful?" my brother asks me.

"Is a girl not allowed to smile?" I raise an eyebrow as I look out the passenger side window, hoping he doesn't start questioning me more. There is only so much I can hide from him, and I hate it.

"It's just nice, I guess," he replies, and I look back at him. His blue eyes are glistening in the bright daylight whilst his hair is flopping over his face.

"You really need a haircut." I reach over, ruffling it slightly. He slaps my hand away before placing both hands back on the wheel.

Finally parking into mum's driveway, I watch as she opens the front door with arms wide open.I run up to her. Smelling so familiar, I squeeze her tighter. She lets go and wraps her arms around Daniel's waist.

"Hope you're both hungry. I'm making scrambled eggs." She beams at us both. I nod in excitement. My mum's eggs are heavenly, and anyone who has eaten them will agree. Stepping inside the large Victorian house, I always wonder if this even feels like home to her anymore. She moved here at the age of twenty-five and gave birth to Daniel in the upstairs bedroom. Her marriage fell apart, and she married Wayne one year later. Wayne's disgusting actions also happened in this home, in almost every room. It's also the same home where she found out the news about her daughter and ex-husband being involved in a car accident. Her first love died instantly. How can she be happy here?

"You okay, sweetheart?" I'm knocked out of my thoughts. Her bright blue eyes look concerned.

"Yeah, just my thoughts rambling on as usual." I chuckle, trying to lighten the mood. She doesn't question it, and she can probably read me like a book by now. We are similar in many ways.

Placing my knife and fork on my empty plate, I let out a deep sigh. "Full?" My mum is sitting opposite me as she beams with pride.

"Yes, so good. Thank you." I tap my bloated belly, earning her laugh in response.

"Any leftovers?" Daniel butts in. Mum's face is full of amusement at his words.

"Yeah, go for it." She nods at him as I watch him pick up his plate, leaving us.

"So, anything new with you?" Her voice sounds almost a whisper, like she's trying to get some dirty details out of me before Daniel gets back.

"Not really, no. Same old really," I lie, not wanting to go into too much detail about my personal life.

"I liked Daniel's new friend. Lewis?" I shoot my eyes up to look at her. She's smiling at me and trying to catch me out. I know it.

"Luca," I answer, hoping she doesn't dig further.

"He's pretty handsome, Rose." She leans over the table.

"Far too many tattoos for my liking, but I'm sure you can look past that." Smirking at me, I'm pretty sure she's hinting something. Surely, she doesn't know.

"I don't know where you're going with this." I'm hesitant, trying to act confused.

"Of course, you do. Makeup had disappeared off your nose and onto his after going to the toilet, unless he wears foundation. Plus the way he looks at you is obvious enough, sweetheart." I close my eyes, nodding my head slightly.

"Right," I say before Daniel appears in the doorway with a fresh plate.

"You both okay?" He steps in with eyebrows furrowed.

"Yes, girl stuff." Mum smiles up at him as he enters the room with a questioning look. I roll my eyes at him, hoping he knows there's nothing to worry about, but he's far from stupid. He's going to catch onto my lie at some point.

Running my fingers over the suede jacket, I almost contemplate trying it on. Dan is standing at the checkout with mum. After breakfast, we decided that it would be nice to go into town for a wander. I'm praying I don't see anybody from school. It's been a while since I left for London, and my heart is racing every single time I see a man over the age of forty walk by, hoping to God it isn't Wayne. He could be anywhere.

"I'm going into Game. I need some new Xbox games," Dan tells my mum as they both approach me by the coats.

"Okay, call me when you finish. Rose, want to go grab coffee?" She looks at me. My heart pounding, not ready to have a conversation without Dan around.

"Sounds good," I answer. After Dan disappears down the busy high-street, my mum links arms with me as we step into Starbucks. I order myself a mocha, and my mum a latte before finding a table outside. The sun beams down on us gracefully as we quietly sip our drinks.

"So how is London?" she asks, as I watch her reach into her shoulder bag, pulling out her cigarette packet and a lighter. She leans over the table passing me a fag and the lighter after lighting up her own. I inhale the smoke, trying to relax my busy head.

"Busy, loud, nothing new," I answer, raising my hand and inhaling the smoke again. I look up into the sky as I blow out the air from my lungs, grey smoke dancing in the sunlight.

"Have you seen Theo?" Her question snaps me out of my world once again.

"Only once recently. Same old bullshit. I'm sorry, I did find out they're engaged though!" I take a sip of my coffee, looking at my mum's face full of pity.

"Good riddance. You deserve much more than what he could give you. After everything you went through, you'd think he'd have more respect." Giving her a warm smile, I think back of Luca. Is he better than Theo? Will he treat me better than Theo ever did? Does Luca care enough to stick around? Do I want that? Does Luca excite me more than Theo ever did? *Absolutely.*

"So tell me more about Luca. Don't you dare say nothing because I can see it all over your face."

"God, fine. If you're not going to let it go but, Jesus, do not tell Dan." I lean closer to her. She nods her head quickly, acting like a twelve-year-old.

"I guess you could say we are seeing each other," I tell her.

"How did it happen?" she asks. I think back to everything, trying to pinpoint the exact moment when I wanted more. *When did it really happen?*

"It was just a buildup of us all hanging out, and we had a connection we couldn't ignore, I guess. I'm going to tell Dan, just not now. I'm happy." Not one ounce of judgement is written on her face.

"You do what you need to do. Be happy. That's all I want." She smiles at me, her blonde hair tied up into a loose bun and her face shimmering in the daylight.

"What's going on in your life then, Mumma? Any men?" I lift my drink, giving her a quick wink.

"Ha! No! No men at all." She laughs.

"Mum, you're only fifty," I say.

"Exactly! I'm fifty years old, most men have lost all their hair and teeth!" I chuckle as she moans and groans about all the men that she has spoken to online.

"Don't give up yet. You're so beautiful." I look at her once again. She doesn't look a day over forty at the latest. For a woman who has had to deal with a lifetime of bad luck, she looks like she's smashed life gracefully—without a scratch.

"Promise me something, Rose. Don't you ever let anyone, even your brother, stop you from being truly happy." She squeezes my fingers for a second.

"I wish it was that simple. I don't know what Luca wants from me," I say, looking at our connected hands.

"He needs to figure it out before it's too late then." Her honesty has me questioning everything, questioning Luca myself. *What do I want from Luca? What do I feel for Luca?*

"I'm so confused as well,mum," I whisper. My eyes are still looking over every detail of our fingers, and her bright red nails standing out against my pale blue ones.

"I think you do, Rose. You're just too scared to realize them yourself." I raise my head, looking into her blue eyes.

She's right, she always is. I swear mums have this magic power where they tell you everything you want to hear just because they know you better than you know yourself. I do know, I know exactly how I feel.

CHAPTER 30

ROSE

With his hot body underneath me and his erratic breathng, I run my index finger over his sweaty, inked skin. "My mum knows about us," I tell him, remembering my conversation with her earlier today. His eyes linger on me whilst his brain ticks like clockwork.

"What does she know?" he asks, sitting up slightly. I fall off his chest. I watch him tense up, unsure how to handle this information.

"She said it was obvious that we had something going on. Don't worry, she won't tell Dan." I sit up, hoping that calms him down. He stands up, running his fingers through his hair as my heart speeds up by the second.

"This is becoming more dangerous, Rose. Nick has everything in his hands." He tugs on his hair, looking at me with eyes full of fear.

"What do you mean?" Sitting up, I slide off the bed and walk towards him.

"I know we're running out of time, Rose. He's going to tell Dan," he says, every word stinging more than the next.

"How can he do that to you?" I growl with annoyance. How has he been in Luca's life for so many years but decides to stab him in the back when he wants?

"He has this obsession with you, Rose. He likes forbidden things. He's not a good guy, and I'm really starting to see it. I spent years of my life with him, and this is the first time he's ever gone behind my back and deliberately messed with me." He reaches out, lacing his fingers through mine. I look up into his blue eyes whilst he watches me fiercely.

"Can I just make the most out of what we have?" he asks. I keep my eyes trained on him.

"Yes," I answer bluntly. *What we have? What is that?*

"What are we, Luca?" I come out and say it. Obviously, I don't have a mouth filter. His eyes are still trained on me. He smiles at me softly as his hands reach out, holding onto my shoulders and pulling me towards his chest. I wrap my arms around his waist as he holds me close.

"All I know is I want you to be mine, and I want to be yours." His warm breath fans my temple as he squeezes me tighter. Being Luca's? Is that what I want? Do I want a label on our 'relationship'? Yes. God yes, I really do.

"Don't let Nick eat you up like this." I pull away, reaching for his sharp jaw. His eyes piercing into mine with so much emotion that I can hardly breathe. Guilt spreads across every inch of his beautiful features.

"I can't help it. Everything's eating me up." His hand wraps around my waist, pulling our naked bodies closer together.

"Relax." I stand on my toes, kissing him gently whilst hoping and praying he doesn't change his mind. It's taken us weeks and weeks to get to where we are—understanding that we want commitment and we want each other. I just hope to God that Nick, or anyone, will not try and stop this. I feel like if this ends badly, everything will fall apart. *Again.*

*　　*　　*

Work has officially finished for the day, and I am in desperate need of coffee. I pick up my stuff and head out of the office. Everyone is rushing to get out of the building for the day. It's been three days since I had that conversation with mum, and I feel tense that something bad is on its way to ruin everything for me like it always has done. My phone ringing stops me in my tracks as I pull my phone out of my bag.

Incoming call: Luca

"Hello, you," I answer sweetly, exiting the lift and marching through the reception towards the glass doors.

"I'm outside. Let's get dinner." His voice is strong and confident. Opening the door, I see him looking flawless as ever in skinny black jeans, a white-fitted shirt with the sleeves rolled up over his elbows, showing off his tattooed hands and arms.

"You're a work of art, Luca." I whistle into the phone as I approach him at a fast pace.

"I could say the exact same thing about you. Damn" He hangs up the call as I reach him in seconds whilst his hands are pulling my coat into his hard body. His lips are hard but soft; hungry, but passionate.

"So where we eating then?" I pull back, raising my eyebrow. I try to ignore the whale noises that have suddenly started to erupt inside my stomach.

"McDonald's." He lets out a laugh as I slap his arm. "I'm joking, unless you want to?" He laughs again whilst I consider eating a Big Mac for a second.

"Honestly, I wouldn't say no," I answer him as I open the car door, letting myself in.

"Have you heard of Giraffe?" he asks after getting into the driver's side and turning on the engine. I shake my head in amusement. He beams as he pulls out of the car park and onto the busy road.

"I know it sounds dodgy but it's so good, I promise!" He breaks at a traffic light, his face caught between the darkness of the car and the sunset behind him. Absolutely breathtaking.

Finishing off my Rodeo chicken burger, I am well and truly stuffed. I watch him struggling to finish off his Smokey Joe burger with an extra side order of onion rings. I've never known someone with a body so sculpted and lean to eat so much bloody crap. I know he runs to the gym every day on his hour lunch break and making it back just in time to carry on working. He also tells me that having me keeps him extra fit and in shape.

"Good?" he asks before shoving the last onion ring in his mouth. I wipe my lips with a napkin, getting rid of any excess ketchup.

"Very pleased. I have a food baby." I tap my bloated stomach.

"How was work?" I ask, changing the conversation. He begins to tell me all about a venue that's beginning to give him more stress then he needs; something to do with extra costs for an event and food supplier dropping out. I tell him all about Emily leaving me alone for the duration of the day until four when she spilt water down my dress. As much as I wanted to rip her dolled-up face off her tiny body, I had to remain calm. If I didn't love my job, it would be a different matter completely.

"On Friday, Daniel and Lee want to go out. Ask the girls." He takes a sip of his Pepsi Max as I look at his face and he's tenser than what I'm used to. His shoulders are raised and his nostrils flare with every breath.

"Only if you'll be there?" I ask. Obviously, he's not asking me to come if he won't be there.

"Of course, I'll be there, you tit." He laughs and I feel my face redden. Looking down at my hands, I study the Pandora thumb ring my mum bought me for my eighteenth birthday. His inked hands reach out, tickling the back of my palms and over my acrylic nails.

"I love this colour. It matches your eyes," he whispers, running circles over my thumb.

"I'll be there," I tell him as his eyes raise to meet mine.

"You wouldn't have had a choice either way, baby." He smirks. Goddammit, I love his smirk.

Locking the front door behind me, I'm greeted with a dark hallway. I look at the time on my phone, and it's only nine. Surely, the girls haven't gone to bed already?

"Anyone home?" I yell, marching into the kitchen and opening the fridge to pick out the milk. Turning the kettle on, I walk over to the cupboard and pick out my favourite mug. It's baby pink with silver writing and it says, "I'm an adult but not like a REAL adult."

I make my coffee in silence and soon find myself alone in my bedroom with neither girls in their rooms. I pull out my phone and text both of them as I undress and jump in the shower. I give myself enough time to let my drink cool down without burning my tongue.

After my shower, I climb into my fluffy pyjama bottoms, an oversized T-shirt, and my bright teal dressing gown. My blonde hair is damp as it falls down my back. As I walk back into the living room, I decide on Netflix. Looking down at my phone, I notice a new text message.

Text Message [From: Darcy]: I'll be home in ten minutes girl, I went to mums for dinner xxxxx

I write out a quick reply before turning my attention back to the film. I decided on *Cruel Intentions*, one of my all-time favourite films. Fancying the pants out of Ryan Phillippe, I can't help but feel like something is wrong, like my luck will run out. It might just be my mind trying to make me feel bad about everything that's happened. It would be typical.

"No Chloe?" Darcy appears in the doorway. Her smile bright as she slips her boots off and flops down next to me. I rest my head on her shoulder as we sit in silence.

"No Luca either?" she asks me again whilst I chuckle quietly. Luca wanted to stay round, but I feel like it will be far too obvious if he's out every night. Daniel will clock on eventually.

"Not tonight," I answer, trying not to dig too deep into my thoughts. Why couldn't Daniel accept us? Will he even accept us? He might not react as badly as we think. Maybe it could work.

"I like Luca, but that Nick friend of his gives me the heebie-jeebies." She shivers at the thought of Nick. It's strange. The more I think about Nick, the more I feel like he's got something cruel up his sleeve.

"What are you? Twelve?" I laugh trying to distract myself from my thoughts once again. My phone vibrates in my dressing gown pocket, and I pick out, looking at the unknown number.

Text Message [From: Unknown] If you have to keep something a secret it's because you shouldn't be doing it in the first place, I've warned you - N x

Scowling at my phone screen, I quickly type out a reply.

Text Message [To: Unknown] Go away Nick, this is getting boring now -R

"You okay?" Darcy asks with her face watching my phone screen.

"Yeah, Nick texted me. He's obsessed with my relationship with Luca," I answer, showing the text. I contemplate sending it to Luca, but I don't want to stress him out anymore.

"Ew, maybe he's like obsessed with you!" She scrunches her face up, amusement with a hint of fear written all over her face.

"Fuck off! Don't freak me out!" I slap her arm, laughing with her.

"I'm just saying. It's odd," she says. She's right, it is odd. Why can't he just be happy for Luca? Unless something is really off, something Luca hasn't told me. And I've been right this entire time.

CHAPTER 31

ROSE

Spraying some hairspray, I take in my appearance; my blonde hair curled into big rings flowing down my chest and back, my eyeliner catlike, and my lips bright red. I decided on wearing my leopard print heeled boots, black skinny jeans, and my new black velvet crop top. Slipping on my leather jacket, I'm ready to hit the London nightlife. I feel like it's been forever. The last time was when I kissed Luca for the first time, which was at least six weeks ago.

"You ready?" Chloe walks into my room, her pink dress hugging her slim figure. She looks annoyingly beautiful.

"Yeah, is Darcy?" I ask, checking myself out one last time.

"Yeah, she's already started the shots. Come on." She laughs before walking out of my room. Picking up my clutch bag, I turn off my bedroom light and walk out into the dim hallway. I hear laughter coming from the living room.

"Finally, Rose!" My brother appears in the doorway of the living room, wearing a denim shirt and black jeans.

"I didn't know you guys were coming over," I say. Behind my brother's head, I spot Luca leaning his back against the rails of the balcony with his eyes watching us. Holding back a smile, I place my eyes back on my brother.

"Yeah, last minute. We decided to pre-drink here." He wraps his arm around my shoulder, tugging me into the living room.

"I need a smoke," I say, opening up my bag. I step out into the surprisingly warm air, leaning over the balcony. I light my cigarette, looking at the city dancing in bright lights below and around us.

"You look stunning, baby," Luca whispers, shuffling a little closer towards me. His body is still facing the living room.

"You don't look half bad either," I mutter. He looks better than half bad; his black jeans hugs his muscular legs and a plain white T-shirt shows off his toned body with a black bomber jacket and his favourite pair of black Chelsea boots.

"This is going to be so hard." He lets out a deep sigh. I turn to face him, trying to act as casual as possible.

"What is?" I ask, even though I know the answer.

"This, us, not being able to hold you, kiss you tonight." He bows his head.

"We might find a way. Don't worry," I say, running many scenarios in my head just so I can kiss him during the night.

"Looking beautiful, darling." Lee steps out onto the balcony, his arms wide open for a hug and his blonde hair in need of a cut.

"Hello, Lee." I chuckle as I hug him quickly.

"I haven't seen you in weeks. Where have you been?" He raises an eyebrow at me and I raise one back.

"Nowhere unusual," I answer.

"How's the love life?" he asks. Giving him a questioning look, I hesitate. Does he know? Of course, he doesn't know.

"Debatable. Yours?" I snap back, hoping the lime light is off me.

"Dead." He chuckles in response. I put my fag out in the ashtray and smile up at him.

"I'm sure you'll find someone soon," I tell him. I don't understand why he hasn't found anyone. The entire time I've known him, which is ten years, I have always known him to pull the ladies on a night out but nothing further than a night. I also have a feeling he has a secret crush on Darcy, but I'm not sure how that would go down with her.

Two hours later, we have visited a couple of pubs and one bar. Everyone wants to go to Lust. Darcy is as drunk as a skunk, and Lee has been slurring words for at least an hour. Somehow, we all get into the club without being questioned on Darcy's or Lee's drunken states. I place a glass of water in both of their hands and force them to drink the entire glass. I thank the bartender for my vodka before stepping out of the way to let Daniel through.

"Can we dance? Please?" Darcy tugs on my hand, pulling me away from the group and towards the packed dance floor. I try to keep up with her moves, but it doesn't seem to work. Instead, I just sway my hips and laugh at her every time she attempts to slut drop.

Everyone manages to find us after a couple of minutes. Chloe grinding up against my brother has my eyes diverting away from them and towards Luca. The flashing red and blue lights have me in a trance, and his eyes are blowing my mind. Why can't we do that?

"You okay?" He leans down, whispering into my ear. I look towards my brother who is kissing Chloe's neck. I'm starting to hate them. Who do they think they are to stop Luca and me?

"Yeah, I just really want to kiss you," I answer, feeling my core ache by the second. He's been around me for over two hours, and we haven't even touched. His breath is warm against my ear.

"Follow my lead," he says. I'm hesitant for a second, watching him look over at my brother.

"Mate, I'm going upstairs. Rob from work just texted me," he tells Daniel. He looks at Luca before nodding. I squint my eyes towards Luca who just nods towards Darcy.

"Girls, I'll be back in a minute. Just going to find a plaster because my feet are killing me," I lie. If I tell them where I'm really going, Dan will find out. Darcy is pissed and Chloe is vulnerable to my brother's touch. I rush off quickly before anyone questions me.

Walking past the dark staircase, I'm pulled into the shadows by the arm. I smell him before tasting him. His lips crash down on me as I'm slammed against the wall. My legs wrap around his waist as he raises me up by my bum.

"God, baby, you are so fucking sexy." He moans into my mouth as I pull him closer, tugging on his hair. His tongue is dancing with mine, and my body is heating up by the second as my pussy aches for his touch.

"Fuck, Luca. I want you so bad," I cry out in pleasure as his hand presses against my jeans. The pressure is blinding me as he teases my clit through the thick denim.

"Why didn't you wear a dress, Rose?" He groans in annoyance. I couldn't hate myself more than I do right now. His strong hand moves up my stomach and towards my breasts. His lips are leaving my mouth and slowly kissing down my jaw.

"I wish we were in your bed right now, baby," he whispers against my neck, and I moan my response as his cock stiffens against my core.

"Does anyone know where Rose went?" I hear my brother's voice. Luca lets go of me as we back up as far into the wall as we can. Our group slowly walks past us as my brother's eyes scan every inch of the hallway.

"She said she was getting a plaster. Maybe she's in the toilet," Chloe says. I can tell by her face that she knows I'm with Luca.

"Okay. Well, Luca's upstairs so I'm going to go find him and meet in the smoking area," Daniel says to Chloe, Darcy, and Lee, who are leaning up against the wall and looking more sober than before.

"Yeah, she's in the toilet. She just texted me. I'll go grab her." Darcy looks at her lit-up phone whilst Luca's hand intertwines with mine as we hide in the corner, praying they disappear. Seconds later, everyone has gone. Chloe and Lee are walking outside while Daniel climbs up the stairs.

"You are so goddamn lucky Daniel wasn't standing where I am." Darcy's voice makes me jump as she appears back through the door.

"Life saver." I chuckle as we step out from the shadows. She smiles at us as we walk outside into the foggy seating area. I sit down, watching Luca light his fag and lending me his lighter. I inhale the smoke; I welcome it into my lungs, relaxing me instantly.

"Where have you been?" My brother steps out, walking towards Luca quickly.

"I've been out here." Luca gives me a questioning look.

"Oh right, I saw your mate Nick with that Emily girl," he tells Luca. His shoulders instantly tense up, and I know Nick's a bit of a dick. Surely, he won't do anything to piss Luca off tonight.

Luca's eyes bore into mine as he smiles lightly at me like he can read my mind, telling me not to worry. His face is a pure work of art. With the bright lights shining down on him, his face is chiselled and flawless. His eyes are glistening like I had never seen them before. I have fallen so hard, and I can't deny it any more. I'm so in love with Luca Haynes.

CHAPTER 32

ROSE

"Hey, Luca. Didn't know you would be here." Nick appears out of nowhere, wrapping his arm around Luca's shoulder. I watch his body stiffen, and the tension building by the second. He trusted Nick. He's been a friend to him for years, so why now? Why has Nick decided to mess with his head?

"Rose, you look outstanding as usual. You are one lucky sod." Nick pulls Luca closer to him whilst I close my eyes, hoping to god Daniel didn't hear that. Daniel's conversation has to be very in depth for him not to react. He's laughing with Chloe and maybe not even realising Nick's out here, threatening to ruin everything.

"Your outfit's a bit trashy even for you, Rose," Emily growls at me as she appears behind Nick.

"I can't even see your outfit, Emily," I snap back at her, taking in her tiny black dress.

"Wow. Now, you have some balls?" She steps closer to me whilst I take a stand, raising my eyebrow.

"Emily, shut up," Nick spits at her, and I watch in shock. As much as I don't like either of them, telling his supposed girlfriend to shut up makes him even more of a dick than I thought. Rolling my eyes, I try to back away from this conversation and move closer to Darcy. Her eyes are glaring at Emily like she's ready to kill.

"Easy there." I tap her shoulder, trying to hold back a laugh as Darcy's face softens towards me.

"I don't trust her, Rose. Look at how she's looking at Luca." Darcy growls. I look over at him with his eyes closed. His nostril is flaring, and his body is tensing as Nick whispers things into his ear. What the hell is going on? I'm going crazy witnessing all of this. I can't just tell Daniel what's going on now. I have to tell him tomorrow. I just need to persuade Luca that it's a good idea.

"Rose!" my brother yells over to me. He smiles brightly as he motions for me. I stand up with Darcy right behind me as we shimmy ourselves through the pact floor.

"What's up?" I ask, and he smiles even brighter at me.

"Where is that bloke of yours?" he questions. I'm taken aback for a second. What bloke?

"Who are you on about?" I ask nervously. Surely, he doesn't know.

"That Jacob guy. That's why we've hardly seen you. You've been hiding him from us." He tugs me in closer to him, his eyes mischievous. Lee laughs next to him, both so unaware. God, he's drunk and in a teasing mood.

"Who's Jacob? Now, I'm intrigued." Emily butts in. Dan steps back opening the group up to all of us again. I look straight into Luca's eyes. He looks worried and scared.

"What is going on?" I mouth to him, hoping he understands. His facial expression is blank, but I can see many emotions behind his eyes.

"Some guy that Rose has been dating." My brother answers, not seeing the tension rise between mostly everyone but him and Lee.

"Wow, this just got interesting, Rose. I didn't know you liked to shag about, poor Luca." Emily snaps. My head turns instantly. I could hear my knuckles cracking as I close them into tight fists.

"Don't start Emily." I take a deep breath whilst Luca's face is turning red by the second.

"She's not sleeping about. What are you on about? What has this got to do with Luca?" My brother turns to face Emily and Nick completely. Oh shit, this is not good.

"Hey, Daniel. Let's go dance again." Chloe tugs his shoulder but he doesn't move. His eyes are looking at Nick's. I look at Chloe, thanking her with my eyes. It was no use whether Daniel find outs if I like it or not.

"How's Rachel?" Nick asks my brother with an evil smirk crossing his face. Luca runs his fingers through his hair. I can see the panic blowing up in his brain.

"What? Who's Rachel?" My brother pulls a face. I can always tell when he's lying. Right now, my brother is lying. His cheeks are reddening and his breathing has doubled.

"Oh, don't act silly. Rachel Silva, your girlfriend." Emily scoffs crossing her arms and I look towards Chloe. Her face is scrunched up in confusion and her hands are shaking by her side. Oh god, Daniel what have you been doing?

"She's not my girlfriend? I haven't spoken to her in years." My brother tries to stand his ground, but I can tell he's going to lose this.

"Don't lie," Luca says. I shoot him a look of confusion, but his eyes are trained perfectly on Daniel. What has been going on? What does Luca know about my brother that he's forgotten to tell me? My legs begin to shake as my anxiety hits the roof.

"Luca, I can explain." Dan steps towards him. Luca glares back not to test him to go any further. I step forward grabbing my brother by the elbow, slowly turning him to face me.

"What's going on?" I quietly question him with his face heating up by the second.

"How did you find out?" He ignores my question, looking back over to Luca. He straightens his shoulders, running his hand over his mouth quickly.

"The day we all went to the beach, I saw her text when you went for a walk with Chloe," he tells evryone.

"You went through my phone?" Daniel raises his voice, angry with the violation of privacy.

"No, it appeared on your screen." Luca deepens his voice. Looking at him, the veins in his neck popping out as his breathing becomes faster with every breath.

"Can we at least go outside the front if we are going to talk about this? I can hardly hear you," Daniel asks. Everyone quickly nods as we make our way through the smoking area. Once we step past the security at the entrance, everybody is tense. Lee and Darcy have completely sobered up. I feel like I might throw up, why has Luca not said anything to me?

"So Daniel, tell us more about Rachel." Nick leans up against the brick wall with his smug face that I want to rip off.

"Okay, fine. I didn't know you, Luca. When I started seeing her again, I didn't know she was in a relationship. When I met you at the bar, I realized what had been going on but I couldn't leave her. I loved her too much." My brother's voice is trembling, and I pity him. My own brother has fucked up in a way I could never imagine.

"And now?" Luca asks, his body relaxing by the second. I feel better seeing him less angry, and I can't handle the idea of him beating the shit out of my brother.

"I don't know what I'm doing. I care about you, Chloe. I really do." He looks towards one of my best friends. Her eyes are teary, and in this moment, I know I have to say something to him.

"How could you be so cruel?" I ask. Hoping I don't mean it but, God, at this moment, I feel so broken for Chloe, even for Luca—the boy I have grown to love. I promised myself I would never fall in love again yet here I am.

"I don't know. Why didn't you say anything sooner, Luca?" He turns back towards him. I keep my eyes on Luca, hoping he doesn't hurt my brother as much as he deserves it.

"I wanted to find out more. I wanted to hurt you. That girl broke me, and you're the main cause of it all, but I knew there was nothing I could do. I honestly don't care anymore," he answers. His eyes soon find mine, and I don't even know how to look at him whether to be thankful, proud, or confused. Why didn't he tell me about this sooner?

"That's not the truth though. Is it, Luca?" Nick steps in again.

"Nick, will you just stop?" Lee steps in, obviously bored of Nick's input. It has nothing to do with Nick anymore. He's just stirring shit.

"Wouldn't you like to know exactly what Luca has been doing? He's lying. He's been planning on stabbing you in the back just as you did to him." Emily steps in and looks at me, ignoring Lee's death stare.

"Rose, any guesses?" She steps closer. I'm clueless of what he has been doing; the boy I have spent every night with for weeks and who I have fallen so hard in love with.

"Can you just stop!" I growl, moving closer.

"You're pathetic." She hisses. I raise my hand, slapping her across the face. She stumbles back before launching herself at me. I fall to the floor as she pulls at my hair. I slap her face and my palm stings instantly. My anger is blinding everything—every push, shove, and comment since the day she caught me in Luca's bed.

"Get off her!" I hear Luca yell. I can see Darcy and Chloe trying to get to me, but Daniel and Lee have their arms tightly around them. I return to Emily who has a fistful of my hair.

"Fuck you!" Emily screams, hitting me. I push her off me, knocking her onto her back. I climb on top of her, and I hit her again and again until I see blood dripping down her nose. Suddenly, someone pulled me off.

"God! Let me rip her fucking head off!" Emily screams whilst being tugged away by Nick.

"Try it bitch!" I wail back, slapping Luca's arms off me.

"Rose, baby. Calm down. The police will be called if you don't calm down." His voice is gentle in my ear. I whimper into his chest as my body trembles with adrenaline.

"What the hell was that about?!" Dan marches over to Nick, pushing at his chest. Nick laughs in his face. My blood is pumping, but I feel warm in Luca's arms.

"Can someone just tell me what's going on?" I yell, tired of everyone's mind games.

"Oh, sweetie. I don't think you want to know." Nick looks towards me whilst Luca's body loosens as he walks back towards Nick.

"Please don't." I hear him whisper.

"'Please don't' what?" I ask as my mind finally catches up with everything.

"Luca's way of hurting Daniel was by breaking the rules." Nick smiles at me. Dan's eyes widen in realisation. Luca's body is tensing again. That's when it truly hits me, *hard.*

"No, you can't be serious?" I beg as my eyes instantly waters.

"What rules? Luca, what have you done?" Daniel steps forward with fists clenched.

"I-I'm so sorry, Rose." He looks at me with fear written all over his face. A cry escapes my throat as tears immediately fall down my face. The sudden realisation that he's been using me, playing with me.

"You know the rules, Daniel. Never ever go for my sister. Your friend Luca has been sleeping with her for weeks. *Weeks.* We wanted proof, something we could send to you but, unfortunately, Luca didn't hand one over." Nick smirks at Dan with pride. My brother's face scrunches up in rage. I watch in horror as he strides towards Luca, punching him hard in the jaw whilst Luca's head snaps to the side.

"You've been fucking my sister?!" Daniel screams before punching Luca in the face again. I cry without even realising. Dan's and everyone's eyes turn to face me. My whole body vibrates. *What the fuck is going on? Oh my god.*

"Rose, let me explain!" Luca tries to walk over but Daniel blocks his path. His hand wraps around Luca's collar.

"Stay away from her," he threatens.

"Rose, I didn't know you the way I do now when I wanted to hurt Dan. I just thought you were an easy target. I'd only met you a couple of times. I swear I didn't mean for any of this," he begs. Looking him in the eyes, I see the beauty and pain.

"You didn't mean for what, Luca? You sure as hell made it a priority to spend as much time as possible with me!" I yell. If this is how my heart is going to break again, then I swear to God, I won't allow myself to open up to anyone again.

"I'm such an idiot!" I cry, covering my face with my hands.

"I fucking knew something was wrong about you!" Chloe's voice echoes through the silence. My sobs muffle in my hands. "I knew there was a reason she shouldn't trust you!" Chloe's voice is getting louder until I feel her arms around my waist, and I cry onto her shoulder.

"Well, isn't this depressing?" Emily's voice cuts through me. I pull away from Chloe, running at her. Swinging my hand back, I connect my first with her eyes and watch as she falls back quickly, completely shocking her. Nick rushes over to her. Her body is wobbly as she tries to stand back up. Her eyes are scowling but she doesn't react.

"Rose," Luca says.

"Why is Nick involved?" I ask him, refusing to keep my eyes off a weak and bleeding Emily. *Serves you right, bitch.*

"I told him about Rachel and Dan, about you. He was all for it," he answers me. Nick's evil laugh breaks me even more. He's finding this funny, hilarious even.

"I like games, simple as that." He looks at me and not one bit of sympathy spread across his face. I turn to look back at Luca.

"So this whole time, I've been your personal gain to get back at Dan? Please tell me you never took a picture," I say with my voice trembling.

"I took one. You were asleep on my chest. Baby, I promise I never showed anyone. I was far too attached to you to actually go through with it." I cover my ears, uninterested of hearing the rest.

"Don't you DARE call me that ever again!" I push at his chest. His face falling with every shove against him.

"Rose, please let me explain myself. I wasn't thinking!" he begs, walking away from him. My eyes are scanning the front of the club; I see taxis beginning to park out front. I need to leave. This is so humiliating.

"Rose! Please!" I ignore his calls, turning and walking away. Chloe and Darcy are next to me in seconds as we approach the line of taxis. Darcy runs ahead, knocking on the window of one of the cars. Chloe's hand interlocks with mine, showing me how sorry she is. I squeeze her cold fingers, thanking her.

"I LOVE YOU!" My feet stops moving. I turn around slowly, and everyone seems to have caught up with us. Luca is only a feet away from me with tearful eyes. My brother's face is full of sadness and fury mixed together. Lee's eyes are wide with shock and he had no idea this whole time.

"Don't say that to me!" I cry out, begging him to stop.

"I'm in love with you, Rose. I love you so fucking much, and I know I've only known you a couple of months, but I do. I love you! Please don't leave me!" I watch the tears fall down his face and my heart aches for him. I want to wipe away his pain. I can't be a fool though; I can't trust him.

"It's a shame I don't love you then," I whisper. My heart shatters as I say the words. I can't bear to hear myself. I love him. I have loved him probably since the night I met him, but he can't know that. Not now. His face falls. I can tell just by the look in his eyes that I have truly broken his heart.

"Rose, he's going to take us home." Darcy's voice cuts through our silence. I nod my head and prepare to leave.

"Okay. I'm coming," I tell her.

"Please, Rose. Fuck! Please, don't leave. I know you love me! I know you do! If you don't love me, then why are you so sad? I've loved you this whole time!" His face is soaking and his hands are trembling. I have broken him like he's broken me.

"Even if I do love you, you've ruined everything. I hate you," I tell him before turning around and getting in the taxi. The driver pulls out of his space. I watch from the window as Luca breaks down on the floor, tugging at his hair as we disappear down the road and out of sight.

CHAPTER 33

ROSE

It's been three days since I found out and realized I had been played. For weeks, I let myself fall in love with a boy, just to be kicked to the curb . . . again. Monday morning hits me hard; I could hardly get up. My eyes are dry and sore. I knew I would have to face Emily, praying she's bruised. That will make me feel a little bit better.

"Rose, can I have a word?" My boss, Mrs. Todd, approaches my desk. Her face is gentle as I slowly nod. I follow her through the office with my eyes catching Emily's. Her make up is overdone to cover up a couple of dark purple bruises. I smile to myself as I follow Mrs Todd into the meeting room.

"Take a seat, Rose." She gestures to the blinding white chair on the opposite side of the large table where she is sitting.

"Is something wrong?" I ask as my nerves start to rise. *Am I in trouble?*

"I am concerned your relationship with Miss Cooper will ruin your chances at succeeding here at Fallon." She holds both her hands out, interlocking her fingers together.

"No! Of course not!" I snap at her with a panicked voice. *God, I'm going to kill Emily.*

"Good because what I've heard around the office is that you attacked her outside of a club last Friday night." She looks at me fiercely. I relax my shoulders. Playing with my thumbnails, I try to think of anything, anything that will help my situation.

"There have been some issues between us outside of work, but I won't let anything like this happen again." I look up at her, trying not to think too hard about Friday night.

"You are a great girl, Rose. Please don't let your personal life get in the way of your work. I will let this slide, but please be more careful next time." She leans back in her chair before standing up. I nod my head as I follow her out of the office. Back at my desk, I try my goddamn hardest not to slam my head against the wooden table.

"Rough day, sweetie?" Her sickly, sweet voice ruining my mood even more as I imagine the terrible things I could do to her right now if I wasn't at work.

"Piss off, Emily." I growl, not raising my head as I go through my paperwork. I try not to imagine her standing in front of me and smiling her perfect smile. Did Mrs. Todd question her too? Couldn't people see she was the one provoking me? I've been ignoring her for weeks.

"Someone's touchy. Things not going well?" I clench my fists, trying so hard not to snap. I can't ruin my career because this psycho has no brain filter. I watch the time on my computer hit five-thirty. I leap up, picking my bag up from the floor. I pull my coat on and shut down my computer all whilst she stands there, watching me amused.

"You deserved everything you got." I hear her as I walk through the office. I squeeze my eyes shut as I run out. I need to get far away from her before I lose my job. If I didn't care so much about my career, I'd probably staple her mouth shut. Literally.

Opening the glass doors, my heart drops and my eyes brim with tears. He isn't there, in his usual space, leaning against car. Warm tears trickle down my face as I stand frozen, wishing to God that none of this ever happened, that we were happy. Unfortunately, that wasn't the case. It never is, is it?

I wrap myself up in my duvet with coffee on the bedside table. My fluffy socks are warming my feet up. With my earphones plugged in and my volume on full blast, I bury myself deep into my bed and cushions. I try to block out any negative thoughts that have come since meeting Luca.

Now that I think about it, every bad thing that has happened in the last two months is because of him. Now, work's questioning me. Emily's going to make this hell for me, and I know it. Browsing through Spotify, I click on one of my favourite songs. I close my eyes, wrapping my body like a cocoon. James Arthur's "Let Me Love the Lonely" plays through my earphones. Listening to the song never had so much meaning until now. I can't help but think of him—of Luca. I opened up to him and let him in.

"Rose! Food's ready!" I wake up abruptly. Darcy is hanging over me and shaking my shoulders aggressively.

"I'm not hungry." I slap her away, covering my face from the bright light.

"You are eating whether you like it or not." She scowls. With a playful smile, I look up at her. Her eyes are bright blue with dark heavy makeup and her pixie blonde hair growing by the day.

"Fine." I sigh, throwing the duvet back and sliding out of bed. I follow her slowly through the hallway. My nose carries me to a steaming plate of chicken and roasted vegetables. My mouth is watering instantly. Chloe is an amazing cook. I watch her serve herself a plate before sitting across from me and Darcy, her eyes deep and sad.

"Thank you so much," I thank her, hoping she's okay—that we're okay.

"Don't be silly, happy to do it." She smiles at me, genuinely making me happy.

"Girls, I love you both, but goddammit, fuck men!" Darcy drops her fork, smashing it against the plate and making me jump.

"Rose, I have to tell you something." Chloe looks up from her untouched plate. I watch her with anticipation. I reach out, squeezing her fingers and letting her know I'm here.

"I slept with Dan a few times. I'm sorry, I lied." A single tear runs down her cheek. She insulted me and made me sound like an easy slut for Luca. I also knew how much she cared for my brother. How she would've done everything and anything to be with him.

"When?" I ask her gently, letting her know I wasn't at all angry with her.

"The first time was about a month ago. I didn't know he had a girlfriend, Rose. I didn't know about anything." A few more tears fall before I slide off the stool and walk towards her, wrapping my arms around her shoulders and pulling her close to me.

"I'm so sorry about Luca. I know you really cared about him. I should never have judged you for it." She rubs my arm as I rest my chin on her head.

"It's okay. I'll somehow cope." I chuckle, trying to make light of everything.

"Do you believe him? When he said he loved you?" she asks as I look over at Darcy. She's resting her chin on her hand with her eyes full of sympathy.

"I don't think so," I say.

"I think he loves you very much." Chloe looks up at me and I'm taken aback. I look towards Darcy as she nods her head. *She agrees?*

"You, out of all people, believed him? You hate him," I tell her, slightly confused. I walk back to my now probably cold food. Sitting down next to Darcy, I pick up my fork and taking a mouthful of the vegetables.

"I didn't hate him, I just didn't trust him, but seeing him Friday night—" She blows out a big breath, her eyes widening in disbelief.

"I don't think I have ever seen someone so heartbroken before." My stomach drops, and my heart pounds as I remember the look on his face when I told him I didn't love him—when I left in the car as he collapsed, pulling out his hair.

"We just want you to be happy, girl. That's all we want, no matter what." Darcy wraps her arms around my shoulders, pulling me in. Chloe's next to me immediately as they both hold me tight. I needed this; I needed my girls. I end up telling the girls about Emily spreading shit at work and my meeting with Mrs. Todd.

"I can fucking hit her for you. I won't get in trouble." Darcy is pacing the kitchen as I shove a piece courgette and chicken in my mouth. I let out a muffled laugh as she scrunches her face up in anger.

"If you see her, you are more than welcome." I look at both girls as they smile brightly at me. My phone vibrates against the marble kitchen top, but I hesitate as my phone dims down until the screen turns black again.

Text Message [From: Daniel] I'm always here, I'm not mad x

Not mad? Why the hell isn't he mad? I lied to him for weeks and weeks. If he's not mad with me, then he might not be mad at Luca? Of course, he's mad at Luca, but I can also imagine Luca's mad too.

Text Message [To: Daniel] Thanks x

I reply quickly. Thinking about it, I'm mad at him. He's messed around with Chloe for far too long, sleeping with her whilst he was secretly dating Rachel, Luca's ex-girlfriend. I don't even know how he could do that. After finding out that she had a boyfriend the whole time, he should have dumped her on the spot but instead, he befriended Luca and carried on with Rachel whilst shacking up with my best mate on the side. I am mad.

"You know, Dan's my brother and I love him to pieces but you deserve a hell of a lot better." I look back at Chloe whilst she's picking at her food. Her smile is soft but sad this whole time he's been playing her. He's worse than Luca.

"Right, let's put on a girly film and eat loads of ice cream. I'll run to Tesco." I stand up quickly. I need to make her feel better, to make myself feel better. Darcy jumps up, picking up our plates and heading over to the sink to wash up.

I rush back into my bedroom, slipping on a new pair of black leggings, my New Balance trainers, and my old oversized yellow sweatshirt.

"Get some wine too!" I hear Chloe and Darcy laughing with themselves.

"Okay! I'll be back in a few!" I yell out as I grab my keys, leaving the flat. The night air is colder as autumn arrives. The streets are busy with traffic as I make my way to the shop. I watch people as they walk by, talking on the phone or listening to music. *Ping*!

Text Message [From: Unknown] You look beautiful Princess

I look up, my eyes scanning everywhere, but I don't recognise anyone. Picking up my pace, my stomach flips, and I only know one person who used to call me that. I was never "Rose." I was always "princess." Wayne called me princess.

CHAPTER 34

ROSE

Tesco isn't busy, but it isn't empty either. People are scanning the microwavable meals for a quick, easy dinner. A group of teenagers huddling round the sweet aisle. I go straight to the frozen aisle, scanning the shelves of ice cream. I reach in and pick out Ben and Jerry's phish food and their new birthday cake flavour, placing them in my basket. I walk over to the alcohol section. I pick up two bottles of Rose, even contemplating on hitting the vodka instead. *Ping!*

Text Message [From: Unknown] You've grown up so much princess, I'm going to make you mine again

And then my screen lights up again.

Text Message [From: Unknown] God, I've missed you

A cold shiver shoots up my spine. I look around the shop again but I can't see him. Looking back at my phone, I open up my contacts. Within three rings, he answers.

"Hey, Rose. You okay?" he asks casually, obviously trying to act calm about everything since the last time we spoke.

"Can you come and get me? I'm in Tesco express. I keep getting weird texts messages and I think it could be Wayne." Honestly, I feel sick to my stomach.

"The Tesco close to yours?" he asks quickly, his breathing picking up by the second.

"Yes. I don't want to walk, even if it's just five minutes," I say. Picking up my basket, I feel calmer by the second knowing that my brother's coming.

"I won't be long. Stay inside," he says before hanging up the phone. I can't seem to calm the nerves that are flipping around in my stomach. I scan every single product in the sauces aisle, just praying traffic isn't bad and he'll be here soon. My phone begins to ring again, but this time, it's Chloe. I quickly answer.

"Hi, where are you?" she asks with her voice slightly worried.

"I'm waiting for Dan to come pick me up. Long story short, I think Wayne's here," I say straight to the point, trying not to let my fear shine through my voice.

"Fuck, did you want me to come down?" she asks quickly.

"No, its cool. I'll be home soon." *Be calm, Rose.*

"Text me when he's with you, okay?" she says with concern laced in her tone.

"Of course," I answer. After I hang up, I walk over to the self-checkout and begin to scan my items after showing my ID for the alcohol. I linger back inside the shop. My eyes catch with the security guard, probably looking very suspicious as I linger around the food awkwardly.

It's been at least twenty minutes since Dan left and I'm starting to get bored, and I'm running out of stuff to look at. This shop is tiny, and I know the security are keeping a close eye on me.

"Rose?" I hear my name being called. I rush over to the entrance where my brother stood. He wraps his arms around my shoulders, pulling me in for a hug.

"Are you okay?" He holds my shoulders, looking me straight in the eyes.

"I just want to get home," I say as he nods his head in response before holding onto my wrist and walking me into the dark night.

"Have you seen him?" he asks while I shake my head, holding my phone out for him to read the text messages.

"You sure it's him?" he asks again.

"I don't know, but it sure sounds like him. I can't risk it," I explain. He closes his eyes, obviously remembering what happened to me. I text Chloe letting her know I'm with Daniel as we walk a couple more feet before we reach his car.

"Did you want to stay at mine tonight?" he asks as I climb in with the leather seats cold against my leggings. A shiver runs over my body.

"No way." I laugh awkwardly. Imagine if I just walked in and Luca stands there all confused. I don't think I would be able to control myself if I saw him again.

"He's gone, Rose." He lets out a deep breath. I shoot my eyes to meet his. *He's gone?*

"Where has he gone?" I whisper, trying to figure where he might be. He shrugs his shoulders, giving me the answer I didn't want. Even if he knew, he wouldn't tell me so that's it. He's just gone? Maybe he's back in Hythe, away from all the chaos and with his happy family. *It's for the best, Rose.* I need to keep telling myself that. I won't see him every time I go to Daniel's. I might see him in Lust or a random bar from time to time. *I'll be okay.*

"I'd rather just go home, if that's okay?" I change the subject as he starts the car, the journey is almost too quiet for my liking. I don't think I have ever felt so awkward around my brother before.

"I'm really sorry about everything." His voice is shaky and I know he's hurt. I don't turn to look at him. I'm still so angry, and now, I'm even more confused that Luca just left.

"He told me everything. You didn't deserve this," he speaks again whilst I still stay quiet. I don't really know what to say or even how to feel. I know my feelings towards Luca haven't changed. I love him, but I don't think I could ever trust him. Minutes later, he turns off the engine and parks as we sit in an awkward silence again. My heart pounds in my chest. I have so many questions, especially to Luca.

"I think you should hear him out, Rose." He looks straight ahead. His voice is sad and distressed.

"Why should I? He used me to hurt you." I scowl at him, surprised that he's even considering this.

"I deserved to be hurt, Rose. I know you didn't but, God, when you left on Friday, I have never seen anything like it." He turns to face me.

"What do you mean?" I haven't heard about what happened when I left. I only know about the pain I felt—what Chloe felt.

"He went crazy. He beat the crap out of Nick, and I got him out of there before the police turned up." He chuckles and I smile slightly at the thought of Nick busted up. *God, I hope it hurt.*

"Why should I talk to him?" I ask my brother. His eyes are the brightest I've ever seen them with a glimmer of hope showing.

"I made you an easy target. So when I fucked up, you were there—perfect to mess with, but God, he loves you so much, Rose. I believe that more than anything." I smile weakly at him. He's right. He's so right.

"That doesn't make it okay. I'll text him, but just to find out more information, I won't let myself be a victim again." I grab the door handle, my eyes never leaving his.

"If you decide to make it work, I'll support it. I think we all will." I bite my bottom lip before opening the door and climbing out.

"Rose!" I hear my brother call out. I turn around to see him running towards me just as I reach the building. He wraps his arms around my shoulders, pulling me in for a tight hug.

"Tell Chloe I'm sorry. Be safe. Call me if you need anything!" He pulls back quickly before turning around and walking to his car.

"Think about what I said, Rose." I was just about to hear him as I walk through the building whilst letting the door slam behind me.

Keeping my phone at a safe distance on the coffee table, I sip on my wine as the film plays on. When I get home, I saw the girls being frantic and worried like hell. They pulled me into a big cuddle and Darcy even cried a little. I showed them the messages, and now, I think I'm going to be locked in this flat forever. The only conclusion I have is that it's Wayne. Nick and Emily don't know this about me and as much as Luca fucked me over. I know he wouldn't tell them out of spite. It has to be Wayne.

"So what about Luca?" Darcy asks, leaning back on the sofa and ripping open a packet of crisps. I look back at my phone, contemplating if it is a good idea. My mind is going through every memory and feeling I have. What's stopping me from calling him? Maybe I can hear him out? But it might be best if we just move on, he's probably doing that right now.

"Are you going to text him?" Chloe nudges my shoulder, snapping me out of my rambling thoughts. I lean into her, not sure what to say or even what to do.

"Do it. Find out the truth," Darcy says as I watch her in fascination. I shove a load of Doritos into her mouth, not even taking her eyes away from the TV.

Just as I am about to lean forward, my phone vibrates and the screen lights up. I'm hesitant, scared its Wayne again but as I look at the name on the screen, my heart bursts.

Text Message [From: Luca] I know you shouldn't forgive me, I love you and I'm so sorry x

My chest suddenly feels too tight. I can barely breathe, and my hands shake uncontrollably. "Rose?" Chloe leans over whilst looking at my phone. A loud sob escapes my throat as the tears fall down my face.

"Come here." She pulls me into a cuddle as I cry, one sob louder than the other. I feel Darcy sit behind me, rubbing my back and resting her chin on top of my head. If I could have anyone helping me right now, it would be my dad. I was his little girl, but he would know what to say to me.

I haven't heard from him in nearly four days. That's not classed as long really, but when everything blew up, I couldn't believe how much I missed him. How much I almost relied on having him around me. I need to see him, even if my heart breaks all over again.

CHAPTER 35

ROSE

I called my mum after work and told her that I'm coming over for a few hours. She accepts my invitation and tells me she will have dinner ready for seven. It's Friday night, and it's been a whole week since I last saw him. I don't know why I haven't texted him back. I almost feel cruel for not replying to him on Monday night. Instead, I have filled up my time reading a couple of sad books and tiring myself out at the gym, obviously with the company of either Chloe or Darcy.

Pulling into my mum's driveway, I rush out of the car as her front door opens wide. Her arms are open, and I don't hesitate to run into them. Smelling her perfume, her soft hair tickles my cheek as I burst into tears. She runs her fingers through my hair as I shake in her arms. She's doesn't ask me if something's happened with Luca. She's my mum and she just knows.

"Let's get you inside. It's getting cold." She gently pushes me into the house as I place my long coat over the banister, making my way into the large kitchen. Hughie, mum's black-and-white cat, is sitting on the windowsill. I make my way over, stroking the slightly overweight boy.

"Hey, handsome." I lean down, kissing his fluffy forehead. His purrs calm me down enough to smile. I wish I was a cat sometimes. They can just sleep, eat, and get cuddles all the time without problems.

"What's been going on, Rose?" I turn to face my mum as she leans up against the counter. Her blonde hair curled down her back, and her blue jeans sucking her in with a teal blue knitted jumper.

"A few things, would Wayne have any possible way of contacting me?" I ask her, slightly concerned with how she's going to react. She frowns and steps closer to me. I open up my phone and hand it to her. She looks through the messages.

"I don't think that would be him, Rose," she says, handing back my phone. I can see the slight change in her breathing. I feel so guilty for everything.

"How can you tell?" I ask, more confused than ever. She takes a deep sigh, her eyes opening up to look at me again.

"That would be very silly of him. He's just come out of prison." I'm not even sure if she believes what she's saying. I hate how every time she looks at me, she sees the girl who ruined their marriage even if I never gave my consent. Surely, that's what she can see. He chooses me over her and that breaks my heart.

"I'm sorry, Mum." I lock my fingers with hers. My mum has only been in love once—to my daddy. I knew my parents still loved each other when they got divorced, but their love turned into a close friendship. Even when she married Wayne, her heart breaks when he died. Wayne seems like a good distraction, especially after dad's death until I told her the truth.

"Baby, listen to me. I know this must be confusing, and I cannot imagine how you feel. He's gone from our lives. I don't know who the hell has been texting you." I hold back my tears. I feel overwhelmed and unsafe.

Sitting at the dining table, Mum makes a roast dinner. Everything looks delicious. I don't know anyone who can make a roast like my mumma. Everything is so fresh and full of flavour, and the meat is always juicy.

"So tell me what's really bothering you?" My mum speaks first. I finish chewing the broccoli, trying to figure out what to tell her.

"He used me to hurt Daniel." I decide against hiding the truth. I can't hide it from her.

"Why would he do that?" She frowns in confusion.

"Because Daniel has been dating Luca's ex-girlfriend Rachel. He was the reason they broke up. You remember Rachel?" I hope mum doesn't kick off. I don't want Daniel to go through too much crap from everyone.

"Daniel's girlfriend from school?" She scoffs. I also remember very clearly that Mum couldn't stand her. She was rude and never thanked my mum for anything.

"Yeah, her. Well, she was cheating on Luca and it turned out to be with Daniel, so he got close to me to piss Dan off," I explain. She nods her head slowly, finally catching up with everything.

"So where does that leave you and Luca?" she asks as I bite into a potato before I reply. I need to figure it out myself.

"Well, I haven't spoken to him since I found out. I'm scared to get hurt again," I answer. Her eyes full of sympathy.

"Let him talk to you maybe? Do you love him?" Her question shocks me. I haven't told anyone how I feel about Luca. It may be obvious but I haven't said it out loud. If I say it, I will have to truly accept it myself.

"I love him more than I ever realized." I try to hold back my tears, but there is no point. I wipe them away as soon as they fall down my face.

"Does he love you?" Her smile is sad but her eyes are shining.

"He told me he does," I answer, remembering the way he confessed it all. How I wish I could go back in time and face it all, I wouldn't have run off. I would have let him explain himself. I would have told him I was in love with him.

"Mum, I need to see him, don't I?" I ask. Her eyes give me the answer as she smiles at me. Picking up my phone, I get up the message from him. I scroll up slightly as my heart aches from every text we shared.

Text Message [To: Luca] Come over tonight, I need to speak to you x

I put my phone down as a sigh of relief escapes my throat before I pick up my knife and for and begin eating my food. It's been one week. Have I dragged it out too long? Will he be over everything because I never answered him? Does he still love me? Will he just ignore my text and never speak to me again?

It's been two hours since I texted him, and I haven't heard a thing. I have spent my time cuddled up on the sofa with Mum and the cat, watching *Somewhere in Time*—one of my most cherished films, same as mum's. *Ping.* Picking up my phone quickly, my heart races beyond belief.

Text Message [From: Luca] I can be over at eleven if that's not too late? x

I smile to myself.

Text Message [To: Luca] See you then x

Maybe it's not too late. Watching the credits roll as the films finishes, I take in my mum asleep on the sofa. My body aches for her. I hate how lonely she is here. I hate that this is all because of me.

"Mum, I've got to go. He's coming over." I shake her lightly. Her blue eyes open wide as a warm smile sets on her stunning face.

"Let me know how it goes, baby." She stands up, kissing my cheek. I walk out into the hallway and pick up all my stuff. I give her a quick hug before opening the front door. Stepping into the chilly air, I wrap my coat around myself and unlock my car door.

"Keep safe!" she yells as I open the door and slipping inside.

"I will!" I yell at her, shutting the door behind me.

On the drive home, I switch my eyes between the road and the clock ticking away until he is at my place. I have one hour and I need to do so much. I need to shower and sort myself out. I look like a worn-out mess and I don't want him seeing that.

"He's coming over?" Chloe asks with a slice of excitement in her voice. This is odd.

"Yes? Is that okay?" I slowly ask, raising an eyebrow. I slip into a pair of leggings and my favourite oversized black top with Harry Styles lyrics that says, "I've been praying ever since New York."

"I think it needs to be done. So yes, girl." She hugs me quickly. My wet hair is slapping her face.

"Now, you have thirty minutes. Sort your hair out." She laughs before winking and then closing my bedroom door. I blowdry before running my straighteners over it quickly, then I hear a knock on my bedroom door. *Shit.*

My heart thumps in my chest as I take one last look at myself in the mirror. My eyes bright with a few coats of mascara. My skin is clear and smooth, and my long hair is shiny. I can't stop the smile that makes its way across my face. He's outside my door and I'm ready.

I take silent steps until I reach the door. I pull the handle down slowly, opening the door. There he stands with his piercing blue eyes that's truly captivating. His jawline is sharp and fierce. The tattoos covering his throat and neck brighter than ever. It's like looking at him for the first time.

"Rose," he whispers.

"Come in." I gesture for him to step in, so we can talk this out. I want to forgive him, but can I?

CHAPTER 36

LUCA

Stepping into her bedroom feels weird, like I've never been in here before. It's like I've never slept in her bed, had late night conversations until she fell asleep on my chest, and where I made love to her. She walked in front of me and sat on the bed, leaning up against her silly number of decorative cushions. She looks beautiful, so exquisite that I can't stand to look at her.

"I came here to say I'm sorry. I don't expect anything in return," I say whilst sitting opposite her but at a safe distance. I can't risk fucking up again. Touching her will do just that. She looks sad as she looks at me.

"Tell me why," she whispers. I can hear the pain I've caused in her voice. Everything runs through my head. Where can I begin? What does she want to know?

"The night I met you, I honestly couldn't believe my eyes. I'd heard about the rule Daniel gave, but I didn't have any intentions on messing with you until we went to the beach with everyone." Her hands are shaking as she picks at the skin around her long painted nails.

"So the day at the beach was the day your game started? Before then was just innocent flirting?" she asks with a timid voice. I've really broken her. I'm an arsehole.

"Yes, my cruel thoughts towards Daniel died down quickly when I found out about Wayne and your dad. I wanted to stop my plan. The night we kissed was never to hurt Daniel. My feelings were there," I speak up again, remembering everything.

"When he nearly caught us in my room and you walked out, I was going fucking crazy. I hated myself, but you had me from the first kiss, Rose." I close my eyes, my voice shaking as my heart thumps over and over again . . . painfully.

"After the kiss, everything became so real, but I had already told Nick and Emily got in the way. They became obsessed with the idea to ruin you. I don't even know why they cared so much. I was so angry with your brother at first." My blood is boiling at Nick's cruel personality, and I know how good it felt to break his nose under my fists that night. "I have never met two people so perfect for each other. They are twisted." I growl, trying to calm myself down.

"Why didn't you show them the picture?" she asks, her voice becoming louder and more confident than before. I take a deep breath, remembering the first time she fell asleep on my chest and her naked body against mine. It only took one second to get the perfect picture; her naked body on show.

"I couldn't go through with it. I told Nick I had the picture but deleted it as soon as he went to grab my phone. I felt protective and foolish for even thinking I could do that to you. I had already fallen in love with you. I don't know what I thought would happen if I betrayed you like that." My body is feeling hotter by the second, and I can't read her face.

"Did you mean what you said?" She looks at me and my heart bursts. Now, I'm scared where this is going.

"Yes. Every word, Rose. I understand if you don't feel the same." I can't look at her anymore. This is a bad idea coming here. I've told her what I needed to. She knows the truth.

"I love you." Her voice slices through me, my head shoots up to face her once again. Her beauty throwing me off the rails as always. I need to control myself. I can't ruin her. I can't ruin myself anymore.

"I have loved you this whole time." Her voice cuts through me again. I realize I never replied to her. Her face is holding so much emotion. This stunning girl has just told me she loves me after everything.

I lean forward, gripping at her waist and pulling her towards me. She obliges, climbing onto my lap. Her lips soft but the kiss urgent and hungry. *What am I doing? I can't do this.* My whole body is betraying me. I need to stop myself.

"Luca, please," she whimpers into my mouth, and I can't even lie to myself anymore. I need her even if she regrets it in the morning. When she realizes she deserves better. I hold her face and take full control. My fingers are raking through her soft hair as I lean forward. Her body follows as I place my elbows on either side of her head, unable to break the kiss.

"You are so beautiful, baby," I whisper, kissing down her jaw. My hands leave her face as I lower them onto the hem of her top, slowly lifting it up and revealing her tight stomach. Lowering my head and kissing just below her belly button, she arches her back as I wrap my fingers around her leggings and knickers, pulling them down her legs and over her ankles.

Leaving her pussy bare, I look at her flawless beauty. Taking in her slender frame and noticing her under boob peeking out from her scrunched-up top, I sit over her and lift the material up and over her head, which reveals her gorgeous boobs. She's naked underneath me, my body ignites as I take in my girls' angelic figure. Her hair sprawled over the cushions, her skin golden and soft as silk.

"Please," she whispers as I sit up, stripping my upper body of any clothing. I feel her getting frantic at my jeans, trying to get them off me quickly. Her fingers gliding over my hard cock as she pulls my jeans and boxers down. I stand up quickly, trying to get them over my ankles. Her soft laugh catches me, my heart flipping with passion as I take her in.

I don't even know how long I'll last; just looking at her has me close. I climb back on the bed until my face is between her legs. I kiss the top of her thighs. Her moans making my dick twitch as I hover over her sweet spot whilst my warm breath has her whimpering again. She knows I'm close to her, but I enjoy seeing her struggle because of me and what I can do to her.

I press my lips against her core as she gasps at the contact, and I begin kissing and sucking her sensitive clit. I let my hands runs up and down her stomach. She flexes and twitches with every movement my mouth and tongue make against her soaking pussy. I enjoy watching her, taking in every inch of her delicious body, her taste, and every sound she makes. I'll cherish and worship her forever.

"I'm going to cum, Luca!" she cries as I carry on pleasuring her with my lips and tongue. Her legs are opening wider, letting me see more of her juicy body as she comes undone.

I sit up quickly whilst she's in a dazed state, opening her bedside drawer and pulling out a foil packet. I take seconds putting the condom on before sitting up between her legs, her eyes wide with lust as she spreads them wider for me to fit. Holding my cock, I press it against her wet slit and slowly thrust my hips as I slide inside her. I close my eyes. *God, I've missed this. I've missed being inside her.* I watch with fascination as I begin to pound her deeper and deeper, her beauty amazes me every time I look at her.

How did I get so lucky? How could I have possibly been so spineless? How could I do this to her? I don't deserve this beautiful girl. I'm an idiot. She'll hate me very soon, I need to make the most out of what I have right now. "I love you so much, Rose," I whisper, trying so hard not to blow my load right now. Her eyes open slowly as she struggles under my pounding hips, her breathing fast as her toes clench.

"I love you, Luca." She moans as I grind deeper; her smell intoxicating, her face unforgettable. I lean down, kissing her hard and showing her how much she means to me. I don't want her to ever forget this kiss, to ever forget she's loved. I cum in my condom as she tightens her pussy around me. I collapse on top of her, my damp skin against hers as she smiles at me. Her gentle fingers reach up, stroking my face.

I'm trying so fucking hard to hold back all the tears I have held in since she opened her bedroom door, my emotions skyrocketing by the second. I know I'll love this girl forever. There was a reason I didn't want commitment, and it doesn't have anything to do with Daniel and my idiotic game. I have been so selfish, and I will hate myself forever.

CHAPTER 37

ROSE

I'm cold, too cold. I turn my body, trying to find heat from his warm body. Opening my eyes, I reach for him, but he's nowhere to be seen. I jolt up, the room still dark. I climb out of bed and walk over to the window, peering through the blinds. It's still pitch black. What time is it? Walking over to my phone, I pick it up. The screen burns my eyes as it lights up. Four-thirty?

"Luca?" I whisper, opening my bedroom door. *Maybe he's in the kitchen?* I wrap my arms around my naked body as I tiptoe through the flat, checking both kitchen and living room. Both are empty. The lamp next to the coffee table is on, lighting the room slightly. A pen is placed in the centre of the table with a few pieces of paper scattered across the top of the oak. Has he snuck out? Why the fuck would he just leave after everything?

I close the bedroom door. I walk back over to my bed, flopping my body down. I hear paper crumble underneath my head. I sit up quickly and turn on my bedside lamp, an envelope resting on his pillow.

Rose.

Why has he left me this? My hands are shaking nervously as I rip it open. My fingers slowly unfolding the delicate pieces of paper. What the fuck is going on?

To my darling Rose,

I know you are probably wondering what is going on, and why I have left this where I should be sleeping. I'm going to tell you everything. I promise you I didn't want to leave. I really didn't. The truth is, I'm leaving London, for good. My flight is at five in the morning, so by the time you have read this, I will be gone. I never told you everything, well, about my work. Months ago, before I met you, I was offered a promotion, an incredible opportunity that I have been dying to have since I started working at the company. It's been five years, and now, it's my turn. I don't know how long I'll be gone for or if I will come back.

When I met you, I didn't think anything of it because I didn't want commitment, and once I got close to you, I knew I had screwed up, not just with the Daniel thing but with my work. I had grown attached to you and I don't want to leave, but I know if I stay with you, I would find some stupid way to fuck this up.

If I told you that I refused the offer of a lifetime, you would have bitten my head off and told me to go. You deserve so much more than what I could ever give you, Rose. I even tried talking to my boss but everything had been sorted. I couldn't back out and I cannot afford to lose my job. I've worked so hard to get to where I am today. Please, please do not think I don't love you. The truth is, I have never, ever loved someone so strongly in my entire lif. Writing this before leaving is breaking my heart in ways I have never known possible.

My intentions were never to hurt you or leave you broken. Knowing you'll wake up alone is killing me, but I know I need to do this for myself—for you. I need to get out of London and start a new life. I just wish I was man enough to have told you everything instead of sneaking out of your flat at one in the morning.

You will find someone who will love every single thing about you. Just like I do, they may even love you more than I do, which I highly doubt, but you will meet someone who will never cause you so much pain like I stupidly did, because they will not be blind. They will see what they have in front of them. I was too late to figure everything out. I will always be internally sorry for that.

Promise me something though, my beautiful girl. Promise me you will stay exactly as you are—confident, strong, intelligent, and kind. God, you are so fucking kind and brilliant with so much life ahead of you. I know you will hate me for leaving you. You will thank me one day though. I'm not a good person to be around, Rose. I used to be good; I never hurt anyone until you. And I hate myself for ever stooping so low and becoming everything I hate. I was not brought up to be a monster. What happened to you is a prime example of why I can't be with you. It will haunt me forever and I deserve that.

I won't tell you where I am going. I haven't told anyone apart from my family, not even Nick. This may not be the end for us, but for now, it has to be. I need to sort myself out as selfish as that sounds, but I know your life will be better without me in it. Our lives may cross again in the future when I'm not such a fuck up and you have gracefully gone through life, smashing every obstacle in your way. Leaving you might not be such a bad thing when that time comes, I may not regret this so much if I ever see you again.

Unfortunately for now, I have to go. For me, especially for you. You are the most beautiful girl I've ever met, and I will never know how I got so lucky, even if it wasn't for long, but I had you. I fell in love with you and you loved me back. It was perfectly short and sweet. It was real. Stay safe, stay perfect, and I will always be yours, like you are and always have been mine.

You are my forever.

Luca Haynes

This moment right here . . . this is the moment I realized I had never loved Theo like this. I never loved Theo this strongly, so passionately. I had never loved anyone like this. My head pounding, my fingers shaking as I reread the letter. This is pure heartbreak. He's gone. He's really gone this time. I can't contain myself anymore as I bury my face into my pillows, tugging on the material and trying to rip it apart. My screams aren't helping the pain inside my chest, the tears not lifting any relief. I don't think anything ever could.

"Rose?!" I hear the girls running through my bedroom towards me, but I can't even look at them. I can't stop the screams. My heart is in excruciating pain. I can hardly breathe. I can't do anything.

CHAPTER 38

ROSE

One week has been one long painful week. I've tried everything to keep myself distracted, but it seems near impossible. Pestering Daniel didn't help either, and he had no clue that Luca was ever planning on leaving London. He never told any of us. I even wanted to ask his parents. The idea of driving to Hythe to speak to people I had never met before sounds psychotic. The girls told me not to. So here I am, on a Friday night, wrapped in my fluffy dressing gown, sitting on the balcony and smoking a whole packet of cigarettes and drinking a whole bottle of wine.

I have truly lost it; I've felt lost before. Only for a few things—the loss of my father, when I confessed to Wayne's sexual abuse, Theo breaking my heart. This feels different somehow; I can't put my foot on it. I have only known Luca a couple of months. I learnt the truth that our relationship was a spineless game. I also know he loved me. He didn't want to but he couldn't stop himself, the same as me. I didn't want to fall in love with him, but I also knew it was inevitable.

The bright city lights dance below me as I take a sip of my wine. I remember when we sat out here for hours one night on a work night, and we didn't go to sleep until three in the morning. We spoke about everything—my childhood with my father and he told me all about his sister and how she broke Luca's nose because of a stolen chocolate bar. It was the little things really, growing to know each other and falling in love.

"You need to get out of the flat, Rose." Chloe's voice almost startles me as I look straight ahead. I don't answer her. I contemplate leaving and going out with them tonight. They have been nagging me all week to join them for drinks.

"Please, Rose. We are so worried about you," Darcy speaks, walking past Chloe and taking a seat on the floor next to me. I look at her, my eyes sting and my throat almost dry.

"I feel like this is worse than when Theo broke your heart," she murmurs.

"It is worse, so much worse," I whisper, trying so hard not to cry, but my eyes cannot hold the tears in any longer. It's only been two hours since I last cried, but I'm a sobbing mess. I bow my head and cry into my hands. I feel the heat of both the girls as they cuddle into me. Surely, they've had enough of this.

"We know. You love him so much." Chloe sighs into my hair. They know how much I loved Theo, but what I had with Luca was so different. I grew apart from Theo. We grew up and we changed as people. Luca met me when I was trying to rebuild myself, and he brought me out of my shell. He made me feel better about myself, even if those intentions were not to at first. He did though. Now, I feel even worse than before.

I know everyone tells you to never rely on a man to be happy, slightly happy. Luca comes into my life, and he has somehow brightened everything just by the way he smiled, how his gentle fingers traced over my skin making me feel beautiful, and how badly he sang to my favourite songs in the car, or the way his eyes glistened in the sun. All I have now are a couple of cheesy selfies we took and his hoodie he left one night. It's all I have of him. His number's changed and he's removed all his social media accounts so I cannot even find out any sort of information.

"Can we please take you out, Rose?" Chloe asks again. I close my eyes before looking at both of my girls. Their makeup flawless and their hair ready to take on the night with half a can of hairspray holding it in place. They are trying to be supportive even if that means we go for drinks. They want me to have fun, so why not?

"Okay. Give me an hour," I tell them, my muscles aching as I stand up slowly. Picking up my wine and fags, I walk back into the flat. Their happy squeals drown out as I walk down the hallway and into my bedroom. Before I close the door, they follow me in. Chloe opens my wardrobe whilst Darcy grabs my arm and guides me to the mirror where all my makeup and hair products sit.

"I can sort myself out," I tell them with a slight laugh. Darcy gives me a warm smile before picking up my makeup bag and sitting down in front of me. I watch Chloe through the mirror as she scans my wardrobe, her smile bright before she pulls out my mini leopard-print dress. I scrunch my face up, causing Darcy to sigh and quickly wipe at my smudged eyeliner.

"You have to wear this with these black heels!" Chloe rushes over to me, holding the dress and my stiletto black heels.

"Fine." I roll my eyes as she claps her hands. I study her skinny black jeans hugging in her petite hourglass figure and her satin white blouse that she's tied at the front, the material dropping on her left shoulder.

For the next forty minutes, my makeup is done to perfection, thanks to Darcy, and my long blonde hair has been curled into big thick waves. You wouldn't look at me and think I have been crying all day and night for a week. I look bloody good. Standing in front of the mirror, I turn body from side to side and take in my figure.

"Did you lose weight?" Darcy asks with concern. I shrug my shoulders. I may have skipped a few meals but not intentionally. I love food. I just can't stomach it right now, and I know how unhealthy that is. Looking back into the mirror, the dress is showing all my assets, and I can't tell if I look cheap or classy because of the leopard print design. I don't even care. I haven't felt this sexy since I last slept with Luca.

Darcy stands next to me, hooking her arm around my waist. Her tattooed arms making me look plain, her red jumpsuit showing off her petite figure amazingly. I have always been jealous of her tiny frame, smallish boobs, and a slender waist. Then again, I'm always being told that I look like a swimsuit model but that's bullshit.

After a few drinks at the flat, we grab an Uber and head out to the city. We decide against going to Lust due to bad memories, and I believe Daniel will be there tonight and Chloe might kill him. We enter our favourite bar by the North Dock—classy and vibrant with bright neon lights and the night life is always crazy.

Finding a table at this time proved to be harder than we thought, so the girls decide to go to the bar and get our drinks whilst I keep looking. After shuffling around groups of people, I find a booth on the other end of the bar. I text Chloe where I am and wait. I open up my Instagram and begin to do the usual scrolling through everyone's images, seeing their perfect lives. Many people I went to school with are pregnant with their second baby and others even married and pregnant. Here I was, nearly twenty-two with no plans for either and heartbroken. I still have my time though, it just isn't now. *Ping*!

Text Message [From: Unknown] You look so sexy in leopard print baby girl xx

My head shoots up, my heart pounding in my chest. I scan the crowd, hoping to God that Wayne isn't lurking behind a group of people watching me. My phone vibrates in my hand again. I look down, hoping its Chloe so they can get over here quickly.

Text Message [From: Unknown] you won't be able to see me, but I'm watching you princess xx

I shove my phone into my clutch bag and look down at my red nails, counting down the seconds until the girls find me. *Please find me.* "You alone?" I hear him before I see him. My eyes widen as

Jacob stands next to the booth. His dark hair longer than I remember, his brown eyes deep. I give him a small smile as he sits down opposite me.

"The girls are getting drinks," I tell him honestly, hoping he goes away but also happy I'm not alone right now. I don't know who could be texting me. Anyone but Wayne would be great.

"Look, I'm sorry about everything. I know I should have texted you after last time," he says. I remember that night. He came over for food, and we had sex—great sex. Unfortunately, I knew my heart was already taken by Luca. I just didn't see it.

"It's fine, really," I answer, trying not to look him in the eyes.

"You okay? You seem tense," he asks, leaning forward. I cannot help but look into his dark eyes. Maybe having him around right now is the best option. Luca promised me he would protect me.

"Someone keeps texting me. I think I'm being watched," I say. What's the point in lying, right? It's the truth, isn't it?

"You serious?" His jaw tenses and I nod. Opening up my texts, I show him the unknown messages I have been receiving. I don't tell him about Wayne. I never have done. This week, I even met up with Mum again, and we had a restraining order put against him, so my family and I are safe. Ever since I told her about my texts, she's been calling me every day. So far, there has been a no-show, but these messages tell me something's going on.

"Hey? Jacob, right?" Chloe walks over with a slightly confused smile. She places my drink in front of me. I begin to sip the pink gin and lemonade, feeling refreshed instantly.

"Yeah. Chloe and Darcy, right?" He returns the smile as the girls sit down.

"I got another text. Well, two actually." I pass them my phone with shaky hands, their eyes wide with worry as they read the messages.

"We can leave?" Chloe begins to stand up but I stop her.

"No, please, I don't want to ruin your night. Let me just go," I say. I don't mind actually leaving, my head's pounding and my stomach's flipping with a really uneasy feeling.

"No. Jacob, stay with us?" Darcy spits out at him.

"Yes, of course. Let me just go grab my mates, if that's okay?" he asks, looking directly at me. I nod as he climbs out of the booth and wanders off to find his friends.

"Rose, if you're not comfortable, we can leave." Chloe leans forward, placing her hand over mine. I shake my head in protest. I can't let Wayne, or whoever it is, control my life any longer. I have the girls with me, and now, Jacob and his friends. I'll be fine. *Everything will be fine.*

CHAPTER 39

ROSE

It's been two hours since I received the texts, and I haven't had one since. The girls and I are getting on with Jacob's friends. Chloe seems to be really hitting it off with one of them—Chris. Of course, Darcy's been flirting like mad with the other two, and Jacob . . . Jacob's been next to me the entire night. When I've gone over to the bar or outside for a cigarette, I haven't been left alone. I couldn't be more thankful right now for him. Even though he has no idea who is texting me and why.

I also have this pain in my heart like I'm doing something wrong being around him because of Luca. He would hate seeing me with him, I know that, but he also would appreciate it. I also know I need to stop thinking about the damn boy. He left me, and I understand he couldn't let go of the promotion, whatever it was, it must have been good. I just wish he told me from the beginning, so we both could've stopped this from happening.

"I need the toilet," I say as he nods, ready to stand up. "No, don't worry. I'll be two minutes." I chuckle, feeling the gin in my bloodstream as I stand up, slowly walking over to the closed doors and up the flight of stairs. The music is drowned out as I reach the first floor and into the girls' toilets. It's empty. Almost eerily quiet, which I hate. Locking myself in the cubicle, I take a deep breath and try not to overthink. I hate my brain sometimes, how it goes on and on when it doesn't need to. I don't need to worry. Nobody's watching me. It's just a sick joke; it has to be Emily or Nick.

After doing my business, I hear the door to the girls' toilets opening, but it feels even quieter than before. My heart beats faster by the second as I flush the toilet, pulling down my dress and taking a few deep breaths. I unlock the bolt and step out. *Be strong. Nothing's wrong. You're fine.*

My blood turns cold. I want to throw up and I need to. His smile is thin and sadistic like it had been all those years ago. His light brown hair is still the same, maybe even curlier than before. He looks taller and more muscular, but he has aged terribly in almost ten years. I can't breathe and I can't even think.

"Princess, you not going to give me a kiss?" he whispers, stepping closer until I'm back into the cubicle. My walls close in around me, my body heat rising, and I know I may pass out very soon.

"Wayne, please leave me alone," I whimper as he steps in and locks the door behind him. How could I have been so stupid to go here alone? Why didn't I drag Chloe or Darcy? The one time I go alone, this happens. Why did I refuse to believe it was Wayne texting me? Why did this man have such an obsession over me?

"I have been waiting nearly six years to see you again. My God, you have not disappointed." He moans, his eyes scanning over my tight dress. I'm a young adult, not a little teenage girl who had no way out. I'm still weak but I'm not alone anymore.

"I have a restraining order against you. You need to leave!" I raise my voice, hoping he just walks out, but goddamn I know that would be too good to be true. This man, who has locked me in a cubicle with him, ruined my life for years. I need to act brave. I know I'm screaming on the inside like the fifteen-year-old he destroyed.

"That won't stop me from being with you. You are such a gorgeous woman." He groans into my ear. I hear his belt buckle underneath his disgusting fingers. His eyes are looking at my chest as I try to think of a way out of here. I hear the bathroom door open, and a wave of girls come in, laughing and chatting to themselves. I open my mouth to scream when his hand covers my mouth quickly and his eyes glare into mine. *I need to get help.*

"If you even make a sound, I will kill you," he threatens. I look down at his other hand, and he's holding a pocket knife and putting slight pressure against my ribs. *He won't kill me, will he?* I whimper with fear as my body trembles. The minutes feel like hours before silence fills the bathroom again and the door slams shut behind them.

I feel frozen. He's really going to do this again. He's going to ruin me, and I'm too much of a pussy to stand up for myself. Why can't I be strong? Luca said I was strong, so why am I not acting like it right now? Why isn't Luca here right now? Tears fill my eyes as I think of him. He would be so scared for me. He promised me he would never let this happen to me, but he left me. I need to defend myself and prove to myself that I'm better off without him.

"Ready for me, princess?" Wayne's hand moves from my mouth towards my breasts. This is it. I have to do something fast. Without warning, I raise my knee, hitting him right between the legs. I know I can't move around him so I open my bag and pull out my phone. I call Jacob and wait for it to ring. My eyes never leaving Wayne as he begins to compose himself again. His face is burning red while veins pop out of his forehead and neck, his hand gripping tighter around the knife. *He's going to kill me.*

"Rose, where are you?" Jacob asks frantically over the phone, relief washes over me quickly.

"Girls' toilets. Help me!" I scream out as a sharp pain shoots through my face. The sound is shocking me as I slam into the cubicle wall. I hold my face, my tears falling down my cheeks.

"Stupid bitch!" His words disgust me as I cover myself up again. I cry louder than I realize as he holds my throat and slams me against the wall. His other hand begins to pull at my dress. My arms are slapping at him but he's strong. He always has been. His grip around my throat tightens the more I fight back.

"Rose?!" I hear Jacob's voice. He's in here, and soon, I can hear the girls yelling my name. My vision begins to blur as he holds my throat, adding more pressure. The cubicle door begins to shake as he pounds and kicks to get in. I can tell it will come off its hinges soon.

"You couldn't keep that pretty mouth shut, could you?" Wayne yells. I'm struggling to breathe, my head throbbing. Everything I have drank tonight wants to exit my body quickly. I have never felt so nauseous in my entire life. Am I going to die? Suddenly, Wayne's body weight is gone and I collapse on the floor, weak and breathless. I sit up and watch him. His body is underneath Jacob. Bloody pours out of his nose as Jacob's fists slam into his face.

I sit in silence as Wayne's body weakens and his face bloody and almost unrecognisable. At this rate, all I can do is watch. This has to be it now surely? The man who has been obsessed with me for years has stalked me and harassed me up till this moment. I almost want Jacob to kill him. I want to watch him suffer.

I can't believe my stupidity. I let myself go alone. When I had a bad feeling that Wayne was here, I had the text messages to prove that I wasn't safe. The alcohol almost made me fearless, or forgetful, but I am an idiot either way.

The ambulance took Wayne to the hospital, where the police will wait until he is able to cooperate, and hopefully, an arrest will be made. The ambulance checked me over, making sure I wasn't in any pain. I explained to them about the hit and him strangling me. I told the police everything. Soon enough, Daniel arrived and shortly after, my mum comes speeding through the city to get to me. My mum is a sobbing mess, and Daniel looks mortified to see me in such a state. He thanks Jacob countless times for saving me. Without him, I don't know what would have happened.

*   *   *

"Do you want me to stay with you tonight?" Chloe leans up against my bedroom door as I lay down, looking up at the ceiling. My mind going over every fucking detail of tonight's events.

"No, but thank you," I whisper, my throat sore and tender.

"We love you, Rose. You are one brave cookie." Her voice is strained, sitting up slightly. I look at her, her make up completely off and her hair tied into a high bun. She looks drained; I look drained. I feel like shit.

After everything and after tonight, I knew I didn't need Luca to be my hero. As much as I love him and he loved me, I could do it without him. It will be hard, but I just managed to survive my evil stepfather's attempts at sexual assault and possible murder. Jacob was my knight-in-shining-armour tonight. I owe him so much for that. How I feel mentally is different. I feel relieved, safe. I feel like if I carry on living like the way I have been, then everything has been for nothing. I want to make my daddy proud. I need to start now; I have been so down and sad for so long. I know Luca broke my heart, but only I can fix it. I need to fix myself. He left for a reason, and I do believe it was the right decision.

I miss him like crazy, but if he can just leave and know it's for the best, then I can sort myself out too, right? I might see him in the future; I might not. We shall see. All I know is that I'm going to be okay. He left so I could be.

CHAPTER 40

ROSE

Two Years Later

The car comes to a stop at the drop-off point. I look behind me to the two girls in the back seats. I give them a toothy grin as my excitement begins to rise by the second. It was time. In three hours, we will be off to New York City. We have been saying for years that we will do this, and we finally are. About six months ago, we decided we needed to stop talking about it and actually book a five-day trip.

"Have you got everything, girls?" Jacob asks, turning his head and looking at us three. I give him a warm smile as I nod. Opening the car door, I step out and wrap my sweatshirt around me tighter. Walking to the boot of the car, Jacob is already unloading our suitcases with the girls hugging him quickly.

"Take care of yourself, okay?" He slowly walks over to me, wrapping his strong arms around my waist and pulling me into him. I stand on my tiptoes, leaning up and giving him a quick peck on the lips.

"Always." I look him in the eyes, his deep brown eyes, trying to find anything. He's hard to read sometimes, but I can see a hint of concern.

"Good, and please let me know when you've landed." He lets go of my waist and quickly kisses my forehead before he walks back over to the driver's side of his car. "I love you, beautiful!" he yells at me, just loud enough for me and the girls to hear.

"Love you too!" I express with a big smile.

"Thanks for the lift!" Chloe calls over to him as we begin to walk towards the lift. He nods before climbing into his car.

"Let's fucking do this!" Darcy squeals as we wait for the lift to take us inside the airport. Once we drop off our suitcases and make it through security, we decide on grabbing some food at Wagamama's. We haven't eaten yet, and I could do with some Japanese food.

"What time's our flight? It's already one," Darcy asks while sipping on her drink. I look in my bag, pulling out all our flight information.

"So our flight's at two-thirty and that gets us into JFK at five-fifteen their time," I answer Darcy before I put a mouthful of chicken into my mouth.

"Are we getting a taxi to the hotel then?" Chloe asks and I nod. I have planned the whole thing; I would be a panicked mess if I hadn't. Taxi to the hotel will possibly cost over forty dollars, and it also counts on how bad the traffic will be.

"Can we go see Times Square tonight, please?" Chloe begs.

"Obviously. Our hotel is like a five-minute walk from there," I answer her with a laugh. I wanted to see every inch of New York, but something about Times Square had me. I didn't know if it was the hectic city night or the vibrant colours and yellow taxis. I just need to see it.

"I want to go into M&M world," Darcy speaks up with a mouthful of ramen noodles.

"They have one in London," Chloe answers her before I could. I love M&M world. Of course we would be going to the one in New York, and we are going everywhere if we can. I look back at my chicken katsu curry, trying to think of every single idea and things I could do in five days. I have always dreamed about moving to New York. My company has an office out there, I might even go and visit.

Tapping the screen in front of me, I check to see how long we have left on this flight. Thirty minutes until landing and Chloe is fast asleep next to me while Darcy is watching some action film on the screen in front of her. I have tried to watch a couple of films, but I decided on listening to my iPod and reading my paperback. Time flies so fast with a good book.

Turning up my music, I close my eyes to James Arthur's "Let Me Love the Lonely" as it fills my ears, and I can't help but think about Luca. This was the song I would listen to when he was around. It's been two years and I haven't heard any news. Everything has changed so much since the night he left. I moved out of London a year ago.

I couldn't risk Wayne finding me again. He was arrested and given a new prison sentence. Unfortunately, he will be out again soon so I moved to a town with a twenty-minute commute to London. Jacob decided to come with me. We had been together for nine months when I couldn't live in the city anymore. We both still work in London, so the travelling isn't so bad.

We rent our own little home, and its perfect. We even got a little Siamese kitten named Simon, and he is the best thing in the entire world—my baby. My brother and both the girls still live in London. Chloe is engaged to Chris, one of Jacob's friends. Darcy and Lee have been a couple for one year, which is a complete shock to everyone, but they are so happy.

I would never have thought that I would be living with Jacob, the boy I met the same time I met Luca. He is gone though, and I am happy with Jacob. He's never given me any grief or hurt me like Luca did, but I still wonder from time to time where in the world he went. It still hurts that I haven't seen him or heard from him. He just vanished.

"So how do we do this taxi thing?" Darcy asks me as we make our way through the hot airport. I can see the sun beaming from outside as we approach the exit. Everything feels different; it's bright and even the smell is new. We're standing outside, waiting and trying to figure out what to do next.

Not long after, we got into a little yellow taxi and began our journey towards the big city. I hold Chloe's hand whilst Darcy sits in the front, talking away with the driver. The traffic is mental and this driver is erratic and crazy, cutting people up with no indication. Everyone seems to be doing it. My heart is going mad and Chloe understands why. It's nearly been eight years since the accident that killed my father, and I still feel a rise of panic when I get in a car.

After a long painful hour in traffic, we make it to our hotel in one piece. Darcy tips him because I refuse to. His driving license should be taken off him, and I even tell him that I feel sticky and tired. We are shown our hotel room, and I hate that we have to tip the man who held only one of our bags. This isn't normal for us English people. We only tip waiters and waitresses if we want to. It's not an obligation but a kind gesture if they give us good service. I feel like we are going to run out of money if we tip everyone. Maybe that's selfish, but it's what I'm used to. Our hotel room is bright and modern, and I just want to shower and sleep, but I also know the girls would not allow me to do that.

I place my suitcase next to my chosen bed as I flop down on my back, my body aching and all I want to do is crack it and release some tension. If I close my eyes long enough, they might just leave me to it so I can sleep for an hour at least.

"Right. Let's get showered, then we can go grab some food and explore! Rose, you go first," Darcy cheers, jumping on the bed with excitement. I open my eyes as I watch her with amusement before standing up from the bed and heading for the bathroom.

I take a quick shower, leaving my hair dry as I washed it before we left for the airport. Wrapping the clean towel around my body, I walk over to my suitcase. Chloe rushes past me to get in next whilst Darcy sits out on the balcony. I step out into the warm breeze as the night begins to fall dark, the city below already alive, and people make their way towards Times Square. Seventh Avenue is only a few minutes walk from our hotel.

She passes me a cigarette as I stand back from the balcony in my towel. The sound of cars beep as they make their way through the buzzing city. From what I have seen already, it's impressive and we haven't even gone anywhere.

"How is everything with Jacob?" Darcy asks. I look down at her as she hugs her legs, watching the street down below. I'm hesitant. I don't know what to say really. I'm happy with him; he's amazing and caring but I just don't know if I will ever find what I had again. Or I'm just being negative and I already have it, better even?

"It's good. He's so nice, you know," I tell her. She nods slowly, her eyes turning to slits as she watches me properly.

"Do you miss him? Luca, I mean," she whispers. I'm almost thrown off by the question. I also forget how well she knows me and how much shit I went through.

"A little, but God knows where he is." I chuckle. Trying to ignore the deep ache in my chest, I'll never admit how much I miss him.

"I get it. Don't feel bad," she answers me. She was always rooting for Luca whilst Chloe stood her ground longer. She officially gave in and got used to our relationship until that night when it exploded. Putting out my fag, I step back inside the bedroom. Chloe's already out of the shower, rushing around in a tiny towel whilst trying to find something to wear. Darcy runs in next whilst I scan through my suitcase. I decide on my mid-thigh black bodycon dress with my denim jacket and a pair of black vans. I apply my makeup and style my now flat hair, giving myself bouncy waves.

“Right, you girls ready or what?” Chloe comes out from the balcony, the buzz from outside electric. Darcy holds out her phone as we huddle next to her, posing on her snapchat. I can’t hold my excitement any longer; I give myself one last look over before picking up my bag and following the girls out of the hotel room.

CHAPTER 41

ROSE

The city is vibrant. Everything sparkles, and I couldn't be more in love with it already. We finish our food, the night sky dark but the city lights everything up. The streets are packed with tourists and locals, people posing in front of every building as we stand in the centre of Times Square.

I look up, advertisement across every building in blinding lights. Its mesmerising, the city square packed, and I'm almost scared I will lose the girls if I'm not careful. "This is actually insane." Darcy exhales with a huge smile on her face. Chloe lifts her camera up, taking pictures of everything she can.

The bright yellow taxis driving past as locals stand on the side of the path trying to sell CDs, artwork, and other merchandise. There are food stalls on every corner, making me wish I could eat again. I walk in a daze as Chloe walks next to me, taking in every second with her lens, whilst Darcy in front looks up to the sky scrapers with wide eyes.

"Excuse me, would you mind taking our picture?" I watch Chloe as she approaches a policeman. He gives her a warm smile and nods. She gives him her camera and walks over to us. We wrap our hands around each other's waists, smiling at the camera. After another three pictures, she thanks him. We head over towards the bright red steps. Taking big strides up to the very top, we sit down on the right side as my body is up against the cool glass rail.

"This is officially my favourite place on earth," I say, looking forward. Everyone looks so happy. I watch the couple in front as he passes her a single red rose. The young family a few steps away taking pictures with their young children. The smile of a stunning brunette looking towards a man with caramel hair and tattoos on the back of his neck. I study his geometric ink as it disappears into his styled hair. I begin to wonder how handsome his face could be. His arm wraps around her shoulder as he pulls her into him, her head resting on his shoulder as they huddle together, watching the breathtaking view in front.

"So where's M&M world from here?" Darcy asks, and I take my eyes off everyone whilst starting to look around.

"I think it's behind us. This way," I tell her, pointing behind her head. She smiles at me.

"Can we just sit here for a little bit longer?" Chloe asks us as I agree with a wide smile. I don't want to move at all; I could sit here all night. I take in the busy steps, and how everyone is either sitting down or trying to move around the people on the steps to get a better view. I hear a laugh, a very natural laugh. I look back over to the couple about six steps down with their backs facing me, her shoulders are moving up and down. She smiles brightly at the guy next to her. He makes her happy.

Soon, she's laughing again; it's real and she seems so joyful. I begin to envy her. I don't remember the last time I felt so content, and the way she's looking at the mystery man, it's like she's never felt so much love for someone before.

His head begins to turn, then it hits me. Why I felt so intrigued to know the man's face, the detail of his tattoos, or the colour of his hair. My heart stops. He's looking at her. His side profile hits me, and I try not to throw up at the sight in front of me. My stomach flipping erratically as I look at him, the way his lips curve when he smiles, or how his dimple appears on his left cheek, or how he runs his inked fingers through his hair effortlessly. He's beautiful. The way he's looking at her hurts me in a way I can barely stand. The boy who left me two years ago. *Luca. Luca is in fucking New York! This whole time he's been here!*

"Rose, are you alri—" I hear Chloe ask, but her voice soon falters.

"Oh . . . my fucking God!" I hear Darcy shriek. I know they see him too. I can see them facing forward. He's smiling brightly at her; his eyes haven't changed. The blue is bright and clear like a diamond. His hair is flopping over them slightly. His shoulders look broader and the tattoos covers his neck fully and up the side of his head but just about covered by his hair.

"Can we go somewhere else, please?" I whisper. My voice is shaking and the lump in my throat rising by the second. I don't even wait for their answer as I stand up and begin to make my way through the crowded stairs. I need to get away.

"Rose, wait! That can't be him surely!" Chloe yells from behind me but I don't listen. I need to get away before I do something stupid. He cannot know I'm here. I have to walk past them. I'm praying and hoping if I step past, he won't see me and my legs wobbling. I can smell his aftershave. He smells exactly how I remember and I almost want to cry. I look down at him through the corner of my eye as I walk past. Oh, mother, he looks even more beautiful than before. I turn my face as he turns his head to look at me walk down. To him, I'm a normal person stepping past to explore somewhere else; he doesn't know it's me.

"Rose, wait!" I hear Chloe again. I take a few steps away, getting a fag out of my packet and lighting it quickly. My fingers shake as I try to hold it still, but he didn't see me. *Good.* I watch from a few feet away as Chloe and Darcy step past him, but he looks up when Darcy's trips over his black boot. His face changes into a questioning look before his eyes begin to scan frantically, looking for something. *Fuck's sake, Darcy.*

Darcy stops and bends down, sorting out her broken sandal. I keep my eyes on him as he watches her, intrigued. Hoping he doesn't recognise her, we can get out of his sight quickly. "Out of everywhere in the fucking world." Chloe's groans into my ear, and my hands are twitching as her eyes widen at the situation.

"I swear, she's doing this on purpose!" I moan in disbelief, tugging on my hair slightly. Since he left, she's grown her hair. It's now reached to her mid back with bright auburn instead of her blonde short pixie hair.

"Darcy?" he asks. Hearing his voice sends shivers down my spine. His eyes find hers instantly as she stands up. I step backwards, trying to get a safe distance between us and hoping to God he doesn't see me. *Oh my fucking God, this is not okay.*

"What are you doing here?" he sounds shaken, his jaw tenses as he waits for her to speak.

"I'm here with the girl," she finally answers as I watch his eyes widen. He knows I'm here; he knows I'm here . . . in Times Square.

Suddenly, he looks up and finds me, my stomach dropping as I try to control the bile rising in my throat. His eyes locked onto mine, icy and as stunning as ever. I can't let this happen; I can't speak to him right now.

"Rose?" His voice gentle as he begins to walk towards me fast. He looks taller. His body is bigger, more defined and grown up. His face sharper, more gorgeous than I remembered. He's only a few steps away and I honestly feel like I'm going to be sick or pass out.

"It's so good to see you!" His arms wrap around my waist quickly and picks me up, squeezing me so tight. His scent invades my nose and, in this moment, I would do anything to cry, but I can't cry. I can't do that to myself. I've come so far.

"You look incredible!" He lets go of me and steps back. His eyes scan over me, making me feel shy and self-conscious. I can't seem to talk. My throat has closed up, and if I make a noise,

I'm scared it will be a cry and that would be so embarrassing. He's looking at me, waiting for me to speak. I need to. I feel so overwhelmed and the anger is rising by the second. *He left me; he left without saying goodbye or even giving me a number so I could call when I needed him.*

"You look good, happy." My voice weak and shaky, looking at the gorgeous brunette standing behind him. She's petite and glamorous, definitely not short of money. Luca is looking sharp too.

"I am. I cannot believe you're here." His voice is still strong, like he is unaffected by my presence. Unlike me, I can hardly breathe, let alone talk. It's like I'm a friend who he hasn't seen in years. Just a friend. *It's like he never left . . . like he doesn't even care.*

"How mad! We didn't even know where you were," Darcy speaks up, hinting exactly that. We didn't know where he was. I give her a warm smile. She knows me well enough. She knows I'm struggling to process this.

"Are you going to introduce me?" The brunette steps forward with a bitchy face, and I instantly hate her. Luca's face is hesitant as she steps closer to him, wrapping her tiny arm around his waist.

"This is my girlfriend Kiara. These are some old friends from London." His confidence drops and so does my heart. *I'm an old friend? His girlfriend?*

"Nice to meet you. I'm Rose," I state without any emotion. *It isn't nice to meet you.* Unfortunately, I can't let this affect me. I'm with Jacob and I have been for nearly two years. I get it, we've both moved on. It's just odd, strange, unplanned, and everything I've ever felt has just come flashing back into my mind.

"You too. I've never heard Luca talk about you before." She cuddles closer into his body, stroking his chest affectionately. I'm so close to losing my mind and ripping her fucking head off. I need to get away. *Fast.*

"We weren't close. He was just my brother's flatmate," I tell her, looking back up at him. His face taken aback with my answer.

"Right, that's nice," she answers. I see her dark eyes roll. *I want to hit this girl.*

"Well, it was so good seeing you, Luca," I say, raising my shoulders and trying to act confident. How pathetic am I? He's watching me intently, hurt evident in his eyes. I cannot take the situation anymore. I turn away from him, giving Darcy a look as my eyes beg for her to help me.

"When do you leave?" he asks but I ignore him. My brain is swelling by the second, and I need to get away before I self-combust.

"Wednesday," Chloe say. He doesn't answer but I feel his eyes still on me. I brave it and turn to look one last time. Kiara is busy typing away on her phone to notice him watching me, like he's trying to talk to me with his eyes. I'm not falling for those eyes again, not a fucking chance.

"See you later!" Darcy calls to him as she holds my hand and begins to pull me away from everything. My breathing becomes more rapid and harsh by the second, and it's not until we walk down the street and around the corner before I burst. She wraps her arms around my waist as I begin to sob into her shoulder. I feel so overwhelmed. I can hardly handle it.

"There you guys are." Chloe's voice appears out of breath. My crying has calmed down by each minute but my heart is still thumping hard.

"I'm okay. Sorry, it's really overwhelming. What the fuck, man!" I cover my face with my hands and slump up against a brick wall. I need to try and chill, like seeing him hasn't just ripped my heart out of my chest.

"He told me he wants to see you tomorrow . . . alone. On the red stairs at one," Chloe tells me, her eyes never leaving mine.

"What did you tell him?" I ask, surprised she actually told me.

"I just said, 'okay, it's between you two'," she answers. I can see what she's really thinking. She doesn't want me to go because she saw what happened when he hurt me before. I also know I'm happy with Jacob and Luca's got Kiara. She's stunning, almost too beautiful.

"I can't go. I'm with Jacob, and what is there to talk about? He left. We moved on," I tell them, trying to persuade them and myself that I don't want to see him. I want to, but I shouldn't.

"Hear him out. You won't be doing anything wrong, plus Jacob is so relaxed. He would understand," Chloe answers me.

"I thought you would be so against this." Darcy chuckles next to me. *Is this really happening? Am I really going to do this? Should I even do this?*

"I am, but you deserve answers. I think you forget we both know you, Rose. You want to see him," she says. The letter he left explained it but not enough. I have been wondering for two years what we could've been if we sorted everything out. I have Jacob and I love him. He's been my rock since Luca left, and he supported me through shit with Wayne. I don't even know if Luca would've come back if he found out what happened that night at the bar.

"Fine. I'll meet him. Now, let's go get some M&M's." I chuckle, linking my arms with both girls on either side of me and walking across the busy street towards the brightly lit building with a huge screen showing all the different amusing adverts to bring people inside.

I know things will be hard tomorrow, but I also know deep down it needs to be done. It's been two years, and he owes me an explanation. Why didn't he tell anyone he was leaving? Why would he let himself get so close to me just to leave? I want to know about his new life, like I'm sure he will want to know about mine. I guess

I will just have to wait and see what the outcome will be because I'm seeing Luca . . . alone. I am so not ready for this.

CHAPTER 42

ROSE

I watch the grey smoke leave my mouth and dance up into the bright blue sky. I feel physically sick. I have to leave the hotel in five minutes. I'm meeting Luca. It's been two long years. I know it's a bad idea but I need closure as daft as that possibly sounds.

"You ready?" Darcy steps out onto the balcony.

"Not at all." I laugh weakly, lifting the cigarette to my lips again. My nerves are driving me crazy. I have smoked at least ten cigarettes, and its only twelve-thirty. Leaning over the rails, I watch as everyone enjoys the beaming sun.

"You look so good," Darcy speaks again. I look down at my legs and decided on my high-waisted light blue denim shorts and a black braless bodysuit that tucks into my shorts. I wiggle my toes as I look at my black sliders. I'm going to get some serious blisters today.

"I'm nervous," I whimper, my voice weak as I take a look at my best friend with her face full of sympathy. She knows how hard this is for me.

"I'm going to be very honest with you, Rose—" She reaches over, squeezing my hand that's resting on the balcony rail. I look up at her, anxious.

"Don't be mad, okay? I like Jacob. He's good for you and he's sweet as anything, but—" She pauses. *Do I want to hear this?*

"Go on." I push at her; I need to know what she's thinking. I don't know what anyone really thinks about my relationship with him.

"But I believe seeing Luca here means something. It has to." She gives me a reassuring smile, and I return one.

"It's New York. It doesn't surprise me he's here," I tell her. It doesn't mean anything. New York is a major city. I don't know why I never thought of it before.

"I'm a big believer on this kind of thing; that's all I have to say. Do what's right for you." She smiles again before leaving me outside alone. I put out my fag, straightening myself out again. Stepping into the cool hotel room, Chloe's applying her make up whilst Darcy's lying down with her phone in hand, waiting.

"I'm going now. Text me where you guys are and I'll come find you or something?" I suggest. Darcy nods.

"Good luck! Don't rush. We have loads of time." Chloe walks over to me and I give her a weak smile.

"Be brave." Darcy smiles. I pick up my hand bag and step out of the room. Walking to the lift, I contemplate on turning back and leaving him hanging. I haven't told Jacob. I spoke to him this morning and I don't know how to break it to him. *Oh yeah, I saw Luca last night and I'm meeting him today to catch up.* How would he react? I don't know but I will tell him later.

I walk towards the bright red stairs where I saw Luca with Kiara. Where everything came flooding back, and now, I'm shitting myself. As I approach, I see him. Standing out like a sore thumb, his plain black T-shirt hugging in every muscle on his body. Black skinny jeans with rips in the knees and black combat boots, and his sunglasses make him look mysterious and so goddamn sexy.

I can't have thoughts like this anymore. He's not mine. "Just don't look at him too much, and you'll be fine," I tell myself. I know full well that it's almost impossible to ignore his gorgeous face. With each step I get closer to him, I know he's clocked on to me. I pray I don't do something stupid like tripping over my own feet as my heart drums in my chest.

"I didn't know if you were going to show." Taking his sunglasses off, I take in a sharp breath as the sunlight beams down onto his face. His eyes bright, almost completely clear. *Jesus Christ, this is a bad idea.*

"I guess I needed my questions answered," I answer him finally. His lips form into a light smile as I stand there awkwardly, looking up at him.

"Did you want to go for lunch or something?" he asks, guiding me away from the steps. I follow him like a lost puppy, but I refuse to let him see me as 'lost' especially now. I follow him in complete silence, not sure where we are heading, but after at least ten minutes, we stop outside a restaurant.

"Are you sure you're okay with this?" He turns to face me. I nod, unsure why, once again, I'm doing this to myself. Maybe I should run now and forget it all. *No, I need to do this for myself.* We enter the brightly lit restaurant. Only a few people are inside as we find a table by the bright window. Sitting down, I take in everything around me. Everyone is so buzzed and full of energy whilst I feel completely drained.

"What do you think about New York so far?" He shuffles in his seat before resting his elbows on the table. I take in the time to study his arms. More ink has been spread across him even when I thought there was no more room, he's managed it. I wonder if he drew them himself?

"Crazy but beautiful. I haven't seen enough of it yet, but I'm sure the girls and I will plan something." My voice slightly shaken. I must look like a fool. He smiles; he has not really changed. His hair still the same, it's either combed back perfectly or its shaggy with his fringe flopping over his eye.

We sit in silence for a couple of minutes as the waitress comes over and takes our food and drink orders. I'm starving but too nervous to eat a big amount so I decide on a salad. I can't stand the thought of being sick in front of him.

"What's new in London?" he spits out before taking a few deep breaths and relaxing in front of me. I almost don't want to tell him anything. I don't want to be reminded why my life is what it is now. Without him in it.

"Well, erm . . . Chloe's engaged for a start," I answer.

"Oh wow, not to your brother, I hope?" he asks with a light chuckle. I shake my head quickly, remembering the whole fiasco with Chloe and Daniel.

"No, his name's Chris. He's great." I sip on my glass of water, hoping he doesn't want more information. I know that's wishful thinking. This was a mistake. I don't want to know about his new life.

"And Darcy? She with anyone? She looks amazing, by the way; her hair really looks great." His voice now relaxed and I can't help but smile.

"She's actually with Lee. They have been together for about a year." I laugh as he opens his mouth wide, obviously in complete shock. Nobody saw it coming really, well from Darcy anyways. We begin to talk about Lee always insulting her, but secretly, we all knew he was crushing, but there is no way anyone has expected her to feel the same.

"I don't want to make things awkward, but how is Daniel?" He clears his throat with a quiet cough. He feels uncomfortable as he shifts slightly in his seat. Running my tongue along my teeth, I ready myself to tell him.

"Well, he's now a married man; a daddy to little Ava," I answer, smiling at my beautiful one-year-old niece.

"He married Rachel?" he asks. His voice is somewhat strained. *Oh god.*

"Yeah, about six months ago. I'm sorry," I whisper, feeling kind of bad. After everything that happened, Daniel still got what he wanted. *Luca never did. Maybe he has now?*

"It's fine. I'm over all of that." He scoffs. I feel a tight pain in my chest. He's over all of that? Including me? He's over everything. Of course he is. He has a great life here now with a beautiful girlfriend. It's been two years. Of course he doesn't care anymore.

"So Kiara seems sweet." I bring her up, hating myself even more. I don't want to know about them, how he can commit to someone and not hurt them in the process. I don't want to talk about my life in London; I don't want to know his story. This was a big mistake.

"Yeah, she is. I met her at work about a ten months ago. We started dating on her second week in the office." He chuckles, reminiscing how quickly they fell in love. I try to control my beating heart but it's almost impossible. Why is this so fucking painful? I was a conquest to him. She somehow snatched him up in a fucking week? *Damn, that's a sucker punch to the chest.*

"That's great," I lie. My throat dry, speaking is suddenly unbearable. I reach for my drink, taking two large mouthfuls as I feel his eyes on me. *Calm the fuck down, Rose.*

"I like your tattoos." His eyes trail across my skin; I look down at my arms. I have a few standalone tattoos scattered on my forearms, wrists, and inner bicep. He reaches out, holding onto my left arm. He looks at my forearm carefully, studying every line of ink on every flower bunched together. I like my tattoos, all so beautifully done. His finger traces over a quote on my wrist. My heart pounds whilst he studies the words.

You are my forever.

Does he recognise it from his letter? Does he think I'm pathetic that I had it inked on my skin? After a couple of weeks of wallowing in self-pity, I told myself I could do it without him after Wayne's attack, but I needed him more than ever afterwards.

"You've changed. You didn't have any on your body, if I remember correctly." He lets go of my arm, I pull it back to me. If he remembers? How can he not remember? Is he deliberately trying to piss me off? I cover my mouth slightly, trying to stop myself from throwing up. *What is wrong with me?*

"Correct. I have twelve now, I believe." I count in my head the few hidden under my clothes. His topaz eyes watch me as I come out of my mind and back to reality. *Just ignore his eyes, Rose. He's an arsehole.*

"So what about you?" He leans back into his chair, not touching the food that's been placed in front of us.

"What about me?" I ask, confused.

"Are you with anybody?" His eyes are piercing into mine. I take a deep breath. Now, this is going to be interesting.

"I am; I have been for nearly two years," I tell him straight, hoping to hit a nerve. His eyes widen. It only took four months after Luca leaving to realize Jacob is a good person who wanted me. It took me a long time to say I love you, but I do love him. He's brilliant and kind and has never hurt me.

"Who's the guy?" he asks, his face still unreadable.

"Jacob." I come straight out with it. He shuffles in his chair, remembering everything about Jacob. The night I met Luca, I also met Jacob. Jacob had me first. He fucked me first, and Luca was always jealous of him. This, for some reason, makes me happy, making him feel like shit.

"Well, I guess the better man won." He seethes before smiling at me. I can't read his facial expressions, or anything. What does he want out of today? Why am I still here?

"Why did you want to meet me today, Luca?" I growl, getting more and more anxious by the second. I look at my salad, not sure If I can even stomach it.

"How could I not see you again, Rose? You're here!" He snaps back at me. I close my eyes, anger building by the second. His current mood swings are giving me whiplash.

"Well, if you fucking told me where you were going, I could have seen you a lot fucking sooner!" I spit back at him. My breathing now deep and fast as I watch him. His eyes are looking back into mine with the same amount of intensity.

"I fucked up, Rose. I know that, but I can't change it now. You have Jacob and I'm with Kiara." He leans back in his chair, running his fingers through his caramel hair.

"If I could go back, I would have never got on that plane. I was in two minds, Rose, but I was selfish. I thought leaving was a good idea. You didn't need me." He looks up at me again, his voice gentle but the anger still blowing up inside me.

"What makes you think you had any right to choose what was best for me? I was so in love with you, Luca, so stupidly fucking in love with you!" I sit up, trying to calm myself down.

"I need a minute." I pick up my handbag, finding my cigarettes and a lighter. He nods, knowing I'm not leaving. I just need a few minutes. Stepping out into the warm air, I light my fag and lean up against the brick wall, my breaths slowing down but my mind going wild.

Why was I getting so emotional? He's only asking me questions. He's so calm, and here I am, acting like a bloody psychopath. He wasn't even batting an eyelid really. He's happy to see me but acting like I wasn't anything to him. Does he miss me like I miss him? Does he love me like I still love him? I always will have a piece of him. It's inevitable.

CHAPTER 43

LUCA

Her hair as bright as the sun, her skin as golden. I watch her chest rapidly move up and down as she leans up against the wall next to the window. She looks incredible—almost too incredible. She's grown up so much. She's not a vulnerable twenty-one-year-old girl anymore but a mature woman. I can see the change in her.

When Darcy stood on my foot last night, I was sure I recognised her with her long auburn hair. It took a while to process who she was. But when I did, I just knew Rose was here, and she was. The way she was looking at me, her beautiful blue eyes wide with so many mixed emotions, I nearly died on the spot. I could see the pain in them; the pain she felt when she looked into mine. The hatred she has for me.

I don't know why I'm being so arrogant, almost cruel. I'm trying to protect her. She's still hurt; I left her without saying goodbye, and I will always regret that. She seems happy though. She ended up with Jacob, the one guy I was jealous of from the night I met her. He didn't deserve her, but he's a good guy. She deserves the best. I think he is the best for her.

Watching her smoke is almost angelic. She looks flawless and she always is. I feel like I've just met her for the first time. Taking in every inch of her, she's exquisite. I haven't seen her face in so long. I refuse to look her up on social media. I refuse to look at anyone I knew in London, not even that dickhead, Nick. I'm happy here and I love my life here. My work has skyrocketed and I'm proud of my achievements. I don't want to stop.

I met Kiara. She's smart, funny, and beautiful, and it feels amazing to have someone around me who cares so much. Just watching Rose, though, has struck a nerve that I began to bury deep down inside me. That scares me to death. I'm content with everything now, and it took a long time to get over everything. Rose is here. I don't know what I'm going to do when she leaves. I know nothing will ever happen, but in this moment, I know I will always love her. I just can't let her know; she's finally happy with the life she has. I can't ruin her again. And that tattoo on her wrist, that quote means something to her, I know it.

I watch for a few more seconds as she puts her cigarette out and walks back into the restaurant. She doesn't say anything as she picks up her fork and begins eating. I taste my food. Everything is now cold, but I still eat it anyway.

"Do you still live in London?" I ask, trying to make some kind of conversation between us. I study her as she chews her food before placing her fork back on the plate.

"No, I moved just over a year ago. I live in Petts Wood, just outside London." She's calm.

"Why did you move?" I ask, taken aback that she would leave the city.

"I needed to get away. I still work at the publishers, and I just couldn't live in London." She closes her eyes like she remembers something. *Why did she need to leave?*

"Did something happen?" I ask carefully. I know I don't have a right to ask anymore. She has every right to hate me, but she's still here. Her eyes are open and her blue orbs are trailing from the table up to my eyes slowly. There's evident pain, and I know something bad happened.

"Wayne found me, or have you forgotten who he is as well?" She snaps and I nod. I deserved that. My nerves are building up though. I do remember Wayne. Her disgusting stepdad. I clench my knuckles under the table, trying to keep calm. *Of course. I remember everything, Rose, every detail about you.*

"He was harassing me over text. One night he attacked me in the girls' toilets at a bar." Her face looks flushed. It's like something's clicked inside me. I want to yell, scream, and punch fucking everything. My adrenaline hitting the roof, imagining his disgusting hands on her. My body shaking with pure rage.

"When was this? What did he fucking do?" I ask, raising my voice. Her eyes are round as tabs of guilt shock my system, but I know I need to calm down.

"A week after you left, Jacob was at the bar and stopped him from almost killing me." She sits up straighter, her voice sad but she looks strong and confident. *A week? Shit, I fucked up.* It's like she almost wants to brag that Jacob was there, and he saved her life. Maybe I'm reading too far into it. I'm so fucking pleased he was there to help her.

"I'm so sorry. I know I promised to protect you from him." I hold my face with both hands, trying to calm myself down. It's been two years. I left her and she got hurt. I've fucked up so bad. How could I break such a promise? I meant it, I really did. *Shit.*

"It's fine. He's locked up . . . for now," she replies. Her face is straight with no emotion in her eyes. How is this girl so strong? It's amazing. She literally amazes me. Since the day I found out about her past, she became someone I truly respected, but how I showed it is terrible. I need to change the subject before I explode with anger. I hate what I did to her.

"So do you live with him?" I ask her, not really sure why I'm bringing it up. All the hate I had towards him building up by the second. Why did I fuck up? I was supposed to be her knight in shining armour. My heart is hammering so hard against my chest. I can barely breathe. *Why do I feel so guilty?*

"Yes. We have a cat." She smiles lightly. I can't help but calm down as I see her lighten up.

"You have a cat? What's the name?" I ask, trying so goddamn hard to relax. Hating myself even more by the passing second.

"Simon the Siamese." She chuckles and I can't help but laugh with her. I've missed her laugh. It's so smooth and real. Her smile relaxes, and I can't help but admire her beauty. I really shouldn't, but from the day I first ever laid my eyes on her, I was struck. A tidal wave of emotions attack. I've never felt so shitty in my life.

"I'm sorry. I really am. I never forgot about you. How could I?"

I always have done. I'm not the cocky man I was when I met her. Showing her that side of me a few minutes ago was stupid of me; I'm not him anymore.

"I know, I'm just glad you're happy." She smiles but I can't read her. She's so calm compared to earlier, and its driving me insane. She picks up her fork and finishes off her salad. The restaurant busier than earlier, so the silence isn't awkward between us. Her blonde hair a little bit longer and brighter. Her face more beautiful with each passing second, and I have not forgotten about that incredible body. I've just tried to bury it. She's definitely lost weight though.

"Are you happy with him?" I ask without processing it fully. *No, I don't want to know.*

"Of course, I am," she says whilst carefully watching me, waiting for some type of reaction. Like she's expecting me to say something cruel and inappropriate like I use to do. I won't say it. I refuse be that person anymore.

"Are you happy with Kiara?" she asks me. I feel the tension radiating off her body. If I think about it, I know my answer, but she can't know it.

"Yes," I answer. She pouts her plump pink lips as I run my hands up and down my inked arms. Studying the tattoos covering my skin completely, I look at my favourite one on my right forearm.

"What's that?" She points at it. My heart rate increases as I stretch out my arm, showing her the design. Her touch burns my skin as she traces her finger over the detailed ink.

"It's a rose." She looks up at me, her eyes full of emotion. I bite my bottom lip, looking back down at my forearm. The rose is the size of my palm. It's beautiful, my favourite. Nobody knows why I have it, but I do.

"Why?" I look up to see them full of tears. Taking a deep breath, I try to think about how to answer this carefully. Does she think I'm a creepy ex-lover? I'm sure I'll find out.

"When I got to New York, I needed something; I needed you. This is all I could think of," I tell her honestly. Remembering the day, I almost went home—back to her. I knew it wasn't a good idea. My job was going so well, and I thought she would fucking hate me. I was so weak.

"Did you draw it?" Her voice is weak, I nod slightly. She knows how much I love my art. She watched me for hours one night, and I felt completely content back then. I'm far from that feeling now.

"I told you I would never forget you," I whimper, my eyes glazing over but I refuse to cry. This is not my life now. She's happy with Jacob, and I'm somewhat happy with Kiara. I can't ruin everything again. This is dangerous territory that I'm heading in.

"It's beautiful." She dabs the corner of her eye with a napkin before blowing out a deep breath. I can't take my eyes off her. This girl in front of me changed everything about me, and she doesn't even realize it. I haven't been honest with her though. Kiara is a great girl, but she's not Rose. I have never met anybody compared to Rose. I fucked up big time. She doesn't know this. I won't ruin what she's got with Jacob, and I can't be selfish. I can't be that man again.

"This quote was written on the letter you left me." She holds out her wrist for me to take. Tears spring to my eyes as I take in the delicate writing. I remember now. She has a part of me with her too. And nothing has changed, those words still mean what they did back then.

"You've changed, Luca," she whispers. *What does she mean*? I need to make light of this situation, I can't cry in front of her.

"Well, I just turned twenty-seven. I had to mature at some point." I laugh.

"The Luca I knew was so cocky and sure of himself. What changed?" she asks, her smile small. She wants to know the truth. Why am I not like that anymore? I may still have a mean streak, but I'm trying to save her from me. I can't control the thoughts and feelings that are rising inside me; I'm not strong enough.

"I broke your heart and that broke mine," I answer. I immediately regret it, but I want to carry on. "I realized I wasn't anything but a coward, that's why I've changed—trying to change," I finish speaking. Her skin flushed and her lips parted slightly, her bright eyes never leaving mine. Why am I holding everything back? I'm telling her I was a coward, but I'm still acting like one now.

"This is wrong. I can't do this. I've got to go," she speaks up, her voice shaky. I nod as I stand up quickly and walk over to our waitress. After paying the bill, I go outside and see Rose is smoking again. Feeling more tense with every step, I light my own fag as we walk in silence. It's excruciating. I've fucked this up; I don't want to do that to her anymore. I never wanted to from the beginning. The walk is quiet, but once we reach the red stairs where we met earlier, my stomach begins to flip. I'm scared, so fucking scared.

"It was so good seeing you, Luca." Her eyes taking me in, she's waiting for something—anything. My head pounding with things to say, but I can't say them. I need to be respectful and let her live her life; I have to let her go.

"Take care of yourself, okay?" She steps closer, reaching down and wrapping my arms around her tiny waist and picking her up, her arms around my shoulders. I can't breathe, the lump in my throat growing massively as I hold in a sob. Her heart beats against my chest; it's going mental just like mine. Taking in a painful breath, I relax at the familiar scent of her perfume, savouring everything about her before I'd never see her again.

Slowly placing her on the floor, I let go of her. She doesn't look at me as her eyes face the ground. I don't even realize what I'm doing until my fingers reach under her chin, raising her face to mine and giving her a gentle smile. I lean down to press my lips against her forehead, relishing the way my lips feel against her hot skin.

"I never want to say goodbye to you, Rose." Taking in a deep breath, I place my forehead against hers. A small sob escapes her lips, and I welcome the tears, unable to hold them back anymore. *What is this girl thinking? Why is she so silent? Why is she crying?* We have so much unfinished business. Our feelings never died. I was so selfish and ruined what we could've been.

Her stunning bloodshot eyes look up into mine, and I take in her beautiful face. How could I ever let this girl go? How could I ever try and think anyone could take her place? I want her to say something; I want her to kiss me or hold me tight. I want her to tell me she loves me. I know she won't do that. She won't hurt Jacob like that, and I respect her for it.

"Goodbye, Luca," she whispers with a shaky voice, then she's not in front of me anymore. I'm standing in the middle of Times Square, watching the love of my life walk away from me. This is it. I never got to say goodbye two years ago, and I can see why I didn't before. It's painful—agonisingly painful.

My mind has never felt so conflicted before. I'm an awful person but I cannot kid myself anymore. I know how I really feel, I've always known, since the night I met her. I want my Rose, and I blew my chance last time. She let down her defences and I took advantage of that.

As the tears stream down my face, I watch her body as she disappears into the crowd and out of my sight. My heart tearing apart as I collapse onto the red steps, with my head between my knees, my arms shielding my head as I cry. I wish I didn't love her, but I always have and always will.

CHAPTER 44

ROSE

We have one more night left in New York before we fly back to London tomorrow evening. Keeping myself busy has never been such a priority before; the girls have been supportive. I told them most things, Chloe not so impressed. She's never trusted him whilst Darcy has always had a soft spot for Luca. She's always seen the best in him. I can't figure out what I feel.

I've still not told Jacob that I saw Luca; I don't know how I can tell him. Or if I even should? Just act like it never happened and go on with my life, forget about the boy with the beautiful tattoos and topaz eyes.

How could I possibly forget? Like do I truly believe I could forget? I've never forgotten about him. Even listening to my favourite artists like Hurts or Harry Styles, I think about him. He's in every word of every lyric of every song. I want to erase him, make him disappear but I know it's not possible.

Walking away from him honestly felt like my heart was breaking all over again. I know how wrong it is. I have a boyfriend back home who has stuck by me, who has truly adored me for so long. I also know my body doesn't crave his touch, his kiss, or to be near him. His kisses don't burn like fire whilst Luca made me hot and ache with pure desire.

I need to get away from this city. It's been astonishing, bright, beautiful, and a completely different experience. It's the most beautiful place I have been to in a long time. I'm almost grateful that I got to see Luca again. To hear what he had to say, to see how healthy and happy he looked, and how well he is doing in life. It was nice, and I feel better knowing I finally got to say goodbye to him. It's all I needed.

There was something else though. The way he kissed my forehead or wrapped his arms around my waist a little too hard. The electricity that sent currents through my body, telling me not to leave, forcing me to stay with him. How his eyes watched my every breath, like he was begging me to hang onto him. Even though I know he doesn't want that, he was being polite.

I decided to tell Darcy whilst Chloe was on Facetime with Chris. I told her how we pressed our foreheads together, like the years never happened and we were still in love. How he said he never wanted to say goodbye, his eyes soaking with tears that he refused to let fall. I had to leave him. I didn't trust myself. Jacob would be heartbroken if I ever did something so spineless, so I left Luca standing there.

"He still loves you, Rose." Darcy tries to get into my head, but I watch the city from below as I smoke a cigarette. My feet aching from all the walking and sightseeing we have done. Central Park was stunning, the sun beaming down on us all day and the views were incredible. I also fell in love with Grand Central station and the constellations mural painted on the ceiling. I sometimes wonder if the people of New York see what myself and every tourist see? Everyone posting their pictures on social media, showing the world how much fun they had in New York City.

Everyone who visits would fall in love. It has this buzz that I have never seen before; the people have so much life and excitement. The food is incredible, the portion sizes are huge. I won't forget the performers on the subways, trying to get some extra cash as they spin around a pole or accidentally kicking a commuter in the face.

"You're not listening to me, Rose. He's not happy with her, I can tell," Darcy's still nagging at me, but I can't think. I don't want to think about it anymore. I'm officially drained from this holiday. I'm drained that Luca has worked his way inside my head after so long of being shut out.

"I have Jacob. Remember that, Darcy," I answer as she rolls her eyes before leaning back in her chair.

"Yeah, but I also remember how much you loved Luca—how much you still do." I drop my face into my hands, I know she's still right. I can't let it happen though, my life in England is so different now, I can't just decide to be with Luca.

"I just wish you could see the way he looked at you on Friday night. It was insane. He still loves you, I know it. He has a rose tattooed on him to remember you, that says it all." She rubs her hand up and down my back, trying to comfort me. I look up, her face soft and her smile sad for me.

"It's not possible if that even was true. Can we just forget about it for one last night and go have some fun?" I ask, she nods as we both stand up. I put out my cigarette, looking over the hectic city again. The night sky lit up by skyscrapers and the people below ready for the what's to come tonight.

"Let's go get some drinks!" Chloe yells as we step into the bedroom, she's off the phone now. I pick up my clutch bag, running my fingers through my hair one last time. My oversized white blouse is tucked into my black skinny jeans, my knee-high boots slick against my jeans. I'm ready for one last night. We've been out every single night. Tomorrow will be a busy day of packing and rushing to the airport for our evening flight back to good old England.

"You look beautiful. Let's go." Chloe stands behind me, honest and as gorgeous as ever. I know it's bad to hide stuff from her; she's been a good friend for years. Unfortunately, every time

Luca has been mentioned, she has to be negative. She told me to see him on Saturday, but refuses to have sympathy for what he says, she knows how much he hurt me. I know she's just trying to protect me, but I'm a big girl. I can make my own decisions.

After a couple of drinks, I can hardly feel any emotion. Except how much I love the city and how much I love my girls. Every night, I've been distracted, but when morning comes, I remember him. The truth is it's pissing me off so much. Just get me back to England and Jacob, so I can forget he ever existed.

It's been two years. It took me two fucking years to stop thinking about him. I moved on, and sometimes, I would go weeks without thinking about him. The first night in New York and I see him, now he's made his way back into my head. It's like a computer virus you just can't get rid of. I'm sick of it.

"If one more guy asks to buy me a drink, I'm going to kill someone." Darcy chuckles. I join in whilst Chloe rolls her eyes before sliding off her stool.

"Round's on me, girls. Gin and Tonic?" she asks.

"Pink Gin and lemonade," I tell her she smiles before turning and walking to the bar.

"So, have you spoken to Jacob?" Darcy asks, her eyes slightly bloodshot. I don't really want to have this discussion whilst slightly pissed. Why does alcohol make everyone so much more emotional? I can't deal with any Luca conversations tonight because I know what will happen. I will cry my heart out.

"Not really. He's super busy at work," I answer her, sipping on the rest of my drink whilst watching the crowds of people enjoying their night. When you grow up in a normal town, pubs and bars are not busy due to people working the next day. London and New York are the same in the sense that no matter what day of the week it is, it never really dies down.

Once Chloe's back with our extremely overpriced drinks, we talk about tomorrow's plans—what time we need to leave for the airport and all the boring stuff that need to be done. I really don't want to leave this place, but I have to for my own sake. Knowing how close he really is, is literally driving me insane. I feel on edge, and I'm questioning everything that has happened since he left me. *I hate it.*

Why couldn't he have been somewhere like Italy? Or Paris? Maybe even Hong Kong. Just not New York. Every time I'm going to think of this city or even hear the words "New York", it's him I'm going to think about now and that pisses me off. He needs to get out of my head. Once I'm back in the UK, he might just fade again and everything will go back to normal.

"You okay?" Chloe pulls me out of my stupid thoughts. I hate how my mind just goes over and over every single detail possible. Overthinking is not going to help me right now. It's just going to kill any buzz I have left.

"Yeah. I'm good, just going to miss this place," I answer, they both smile warmly at me as I look down at the table. Hoping they don't see the tears falling down my face, I'm going to miss this city. I'm going to miss Luca all over again, and I hate myself for it.

CHAPTER 45

DARCY

Packing my suitcase sucks, I want to stay here forever. The holiday hasn't gone exactly as we planned. It's still been brilliant, but I don't know if Rose feels the same. On Saturday, when Rose came back from meeting Luca, I could tell what her face was saying, the emotions behind her eyes. Chloe was almost oblivious, or she just didn't want to think about it. I know she does, she's just got this bitchy way of showing it sometimes.

When we forced Rose to tell us everything, I knew she was holding some stuff back. She didn't want to tell us everything, and I knew that. Chloe rolled her eyes and scoffed when she explained their conversations during lunch. She almost laughed when she mentioned his rose tattoo. I almost cried. Is Chloe blind? Is she just being stubborn? I can see it clear as day, I always have.

I watched from the beginning, from the night they met. I saw how he looked at her and how he studied every detail of her beautiful face. Until the day he left, even if it started off as a game to him, I also knew how quickly he fell in love with her. He didn't even know it, but I saw it.

I know Chloe's only acting this way because Rose is with Jacob. She's always preferred Jacob than Luca. He's a great guy but he's not for Rose. Anyone who really knows Rose can see that. She's been unhappy, not obviously unhappy. She's just not whole and I don't even think she knows this herself. She doesn't laugh with Jacob like she did with Luca. I never see her smile like she did when Luca was around. I want her to see it—the truth. Luca is her soulmate. I believe that completely.

My phone ringing pulls me out of my thoughts, looking down to see Lee facetiming me. I smile to myself before picking it up and going outside for a fag. "Hey, you," Lee speaks first as I light my cigarette.

"Hello." I smile at him, his blonde hair growing darker by the day. His blue eyes bright and beautiful.

"How has it been? You packing?" he asks with a wide smile across his cheeky face. *God, I miss him.* I begin to tell him our plans. We are leaving in one hour, and our flight's at six so we have plenty of time to chill out at the airport.

"What's wrong?" he asks, catching me off guard.

"Nothing." I smile gently at him, hoping he drops it. I don't know what he would think. He loved Luca as a mate, and I know he still misses him from time to time.

"Come on, what's wrong?" he asks again, his sweet laugh making me weak in the knees.

"Fine. Please don't tell anyone, but Luca's here. He lives in New York," I answer. His eyebrows furrow in confusion.

"What? Luca Haynes?" He leans in closer to the camera.

"Yes, I think Rose is so conflicted right now. They went out for lunch, and I know she's struggling to deal with it all," I explain. I don't know how she's doing it.

"Shit! I'm sure she will figure it out when she comes home." I nod in return. Maybe it will help. We dismiss the conversation; I don't want to get too involved in Rose's life. Even though I want to shake her head until she sees sense.

After getting off the phone with Lee, I go back inside whilst Rose is out of the shower and getting dressed. Chloe is in the bathroom freshening up before we leave. "You alright, girl?" I ask, walking back over to my suitcase and just about managing to zip it shut. She gives me a wide smile as she slips on her grey sweatshirt.

"I don't want to go home." She struggles to speak. Her voice trembling as she tucks a piece of hair behind her ear.

"We had a good time, didn't we?" I give her a warm smile, remembering everything that's happened. All the places we got to visit. I can't wait to get home and take a close look at all our photographs.

"I don't think I will forget that man you almost dropkicked for following us around on the subway," she reminds me with a real laugh and I laugh with her.

"The people here are a bit weird and forward, I must admit." I smirk. Well, not everyone but there are a few odd apples. Everyone's a bit too forward for my liking.

"When we get home, can you send me the pictures on the Staten Island ferry? I want a new profile picture," she asks and I nod. The photos I took of Rose in front of the Statue of Liberty or the one with city lights behind her are incredible.

"You know, we can always come back soon," I hint. Hoping she knows what I mean, what I'm really saying to her. Her jaw tenses, turning to her suitcase, obviously trying to ignore me. I know I'm pushing her, but I'm extremely worried.

"I can't . . . for a while." She's so quiet.

"Why?" I ask, intrigued. I want to know what's going on in her mind. She's never shut me out so much before. I don't want to nag her or piss her off, seeing Luca really has severed an old nerve.

"I want to get over what happened. I need my time," she says. I nod, but I also don't understand what she's doing. Why is she fighting this? Why can't she see what she's got? Someone loves her so much and she won't accept it. *Why*?

"Okay, if you say so," I answer. She's walking out onto the balcony seconds later, lighting a cigarette. I know I shouldn't force her. I just know she's going to regret this. Not fighting for him, I know he was trying so hard not to tell her the truth, how she told me he kissed her forehead and held her tight. I know he loves her. I'm so sure of it.

"You almost ready to leave?" Chloe walks out of the bathroom with a towel round her. I nod as I sit down on the bed, scrolling through my social media.

"What's up with Rose?" Chloe asks as she gets herself dressed and ready. I look back out onto the balcony. She's hunched over, smoking her second fag in under ten minutes.

"She's struggling. I think she doesn't want to leave," I tell Chloe, looking up from my phone. I hear it vibrate but I ignore it, Chloe's eyes questioning mine.

"You mean, leaving Luca," she says. She slips her leggings on from behind the wardrobe as I look back out at Rose. She's hugging her knees whilst looking out towards the city.

"I reckon so, yes." I'm blunt. *What can she possibly expect?*

"She'll be fine once she's home." I watch Chloe as she rolls her eyes, packing the last bits into her bag. If I wasn't going to spend the next how many hours with her getting home, I would consider slapping the bitch out of her.

"Why can't she be more than fine? Why can't she be so happy that she can hardly handle it? I want her to feel how we feel—how she used to feel." I sit up straighter, never taking my eyes off Chloe. Challenging her to say something mean and unaffectionate towards our best friend's feelings.

"She's happy with Jacob. Luca's just found another way to fuck with her head. He's a tool!" she snaps back at me. I stand up, walking towards her.

"What I can't stand about you, Chloe, like literally cannot stand about you, is your inability to see past your simple-minded opinions." I hiss in her face. I'm not used to being around her anymore. I don't know how I've lived with her for so long. She's a great girl, but she's so opinionated and black and white. It can be shocking.

"I'm just saying how I fe—" she starts but I cut her off again.

"You don't always have to say it. Just let it fucking happen, and be a supportive fucking friend even if it does end up like shit!" I glare at her before I go back to the bed. She stands there silent for a few seconds before carrying on with her packing. I pick up my phone, trying to ignore the anger boiling up inside of me, but my heart stops and my eyes widen at a Facebook message that was sent only three minutes ago. I can't say anything; I need to keep it quiet. It's from Luca Haynes.

CHAPTER 46

LUCA

My hands are shaking with fear. My head is throbbing, and my lip is stinging as the skin ripped with the impact of her fist. I throw that to the back of my mind and think about right now. Standing and waiting, hoping everything goes to plan. I need it to.

It took me until a few hours ago to realize that I was a fool to think I could ever live without her. I couldn't let her go without her at least knowing I am unconditionally in love with her.

So I found Darcy on Facebook and I messaged her, asking what time they were going to be here at the airport. She wasn't even hesitant. She told me to be here. I know she doesn't want to get involved, but she also knows how desperate I am.

I bite my bottom lip, regretting it instantly as the cut reminds me of what happened today. I went over to see Kiara; I had to tell her the truth. I apologised and apologised, but she still hit me, which I deserved. She knew who Rose was. She wasn't stupid. When I told her the truth that I needed to see Rose and that I wanted to be with Rose, she flipped—throwing anything she could get her hands on and smashing up vases and a couple of plates.

I feel bad, but I knew that was going to happen at some point in my life. If it wasn't the past couple of days, it might have been in a few years or sooner. I would have figured it out that I needed to be with her again. I needed her to let me love her like I should've done from the beginning. I have seriously cocked up everything since meeting Rose. I have been so blind and stupid. How has it taken me so long to come to my senses and really tell her I love her? I should never have left for New York. Why didn't I go back to London sooner? Why have I let this run on for too long? I watch as the doors open and more people come walking in with their bags and suitcases. *I can't take it. I need to see her. I need her.* I look down as my phone vibrates in my hand.

Messenger [From: Darcy] Getting out of the taxi now, good luck!

My throat closes as I read the message again. Putting my phone into my back pocket, I look back up to the automatic doors. *Which one is she coming through*? I scan between the two doors until I see her approaching. Her blonde hair straight, hanging over her shoulders, wearing an oversized sweatshirt and black leggings with blue New Balance trainers. She looks so beautiful. I take a deep breath as the doors open. All three of them step inside the busy airport. She looks so tired and conflicted.

Darcy clocks onto me first. Her face sad and worried, but she gives me a reassuring smile—the smile to tell me it's time. I take a couple of steps, trying not to falter as I walk over. She's looking around the airport. I want to know what she's feeling and why she looks so lost.

"Rose." Her head snaps up and her eyes meet mine instantly, her cheeks flush red as she takes me in.

"What are you doing here? What happened to your lip?" she asks, stepping closer. My heart drumming in my chest. *Don't fuck this up, Luca. Stop being a coward and fucking tell her.*

"I'm fine. I had to see you. I need to tell you something," I whisper, taking a few deep breaths. Her face full of surprise. *Can she see how rough I look*? *How tired and stressed I have been for days*? I'm willing to give this life up for her. Chloe and Darcy are standing a few feet behind her, watching with curious eyes.

"Okay?" she answers me. I can see she's hesitant, maybe even a little scared.

"I'm sorry that I fucked up. I'm sorry that I left you and you had to go through shit with Wayne." I feel sick, I feel faint, and I'm ready to pass out. I can't stand the thought of her rejection, but it wouldn't surprise me if she does.

"You told him?" Chloe butts in. I close my eyes, trying so hard not to tell her to shut up. Why has she always got to ruin everything?

"Yes, I told him!" she snaps at Chloe before looking back up into my eyes, begging me to go on.

"I'm sorry that I played with your brother. I'm sorry for everything that I have done to ruin your holiday." I clench both of my hands into fists, my nerves are going wild. She's only two feet away, her breath warm and minty.

"You haven't ruined my holiday, Luca." She smiles with so much certainty that I almost believe her. I know she's been stressed; I can see it on her face. Her skin soft and pale, her blue eyes bloodshot and deep. *Always so beautiful.*

"I know I'm probably the last person you wanted to see again, but I'm so glad you did." My body's shaking, I have never felt so petrified in my life. I have to do this, so why is it so hard to say the words? I take in a deep breath, never taking my eyes off her.

"Rose, I love you!" I burst with so much confidence, even though on the inside I'm screaming, crying, tearing my heart apart. Her face blank but she's now panting, her eyes never leave mine. She doesn't say anything. I'm waiting and watching. I know this must be hard for her, and I need her to know that I understand that.

"You don't have to say anything now. I just need you to know that I love you . . . that I have never stopped loving you." I look down at my feet, trying to breathe steadily. *Why isn't she saying anything? Love me, please, love me.*

"I've never been so scared of losing something in my entire life. I am so scared that this is going to be it. Seeing you has awakened something that I tried to forget. I can't lose you, Rose, please." I rub my hand over my mouth, trying to hold back the tears.

"Luca, you know it's not that easy. I have Jacob and you have Kiara. Everything will be fine," she says. Her voice soft, trying to reassure me that I have Kiara and I will be fine? *Is she mad? I've just told her I love her.*

"Rose, you are not listening to me. I left Kiara. I refuse to let this be it. I cannot let you go home without you knowing that I am so desperately in love with you that I can hardly breathe. I am begging you to love me again. I have been trying to move on for two years, and I thought Kiara was the right person for it, but this whole time, I've been comparing her to you, wishing she was you. I know how cruel that sounds but I have been trying every day to move on. I hate myself that I never just got back on a plane to find you. I hate myself." I run my fingers through my hair as the tears appear in my vision. I don't care anymore. She needs to see this, she needs to understand that I'm not bullshitting her.

"I just can't do it. It's been too long." She wipes a single tear that streams down her soft cheek.

"We can fix everything. Let me prove to you that I am the man for you. I want to spend the rest of my life showing you who I can be, that I am meant to be with you. You're my soulmate." I let out a sob, my heart breaking with each word. *She's not taking everything in, she's trying to deny everything.* I can see her brain ticking away, trying to find any excuse to why this isn't a good idea.

"Please, Rose," I whisper, my throat dry and my eyes stinging with tears.

"Luca, I'm sorry. I can't." She steps closer. She's not crying, her face unreadable. She leans up, wrapping her arms around my shoulders and pulling me into a hug. I quickly hold her waist close to me. Her scent invading my nose; she smells incredible, sweet, and delicious. She always smelt so fucking good.

"I'm so in love with you," I breathe into her ear. I watch as goose bumps raise on her skin. I'm praying she changes her mind—praying so hard. She whimpers into my neck before pulling away from me, her cheeks soaking with tears.

"We have to go." She steps back quickly, bending over and picking up her bags and taking one last look at me. Her stunning face, her absolutely incredible face, will be burned into my memory. This girl will haunt me. My heart shattering into a million pieces hurts more than I ever thought. She's leaving, she's actually going to leave. *Oh my fucking God.*

"Please, Rose." I crouch down, pulling at my hair as my cries become more aggressive with each passing second.

"Don't, Luca." I hear her whimper. She's holding onto my shoulder, giving it a tight squeeze. I can't answer her; I can't even look at her. I'm feeling every ounce of rejection, every piece of splintering pain as it stabs through my body.

"I'm so sorry." I open my eyes. Darcy's crouched down in front of me, her eyes bloodshot and her smile sympathetic. I watch her as she stands up, giving me one last look of pure sadness before she starts walking. I stand up quickly, turning around as Rose and the girls are walking ahead, the crowds getting busier.

"Rose! Please!" I yell in pain, hoping to God she turns around and changes her mind. *Please change your mind.* She doesn't turn around. Everybody looks at me, except for her. I watch from afar as she walks deeper and deeper into the airport. I collapse to my knees again, begging that she will come back as my body heaves with each cry.

I think I see her turn back, but I'm not sure. My eyes blurry as the tears carry on falling. Standing up, I walk out quickly. The fresh air hits me as I find an empty seat. Lighting a cigarette, I pull up the hood to my jacket so I can cover my face. Crying so hard, my head feels like it's going to explode, not caring who walks past.

Maybe this is how she felt when I left her that day. Maybe I truly deserve this. I have done this to myself.

CHAPTER 47

ROSE

We've been in the air for two hours, and I've hardly spoken a word since we arrived at the airport, since Luca told me he loves me and that he wants to be with me. I walked away from him. I had to. I can't just give up my life for him. He left me and I had to move on. I had to sort my head out, and that's when Jacob snuck his way in.

I love Jacob. He's sweet, caring, and we have so much in common. I have felt safe with him since the night he helped me in the bar. He's stuck by me since. Everyone said I rushed into being with him, even though it took at least four months to make our relationship official. I also know a part of me has never been sure if that was the right thing to do. I knew getting over Luca would take a while. I also know everything happened so fast with Luca. It was intense and passionate and nothing I had ever experience before. We only knew each other not even three months before our relationship came crashing down.

It's also surprising how someone you barely know can change everything and someone who can make anything seem so easy and peaceful. He is cruel, spineless, and completely unaware of the damage he caused. But no one really saw the other side to him; he was gentle, affectionate, and so romantic. I know he really loved me. He also told me everything about him. His childhood was the perfect family dream; his happy life was everything I ever wanted. When Rachel has broken his heart, he became a playboy with a serious attitude problem. But I somehow changed that, he became the person he told me he was before.

Pulling my earphones out as the flight attendant passes over my pasta, the sight of food makes me want to throw up. I'm not hungry. Far from it. My stomach is constantly flipping every time I think of him, my head pounding so bad I can barely keep my eyes open.

"You okay?" Chloe asks, suprising me. I look over at the girls who are eating their food. I don't even know how to answer it. *Am I okay? Do I just say I am so they don't ask any questions?*

"I told him to be at the airport. He messaged me on Facebook and I couldn't say no," Darcy spits out. I can see the guilt creeping its way across her face. *Does she expect me to be angry with her?*

"I'm not angry, just confused, I guess." I smile at her, a real fake smile but it's the best I can do right now.

"Can I say something?" Chloe asks as Darcy and I look towards her. Anxiety rushes through my body. I can't handle the thought of her going off on one like she used to about Luca. I need my friends to be loving and supportive right now. I know I'm pissing them off; I've been such a downer since I saw him. I've been trying so hard to have fun, and I feel awful with the way I've been acting. But right now, I need them to just be nice.

"I'm really not in the mood for you to drill into me right now, Chloe." I lean my head back against the headrest, closing my eyes. My headache is getting worse by the second. I need some strong painkillers. Vodka, something that can knock me straight out for a few hours so I can give my brain a rest.

"I just want to say sorry. I know I've never been supportive when it came to Luca, but Jesus, Rose, what are you doing?" Chloe's voice hits me. I sit up straight and open my eyes to properly look at her. Her blue eyes sympathetic and Darcy's sitting further back into her chair, giving Chloe the room to speak.

"What do you mean 'what am I doing'?" I ask her. She rolls her eyes dramatically, causing Darcy to laugh a little. I ignore it though. I'm confused, and battling this inside my mind is killing my brain cells.

"Exactly. What the hell are you doing? Luca dumped his girlfriend. He waited for you at the airport and begged you to love him again. He cried on the floor in the middle of JFK, and you're on this bloody plane with us. I almost fell in love with him just by seeing that." Her eyes fierce. I can tell she's trying to read my mind.

"How are you coping, Rose? Please tell us the truth," Darcy butts in. Closing my eyes, I look down at my wrist. Stroking over the words he wrote to me when he was leaving. *You are my forever.*

"I can't be with him," I answer. Trying to figure out what I am really thinking, I know it's not a good idea. I know I love him, but is that enough?

"Why fucking not? Because of Jacob? Seriously, Rose, I like Jacob a lot but I would rather you be with Luca. He's perfect for you, and you cannot bullshit us and say you don't love him! I know it took me sometime to really see it, but you must see it too?" Chloe says in annoyance. Burying my head against the window and hoping it breaks, and I get sucked out. I feel suffocated, unable to breathe.

"We don't want to stress you out, Rose. We just love you too much to see you throw this away." Darcy squeezes my hand as I look out the window. The darkening sky looks so beautiful from up here. I always loved being in the sky, looking out of the window. The incredible views you can see from a plane window can be breathtaking.

"Just think about it, you're going home to Jacob. He should be your comfort, your home, but he's not. Luca is everything you need." Darcy leans in closer. I close my eyes, trying to block it out. I pick up my earphones and plug them in, hoping I forget and they can stop. I know they're just trying to help, but do they understand this? I can't just leave Jacob. My life is so comfortable. I've been doing fine without Luca since he left. I'm sure I'll cope without him again.

Minutes go by, maybe even hours, as my forehead rests on the window. My eyes are closed but I'm at peace with my music playing, blocking out any sound that could disturb me. The next song starts and I smile to myself. It's one of my favourites, "Can't Help Falling in Love" by Elvis Presley. I struggle not to sing along as I take everything in. His mesmerizing and passionate voice, the angelic music, and the lyrics. Those goddamn beautiful lyrics:

Take my hand, take my whole life, too, for I can't help falling in love with you . . .

Tears fall down my cheeks as the song plays through my headphones. When it finishes, I play it again and again. I cover my mouth with my hand as my body jolts forward. I can't breathe.

He collapsed on the floor but I fucking left him. He told me everything I have wanted to hear since the night I met him. My heart begs and cies for him since our first kiss, the first time we made love, and when he left me. I walked away, his body shivering as he sobbed on the cold tiles. I walked away from the only man I could ever truly love. The lyrics running through my head again and again, looking down at my wrist one more time as I let everything sink in. *How could I just leave him like that?*

I'm not happy. Jacob is a great person, but I'm not happy. I don't think I've ever been truly happy with him, and I feel awful about it. I do love him and he really is amazing, but that connection I had with Luca could never be replaced and I've always known that. I hate myself for leading Jacob on. I really did believe we were great, but seeing Luca has magnified the problem in our relationship. I'm not in love with him and I need to end it. *I've been so selfish.*

He's not Luca. He's never compared to him. I also think deep down he knows this. He knows everything about my relationship with Luca. I don't even know why he stuck around me. I'm sure he could tell that I wasn't affectionate enough. He just didn't cut it for me. As cruel as that may be, I'm not in love with him. I love him and always have, but it's not the same love I have for Luca. He's been my friend and comfort blanket. He doesn't make me feel like I'm walking on water. He doesn't make me see the universe. He's never felt like my home—my soulmate. *Luca is my home.*

This inner conflict between what I have and what I really need and what I really want is tiring. Luca didn't see how worthless he made me feel when I found out the truth that he used me. He broke my heart when I let him back in, giving him the chance to regain my trust. He left me to start a new life. I'm still irrevocably in love with him. He's my other half.

I love him. I love Luca so much. The guilt spreads through me with every second that passes. *Oh my God, I left Luca on the floor.* I left him crying because I didn't tell him the truth. I've been lying to everyone. How could I be so spineless to do that to him?

"Rose?" Darcy pulls out my earphones. I'm crying in my own world, shadowing the reality that I'm sitting on a plane. I need Luca in my world. I have to have him or I'm going self-combust.

"What's wrong?" Chloe leans over, both of them studying me as I wipe my tears away from my cheeks but more keep falling. I can't help the smile that makes its way across my face. *Am I mad? Have I truly lost the plot?* Darcy shakes my shoulders, pulling me back.

"I made a mistake." I cover my face with my hands. The pain in my chest uncontrollable. It's like I have been blind for so long. The truth hits me so hard. Why did I dismiss everything he said? Why did I act like I couldn't accept it?

"What do you mean?" Darcy asks, their support overwhelming me even more. My friends have known longer than I have. How could I have been in such denial?

"I love him. I love him so much! Why didn't I tell him? Why did I fuck this up?!" I cry between each word. Trying to stay calm feels impossible. I didn't tell him how I feel. I've messed this up so badly. He begged me to love him, when I have never stopped loving him. I just got used to his absence; I got used to being with Jacob. I never forgot. I just ignored it. I love him; I always have and I need him to know.

"I have to tell him." I look at the girls anxiously. What if he hates me now? What if I truly screwed this up? How could he forgive me for embarrassing him like that? I watched his own heart break under my foolish words. How can I tell him? I need him to know right now, or I will go insane throughout the rest of this journey.

"We can figure it out when we get back to England." Chloe smiles at me softly. It's like she finally realizes. It took Luca begging on the floor for her to see he loves me and for her to understand it wasn't just a game for him. It was real for him. It's always been real. *And I couldn't see it, is it too late for us?*

CHAPTER 48

ROSE

The ride towards home is long. I need to get home and figure out what I'm going to do next. I need to figure out how I'm going to break the news to Jacob. What can I tell him? That I can't be with him because I still love Luca? That I saw him in New York, and I changed my mind so suddenly? He's going to think I cheated, that I betrayed him. I wouldn't do that. I've been on the other end of the stick to know firsthand how heartbreaking it is.

How is he going to take it? I have to be honest. I have to be selfish. I don't want to hurt him, but being with him when I my heart isn't there is cruel. The girls are quiet. Lee can obviously tell something's wrong. He has hardly spoken a word since he picked us up.

"Do you want to call him?" Darcy turns around in the passenger side, holding her phone out for me. I shake my head. I have to end things with Jacob before I do anything. That's only fair.

By the time Lee parks up outside my house, it's nearly 9AM. The bedroom light is on and that's when my heart goes crazy. This is it. I need to just pull the plaster off, get it over and done with. Everyone turns to look at me as I take off my seatbelt. I feel sick, seriously close to throwing up at this point. I've never had to do this before. I really don't want to, but I have to.

"Goodluck." Chloe squeezes my hand, her smile sympathetic. I smile at everyone, nodding at Darcy. I told her when it's done, I will call her, so that we can get in contact with Luca. I don't know what I'm going to say to him when I actually call him, but I have to let him know that I want him. I need him to be mine.

"Thank you for picking us up, Lee," I say as I open the car door.

"No problem, Rose. If you need me to pick you up later if things get a bit overwhelming, just give one of us a call." He smiles warmly at me.

"I knew there was a reason why I stayed friends with you," I joke before shutting the car door and rushing over to the boot, pulling out my suitcase.

When Lee drives off, I'm left standing at the front door, not even close to ready. I'm excited to see my baby Simon yet petrified at how Jacob is going to react. I pull my keys from my handbag, my nerves getting stronger by the second as I turn them in the lock.

The hallways is dim and no lights are turned on downstairs. No sound of Jacob. Maybe he's in the shower? I walk through the hallway and into the living room. The beautiful sound of my boy meowing at me hits my ears as he comes walking in almost majestically. His fur is like silk as I bend down to pick him up, his eyes bright, reminding me of the blue in Luca's eyes.

"Hello, baby boy." I cuddle into him, trying to hold back the tears. His soft purrs calm me down before I hear a thud from upstairs. I place him down gently before walking back into the hallway and slowly up the stairs. On the upstairs landing, I approach the bedroom door as the light shines through from underneath. Reaching the door, I pull down on the handle with this uneasy feeling settling in my stomach.

This is it. You've got to do it, Rose. Rip it off. I can't hold this in. The longer I hold it in and the harder it will be for both of us. The room is bright as the chandelier sparkles, but that's not what surprises me. It's the beautiful girl sitting on my bed, a blue towel wrapped around her naked body with her dark skin dripping wet, her hair long and black as the night sky. Her face is in shock. Her deep brown eyes watch me as the sound of the shower tells me Jacob's unaware of my arrival.

"Who are you?" I ask her calmly, trying so hard not to make a scene. *Maybe I should? Maybe I should react how I did when I caught Theo and Lauren at it.* I'm hurt, caught off guard once again. It doesn't sting though. It doesn't hurt like it should, and that says it all, right?

"I'm Tia. I didn't know. I'm so sorry, I should go." She sits up quickly, rushing over to her bag on the armchair by the window.

"No, you can stay. I just need to talk to Jacob before I go." I stand in the doorway, refusing to move until I hear what he has to say. He can hear what I have to say. She sits back down on the bed, picking at the skin around her nails. I keep my eyes on her, picking out every detail of her. It's typical really, she looks like a model.

We wait in silence as my heart thumps. I can't even tell how I feel about this. I feel betrayed, and I'm also in shock that he would do this to me. I didn't think he was this kind of guy. After what seems like hours, the shower stops, and that's when all my anger boils over. He's going to be in for a shock when he catches me in the doorway.

"Baby, what did you want to do today?" His deep voice clear through the other end of the door, I almost laugh. The door opens, and he steps out in a towel low on his hips. His smile drops the moment his eyes move from Tia to catch mine.

"Hello, didn't you expect me home so soon?" I cross my arms, resting my body weight on the door frame. He runs his hand through his wet hair, his wide eyes move back to Tia before landing on mine again.

"I can explain, Rose." He steps closer to me. I can hear the fear in his voice.

"What can you explain exactly? Because I've heard that before, and it all comes down to the same thing!" I snap back at him, clenching my fists and trying not to swing at him. Surely, he fucking knew I would catch him?

"I didn't think you would be coming straight home. I thought you would be staying with Darcy for the day," he explains. I can't help but laugh at him because that makes no sense whatsoever.

"Why would I when I could come home? I don't live with her anymore. I didn't think you would be so foolish to still have Tia here." I look over at the girl, her body tense as she looks at the floor, timid and slightly scared.

"London's closer to the airport so I thought you would stay with Darcy for a bit. I'm sorry I wasn't thinking," he answers. With eyes full of worry, Tia's head shoots up in pure anger.

"Nothing you can say will fix this fuck up. You fucked up big time." Growling at him, his shoulders drop. Tia stands up quickly and grabs her bag and hides herself in the bathroom to get dressed.

"I'm so sorry, I didn't mean for this to happen." He looks down at the floor, but nothing he can say will work.

"Who is she?" I ask, intrigued. My eyes glaze over. How is it possible for this to happen to me again? Am I that horrendous to be in a relationship with?

"Tia's my ex-girlfriend," he murmurs. I know he's refusing to look up into my eyes.

"Oh yes! Tia! How could I forget! The girl you ditched me for on our first date!" Laughing to myself, this day just keeps getting better and better. I wonder how I would've reacted if I never bumped into Luca. Would I have cried and cried and beaten him with my hairdryer? Or would I be how I am now? Upset but slightly relieved?

"I saw her last night in the pub, and it just happened. I didn't mean for it to. It was a terrible mistake." He looks up and steps closer to me. The smell of his body wash making me want to gag, and his scent suddenly unbearable. I can't be around him. He's not what I want; he's not even close to who I want.

"Fuck you, Jacob! You lied to me. You told me she dumped you!" Tia bursts through the bathroom door fully dressed, storming towards us with a face that could kill. She stops just in front of him, her eyes furious. It's the sharp sound of her hand across his cheek that shocks me. He grabs his face and crouches down, taking a deep breath she turns and looks at me.

"He said you left him recently. I'm so sorry, I would never do this intentionally." I can see the hurt and pain in her eyes, and I believe her. I know I shouldn't but I can see it; I can see her anger and mixed-up emotions. I nod, giving her a weak smile. She returns it before walking past me and running down the stairs.

I look at the disrespectful man that everyone seems to like so much, the guy I thought cared about me. I was so scared to break his heart because I respect him, but now, I don't care. "I want you out by the end of the day. I don't care where you go but you need to leave," I say with my arms still crossed. I need to stand my ground and let him know who's boss. I'm not leaving my own home for this muppet.

"This is my house too!" He growls, standing closer than before. I keep my eyes strong. I refuse to back down from this.

"No, this house is in my name so don't even try it! You fucked up! This is your own doing!" I snarl at him. I will not leave a place I have made mine again like I did with Theo. He huffs, walking over to the bed and sitting down.

"I'm sorry, Rose. You didn't deserve this," he whispers. My heart aches from the shocking betrayal. He knows my past with Theo. Now, he's gone and done it.

"I really didn't expect this from you, Jacob. How did you think this would turn out for you?" I ask. I want to know how he really feels, if he loves me like I always thought he did. Obviously, he doesn't but I need to hear him say it, to push me forward into calling Luca.

"Are you still in love with me?" I walk over, sitting down next to him. His body tense, his mind ticking away, trying to think of the answer I now know.

"Yes." He looks at me, his eyes sad and slightly glazed over.

"You don't have to lie to me." He lowers his head, shaking it.

"I don't know when it changed, but I'm sorry." His honesty hits me deep.

"We gave it a go, but obviously, it's not meant to be, but you did it in a really shitty way and that's not okay at all," I answer. Even if I went to New York and didn't see Luca, I know this would have still happened. We would've broken up, because we are not in love. We liked the idea of being comforted and safe, but that's it. It's obvious now.

"How are you so calm? Shouldn't you be hitting me?" He laughs, shrugging my shoulders.

"Tia kind of beat me to it." I let out a weak smile. I might as well tell him the truth, the honest reason why I'm not heartbroken.

"I saw Luca." I breathe. I don't know what this will achieve.

"What? Like in London?" He looks up at me, confused. I shake my head quickly, regretting this slightly.

"No, in New York. That's where he lives," I answer. His deep brown eyes watch me carefully. Looking down, I play with my thumb ring.

"Did you know he was there then? How is he?" he probes. Out of everything he could say, he asks me how he is? He's always known the impact Luca had on my life yet he's never been jealous.

"No, I bumped into him at Times Square and we went out for lunch, but nothing happened if you're wondering." I chuckle.

"I believe you. You're too good of a person." He smiles at me. Closing my eyes and trying not to let any tears fall, it's weird. I love Jacob as a person but this must mean something. I can finally call him.

CHAPTER 49

ROSE

Jacob left about an hour ago after packing up most of his stuff. It's been three hours since I walked in and found out what kind of guy he really is. The kind of person I never expected him to be. He blamed the alcohol. I also know that alcohol can make you do and say stupid things. Bringing your ex-girlfriend home to have sex isn't just the alcohol; he wanted to do it, no matter if he was super drunk or completely sober. He would have done it, or wanted to at least. I don't know where he's going, and I honestly don't care anymore. All I care about is sorting out what I'm going to do from here, what I'm going to do about Luca.

I called Darcy as soon as he left, telling her everything. She's beyond pissed off but she's also happy. Happy that I can contact Luca and feel no shame. It's like this was meant to happen. I was meant to see Luca, and everything would fall into place from here. *How cliché.*

She sends me the link to his Facebook account within seconds of hanging up the phone and wishing me good luck. I open up his page, shocked to see the name 'Luca Jay.' His middle name. How did I never think to look for that? I go through his page for a few minutes, seeing posts he's been tagged in over the last couple of years. Group pictures with new friends and work colleagues, drunken bar nights. He looks so happy, like he's known them all his life. Like he never left the girl he supposedly loved to start a new life with them. I close my eyes, trying not to think about it. Why do I let my brain do this? Why can't I just stop overthinking? *He still wants me, he's always wanted me. Please still want me, Luca. Please.*

He doesn't answer my first call, and he doesn't answer the second. I hang up before leaving a voice message. Maybe he's just not active on Facebook right now? Or his phone's not connected to the internet at the moment? I type out a message, then another message, not sure how I can word it. I need to tell him that I regret how I left him, that I love him and always have and I want to be with him. My biggest fear right now is that I messed up so bad at the airport that he's ignoring me. He doesn't want me anymore, or he even hates me. So I type out a message, simple and to the point.

Facebook Message [To: Luca Jay]: Call me when you can, I am so sorry I messed up. I love you and I always will x

The wait to hear back from him is unbearable. I have unpacked and finished most of my laundry including washing my bedding and I even had a long relaxing shower. It's three in the afternoon at this point and my body is dead. I need to sleep, at least for a couple of hours. Jetlag is a bitch, and I can hardly keep my eyes open as I wrap myself in my fresh duvet with Simon by my side. My phone on loud with vibrate on, so when he calls, I will hear it. That's if he even calls me. Will he call me? He has to call me, right? I need him to know that I want to be with him; I want every bit of him. He has to call me back.

If we did decide to work this out between us, what would we do? How could we? I'm here and he lives in New York. It's worlds apart. I don't know if I could leave this place. My home, my family, but could I do it for Luca? Could I move for him? *Yes*!

The doorbell rings throughout the house, my body reacting slowly as it rings again and again. Sitting up, I notice I have been asleep for a while now. The sky outside is black and the air is cold. I check the time on my phone, it's nearly eight. The doorbell keeps on ringing, and I try to ignore it. Jacob's probably back to find more things to take with him. Looking at my phone, I hope I see a message from him, but I only have a message from Darcy asking if I've heard from him yet. I reply with a quick 'no' before climbing out of my bed and walking out of my bedroom and down the hallway.

Simons meows get louder with each step I take down the stairs and towards the deafening doorbell. I swear if Jacob's back, I might go mental. I took his keys and that was that. The door begins to shake against powerful fists as I slowly approach. I hope if I stay quiet, he will just go away. I look down at my phone as it vibrates in my hand.

Text Message [From: Darcy] Let me know when you hear from him x

I don't reply as the knocking continues, getting louder, faster, and more desperate. I don't even care who it is anymore. I reach for the lock, turning it quickly and slipping the chain off. Swinging the door open quickly, my blood is rising but I stop yelling. My eyes land on a single red rose held delicately by a tattooed hand.

CHAPTER 50

LUCA

My stomach flips at the sound of the door as it unlocks. I unclench my fist, moving it away from the door to my side quickly and holding onto the rose with my other hand. *Deep breaths, Luca. Be calm.* The door is sweeping open violently revealing her, so beautiful and natural. Her wavy blonde hair is flowing down her chest, face bare of any makeup, her eyes round and sparkling blue. Gosh, her stunning eyes are so big and breathtaking. I've missed looking at her. She looks angry, so angry. Until her eyes catch mine, her face softens instantly.

"Luca? What are you doing he . . . how are you here?" she stutters, holding onto the door handle until her knuckles turn white. Her body frozen whilst her eyes roam every inch of me. What is she thinking? What does she want? Have I made a mistake coming here? Be smooth; be very honest. This is your last chance to make things right.

"You need to listen to what I have to say, Rose, then I can leave if you want. I just need to tell you that when I saw you a few days ago, I couldn't believe I made you feel like you were not enough. I was stupid and blind. You're my everything and you always have been. I love you, Rose. I love you so much," I spit it out, hoping and praying she believes me, that she loves me too. *I need her to love me or I won't be able to breathe.*

I watch her teary-eyed as her body freezes in place. My heart pounding so hard against my chest, I look down at the rouge red rose. Its beauty reminds me of the girl standing in front of me, the girl I would die for. I would do fucking anything and everything to have this girl love me.

Suddenly, she's stepping towards me and I lose myself. Cupping her face, I lean down and press my lips against hers hard enough that I'm sure the skin might split. *God, yes, Rose. I love you so much.* My inside's screaming as I grip onto her waist, pulling her closer to me. She doesn't pull back or push me away, her lips as hard and as passionate as mine. Her arms wrapping around my shoulders, tugging herself closer to me. I missed the way her soft lips feel against mine, the way she smells and tastes. *I've missed you so much.*

Stepping forward, I make sure not to break the kiss. I push her inside the house, using my foot to slam the front door behind me. Her lips are intoxicating. I want her to give herself to me but I can't push her. Does this mean she loves me too? Or is this all some random impulse and she will stop me soon? I need to know what's going on in her head; I need to know now before this goes further. Her lips are swollen and dark pink when I look down at her, her cheeks reddening by the second. I place the red rose on the hallway cabinet next to her, her eyes watching my movement.

"Do you love me, Rose?" I ask, running my fingers through my hair. I can't look at her. I don't want to see the truth in her eyes. *What if the truth isn't what I want to hear?*

"Luca." She sighs and I interrupt her quickly. I can't handle rejection. With my heart in my stomach, my nerves building up with every breath.

"Do you love me? Because if you don't, I can't go through with this." Looking into her bright blue eyes, I can't see anything to indicate how she's feeling. She needs to tell me now. Did I make a tremendous mistake coming here? Should I have listened to her at the airport?

"Luca, I've never stopped loving you. I'm all yours if you'll have me." She looks up at me with a smile so honest and her eyes so happy. I reach for her, cupping her face and shoving her against the wall. I dive for her lips, not letting another second go to waste. I growl into her mouth as her hands pull at my hair, driving me batshit crazy as my cock twitches in my jeans.

I move my hands from her face quickly, cupping her arse, and squeezing tightly. I lift her up against the wall. My heart is pounding like mad. I need her so badly, I can hardly stand it. Pulling away from her lips, I take in her beautiful face, her lips forming into a mischievous grin.

Dropping her body gently, her hand reaches out as she begins to run up the stairs. Linking my fingers with hers, I follow her upstairs and into a dimly lit bedroom. I don't even wait another second, pushing her onto the large bed. Her hair sprawled out on the baby blue bedding, her T-shirt risen to show her soft stomach.

Sliding my jacket off, she watches me and our eyes stay connected as I lift my top up and over my head. She leans up on her elbows watching me take my jeans off. In my boxers, I feel exposed as she studies my body carefully. Stepping forward, I climb onto the bed whilst resting my elbows either side of her head.

Leaning down, I kiss her lips hungrily. I need her more than I've ever needed anything in my life. I need to see and feel her body. I leave her lips and begin to kiss down her jawline. Her neck smelling sweet as I kiss and suck gently underneath her ear. Her moans have me rock hard in seconds. Her body reacts against mine as my hands glide up her stomach, holding onto her T-shirt until it's up and over her head.

Tracing my fingertips over the quote tattooed across her right rib cage that says, 'It was her chaos that made her beautiful'. I kiss the inked skin, remembering everything she's had to deal with in her life, all the hurt and pain and suffering and I helped cause that. I hate myself for it every single day. She still stands tall, powerful, and as beautiful as ever.

Unclipping her bra, I take off the material, revealing her chest. Her boobs are bigger and even more perfect than before. I lean my head down, taking her nipple in my mouth. Her back arches as I kiss and suck on the delicate skin. I move my mouth to the other nipple, creating the same action.

"Please, Luca," she moans in response. I smile against her skin. Moving my hand down and hooking my fingers into her leggings, I move my mouth back up to hers, kissing her again. My fingers tug down her leggings and underwear, revealing her silky legs. Throwing the dark material across the room, I take in the exquisite view beneath me.

"Luca," she moans my name, and I begin to pepper kisses along her throat as my fingers sink into her soaking core. My cock twitches in pleasure as I feel her and the way her body arches against my touch. I haven't touched her in so long. How could I live so long without looking at this incredible girl? I can't waste any more time. I need to feel her and I need to make love to her.

I climb off the bed whilst pulling my boxers down and throw them across the bedroom. I take her in again. She's reaching over the bed and into the bed side table. Her body hasn't changed much, just a few dark tattoos that I want to look at later. I hear the familiar sound of foil between her fingers as she rips it open. Climbing on top of her again, she wraps her hand around me, and my legs are trembling at the contact. She takes the condom and slides it over me completely. Sitting up straight, she widens her legs for me.

Holding onto her hips, I pull her body closer to mine with her legs spread, revealing her pink juicy pussy, soaking wet for me. I tease her clit with the head of my cock as her eyes roll with pleasure.

It feels like I never left her. It feels like this never ended, that we never ended. She's still a goddess—soft and beautiful with curves. She has angelic looks that I could look at her forever. I begin to pound into her at a hard pace, unsure if I should keep it slow, or show her how much I missed her. Her moans becoming louder as I hold onto her thighs. Her toes clench as push myself deeper.

Everything in this moment shakes me to the core. The girl underneath me, moaning with every thrust, is the only girl in the entire world I want to be with for the rest of my life. The way her body reacts when I touch her soft skin and how her mouth tastes. She's my drug. I can't and won't ever get enough of her.

Leaning down, I kiss her lips as I continue to drive into her. Her nails are clawing at my back as I pleasure us both in every way possible. Her hands are forcing their way to my arms and pushing me off her. Lying on my back, I watch her climb onto my lap and sink onto my cock. Her tight wall is pulsing with every inch, and her skin is hot and clammy as she rides me. Our skins slap together, and our eyes are never losing contact.

"I love you, Luca. Never leave me again," she moans as I close my eyes. Unable to handle the happiness surrounding me. She loves me. My angel loves me.

"Never, baby. I promise I love you, Rose," I whisper as ecstasy takes full control of my body. Holding onto her gorgeous waist, I let her ride me. I honestly didn't believe this would ever happen to me. I remember every time we had sex in the past and every single minute of each time. I was overwhelmed and I still am. How can I love somebody so much? How could I love somebody so much and still hurt her like I did? I will never let that happen again; I will treat her like she deserves. I will love her forever.

CHAPTER 51

LUCA

"What made you come here?" she asks. I close my eyes, remembering every emotion I felt at the airport. I felt lost, empty. I knew how badly I screwed up two years ago; I thought I could get over it. I never did, and when I saw her again, something woke in me and every feeling I felt for Rose doubled.

"When you left, I went home and looked round my apartment, and I just knew this wasn't where I should be, so I packed a bag and got a taxi back to the airport. I sent Darcy a message just before your flight and she sent me your address. I got in the next flight," I say. Maybe it sounds weird, stalkerish even.

"She knew the whole time? And you just decided to come find me?" Her voice just below a whisper, weak and full of emotion.

"Yes, I needed to prove to you that everything I said at the airport was true." I lean my head down, kissing her temple.

"I would have gone back to New York to find you," she says with a light laugh. When did she realize she needed me?

"What changed so suddenly?" I ask.

"On the flight, I just sat there listening to music. I broke down; I knew I had fucked up. Big time." Her soft breathing quickening with every word. I'm so happy and relieved. I'm also confused, confused that I'm here in bed with her when she told me that she was in a relationship. *How did I not think about Jacob? I can't share her.*

"Where's Jacob?" I ask. What if they're still together, and I've just had sex with her? Surely, she wouldn't do that? I didn't even think about asking her before. I was so caught up in the moment when she told me she loved me. I won't be able to handle it if she's still with him.

"He moved out earlier today," she replies and I take a deep breath. *Thank fucking god.*

"What happened?" Intrigued but over the moon with the sudden change in her relationship status.

"I came home to end things with him and found his ex-girlfriend in a towel instead. It kind of saved me from being the bad guy, as evil as that sounds. I knew we weren't right for each other." She smiles. This girl really goes through some bad shit with men. *God, I hate myself.* It will never ever happen again.

"Can you tell me everything?" I ask her, my fingers running through her silky blonde hair. Her head resting against my bare shoulder, her fingertips tracing over my inked chest.

"What do you want to know?" She leans up on her elbow, looking up at me. Biting her bottom lip, she's obviously unsure if I want to know everything, but I do.

"Everything. I hate myself every day for what I did to you. Look how much time I've already lost with you." I close my eyes, thinking everything we could already have if I wasn't such a dick.

"Luca, you're only twenty-seven. We have so many years ahead of us," she whispers, leaning into my lips as she touches them gently.

"Tell me about Daniel and Rachel," I say, hoping she doesn't think I still care as my eyes pierce into hers. She just smiles at me. She knows I'm just interested.

"Not long after you left, she got pregnant and then six months ago, they got married. Strange. It's like after you left, Daniel grew up and matured. I still wonder if Rachel ever found out that he slept with Chloe. It's like nothing ever happened, like you never existed. I haven't seen Emily since she got fired nearly two years ago, and Nick just disappeared, just like you." She gives me a warm smile. I can see the sadness in her eyes. I just disappeared from her life. *I'm so selfish.*

"I'm happy for him. We'll have to bury the hatchet at some point. I want to be in your life, and to do that, I need to sort it out with him. I'm so sorry about everything." I groan, thinking about the last time I saw him. He was so angry, and I moved out so quickly, but I need to do this. I need to make amends . . . for Rose.

"What else do you want to know?" She sits up completely, wrapping the duvet around her naked body.

"There is so much that happened to that ex of yours. Theo, wasn't he?" I ask. Out of all the things I want to know, I ask about him? I remember when I first met her, how heartbroken she was because of him. I feel like I caused more heartbreak. I can't judge him when I hurt her too.

"I heard from Darcy a couple of months ago that he was cheating on Lauren with her cousin Jenny. I know I shouldn't laugh, but I'm also happy that it fucked up. Serves them right." She tucks a strand of blonde hair behind her ear, her smile making me warm inside.

"Even if that sounds bad, they both deserved crap for what they did to you. I also deserve crap for what I did to you, Rose. I don't deserve you and I know that." I reach for her face, stroking her cheekbone lightly with my thumb. Her eyes closed but a slight smile playing on her pink lips.

"I don't want you to go back," she whispers, I watch her face as a tear leaves the corner of her right eye and rolls down her cheek slowly. Pulling her towards me, she breaks out into quiet sobs. Her skin is warm against mine as I hold her body close.

"Rose, listen to me, baby. I have to go back. I need to pack up my life, but I will be coming home to you. I will be with you, just give me a few days to sort everything out," I say, cupping her gorgeous face whilst holding back my own tears. I need to go back. I need pack to everything and leave my job. I will be coming back to her. I always knew I would . . . someday.

* * *

My stomach is eager to eat as we head downstairs and into the kitchen. The loud cries of a cat ring in my ears. I look down at the light-haired Siamese walking into the kitchen. His body is thin and long but majestic. His eyes are dazzling blue, so bright.

"I guess this is Simon?" I ask her with a light laugh. I remember her telling me about him at the restaurant. She smiles at me with a nod before walking over to him and picking him up. He places his paws on her shoulders and one on either side completely at peace with her holding him. His fur is soft and clean. I've never really liked cats. I'm more of a dog person. He is odd but insanely cute.

"Do I have some competition?" I joke, stroking his smooth fur. His purrs get louder as he cuddles into her. There is so much love and affection between them, it's admirable. He's more loyal than I ever was.

"No competition. He's my main boy." She chuckles lightly, putting him down onto the floor. I watch him as he looks up at her, meowing like he's talking to her.

"He's a character. He won't get jealous, will he?" I joke, wrapping my arm around her waist and pulling her closer to me. She welcomes my hold and cuddles into my side.

"Probably! So what do you want to eat? I can make something or we can order in?" she asks, playing with her long blonde hair. Completely content.

"Is this real? Am I really with you again?" I ask, looking down at her and ignoring her question all together. My brain is frazzled. I feel like I'm dreaming and I'm going to wake up soon. My thumb stroking her cheek. *She's stunning, so bloody perfect.*

"It is real. I'm hungry so what are we ordering?" She pulls away from me, picking up her phone and opening the food app.

"Indian?" I ask, hoping she says yes. From what I can remember, she loves it and I crave Indian food so much right now.

"I'm so glad you said that!" She smiles brightly at me. I watch her scan through the different Indian restaurants on her phone. Once she chooses a takeaway, we go through the menu and order more than we can handle. Our eyes are bigger than our bellies, but I'm paying so I don't care. I have never been so excited about sitting with her and eating food in my life, because I'll be with her—my Rose. I'm back with my Rose.

As soon as our food arrives, we go back into the kitchen. She points at the cupboard with the plates in whilst she gets the cutlery out of the drawer. Leaning up against the kitchen counter, I watch how she moves gracefully. Her tiny shorts showing off her tanned legs and the crease of her bum cheeks. The oversized sweatshirt making her look so warm and snug. I mentally scowl at myself for letting her go. She's only twenty-four but has matured so much. She's this gorgeous, goddess of a woman. Absolutely breathtaking.

"Will you stop looking at me like that and come here and sort your dinner out." She has a playful smile. She reaches her hand out for me to take as our fingers intertwine. Walking towards her and bringing the two plates with me, her body now back up against the counter and our chests pressed together. I gently place the plates on the counter next to her, her eyes never leaving mine.

"Do you trust me, Rose?" I whisper, my neck bent down so I can take in her remarkable face. Her eyes shimmering in the kitchen light, her skin clear and her lips slightly parted.

"Yes," she murmurs, breathless. Her palms are running up and down my chest, my fingertips gracing the curve of her waist.

"Will you be mine? Will you give me the chance to love you forever?" My free hand reaching up, stroking her face until I cup her cheek in my hand. I watch as she bites down on her bottom lip so gently.

"I've always been yours, Luca. No matter what, I'm yours," she answers me. I can't control the smile that forms before I bend down. Our lips connect in such raw passion I can hardly breathe; her lips taste incredible. Her hands hold onto my hair, tugging slightly as I hold her hips, keeping her close to me.

All I care about in this moment is showing the girl I have been in love with from the moment. I first kissed her, that I will give her my life, my soul. I will love her until the day I die and a long time after that. Someone out there is looking out for me. I don't know if I've ever felt so blessed in my life to be given this chance to make things right for us.

CHAPTER 52

ROSE

Three Years Later

"Are you sure you're okay, darling?" My mum holds onto my shoulders gently, looking up at her and trying to calm my breaths. Her once blonde hair now a deep brunette. Her blue eyes are vibrant and her makeup is flawless. I give her a warm smile. *I'm fine. I'm great even.*

"Just a little nervous," I answer. She gives me a reassuring smile before walking to the other side of the bedroom, slipping on her silver stiletto heels. Looking at my reflection, I keep blanking out, forgetting that anyone else is in the room. It's just me in the full-length mirror.

The bedroom door opens; and Darcy, Chloe, Lola, and Kelly walk in, all looking bloody stunning. "Oh my God! Rose, you look incredible!" Darcy almost runs over to me, lifting her baby blue dress slightly off the ground. She embraces me in a tight hug, soon followed by Chloe.

"You look gorgeous, Rose. My son is one hell of a lucky boy." Kelly looks at me from a couple of feet away, her eyes watering and bloodshot red.

"Thank you," I answer, unable to hide the happiness that overwhelms me.

"He's not going to be able to keep his hands off you!" Lola laughs as she pulls me in for a cuddle. I squeeze my eyes tight, trying not to let any tears fall.

"Seriously, Rose. My brother is going to feel like the luckiest man alive when he sees you." I pull away from her, a couple of tears falling down her makeup-covered face.

"I think we all know he feels like that already." Kelly steps closer, wrapping her arm around her daughter's waist.

"Don't cry. You'll ruin your makeup." I whimper, trying my hardest not to cry. Lola cracks into a wide smile before dabbing her face with a tissue. I take a step back, studying my two best friends, Darcy and Chloe. Both wearing silk floor-length baby blue dresses, their hair long and wavy. Lola is wearing a baby pink belted wrap front midi dress with matching coloured heels, her jet-black hair is straight, flowing down her back.

"What's the time?" My mum asks, pulling me out of my daze once again. My heart begins to pound in my chest as I walk over to the mirror.

"It's twelve-thirty. It starts in thirty minutes. Rose, are you ready to get going?" Kelly asks me, resting a reassuring hand on my shoulder.

"I'm so ready," I answer her. Not feeling one ounce of doubt in my mind, I can't wait to see him. I'm ready to do this. A gentle knock on the door stops everyone, the door opens and my brother steps in. His brown hair pushed back into a nicely styled quiff and his black suit fitting him perfectly. Followed behind him is my gorgeous niece Ava. Her pink puffy dress and floral headband making her look so delicate and beautiful.

"Rose, you look absolutely breathtaking." I smile at him as he walks over to me quickly, wrapping his arms around my shoulders.

"Dad would be so proud of you," he whispers into my ear before kissing my temple gently. I hold back the tears as my eyes well up.

"I wish he was here." I take a deep breath and he takes a moment to just hold me.

"He is," he finally answers, giving me one final squeeze. I know he is and I can feel him. I always have but, in this moment, I know my daddy is here with me.

"Are we ready?" Kelly asks, her smile calming me for a second. The photographer quickly comes in taking a couple more photographs of us as we pretend to finish up getting ready.

I feel sick, nauseous, and seriously scared, but I don't care. I am doing this. I will never question anything when it comes to him; I am ready. Daniel links arms with me as we leave the bedroom, walking down the grand staircase with my mum holding hands with Ava in front of us

As we reach the bottom of the stairs, my mum walks over to me. "I love you, baby." She cries, kissing my forehead gently. Kelly giving me a quick cuddle next, her eyes brimming with tears as she looks at me. Lola hugging me soon after, squeezing me tight.

"Love you, girl," she whispers into my ear.

"Love you, too, sister-in-law-to-be," I answer her with a wide smile.

"Hell, yes!" she cheers quietly before walking after Mum and Kelly. Taking in a large breath, they step outside and disappear from my sight. I stand still, not sure when to start walking—that's if I can even walk.

"You've got this," Chloe speaks up. I nod as I bite down on my lip. Daniel leans down, whispering to Ava with her straw basket in her hands. Darcy and Chloe in front, Daniel now at my side with his arm linked with mine. The gentle sound of my favourite music starts to play.

"You ready?" He leans in, whispering in my ear as his hand lightly squeezes my arm.

"So ready," I answer him. My heart is racing as we begin to walk, and my adrenaline is kicking in to full gear. *This is it. I'm about to do this. There is no going back.* Stepping outside and into the warm summer breeze, I see the rows and rows of seats around the corner. Ava walks in front with Chloe and Darcy following her. Rounding the corner, I take in a deep breath. My body is coming to a complete halt. The view is beautiful. The lake behind the floral arch shimmers in the sunlight as white and pink roses scattered across the chairs and the grass an intense green and the sky radiant.

The crowds of people turn to look, smiles brightly, and their faces full of happiness as they watch little Ava throw rose petals out of her basket. Their eyes soon follow my bestest friends in the entire world . . . until they all land on me. It's like the air is being knocked out of my body when I find his eyes already locked onto mine. *Luca.* My love, my best friend, and my soulmate, standing on the other end of the aisle waiting for me. I'm ready. So I step forward and I don't look back.

CHAPTER 53

LUCA

I watch carefully as Ava walks down the aisle in a puffy pink dress, sprinkling rose petals everywhere. My pulse increases with each second. Rose's favourite music playing beautifully as Darcy and Chloe follow behind Ava. My heart stops, my knees buckle, and my arms begin to tremble. Daniel is by her side as she comes around the corner shortly after her bridesmaids.

My happiness is beaming. I'm the luckiest man in the entire world. My breathtaking bride is standing on the other end of the aisle, her bright eyes shimmering in the sun light. Her skin is glowing; she's a goddess, beyond anything I could ever imagine. Her dress shapes her figure in such a sexy but elegant way, her arms and shoulders bare of any material.

As she begins to walk slowly towards me, I can't seem to get my head around it—any of this. How did I deserve such a gorgeous woman? I messed up in the past, majorly. Yet she still forgave me. And now, here we are. Nearly six years ago, we met in a gross club in London. Now, I'm standing here in an incredible garden looking over a lake and a luxurious manor house behind her.

I can't control the muscles in my face, I cover my mouth with my hand as every powerful emotion and feeling I have for this girl doubles. My eyes well up uncontrollably, and that's when the tears fall. I feel my shoulder being squeezed as I sob into my palm.

Trying to keep calm, I turn slightly as my dad looks down at me with a smile so proud and genuine, I almost burst into tears.

"I'm so proud of you, my son. She's remarkable," he whispers into my ear. I smile at him, his eyes slightly glassed over. He gives me another shoulder squeeze before diverting his eyes back towards my girl.

Both of our family and friends watch in awe as she gracefully walks down the aisle—towards me. Her blonde hair curled beautifully and her makeup flawless yet natural. Her smile is overpowering, causing my stomach to flip. This right here is sweet agony. Every step is taking forever for her to get to me. The closer she gets, the more beautiful she becomes . . . until she's standing in front of me, overwhelmingly stunning. This angel, dressed from head to toe in white, is my bride.

I reach her face, cupping her soft cheek. Her eyes bold yet teary as I press our foreheads together. I close my eyes, taking in a deep breath. Her smell as sweet and delicious as it was the night I met her all those years ago. This feeling is crazy, suffocating almost. She's going to be my wife. Rose Harrington will be mine forever.

I lean down, kissing her pink lips gently before pulling away, never leaving her gaze. My mind dazed and my body relaxed. This is everything I have ever wanted. "I love you so much." I press my forehead against hers again, stroking her jaw with a light pressure. Her warm breath fanning my face. I've never felt so sure on anything in my entire life.

"I love you, Luca, so much," she whispers. I can't hold in the smile anymore. I never imagined this would ever happen to me. I am marrying the love of my life, my soulmate.

The room is blindingly white with chandeliers hanging from the ceiling and grand circular tables scattered across the stunning room. Roses in different colours placed on every table with our guests seated accordingly. Daniel stands next to me, the microphone to his mouth. Everyone laughs with every word as he makes his speech. I try to listen but everything's become a blur. I lay my eyes on my Rose—my wife.

"Will everyone raise a glass to Luca Haynes and his wife, my baby sister, Rose. I hope your life is full of endless happiness. I love you both." I step out of my thoughts as everyone's glasses raised in the air. I quickly copy everyone, and that's when Daniel sits down, passing me the microphone. *Here it goes.*

Taking a deep breath, I push my chair back as I stand up slowly with everyone's eyes on me. Reaching into my suit pocket, I pull out a piece of paper with my speech on two sides.

"Evening," I speak into the microphone, my hands trembling. I clear my throat quietly. I don't know why I'm so scared to speak in front of everyone. I've made many speeches in my time at work. But this is different; this is my wedding day.

"Thank you, Daniel, for those kind words. I had prepared a superb speech for you today, but unfortunately, now that I am married, I've been told to read this one instead." Everyone laughs but I draw my attention to her. She's watching me so intensely I can hardly breathe. I give her a warm smile before looking out towards our guests.

"Family and friends, on behalf of my wife and I, I would like to thank everyone for coming here today. It means so much to have everyone we love and care about here to share our special day. I would also like to take a moment to think about those absent today." I look down at her again; she's biting her bottom lip. *Jesus, she's perfect.*

"Rose's dad, who I can imagine is looking down on us with a smile. He would be so proud of the gentle and incredible woman that you are. I never had the honour of meeting him, but I know he was a great man and he loved you very much." Her eyes soak with tears. Reaching down and holding her hand, I squeeze it tight.

"Today is everything I ever hoped for and so much more. I never want it to end. I would like to say thank you to Sonia, my mother in-law, for welcoming me into her family. Daniel, my best friend and now brother-in-law, I promise with every part of my soul that I will love, protect, and cherish Rose until the day I die." I look towards him. He nods gently, smiling up at me and believing every word. We buried that hatchet only days after I came back from New York. He welcomed me with open arms, and we sat and talked for hours.

"Rose, my darling." I look down at her again, trying to keep a calm breath. I study the words written on the paper, realising I've not looked at the speech since my opening line. I place it on the table, turning my body to face her and gripping the microphone with both hands.

"The night I met you, almost six years ago, I never expected this. I thought you were hot—" I tell her, and everyone begins to chuckle including Rose. I join in for a second before bringing the mic back up to my mouth.

"Seriously, I thought you were hot, but never in my wildest dreams did I see this. I messed up, not far into our relationship, and I still regret missing two years of what we could've had. I'm trying to make it up to you, so here I stand before you and everyone we care about to say that I couldn't be more in love with you. You are the most beautiful person I have ever known. You are strong and brave and so gorgeous, it's unbelievable. You are my soulmate, my best friend, my world, and I cannot wait to cherish you forever." My voice shaking, my hands trembling as I hold onto the microphone, but I never take my eyes off hers. Tears rolling down her face, my own falling from my eyes.

"I promise to love you, respect you, treasure you, and honour you forever. I feel like the luckiest man alive. I love you. So if everyone could raise a glass to my beautiful wife, Rose Haynes! You are my forever!" I lift my drink into the air, our eyes still locked. Cheers and claps fill the room as she stands up, wrapping her arms around my shoulders, connecting our lips in a passionate kiss that I know I will never forget. I finally have my forever with the woman of my dreams. My angel, my stunning and delicious Rose.

EPILOGUE

ROSE

With every year that passes, our marriage grows stronger. Luca stays true to his word. He shows me every single day how much he loves me, cherishes me, and adores me. Not even a month after our wedding day, I get pregnant with a baby boy, and we name him Oscar. He is the splitting image of Luca. His eyes are bright. Two years later, he becomes the older brother to our little girl, Isla.

My life has become everything I have ever dreamed of, maybe even too good to be true. I never doubt my love for the man, and he wouldn't break my heart again. The years go by fast—too fast. My girls stay my girls. Chloe marries Chris, and Darcy marries Lee a couple of months after my wedding. We raise our children together, with the same age. They become friends like we are all one big family.

I wonder what everyone else has done in life. Where is Lauren? What could have happened after Theo broke her heart? Chloe's husband Chris told me that Jacob is happily married with three kids. Everything has fallen into place for me. After all the shit I went through whilst growing up, I am finally happy. Wayne has never contacted me since coming out of prison, making me at peace.

It has been scary though. As the years go on, we grow older and our children will fall in love and have their own children.

I want time to stand still, and I don't want this life to end. I know it's impossible, but we have to grow up.

My mother is gone. She died at the age of eighty-eight, and it has been horrible and heartbreaking. That is unfortunately how life works. She watched my children grow and even attended their weddings. I never forget about my dad. What would've happened if he never passed? Would he have died of old age? Would he have approved of Luca? I believe he would have.

My Luca aged beautifully. As his hair changes to grey, soon after, mine have begun too as well. I wish that it isn't happening, but I watch everyone I grow up with age, skin wrinkling, and bodies changing. My brother has grown old with Rachel by his side.

I feel my body become weaker in every day that passes by, and my days are numbered. All of our days, that's when my world stopped. My brother then dies of heart attack at eighty-two. I feel lost and scared. It's the time in my life when everyone you love, who supported you as a young girl, begins to leave. I never show the fear I felt though. I spend as much time with my family as possible. I watch my grandchildren grow and turn into lovely young adults.

My marriage is still full of love, admiration, and support in every hospital appointment and pain we experience until Luca collapses one day and is rushed to hospital. His heart is weak, and his life is slipping between my fingers. I still remember his birthday, lying on the hospital bed. His skin is pale and thin. His tattoos blurs with age. He looks as handsome as he did the day I met him. He cries so hard. The hardest I have ever seen him cry after fifty-five years of marriage.

"I don't want to leave you all alone." His lips quivering in fear. I close my eyes and take a deep breath.

"Don't think like that. I have Oscar and Isla and the grandkids to look after me. I won't ever be alone." I sit down in the armchair next to the bed, never taking my hand away from his. His eyes are now closed, but his lips are still shaking with tears streaming down his face.

"I still remember the first time I saw you, Rose, like it was yesterday," he whimpers. I raise my head slightly with a smile tugging on my now thin lips.

"Tell me about it." I give him the 'go ahead' gesture. I want to hear it. I need to hear it, even though he has told me many times over the years. I need to hear it one last time.

"When I first saw you, I had never seen someone so beautiful, so bloody beautiful. I tried not to get attached to you, but you were like an angel, an angel with a heart so precious and I loved you for it. I've always loved you for it." He turns his head, his hand pinching each one of my fingers before tracing over my tattooed wrist. The ink blurry but the quote fresh in our minds.

"You are my forever. I don't want to go," he whispers as his eyes shed more tears. I close my eyes, trying to block my own, but there was no use. I couldn't stop it.

"You'll always be with me, but don't think so negatively," I reassure him and myself. I try not to think about what's going to happen. How much longer do I have with him? I know it's not long. I know he's leaving me.

"I don't want to go. Please know that, Rose," he sighs, his eyes fluttering and my fear heightens. All my emotions heighten as I sit up as quickly as possible.

"Sweetheart, stay awake, please." I lean over the bed, my tears blocking the full view of my man. "Stay with me," I beg, his eyes twitching but his hand limp against my own, his face blank.

"Please stay with me!" I cry into my free hand, nurses checking the monitors around me, but I don't move from his side.

"Rose?" he says. I never take my eyes off his, his blue eyes so magical and full of love. I study the astonishing colour, the colour that has burned into my heart since our first encounter. So beautiful. I need to cherish these eyes for a few more seconds. *My man is so beautiful.*

couldn't imagine a life without him. He is my soulmate, and I am his." My throat dry, the lump getting bigger.

Before I met Luca, my mum has told me that I am going to meet someone who will make sense to everything. All the sleepless nights I have cried for Theo, the heartbreak, and rejection that I have felt catching him with Lauren has been washed away. When I have doubted myself and say never wanted to fall in love again, everything is dissolved the moment I kiss Luca. Meeting Luca has opened up to new possibilities. When he left, I was broken, but when he comes back into my life, I have known that I am waiting for him. I don't question my feelings. I never question what love could feel like and if butterflies are a myth.

All the shit that I have gone through becomes a distant memory because all I could focus on is him. He has loved me so wonderfully and completely, and that was all that matters. I deserve to be loved and to be cherished the way I've always wanted to be. It's a love so pure and magical that it put my mind at ease. My heart has found its home.

I watch the couple in front of me, my granddaughter Millie's eyes are as blue as Luca's. She has long blonde hair and I can see myself in her. The love she has for James is remarkable like my love for Luca. I just pray that she finds that happiness with him, the happiness I have finally felt with Luca. I hope she gets her happily ever after because it doesn't happen for most people, but it has happened to me. I have married him. He's gone but he's always going to be with me. He lives in our children, our grandchildren, and soon, I'll be with him again so our forever can live on until forever's gone.

The End.

Do you like new adult romance stories?
Here are samples of other stories you might enjoy!

INTRIGUED
BOOK ONE OF THE INTRIGUED SERIES
ANNA KENDRA

CHAPTER 1

GRACE

The pounding music blasting from the inbuilt speakers gave me a headache. It pulsed through my veins, vibrated in my blood stream, and slammed straight to my heart until the organ beat with the same intensity, a merciless tattoo against my ribs.

But why should I complain?It is, after all, the reason why I was inside Hell Hole, not the literal one, but my favorite bar to hang out on Friday nights with my girlfriends. And for a time, one of them was nowhere to be found.

Ah! There's Ken.

She was theslender blonde with killer legs and an extremely short black dress on the dance floor, devouring the face of a guy in an orange jacket. A very orange jacket. Trust Kendra Millar to have otherworldly tastes.

My other girlfriend, Ty, short for Tatiana, sat next to me on a barstool. She sipped from a glass of Bloody Mary—trust her to add veggies into a cocktail—while bobbing her head to the music, singing along, and texting her boyfriend of two years, Connor. Multitasking at its finest.

I was doing the same too, minus the texting the boyfriend part since I didn't have one. But somehow, the it's-freaking-Friday excitement had gone out like a light bulb in my head. As always, Ty noticed.

"What's with the sulky face?" she asked.

Tatiana may be a bit shy around strangers, but she's popular for her bossiness among her friends. And we try our best to obey her because hell hath no fury as a Tatiana scorned. But we all love her, so it's okay.

My first instinctive thought was to lie, but Ty's my best friend, and she deserves the truth.

"I think I'm getting fired," I told her what was turning me into a nervous bundle.

The bosses of our company had trusted me with a rather complicated case, which I had delivered before the deadline with maximum accuracy. But in doing so, I'd ignored the projects I already had on hand, and now I'm on a deadline with a ton of work to do and no time to ponder. And to top it all off, Vincent, my senior, would love to see me kicked out into the streets and take credit for all my work, so he's done the good deed of "reminding" our bosses that my initial job came first.

"My head's so full right now," I told Ty. "I know what I have to write, but I cannot fathom where to start!"

"You know what"—Ty leaned in slyly, her auburn hair sliding over her nude shoulders and a wicked gleam in her eyes—"I have the perfect solution for your little problem."

"Really? What?"

I leaned toward her, anticipating her magical remedy.

"Sex."

"Sex?"

"Why, yes! What else?"

She leaned back with a grin stretching from ear to ear, leaving me dumbfounded.

"How on Earth is sex going to help me with my problems?" I lowered the volume of my voice when the bartender passed me another bottle of ice-cold beer.

"Honey, there's nothing like a mind-blowing orgasm to clear your head of all thoughts…instantly!"

She snapped her fingers with a flourish, like that explained everything.

"Really?" I raised a dark eyebrow.

"Even if I do believe in that ridiculous notion of yours, where am I going to find a partner for this mind-blowing orgasm to clear my head? Last I checked, it takes two to tango…Unless, of course, we're taking a trip to the sex shop."

"Oh no, silly! With the hottie over there, of course!"

She shamelessly pointed at someone behind me, like the person was the most obvious of choices.

I didn't follow her lead.

"And why is he the rightful candidate?"

I took a wild guess in thinking that the hottie she'd so boldly pointed at in her drunkenness was a guy. The last thing I needed was an invitation from the same sex.

But Ty's voice was coherent when she said, "Because he's been giving you a once-over since you got here."

"And how do you know that?"

I raised an eyebrow while taking a sip from my beer.

"Because I've been giving him a once-over."

I nearly spat out my drink. Coughing, I dabbed a napkin on my chin and tried to make sense of what Ty was telling me.

"So, you mean, you were giving this guy a once-over, who's giving me a once-over. Remind me, why exactly are you setting me up with him again?"

Ty blinked.

"You're drunk. And I have a boyfriend."

Shit! I really am drunk.

Which really wasn't all that surprisingonce I realized Ialready had three bubblegum vodka shots and was on my second bottle of Anheuser-Busch O'Doul's Amber NA.

Taking the opportunity of a distracted Ty, who was smiling goofily at her cell phone, I glanced behind me. I was hoping that she was just hallucinating and there actually wasn't anyone therebut instead, I met eyes of endless blue, visible from even that wide a distance. The face they belonged to also had seductive, plump lips, and it evoked wicked thoughts of dark rooms and ruffled bed sheets. I felt my throat dry up. The attraction was instant and—I blame it on the alcohol—made me want to take up the offer clearly visible in his eyes.

He stood in a far corner between the private booths and the dance floor. Black hair spilled over his forehead, and his jaw was dimmed undera five o' clock shadow. He wore a full-sleeved shirt in the darkest of blues that almost seemed black in the dim disco lights. He held a glass of whiskey in one hand while the other was tucked into the pockets of his charcoal dress pants. From what I could tell, his skin had an olive tint to it, but it just might be the flashing lights.

"Hey there, crazy frienemies!"

Ken came bounding to our stools. Her tangled corkscrew curls and her smudged lipstick didn't leave much to the imagination; I knew right away what she had been up to.

Leaning over the bar, she ordered another round of shots, and once they were delivered, she placed three suspiciously green glasses in front of us.

"What on Earth is this monstrosity?" Ty scrunched up her nose.

"Something called celebration," Ken answered with a flip of her hair.

"And what are we celebrating?" I asked, although I already knew the answer.

"Why, me hooking up of course!"

She gave us a contagious grin.

Ken wasn't a slut, but she really loved sex and took it as it came. She wasn't really the relationships type. People she dated claim to find her too adventurous, too bold, too aggressive, too free-spirited, and a bit too much of everything.

"Great!" Ty exclaimed while giving me a sideways glance. "So is Grace."

"You are!" Ken gasped while placing her hand over her heart.

"My little girl is all grown up!" She pretended to wipe tears from her eyes.

"Hey! I said no such thing!"

My complaint fell on deaf ears, as Ty was already pointing at the guy with the bluest eyes.

"Hmmmm."

Ken made a moaning sound as she too gave the guy a once-over.

"I approve."

I wanted to dunk her head into the shot glasses. The guy was looking at me, for God's sake!

"To hook-ups it is then!"

Ken picked up a shot glass and waited for us to do the same.

I must be really drunk if I'm even agreeing on a toast to myself hooking up tonight. Oh well, it's Friday night, might as well.

I shrugged.

Tipping back my glass, I let the familiar burn of the alcohol run down my throat…and gagged.

"Gods! This is horrible!"

"Monstrous!" Ken seconded.

"I liked it!"

Ken and I both looked at Ty in horror.

"You know what," Ty chirped in. "I think it's time to hit the dance floor."

Agreeing, we all got out of our seats and headed toward the mass of sweaty swaying bodies.

Ken blended in instantly. She swayed her hips to the music and moved her head from side to side as her curls flew in every direction. It wasn't long before the guy—let's call him Orange shall we? Yes, that sounds much better than calling him "the guy she'll be hooking up with tonight." So, as I was saying, it wasn't long before Orange was right behind her, grinding his junk against her hips, giving us an unwanted trailer of what was to come.

Ty and I both gave a synchronized shudder and moved to a less crowded spot and began to sway awkwardly, both more deplorable at dancing than everyone on the dance floor. Before long, we too were dancing the night away, making weird alien-like gestures and doubling over.

See, who needs sex when you have crazy friends to clear your mind? I thought to myself.

"Bella signora," a heavy Italian accent whispered into my ears, sending shivers down my spine.

"May I have a dance?"

Forget friends. I'll take sex over friends anytime if the guy has such an accent.

I turned around and looked at a devilishly delicious and mesmerizing face. Suddenly, I felt something lodge in my throat.

Because it was him. The guy with the endless blue eyes.

My hook-up for that night.

melissa bender

HIS REBOUND LOVE

PROLOGUE

My cock throbbed.

The hot water spilled down my head, seeping into my shoulders and running down my back as I stood in the shower. I was unable to focus on anything but the familiar ache in my balls—the need for release.

It had been too long since I had a good fuck, and just thinking about it could no longer cut it anymore. My dick needed some attention. I had tried putting it off, but as I closed my eyes and wrapped my hands around the base of my cock, it was too much to ignore.

I needed to come before I lose my fucking mind.

There she knelt before me. Her tongue slid across her upper lip, and her mouth opened just enough to take me. Her tongue flicked back and forth against the underside of my hard cock. It drove me wild.

The vibrations of my cock from her words drove me insane. She was making love to my dick, the same way I wanted to make love to her pussy. Slowly and lusciously, her mouth took me fully in. My head fell back instinctively, and my eyes closed.

"Fuck me," I moaned, my shaft growing stiffer.

The pace was too teasing. My balls twitched, and she stopped. My eyes opened, and I asked her to continue. I didn't beg, though. I never begged anyone for anything. Her green eyes widened, and they are teasing but still adoring as she pulled back and blew warm air on the tip of my cock.

I wasn't a patient man. I throbbed harder. Her thumb drew circles around my swollen head glistening in pre-cum. The teasing was almost too much. I needed to blow so hard. Her mouth fully engulfed my cock, sucking me in, licking and moaning against my cock. Her hand was stroking faster, up and down. Faster and faster.

All I wanted to do besides come was to taste her, to fuck her…to eat and fuck.

Reaching down, my hands combed through her red hair, taking a firm handful as I begin to fuck her mouth. My hips rocked back and forth as she sucked harder. Her eyes bore into mine. It was too much to handle, and I lost it.

Oh, fuck yes. I exploded with the build up from the week. Semen burst from my cock and coated the inside of her mouth. Her tongue stuck out, swirling around the head of my cock and taking every drop I had to give.

As I slumped against the cool shower tiles with my eyes half-opened, reality hit me. I was alone, with my cock in my hand and the load a fucking mess on the glass in front of me.

What the fuck.

I cupped a handful of water and splashed the screen until there was no trace of me jerking off like an adolescent teenager. Those years should have been long gone by now, especially if my girlfriend had something to say about it.

Both my hands ran through my dark, wet hair as I slumped with my back against the wall again, trying to control my breathing. What the fuck just happened?

More importantly, who the fuck was that girl I had just jerked off to?

CHAPTER 1

Jasmine caught my attention from the corner of my eye as she walked by in a red, figure-hugging dress that barely covered her pert ass, let alone her pussy. Her blonde, freshly curled hair, for which she paid hundreds for, cascaded down her back. *Oh, what I would give to grasp my palm around that hair and bend her over…*

"Well?" My trail of thought stopped as she gave me a pointed expression.

This was one of those times she had spoken and I really hadn't paid any attention to her. I wasn't sure which route to take as I let out a low groan and my eyes skimmed over her small frame. I cleared my throat, trying to think of something else as my cock stiffened in my sweats. "Do you really need to dress like that?"

"What do you mean?" she said, her voice lower than a moment ago. I knew where this was heading before anything more was said. "You're saying that I'm not hot?"

How could I put this without pissing her off? "I never said that. I just meant you're not going out to impress anyone. Why the need for all the makeup?" *Or that fucking dress*, I added in my head.

Not bothering to hide her annoyance, she rolled her eyes. "You'll never understand. I must appear well-dressed. Don't you want a girlfriend who likes to appear her best always? Better than being a slob in a shirt and sweats."

That remark was towards me, as I currently wore them. I shrugged, brushing the remark off. "I'm comfortable."

"It's gross." Her nose crinkled in disgust. "I wouldn't be caught dead wearing sweatpants."

I let out a low chuckle as I walked towards her until my arms snaked around her waist. "You do know that I don't care what you wear, right? You're beautiful in anything." My cock twitched as my eyes zoned in on her perky tits when I pulled her closer, wanting her to sense how much I needed her. "Stay in. Let me undress you and show you how fun it is to be lazy."

Her palms laid flat against my chest, pushing me away. "And that is why I buy your clothes." She pursed her lips and sighed. "You should dress nice all the time. I miss that about you."

"You know what I miss?" I had the need to point it out again. I missed sex. Five months had passed, and I fucking missed having sex.

Her blue eyes turned from playful to squinting. She shook her head and walked away. "Is that all you think about?"

"I'm a man, after all, baby. Can't blame a guy for trying." I grinned. "So how about you skip the girls' night and stay in?" I damn well half-pouted. At this point, I would have done just about anything to keep her home with me.

Her red lips broke into a wide smile, her perfect white veneers showing. "You can wait. I want to hang out with the girls. Lisa and I haven't caught up in forever. I won't drink too much."

"Since when have you followed that rule?" I raised a brow in question.

Her smile faded, and she took a scolding tone. "Jackson, don't." It reminded me too much of my mother. So much for my long gone hard cock.

"Sorry, Mum."

Jasmine didn't find it funny. Instead, she rolled her eyes with a sneer. "I'm nothing like her."

Yeah, you've got that right.

Seated on the black leather dining chair, she crossed a leg over the other and proceeded to put on her red-soled heels. I leant against the wall, watching, silently wondering why she was so dressed up. Her lipstick got my attention as she pursed her plump, red lips, focusing on clipping the buckle up. My cock began to wake once again.

This is when I should have shut up. Instead, I couldn't help myself. "You know, you could give me a quick—" I glanced down to my crotch, my dick straining against the fabric, then looked back up at her, "—before you leave?"

Her foot fell to the light grey tiled floor with a thump. Her blue orbs widened as she looked up at me with an incredulous glare that gave away her answer before she had to speak. "Are you kidding me? You're such a pig."

"Well, fuck." There goes that idea.

Mission accomplished. She had the ability to make me as stiff as a rod but also make me limp with just words.

"What's that meant to mean? Jesus, I'm sorry if I'm not really in the mood right fucking now."

"When are you ever in the mood?" I muttered, pushing off the wall and readjusting. "It's not my fault that you're so hot."

We were heading towards another fight neither of us wanted to have. It always ended up this way. The little things caused the biggest of arguments. To be honest, I wasn't looking forward to another one.

Her body pressed against mine, her arms draping over my shoulders and sliding around my neck as her perfume hit me. It's a strong scent of flowers. I hated the smell, but she loved it. "Hun, relax, okay? Nothing bad is going to happen. I'll be home before midnight."

I grimaced at her words. Why the fuck would she even bring that up? I wasn't even considering anything bad happening. "Relax? I am relaxed. But I'd be more relaxed if you stayed in."

I was the pathetic bastard who wanted to keep my girl home and get laid.

"You're trying to guilt me into not going. I can't believe this! That's low, even for you." She sounded hurt, which made me feel like shit. I shouldn't be making her feel bad for wanting to go out. I had to lay off the guilt. It wasn't fair for her.

She fought my hold, wanting to push away. I let her go until her touch was almost gone but not for long, as I soon pulled her. My arms tightly held her close. "I'm sorry," I said, cupping her face. "Go and have fun. I'll be here with the Xbox and Colt."

She heavily sighed. "Hmm. Sounds like a perfect night-in for you then. I'm sure that's all you'll be doing."

I disregard her accusing tone as her crystal blue eyes refused to meet mine, evading eye contact altogether. I shrugged, annoyed at the way she spoke. "Yeah, because every man dreams of spending the night in with his dog and video games." My own reply was sarcastic.

She managed to break free from my hold, picking up her black leather purse from the glass dining table. "I need to leave. I'll see you later."

"Hey," I said, capturing her once again and pulling her in closer. I couldn't let her leave this way, in a silent war against each me. Resting my forehead against hers, I traced the curve of her hip with my thumb and touched the bone protruding there. "Don't I get a goodbye kiss?"

When her head shook, it only made me frown until my smile had completely disappeared. *What the hell?*

"I just put lipstick on. You can wait until later for a kiss."

"You're joking, right?" I didn't buy it. Since when didn't she want a kiss?

Jasmine was already walking towards the door when she glanced over her shoulder with a playful wink. "I'm running late. I promise I'll make it up to you."

Curiosity got the better of me. My attention span was low when it came to sexual innuendos. "Oh yeah? How?" This would be interesting.

Her expression was flirty as her hand held the door open. Oh, I missed this side of her. "Sex. Any way you want."

"Any way?" I asked, my voice lower. Immediately, my sight fell straight to her ass as I cocked my head to the side. "No objections?"

A soft sound of laughter filled the room as she let out a giggle. "None."

"Let me have you now," I suggested, my dick back on high alert once more. "I'm ready to go. Might be quick, but you'll still get off."

Shaking her head, she laughed again. "You're always ready to go, but Lisa is waiting for me."

"Lisa can wait." For the love of God, she could wait.

I realised I was getting nowhere with her as she gave Lisa, who was waiting for her, a wave. She leaned in, brushing her lips against my cheek. "I'll be home in a couple hours."

"Call me if you need a lift back home," I called out, watching her walk down our footpath towards Lisa's blue Ford Focus. "I love you."

"Yeah, you too," she called back without a second glance as she pulled open the door and sunk into the front passenger seat.

My back was against the front door when it closed. *Yeah, you too? What was that?* I felt like I was the only one trying in this relationship. I had tried for weeks, months even. Things weren't what they used to be. I guess the lack of sex was the main clue, but she'd been working a lot and traveling. I put it down to being tired. I was trying not to push that subject, but lately, I just wanted to fuck.

I *really* just wanted to fuck.

My hands gripped the marble counter top as I shook my head. There was no effort from her whatsoever.

We had met through mutual friends almost two years ago, and she was the girl I thought I could never get. Sure, she was not my first, as I have had others before, but Jasmine was different back then. She was down to earth, and—believe it or not—she was loving. We clicked. She played hard to get, and then, funny enough, she asked me out. She planned the entire date herself too. It was cute in a way, or so her friends thought. I thought she was eager, and although I wasn't keen on being told what to do, I kept quiet. I had enough of that growing up from my mother. By the time we had our third date and she paid, that was when I told her it bothered me. She apologised and told me she was used to being in control and on her own.

I allowed it to slide even though it had pissed me off. It still pisses me off at times.

We moved in together after eight months of dating. Sometimes I wonder if it was a rash decision. Then again, I would have done anything to put a smile on her face, and living together was something she eagerly wanted to do.

We had a few fights, and I had spent a couple nights on the couch here and there. I finally figured out when to avoid her, knowing the signs before she flew into a hormonal bitch fit. She could go from fine to lethal within three seconds, all from leaving a shirt on the floor or my shaver out on the sink.

Well, it needs to fucking charge somehow.

You'd probably assume the makeup sex was always worth the fights. Ha! What was sex again?

It had been so long since we had last fucked, and oral was out of the question for both of us. The sex could be great if she moved from her flat on the back—favorite position. But I shouldn't complain too much. It was better than what I was having now: none. She had caught me having a wank in the shower last week. Who knew that using my hand was not only classified as cheating, it was also considered vile and disgusting.

My jerking off seemed to be more frequent ever since I had fucked some pretty redhead's mouth. A knot in my stomach formed as I thought about her. I had no fucking clue who she was. I blamed it on me watching porn too much. But damn, if she wasn't in my thoughts each day. I wasn't cheating, but I felt like I was at times, and that's when the guilt set in. I was a fucking bastard.

But with the crazy, we did have a lot of great times together. We had plans to travel and explore the world.

I was looking forward to the future, to those talks about marriage and babies. I couldn't tell at times if she was as excited about them as I had been. I had already bought a ring but kept it well hidden in my sock drawer. It was not much of a hiding place, but it would be there until I have planned the perfect proposal that she deserved.

Whenever that would be.

I loved her and was fully committed to our relationship.

Jesus. I sounded pathetic. No, I sounded pussy-whipped by a woman who had me by the balls.

Pulling open the fridge door, I scanned for the alcohol I brought earlier. I carried the six pack of Boags Draught and headed to the couch. Colt jumped up and immediately rested his head down on my thigh as I picked up the controller. This was probably one of the rare times that I got to relax and not feel like a lazy fuck.

I should have jerked off, but the promise of a good fuck after Jasmine came home made my dick more interested in waiting.

A large pizza, a six pack of beer, and two hours later, I was starting to pass out mid-game.

It was dark when Colt let out a low snarl, jolting me awake. He took off down the hallway as keys rattled and the front door opened. Her heels clicked loudly against the wooden floorboards with each step she took. The LCD was still on with my paused Call of Duty game, and I turned it off as I noticed it was well after midnight.

I was half-asleep as I sat there sprawled out, yawning. "In here, babe."

Her steps came to a slow stop, then started once more as she made her way into the room. "I didn't think you would still be up."

CHAPTER 1

AMIRA

Gazing at the several unknown faces, I began to feel as if I was living in the shadows once again. I was left bearing a secret that made me feel like I was living in a lie.

Innocent humans watched as our college professor continued to lecture about Accounting and Finance. I looked to my left; beside me was a girl. Her blonde hair was draped over her brown eyes as she continued to scribble insignificant pictures on her notebook. What amazed me the most was how unaware she was of the nonhuman creature seated only inches away from her.

She sighed. My useful heightened senses allowed me to listen to her heartbeat and breathing that would accelerate every time the professor searched for a student to answer a simple question. Her heart rate would regulate once the professor called someone else. She slouched in her chair, her eyes occasionally wandering off from her work to a boy sitting in the far corner of the room.

"Amira? Are you paying attention?" I looked to my right, finding the eyes of my friend, Eric.

Eric and I have been friends since we were thirteen. Six years later, we were still going strong. We had a lot of classes together over the years, so our friendship continued to grow. However, despite us being friends, I could never find it in myself to tell him who I really was. Or should I say, *what* I was.

"Yeah…no," I admitted before we both shared a low snicker.

"Eric, you know I got all of this stuff already," I reassured him, slouching down in my chair.

I was known to be very intelligent in school. Unlike most, it was very easy for me to remember and comprehend any given task. This skill has been very helpful to me.

"Well, then, if it's so damn easy for you, you can teach it all to me because I'm lost as hell." Eric sighed. His eyes narrowed in on the textbook in front of him as I chuckled at him.

"Okay, ladies and gentlemen, class dismissed," the teacher announced as she wrapped up her lecture. I stood from my desk. Students began gathering their things before everyone scrambled out of the door.

"So, lunch on me today?" Eric offered.

"No, sorry. I have to help my mom prepare for this dinner we are having tomorrow. Just a few out-of-town guests." I sighed heavily.

"Okay, cool. Well, I'll text you tonight?"

"Sure."

* * *

The appetizing smell of food danced its way around me, clouding my nasal passages with the mouth-watering aroma of my mother's home-cooked meal.

I walked into the kitchen to see my mother running back and forth. She was cutting vegetables, stirring food in the pots, and measuring the temperature of whatever she was roasting in the oven.

"Mom, is it this serious?" She was acting as if the president was stopping by for dinner.

"Yes, sweetie. This is when you'll see your new alpha for the first time." My mother was more cheerful than the rest of us were.

It was amusing how my mother cared about the alpha's arrival more than the actual werewolves that lived here. I expected her to feel uncaring about his presence as if he was just another regular visitor, her being a human and all.

I guess being married to and being the mother of a werewolf really had her interested in the supernatural world. Unlike her, I couldn't care less about the werewolf society. I found human life to be much better. Accepting. I enjoyed not living under the command and authority of some male who was determined to show his dominance over everyone because of a title.

That was why I loved living in the city. Majority of our pack, including the alpha and beta, lived far out in the country somewhere.

Honestly, that's how I liked it. I loved being away from the group who allowed their title to get to their overgrown skull.

I preferred the distance. However, my father seemed to not feel the same way I do. Recently, he had invited the previous alpha and luna, and their son—the new alpha—over for dinner. Only my father could ruin such a beautiful thing.

"But Mom, they aren't coming until tomorrow," I reminded her again.

"I know, I know, but I prefer to get things done now."

I sighed. Looking over everything, I could see how she had handled things.

"You seem to have everything done." The chicken was roasting in the oven; the vegetables were boiling in the pots; and she seemed to be starting on dessert. "Call me if you need anything then."

I snatched up my bag from the kitchen counter. Reaching into the cupboard, I pulled a granola bar from the box before I left the kitchen.

I silently cursed my mother and father again. I don't even know why I have to be here. If I could, I would disappear before the guests even made it to town. Sadly, my father requested that I should be present for the attendees.

Why did I seem so against the presence of the new alpha? I would say our past was just a tiny piece of the reason that I wanted to disappear. Even though my mother said it's the first time meeting the new alpha, it's actually not. We had already met before he had taken over the title, alpha.

When I was about eight years old, my father and I would visit the main pack house for some business. Since my father was one of the strongest warriors of our pack, the previous alpha would need him by his side during decision-making.

That's when I had first met eleven-year-old Xavier, the soon-to-be alpha.

My father said—to keep us busy and out of their hair while he helped the alpha—Xavier and I should go play, and we did. Honestly, I thought Xavier was cute. I was actually very fond of him. Stupidly, I asked him if he felt the same way. Let's just say it was not the answer I hoped for.

To impress his friends, who were the children of other higher ranked members, he knocked me off the swing. I remembered crying on the ground as he and the other kids laughed before they left me soaking in my own tears.

That fucking bitch.

Yes, I knew that it happened many years ago, but for some reason, I just couldn't forget and forgive. I guess I just didn't take rejection or embarrassment too well. I still don't.

Luckily, after that, I never saw him again, and I was perfectly fine with it.

I quickly shook the thoughts off before I disappeared into the bathroom.

I stood in front of the mirror in my room after I finished taking a shower. I ran my hands down my hips as I stared at my reflection. I adored my frame. I didn't consider myself fit or slim like the other female werewolves I had encountered. Other she-wolves had a fit and athletic physique, the type of body that would look exceptional in anything. I, on the other hand, did not have that. I was a curvaceous woman—full breasts, thick hips and thighs without such a slim waist. I would always assure myself that I would soon diet. At least, after I finish off the pizza I was enjoying.

I began to smile. My full pink lips looked well with my silky smooth skin and brown eyes.

I pulled out my blow dryer and started drying my shoulder-length black hair. When my hair was already dry, I pinned it up and leaped into my bed. Turning my television on, I searched through various channels until I finally landed on a show I could finish my night with.

* * *

Wrapped up in my comforter, I felt at ease. No classes. No early morning wake-up calls. Just the perfect time to oversleep.

"Amira, wake up. Let's go the mall." I heard my mother's all too familiar voice as she pushed through my bedroom door.

"No, thank you," I rolled away from her. "It's too early."

"Too early? It's 12:30 in the afternoon. Now, get your butt up."

I turned to my mother and an annoyed snarl escaped me. She narrowed her eyes and shot me a warning glare before walking away. It was a warning, convincing me that her wrath was more powerful than my teeth.

"Make it an hour, or I'm coming back."

"Fine." I sighed.

I stayed in bed for another fifteen minutes; I just did not want to get up. Mustering up some energy, I swung my legs and sat up from the bed. Tired and drained, I dragged myself to my bathroom.

After finishing my routine, I picked up my bag and made my way downstairs.

"Hey, Dad," I greeted my father as I walked into the kitchen. He glanced up from his paper to meet my gaze.

"Hey, where are you two headed?"

"She's dragging me to the mall." I slipped into a chair beside him. I reached for his paper and pulled the comic section from the crumbled pile.

"Oh, good luck." I could sense the humor in his comment.

My father knew how things went when it involved accompanying my mother to the mall. He had found a way to get out of it. During their mall trips, he would make her shopping experience hell. He complained, dragged his feet, and gave opinions my mother found useless. Occasionally, he would become 'ill' during their mall runs.

I could only admire his tactics for escaping.

"Okay, sweetie, I'm ready."

"Okay." I sighed and stood up from my chair.

I followed my mother out to the car and got in. I slumped down in my seat as I listened to the vehicle's engine roar to life from under the hood. I slipped my earbuds on and drifted into my own thoughts the entire ride.

* * *

We roamed the mall for hours, not looking for a specific item. My mother just wanted to buy random things. With the help of my complaints, my mother wrapped up her shopping journey, and we finally left the mall.

"Sweetie, can you tell your father to come help with the bags?" I scowled at her. *What am I? A personal beeper?*

Reaching into our mind link, I urged for his assistance. A few seconds later, my father emerged from the front entrance. He grabbed my mother's bag, refusing to have her carry her own.

He should have joined us in our mall run then. With his petty whining, I would have been home already.

By the time we arrived home, I made my way to the kitchen and walked over to the refrigerator, pulling a bottle of water from the shelf. As I turned to leave, I witnessed my parents sharing an intimate kiss in the living room. "We all have rooms for that, people."

"Sorry, honey." My mother's cheeks flushed red as she pulled away from my father.

"You will understand once you find your mate," my father explained.

A mate. To us werewolves, our mate would be someone the moon goddess has blessed us with. A mate would be someone we plan to spend the rest of eternity with.

Love. A destined bond that was almost unavoidable and hard to break. My mother and father were mates. He shared his secret with her, and she accepted his life and him as well.

However, some weren't that blessed. Some were cursed. Some were given a mate who could be careless, cold-blooded, and downright disgraceful.

There could be some who don't want a mate. Some who would rather remain unrestricted than fall into the spell of the mate bond.

Rejection. Some would rather reject their mate; it's their way of freeing themselves from the world they consider a prison. However, it's not always accepted by the other. The rejected mate may not fully accept it, leaving them with a broken heart and the feeling of desertion. Some would begin to feel as though it's their own actions that caused the rejection, and feel self-loathe and hatred for their wolves. Finally, another dangerous aspect was pain, hatred, and even suicidal ideation.

Honestly, I didn't care about finding my mate. I didn't want to find some wolf who probably believed that I my only purpose was to bear his children and sleep with him. A man who would probably only use me as his chew toy. I couldn't allow someone to have so much control over me, so much power. And then give me so much heartache.

"No, thank you on the mate thing, Dad." A waved my hands frantically. I didn't want that curse.

"Honey, go, get dressed. Our guests should be arriving in about an hour." My mom pressed.

Shifting my eyes toward my father, I shot him a venomous glare once again.

"Oh, honey, you will love them. They are nice people, so relax."

Disagreeing with him, I picked up the small bags I had gotten from the mall and ran up to my room to prepare for an unwanted arrival.

ABOUT THE AUTHOR

I am very passionate about reading and writing. I spend most of my time with my head phones in listening to music with my head inside a book or planning my next novel. I also love spending time with my friends and family or just relaxing and watching something scary on Netflix.

am

sister
obses
and a
would
I get i
and w

rece
ho
yo

Printed by Amazon Italia Logistica S.r.l.
Torrazza Piemonte (TO), Italy